A MOTHER'S HOPE

Rachel took another calming breath and looked to her left to find people watching her, staring, contemplating.

When she faced them, they glanced away, uncomfortable and nervous. Were they able to do the math and realize that her daughter should be graduating today, too?

You should be here, honey. Rachel sent the message out the way most people transmitted a prayer to the heavens. Somewhere out there, Lauren was alive and receiving at least a flicker of telepathic activity.

Like the flyers that shouted DON'T STOP BELIEVING! Rachel held on to the conviction that her daughter was alive. Sure, people thought she was deluded. Living in denial. Let them think what they wanted.

Lauren was out there somewhere; Rachel knew that. She could feel it. And one of these days, she was going to come back to them . . .

Books by Rosalind Noonan

ONE SEPTEMBER MORNING

IN A HEARTBEAT

THE DAUGHTER SHE USED TO BE

ALL SHE EVER WANTED

AND THEN SHE WAS GONE

TAKE ANOTHER LOOK

DOMESTIC SECRETS

PRETTY, NASTY, LOVELY

SINISTER
(with Lisa Jackson and Nancy Bush)

OMINOUS
(with Lisa Jackson and Nancy Bush)

Published by Kensington Publishing Corporation

AND THEN SHE WAS GONE

ROSALIND NOONAN

KENSINGTON BOOKS
www.kensingtonbooks.com

KENSINGTON BOOKS are published by

Kensington Publishing Corp.
119 West 40th Street
New York, NY 10018

All Kensington titles, imprints, and distributed lines are available at special quantity discounts for bulk purchases for sales promotion, premiums, fund-raising, and educational, or institutional use. Special book excerpts or customized printings can also be created to fit specific needs. For details, write or phone the office of the Kensington Special Sales Manager: Attn. Special Sales Department. Kensington Publishing Corp., 119 West 40th Street, New York, NY 10018. Phone: 1-800-221-2647.

Kensington and the K logo Reg. U.S. Pat. & TM Off.

ISBN-13: 978-1-4967-0827-4
ISBN-10: 1-4967-0827-X
First Kensington Hardcover Edition: January 2014
First Kensington Mass Market Edition: July 2017

eISBN-13: 978-1-61773-026-9
eISBN-10: 1-61773-026-2
First Kensington Electronic Edition: January 2014

10 9 8 7 6 5 4 3 2 1

Printed in the United States of America

For my niece, Elizabeth Hartley
Artist, Reader, Shiny Bright Thinker
Thank you for sharing your inspiring sketches

"It is better to laugh and cry than to just cry."

—Jaycee Dugard

PART 1

Long Ago and Far Away

Prologue

It was a nothing day.

Nothing exciting had happened at school, and nothing good was going to happen tonight with all the homework weighing down her backpack as she plodded along Wildwood Lane, heading home. Homework was annoying because it took Lauren away from fun things, like reading about dragons in ancient kingdoms or sketching the gargoyles and winged beasts that decorated her thoughts. Lauren imagined sliding the heavy pack off and kicking it down the street. That would be fun, except it might mess up her sketchbook inside. She wiped the damp blond hair from the nape of her neck and sighed. Looking on the good side, at least Mom was letting her go home on her own instead of sitting in that stuffy classroom of babies in the after-school program.

Why-oh-why did Mom and Dad think she needed after-school babysitting? She wasn't like Sierra, six years old and still a baby. Lauren was eleven and perfectly capable of walking home on her own, one foot in front of the other. And she didn't mind the walk, even when it was raining, which was pretty often. Thirty-seven inches a year in the city of Portland; that was a fact. Some people acted like the rain would melt them, like the Wicked Witch of the West.

That would make a cool sketch. A melting creature.

More than anything else, Lauren liked to draw. Her new obsession had overtaken her passion for reading a few months ago when she'd realized that nobody was going to give her a job for reading, but sketching had possibilities. She could see herself sitting at one of those artist's drawing tables, creating graphic novels or animated characters for movies. Already she had two sketchbooks filled with gargoyles and winged beasts, fairies and elves, and illustrated phobias. She was proud of her illustration of thirty phobias; from acarophobia, fear of itchy, crawly insects, to selachophobia, fear of sharks.

Someday, someone was going to discover her talent, and then she would get a chance to complete her phobia illustrations, because there were many, many more.

The Eastons' overgrown bush blocked the sidewalk, and Lauren reached one hand out to bat off the leaves as she sideswiped it. The bush had grown into a giant mushroom shape, which attracted the neighborhood kids like catnip. Sierra and her friends would run underneath the springy twigs, shrieking like hyenas. Lauren grabbed onto a crisp leaf and imagined the bush coming to life: a giant mushroom with a cap that curled down over the unsuspecting children huddled under it.

Just what Sierra deserved. Mom got mad when Lauren talked about it, but Sierra was a six-year-old dodo birdbrain. In fact, because of her pesky sister, Lauren had almost been stuck in Aftercare with Sierra and her first-grade friends. Dad totally didn't get why Lauren wanted out. He was disappointed that she didn't like spending time with her sister. At least Mom was beginning to understand that the five years between her and Sierra made a huge difference. Huge.

She let the branch snap back. Just two more weeks of this. Sixth grade was boring—more of the same stuff they'd done before with the same teachers. She doubted that junior high would be any more interesting.

But summer . . . summer vacation was going to be awesome.

This year Lauren was old enough to stay with her grandparents on Mirror Lake. She longed to wake up on the lake and spend the day drawing birds and flowers and magical creatures that rose from the lake or formed in the clouds. Maybe she would get to sketch some more phobias.

Eleven was a good age to get away from your parents for a while. Definitely a good age to get away from Sierra.

Just then a hummingbird zipped over her head and darted toward the Millers' house. Lauren watched in wonder as it hovered over their porch—a flash of iridescent green—near a feeder shaped like a spaceship. The Millers didn't seem to be home, so she edged closer; besides, they probably wouldn't mind as long as she didn't trample anything.

"Oh, little hummingbird." It seemed like a sign of good luck and affection. The hummingbird wouldn't have dipped so close to her if it didn't know how she loved creatures. Although she knew the little bird was too fast to sketch, she dropped her backpack to the ground and took out her sketchbook. The cloud of glimmering green—that was what she wanted to capture in a speed sketch.

The hummingbird lingered, and Lauren sat down in

the grass with her pad in her lap. Why shouldn't she stay a minute?

She gasped as the little bird darted close again, buzzing her pulse to a rapid pace. And then, he flew off.

Lauren twirled strands of golden hair around one fingertip as the volume seemed to turn up around her. Birdsong and the smell of warm soil. Insects bouncing in a cloud over the yard and so much green. Leaves and ivy and grassy lawns. Tiny violet flowers wove through the grass beneath her in a random pattern that she found irresistible. This she could sketch.

"Hey, there." Although it was a friendly voice, with the steady timbre of a teacher or a dad, Lauren was startled.

A man stood over her, a hulking figure backlit by the sunlight. She squinted up at him just enough to decipher the uniform shirt and the brown paper package in his hand. A white van idled by the curb.

Some delivery guy.

"Do you want to sign for this?" Clutching the package awkwardly, he hunched down beside her.

Too close. Lauren didn't like people that close, especially strangers. The sun glinted off little slivers of gold in his short hair, but his face was in shadow.

Pressing her sketchpad to her chest, she leaned away. "I don't live here."

"No? You look pretty much at home."

He was teasing. She knew that. Adults said stupid things like that all the time, even when they didn't know you. Still, she wished he would just go away. "Is that for the Millers?" she asked.

"Yeah, the Millers." He fumbled with a black gizmo beside the box. One of those electronic pads that scanned the packages. The man didn't look creepy, but something about the way his blue eyes pinned her down made Lauren squirm.

She clambered back, away from him, and shoved her sketchbook away. "I got to go."

"What's your hurry? It's too nice a day to be rushing around."

Bowing away from the pressure of his stare, she fumbled with the zipper on her backpack. She heard the whir of a lawn mower nearby but didn't see any neighbors or kids out on the block. Now she wished the Millers were home. She wished she hadn't stopped. She had to get home.

Suddenly the man's hand clamped over her arm, cruelty in his grip.

"Let me go!" she ordered, adrenaline shooting through her body. She yanked back, determined to shake him loose. But as she tried to pull away, he pressed something to her neck and . . .

Brrrr . . .

She sucked in a breath as her whole body cramped up in a cold jolt of pain.

Terrible slamming p-p-pain!

The instinct to get away was strong, but her body was useless, hunched and rigid and sprawled on the green lawn. Somewhere in her mind it registered that she had peed in her pants, but that didn't seem to matter. Her mind didn't have the strength to be embarrassed because it was wrapped around the pain.

How long did she lie there—seconds? Minutes? The sound of him near her pierced through her daze. She had to get up!

Face-to-face with the tiny purple flowers, she pressed into the earth, tearing at grass and clover as she tried to get up. Get up and get away!

But the best she could do was to tear up a handful of green clover.

She grasped it in one fist, holding on to the last trace of home as the man lifted her under the arms and dragged her away.

Chapter 1

Six Years Later

Rachel O'Neil watched from the bleachers as one by one the members of the senior class crossed the stage to receive their diplomas from Dr. Kendris, principal of Mirror Lake High School.

"Nora Berton."

Rachel applauded and whooped it up with her friend as Julia's daughter crossed the stage. Julia shifted forward on the bleacher seat and snapped some shots with her digital camera as Nora accepted her diploma.

"Congratulations, Mom," Rachel said quietly as Julia's lower lip rumpled into a pout.

"I can't believe it." The two women exchanged a quick hug, and then settled back into their spots.

As other graduates were called, Rachel watched Nora make her way back to her seat, hugging classmates along the way. Such a good kid. A memory from years ago flashed across Rachel's mind: overhearing Nora asking Lauren if she wanted to be best friends. Would the girls have remained friends through high school? Grown closer or drifted apart? The "what-if" game always taunted her this way.

"Trevor Feron." Amidst applause, it was announced that Trevor would be heading to the University of Oregon next year.

As the tall boy moved in measured steps across the stage, Rachel smoothed back her hair, once the color of caramel, now layered with streaks of gold to blend with the gray. She had aged, but so had the students. Although he'd grown a soul patch since Rachel had been his seventh-grade English teacher, he was still the same unkempt Trev. "Still blinded by those bangs," Rachel muttered.

Her friend Julia leaned close to add, "It's a wonder he can see to make it across the stage." Julia Berton knew all of these characters as well as Rachel. It was Julia, parent of a graduate, who had scored these seats in the bleachers for Rachel and Dan, who had bowed out at the last minute.

"I can't do it," Dan had told her that morning as he'd stared into his coffee. "I can't sit there and watch every other kid in that class graduate just because my daughter should be there with them. I can't stand to look at the faces of Lauren's classmates and long for what could have been. What should have been."

"That's not why we're going. Don't you want to see Nora graduate? She and Julia are like family."

But Dan had not budged. "You go. They were your students; you taught most of them in junior high. They'll be happy to see you."

Rachel doubted that anyone in Mirror Lake was happy to see her these days. She knew she had gained a reputation as a bulldog mom, voraciously chomping at city and state authorities to keep the search for her daughter open and active. When parents dared to make eye contact with her, there was pity in their eyes . . . pity and hopelessness and relief that it had not happened to *their* daughter. Rachel understood their discomfort. Some kept their distance out of fear that her tragedy might be contagious. Others didn't know what to say to her, the parent of a child of uncertain destiny.

Lauren had been in a class with achievers. On stage now, Brooke Fitkin towered over the administrators. She was headed for Stanford on a basketball scholarship. Kara Gaines was off to Southern Oregon University. Jordan Gilroy was going to UVA for swimming. And Erica Glass had earned a javelin scholarship to a university in Hawaii. "A full ride," as Julia kept saying.

Mirror Lake had one of the top-ranked high schools in Oregon—of course it did. It was one of the reasons she and Dan had scraped and saved and borrowed money from Dan's parents to buy a modest house here when they could have afforded a nicer place with property just about anywhere else in the Portland area. Great schools, plenty of parks and green space, responsive police force, low crime rate . . . these were factors that wooed young families to the lake community. Outsiders mocked Mirror Lake residents for their "life in a protected bubble," but who would not choose a town where the "civil war" was between rival football teams instead of rival gangs?

Seeing these students now, Rachel recognized them all with their little quirks. Yes, she cared about these kids, but Dan was wrong about one thing. They were not her kids. They were not Lauren. She had not come to any other ceremonies to watch her former students graduate. Sitting here beside Julia, the mother of Lauren's best friend of long ago, Rachel knew that Dan had been right the first time. She was not here for these kids; she was here to represent Lauren, in some sick way. Lauren, who should have graduated from high school today. She couldn't let go of that. She couldn't give up on her oldest child. This was Lauren's class. What if Lauren's abductor had let her continue school somewhere else—in another state? Maybe Lauren *was* graduating today.

Since the day Lauren started kindergarten, Rachel had pictured this day. Her bright, artistic daughter had started school a year before most and would be graduating high school at the age of seventeen. "I can't hold her back," Rachel had told people. A teacher herself, Rachel could see that her daughter was ready for school, hungry to learn, pushing for routine and independence at the age of four. Rachel and Dan had shared high hopes for Lauren. An Ivy League school. A dynamic career. "How high can you soar?" she and Dan used to ask Lauren when they pushed her on the tree swing. Lauren would kick her legs and lean back to propel herself high in the air as she answered: "Up to the stars!"

Throughout grammar school, Lauren had been a highflier. Maybe not the most social kid. But Dan and Rachel had vested so many hopes in their oldest daughter, looking toward this day. Graduation day . . . but not for Lauren.

No, Lauren's day had been little more than a week ago, the sixth anniversary of the day she'd disappeared, when the grounds of Mirror Lake Junior High had been crowded with people, hundreds of them, assembling to honor the six-year mark of Lauren's disappearance and continue the search for her. Messages like *We will find you!* and *We love you, Lauren!* had been attached to hundreds of balloons that the searchers had released to the sky, shouting: "Find Lauren!"

Rachel would never forget the sight of those hot-pink balloons—Lauren's favorite pink—rising into wide-open blue until they became small dots. It had been touching that so many people showed up for her, even six years later. They didn't think Rachel was crazy. They believed she was out there, alive and waiting to be rescued.

Dan still went looking every morning as he jogged along the paths that cut through the town's parks and neighborhoods. Every six months the local television stations broadcasted images of Lauren: photos from sixth grade and computer renderings of how she would probably look now.

Squinting over the graduates below, Rachel could see her down there, crossing the stage, her honey-blond hair streaming out beneath her mortarboard cap. If her hair hadn't been cut in these past six years, there would be flaxen gold spilling over her shoulders and down the back of her royal blue graduation gown.

Rachel could hear the principal calling her name . . .

Lauren O'Neil.

Would she be attending U of O, Dan's alma mater, or Brown? Stanford or Northwestern? Lauren had been an excellent student, more interested in reading and learning how things worked than parties or boys.

How high can you soar?

Rachel pressed her lips together, trying to tamp down the swell of emotion. These days, the only things soaring were latex balloons. The memory of those fat pink balloons, swaying and rising, made her mouth go sour.

She bit her lower lip and turned to Julia. "It's hard to believe our babies are old enough to graduate from high school."

Julia's eyes glimmered with compassion as she squeezed Rachel's hand. "Hard to believe. Time really flies."

And sometimes it drags, second to second, day to day. Time was a race through molasses when you were waiting for your daughter to come home.

At the podium Natalie Miller's name was announced, and Rachel held her breath as she watched Russ and Trudy's granddaughter cross the stage. The Millers were neighbors, two doors down. The police believed a van that had stopped in front of the Millers' house had been used to abduct Lauren when she was walking home from school. One woman saw the van at the curb, its motor running. A plain white van, but the man who emerged was wearing a uniform.

As if that made it all okay. Rachel still seethed over the way our society teaches us to trust a person in a uniform.

"And I saw him carrying a package," the woman, Allie Cotter, had insisted. "It was a delivery for the Millers. Just a deliveryman with a package."

Nothing out of the ordinary.

Except that, when the Millers arrived home from their oldest son's house in Bend, they were mystified by the brown paper package that contained no address, no postage, and no markings whatsoever. The package had been a cover, a way to park a van on Wildwood Lane and drive away without attracting attention. There was a slightly trampled section of the lawn. A section that might have been torn up by a digging squirrel. Had Lauren run to knock on the Millers' door when she sensed danger, but then struggled with the abductor on the lawn? And somehow, without anyone seeing, he had managed to get Lauren into his van.

Or at least that was how the theory went. Rachel refused to believe that her daughter would get into a stranger's van without a fight, but there were other factors involved. Maybe he wasn't a stranger. And it was too painful to think about the weapons an abductor could use to subdue a girl who fought him.

Beads of sweat were forming on Rachel's forehead, and she had to remind herself to breathe. Was the gymnasium hotter than usual? Was she suffering a hot flash at the age of forty-two, or was the heat because of her own voyage to the Inferno, the serpentine layers of hell surrounding Lauren's disappearance?

Julia leaned closer. "You okay?"

Nodding, she swiped the back of one hand over her forehead and accepted a small bottle of water from Julia's bag. Even tepid water was a relief in this hotbed of community. It helped Rachel focus, helped her remember the positive reason she had come, to celebrate the graduation of Julia's daughter Nora.

She took another calming breath and looked to her left to find people watching her, staring, contemplating.

When she faced them, they glanced away, uncomfortable and nervous. Were they able to do the math and realize that her daughter should be graduating today, too?

You should be here, honey. Rachel sent the message out the way most people transmitted a prayer to the heavens. Somewhere out there, Lauren was alive and receiving at least a flicker of telepathic activity.

Like the flyers that shouted DON'T STOP BELIEVING! Rachel held on to the conviction that her daughter was alive. Sure, people thought she was deluded. Living in denial. Let them think what they wanted.

Lauren was out there somewhere; Rachel knew that. She could feel it. And one of these days, she was going to come back to them.

Chapter 2

Sis's foot twisted in the loose soil, and the pain that shot up her leg sucked her breath away. She braced herself against the hoe and used it to edge back, out of the dirt and against the fence, where she collapsed with a sigh.

She closed her eyes and let the tears flow down her cheeks. Kevin would be mad if he found her crying, but he was off at the Portland Saturday Market right now, and the tears came automatically when she wrenched her bad leg. Bad because Kevin had made it that way. Even after all these years, six years of minding him most of the time, he still let her have it when he thought she was disobeying him.

She shifted her leg, and winced. It still hurt, but she couldn't let it slow her down. Kevin would be mad if he came home to an untended garden. Silly girl.

She swiped at her cheeks and took a breath. No use in crying. Besides, it wasn't so bad, out here in the sun. Using the hoe as a cane, she propped herself up, back on her feet. Testing the tool against the moist earth, she imagined herself pushing off the stick and bouncing over the fence like one of those pole vault guys.

Just thinking of it made her smile. She would bounce over the fence and just keep bouncing from one green hill to another, bouncing into the deep blue sky.

She had hopped the fence once, jumping from a nearby tree. It had been one of those hot summer days when the sun pounded down mercilessly from a clear sky, and all she had been able to think of was the cool gurgle of the little stream a few yards from their compound. The spring that ran over the rocks at the bottom of the hill had just enough water to cover your body in the summer. When Kevin had found her down by the creek, he had been real quiet as she had explained that she wasn't breaking any rules. She hadn't been running away, just cooling off. Later, back behind the fence, he had beat her hard and chopped down the poor little beech tree.

The sun was hot on her head, and she wished she could slip into the river right now and wash her hair. "Not until Kevin gets back," Sis said aloud. Sometimes, you needed to remind yourself of the rules. She was limping because she'd broken the rules.

"You should know better," Kevin had hissed. "I haven't had to lay a hand on you for a long time. I thought you stopped trying to git away."

Because of Mac . . .

She couldn't leave her daughter behind, and even if they could have gotten away, who would take in a teen mother and her baby? She couldn't risk it. It was her job to protect her baby.

As pain flared in her ankle again, she could still see him, the metal wrench silhouetted over his head as he'd swung it up. And then down on her bad leg.

The wound that was never allowed to heal.

"That's so you'll remember the rules," he had told her. It seemed like he'd told her that a thousand times.

Kevin was a stickler for the rules. With a hack of the hoe, she flashed on the first time she had broken the rules, that day in the beach house when he had pushed her out to the edge of the jetty.

Her knees still trembled when she thought of the icy shock of the stun gun and the long finger of boulders jutting out into the ocean.

Sharp, slippery rocks. But Kevin didn't care. She'd been eleven years old, and he had pushed her out on those rocks.

The jetty was a long mound of boulders, some of them the size of coffins, many of them pointy and unforgiving. They were lined up at the edge of that beach, as if a giant had stacked his rock collection at the water's edge. "How did these get here?" The magnitude of the rock pile, with seawater splashing over the jagged stones, had momentarily eclipsed the knowledge that he was mean and angry and hurtful, that she shouldn't ask him any questions because she didn't trust his answers anyway.

"That's the Army Corps of Engineers for ya. They come in here and build a wall of rocks on the beach and spend millions of dollars doing it." He loved to show off that way, when he knew something.

He was mad at her for telling him to mind his business and keep his hands off her. She had tried to slap him away when he'd followed her into the shower and put his hands on her private parts. She wrenched away, slashing at him with her fingernails, and he threatened her with the razor, telling her he could do much worse.

He'd been waiting for her outside the shower with a stupid flowered dress for her to put on, along with a gray hoodie. And no panties. That was his way of making her feel uncomfortable and naked. She really wanted her underwear back, but she was too embarrassed to ask him for it. Without a word he had stuffed her into the back of the van and driven to the beach. The short ride told her that the house he'd locked her up in must have been close.

When the van door opened at the beach, he greeted her with a cool smile. His hand held the stun gun, a black object that reminded her of Dad's electric razor. Only the stun gun held a cold, electric sizzle that made a person curl up and die inside. She knew, because he'd used it on her in the Millers' yard.

He held it up to her, an angry squint in his eyes.

"N-no!" She scooted back on the van's rough carpet.

"Then get out of the van, or I'll zap you good."

She scrambled quickly and did as she was told. She pulled her hood up and walked along the packed sand that filled the center of the jetty.

"Do not look around, and do not walk out of line, unless you want the shock of your life."

Knowing she couldn't take another cold blue shock, she walked out toward the ocean. Were there people on the beach around them? She didn't think so, not in this cold wind that slammed the water against the rocks, sending salt spray into the air.

Where are we?

She didn't know. They didn't walk past a sign, and she wasn't allowed to look around. The jetty curled around one side of the beach and jutted out into the ocean for twenty or thirty yards. She imagined this would be a spot for fishermen on a calmer day, but it was isolated in today's chilly June gloom.

At the end, where the packed sand path ended in a ring of jagged boulders, she paused.

"Keep going!"

That gun . . . it jabbed her back. Painless, but if he

turned on the electricity, she would collapse out here in the wind and ocean spray.

And then what? Would he kick her body around and toss her into the ocean?

No. *No.* Then he would lose power over her. He needed someone to kick around. Someone to yell at. This she knew. She was learning him, faster than he was learning her.

Because he was wrong about her. He had brought her out here to scare her, and the ocean didn't scare her at all. The roiling black water was mesmerizing, soothing in a dark sort of way.

"I said go! Climb down on the rocks." She left the sand path and scrambled forward onto the rocks, just as a wave snapped over the crest of stone and splashed them.

"Goddammit!" Hearing him sputter behind her, she wanted to turn and run for help. Wouldn't someone help her?

But he had the stun gun, and the path was narrow. She would never get past him. There was no getting past him without getting zapped by the gun. Her nerves tingled at the memory of that terrible pain. Her whole body cramping up. Losing her balance and peeing her pants and hunching up while pain rippled her spine.

No. She couldn't risk the stun gun again.

"Stop right there and take a look. Take a look at where you're gonna end up if you act up again. Is that what you want? Here I'm giving you food and a warm, dry place to sleep and you thank me by crying and scratching like a mangy cat."

Lauren stared out over the dark sea, the roiling waves, shifting and spitting like the bathtub when she and Sierra used to churn it up.

Maybe the ocean could be her escape.

She imagined herself slipping into the black water and swimming away like Ariel, the Little Mermaid. Wouldn't he be surprised when she slid under the surface of the water and never returned? Just like Ariel . . . or Harry Potter, when he grew gills for that competition. In strong, broad strokes she would swim straight down to the ocean floor, beneath the riptides and undertow. In the cold, inky darkness she would wait with her hair splayed out around her. Counting to one hundred . . . to one thousand, she would hide from him.

"You got to learn that I'm in control. I'm in charge of you now. Do what I say and I'll take care of you and feed you and make sure there's a roof over your head. But step out of line . . . any more fighting and you get this."

Blocking out his words, she thought about diving into the water. Not the fantasy, but the reality. The water was dead cold. She wasn't a good swimmer, and she didn't have supernatural abilities. She would probably drown or conk her head on the rocks, and that wasn't the point, was it? She didn't want to kill herself.

The point was to survive. Get away and get back to Mom and Dad and Sierra.

A swell rose near the jetty. With a fierce, sudden strike it smacked over the rock where Lauren was standing. Water exploded in the air as the wave swarmed over the boulder, rising up to her knees and shooting up her legs.

One second she stood there dreaming of escape, the next the water grabbed her like a fist around her ankles and yanked her legs out from under her. She went down, gasping and choking and groping for something to hold on to. The rock surface was slick and she began to slide.

And then, he grabbed her.

"Come on. I got ya."

She coughed up a mouthful of saltwater and let him help her up as the little kernel of realization stuck in her mind.

He didn't want to kill her.

At least she had that going for her. At least, he wanted her to live.

Chapter 3

"**I**'m getting a little old for this. I'm going to be thirteen in a few months," Sierra O'Neil told her father as they waited in the queue at the outdoor amusement park. She gave her head a toss, trying to get her side bangs out of her eyes without touching them, because every time you touched your hair, your fingers made it oily. She'd learned that the hard way.

"Yeah, you're an old lady," her dad teased. "Next you'll be telling me you're giving up ice cream and burgers because you've gone vegan."

She knew he meant it as a joke, but it really wasn't funny. Half the girls in her grade were vegan. Nobody wanted to think that they were eating an innocent animal with a cute face, and if you researched it online, everyone was at least a little bit lactose intolerant. Sierra bit her lips together as she scanned the antique car racetrack for familiar faces. Some of her friends said they would be here. Where were they?

"See that? The line is moving fast." Dad nodded as

they moved up. "Boondoggy's is usually packed on weekends, but today, this is good."

"It's pretty empty. Probably because half the town is at the Mirror Lake graduation ceremony." Where Mom was.

"Yeah, maybe you're right. Lucky for us."

Sierra wanted to take a shot at Mom for choosing Mirror Lake High over this, but she knew Dad didn't want to talk about Mom's obsession. "It would have been your sister's graduation," she'd told Sierra last night. Her breath was wispy with forced patience, as if her composure was held together by a few flimsy stitches. That was the way Mom acted when it came to Lauren. Distracted, fragile, distant. Sometimes it hurt Sierra, and sometimes it pissed her off.

Remember the daughter who is here!

What about me?

Am I invisible? Don't I matter?

She knew she mattered to Dad. Where Mom kept her focus on the missing person case from six years ago, Dan O'Neil kept a tight leash on Sierra. Way too tight, even if he was just trying to be protective.

Like now, with his hand on her shoulder as they waited in line. *Really, Dad, do you think someone is going to snatch me away from your side if you don't hold on?* She came this close to actually saying something, but she knew it would hurt him, and Dad was the only one who was trying, *trying* to move on and be a normal family.

Normal meant making it through dinner without talking about new places to search.

Normal meant going a whole month without conducting a search in one of the state parks or hosting a fund-raising 10K race to raise money and awareness for the Lauren O'Neil search and recovery effort.

Normal meant watching one of Sierra's soccer games

from the sidelines without distributing DON'T STOP BE-
LIEVING! flyers to parents and tucking them under every
windshield wiper in the parking lot. Ooh, and if Sierra
heard that song pumped up loud one more time, her
eardrums were going to explode!

Dad guided her forward, giving her tense shoulder a
little massage. "You okay?"

"I'm fine," she snapped, tamping down the ugly little
feelings that no one wanted to hear about. "But I'm getting dehydrated. Can I go get a bottle of water while
you buy the tickets?"

"Just hold on. We're almost there and I'll go with
you."

Sierra crossed her arms. He didn't trust her to go
four steps away from him. Really, she should have
bought her parents a dog leash for Christmas.

"You'll feel better when we're on the bumper boats.
You're never too old for bumper boats, and it's a great
way to cool down."

She rolled her eyes, but stayed by his side. "Yeah, but
still, you can't drink the water by the bumper boats."

"We'll get you water, kiddo."

It turned out Dad was right about one thing. She did
feel better on the bumper boats.

This was one of the first times that Dad had let her
drive her own boat, and it was fun motoring out on the
clear water, steering around the squirting fountain and
drifting close to the stone waterfall that smelled of chlo-
rine and hot stone. The boat moved slowly and only
after you pressed the pedal down hard, but hey, freedom was freedom.

Of course, Dad was trying to follow her, but he didn't
have total control. Some man with his little son bumped
into Dad's boat and got him spinning. Dad gave the duo
a squirt, but Sierra saw her chance. She drove around

the back of the fountain and managed to sneak up on Dad.

Well, sort of. The element of total surprise is lost in a wide open pool of bumper boats.

Sierra steered her boat into his—rocked him good—and blasted him with the water gun until he was soaked. He got in a good shot, too, but the cold water felt good in the sun.

The session ended, and as they docked the boats, she spotted her friends from school waiting their turn in line.

"Sierra!" Jemma shrieked, pointed, and then they all shrieked.

"Wait for us!" they called.

"Do not go anywhere!" Isabelle ordered. "Stay there. We'll be right off."

Sierra smiled from deep inside. It felt good to be wanted.

"Wow. Somebody's happy to see you." Dad was wiping his sunglasses on the tail of his T-shirt.

"Hold on a second. I have to see what they're doing next."

Sierra jumped over the metal divider to press into the line. "Don't worry," she told two annoyed-looking boys, "I'm not cutting."

"So, guys?"

Jemma, Isabelle, and Lindsay turned at once and surrounded her for a hug. She asked them what they were doing next, and they invited her to play miniature golf with them.

"I'll ask my Dad," she said, then ducked out of the line as they got a chance to board their boats.

Her sneakers felt heavy as she returned to her father's side. Of course, Dad was not invited to tag along, and Sierra didn't know how to run that one by him. Sierra knew the answer would be no.

It was always no. Her parents watched her like a hawk. No alone time. Because bad things happened when you left your daughter alone.

Dan and Rachel O'Neil couldn't get over the fact that they had let Lauren out of their sight; they still thought it was their fault. They probably always would. Sierra got that, but she wanted to be alone sometimes. She wanted to do stuff with her friends.

"So . . . ," Dad leaned against a post. "I guess Isabelle, Jemma, and Lindsay aren't too old for the bumper boats."

"Guess not." She folded her arms across her chest and looked toward the bumper boats. She caught a glimpse of Jemma spraying another boat, but then it blurred as tears filled her eyes.

"Honey, what is it?" Dad straightened and tilted his head. "What's wrong?"

"I just want to hang out with my friends." Her chin wobbled, and she knew she was making a puckered froggy face, but the tears had come out of nowhere, hitting her hard. "We want to play a game of miniature golf and go on the antique cars and play some games in the arcade. And all the other parents dropped their kids off and left. Why can't you do that, Dad? Why can't we ever be normal?"

"Sierra, you know that your mom and I keep an eye on you because we love you."

She sniffed, turning away from the bumper boats so her friends wouldn't see. "Yeah, but you can strangle a person with love like that."

Her dad started to answer, but then he stopped and shifted from one foot to another. His eyes were unreadable behind those sunglasses, but she sensed that he was a little hurt. Or maybe he was mad at her for asking for something he couldn't give.

"Can't we try it, just this once?" she suggested. "You can go and do errands and I'll be fine. And I won't say anything to Mom. She'll never know!"

"This is not about sneaking behind your mother's back. If we give it a try, I'm going to fill her in on it."

Sierra squinted at him. "So . . . I can do it? You'll leave me here and come back later?"

He scrunched up his lips, then sighed. "Sure. Why not."

"Thanks, Dad." She hugged him, seeing a glimmer of hope.

Maybe things could change.

Chapter 4

Through the checkered latticework of a rose trellis at the edge of the amusement park garden, he watched the four girls. Laughing and shrieking, exclaiming "I love you!" as they flung themselves into each other's arms.

Four girls, soon to be teenagers. Man, he was slipping into a strange land without a road map.

Dan O'Neil stepped around the trellis as Sierra moved out of his line of vision, behind the spike of a windmill. A moment later, he relaxed as she came back into view, plucking a purple ball from the cup and doing a little victory dance on the putting green. The sun brought out red highlights in her warm brown hair. Caramel hair, just like her mother. Every day Sierra was looking more and more like Rach. A good thing, though sometimes it made him yearn for Lauren, who had inherited the O'Neil blond hair and pale skin.

Dodging the hot sun, he sank into the shadows to wait. At first he had worried that the two guys playing ahead of the girls could be a problem, but then they were with girlfriends. Should be nothing to worry about.

Should be.

He had promised her he would leave, but that was a lie; these girls needed someone to watch over them. Besides that, Rachel would never let him live it down if he let their daughter loose on her own at Boondoggy's. Therapy had gotten Rachel and him beyond the blame stage for losing Lauren, but the murky waters of guilt never completely receded.

But this was normal, he told himself. Just a normal dad, watching over his twelve-year-old daughter. Okay, a normal dad with a touch of OCD, but he imagined that other fathers did this—guys like Larry and Hal. Guys whose daughters hadn't disappeared from the face of the earth. They didn't see ghosts of their daughters whenever a windowless van cruised through the neighborhood. Their teeth didn't grit at the sight of a grown man talking to a child. They didn't see the dark underbelly of danger that accompanied life in suburbia.

As Dan straightened out one of the slats of the latticework that had worked loose, he thought of his wife at the graduation ceremony, clinging to what might have been. Sometimes, he worried that his family was spinning out of control, that they were planets circling a sun that had burned out, and it would be a thousand years until they realized it was all over.

Lauren was that missing sun. When he dug deep, he believed she was still alive somewhere, though he didn't hold out the hope that he would ever be able to see her again. He didn't believe he would ever be giving her long blond hair a playful tug, calling her "movie star," serving her up a s'more from the fire pit out back. That was the fairy-tale ending. But then, when he fell to the lowest of lows, Rachel would rally and make his favorite sherry chicken. Or he would get distracted by a movie, and she would snuggle up beside him on the couch and put her head on his shoulder, the way she used to when they were teenagers. And for a few fleeting moments he felt right again. Until reality pinched him, reminding that something was missing.

Lauren.

He thought of those first wretched days, of lines of volunteers, side by side, crossing fields. Stirring weeds and poking bushes. Canvassing door-to-door and begging people to answer and take a minute—just one minute—to look at Lauren's photo. Thank God for the guys from the firehouse, who knew how to handle all sorts of people. They had gotten the word out, and within twenty-four hours they'd had firefighters from all over the state of Oregon helping in the search.

A good thing . . . because when they'd activated the beacon on Lauren's cell phone, they'd learned it was coming from the Tillamook State Forest, a vast tract of land between Portland and the coast. Finding a person there would be like finding a needle in a haystack.

But they had combed the lush, green woods that swept over the northern Coastal Range. Tuna and Sully had worked with the state rangers, leading search parties from dawn till dusk. They had found Lauren's cell phone just twenty yards from the side of the highway, as if someone had stopped along the road to cast it off while driving west.

So the search had moved down Highway Six to the raging Pacific and the small beach towns that were just coming awake that June. Volunteers headed south to Netarts and Oceanside and north to Bay City and Garibaldi, all the way through the crowded city of Seaside and up to the Washington border at Astoria.

Lauren . . . Lauren. Find Lauren.

It was the mantra that kept him on the edge of nausea most of the time. The search that began six years ago was still going on, every day, every minute that Dan was awake.

It was the focus of his morning run that took him through the streets and hills and woods and fields of Mirror Lake. It had him peering into the backseats of cars in store parking lots. It had him watching neighbors' garages and playhouses. It sent his dad out on the boat every morning to eyeball the shoreline of Mirror Lake.

It kept the guys at the firehouse busy slapping stamps and labels on postcards with an aged sketch of Lauren and the headline: MISSING: LAUREN O'NEILL, SEVENTEEN YEARS OLD. It had been Sully's idea to send postcards to every filling station in Oregon and Washington. As Sully had pointed out, anyone who wanted to move around was going to need gas. Good men, Sully and Tuna. They had proven to be good friends, just when Dan needed them, and, like Dan and Rachel, they had refused to give up.

There was no telling when you might find your daughter coming out of Walmart or searching the dairy cases for the cheapest milk. You had to be ready, watching, on alert. As his father always said: "You never know."

Chapter 5

When Paula Winkler got the call from the Clackamas County Sheriff's Office, she was sipping café
au lait from a huge mug and wondering if she should
rethink her painting of the three red hens.

She backed away from the easel, paused in a stream
of lemony sunshine that shot through the skylight of
her garage studio, and tucked a long strand of silver
hair behind one ear. Too much red?

She could easily make one a dark shade of orange,
leaning toward burnt umber. Or maybe a zesty shade of
tangerine.

"Such a problem to have," she said aloud to no one.
Since George had passed and her kids had flown the
coop, Paula was on her own now. She had come to embrace the change with this second career—art. Ten
years ago, at the age of forty-eight, Paula had cracked
open the dozens of paint buckets George had stored in
the garage and, mixing and tinting, she had begun to
paint on scraps of plywood.

She'd had a modicum of success selling her work, but mostly it was her therapy and her path to joy. With budget cuts and tons of red tape binding a social worker's every move, working for the Department of Human Services did not put a gal on the fast track to fulfillment.

But painting did.

Some days it was about the feeling she wanted her topic to express. Some days, like today, it was all about the color.

"A happy apple red is one thing," she said as she stalked the canvas. "But fire engine red? A five-alarm fire?" She shook her head. It needed some adjustment.

That was when the phone rang and the desk officer at the sheriff's office asked her to report in for an urgent matter.

"To the sheriff's office?" Paula blinked. Usually when she was on call, she responded directly to the scene of an emergency: a home where children needed to be taken into custody, a crime scene where youth needed to be safely apprehended.

"This is a special case," the desk officer explained. "The sheriff and a police chief would like you to ride along with them. How soon can you get here?"

"I'll be there in two shakes of a lamb's tail."

Paula was the queen of the quick response. Her home in West Green was centrally located in the county, she knew her way around, and when you lived alone there was no child care to arrange or meals to tuck in the oven. Within fifteen minutes, she was standing in the lobby of the Clackamas County Sheriff's Office, shaking hands with Hank Todd, the Mirror Lake police chief, Jacob Darius, the county sheriff, and Pete Wolinsky, a patrol officer she had worked with before.

Paula had never worked directly with high-ranking officers before, and certainly not on a Saturday. Her radar was blinking like the town square on Christmas Eve.

"Thanks for getting here so fast." Pete closed his black notebook. "Guarantee, you're gonna like this one."

Hank nodded toward the parking lot. "If you don't mind, we'll brief you on the way there. You want to ride with me?"

"Sounds good."

"We've got a unit out at the farm right now," Jake advised as she pushed back her sleeves to buckle into the department Jeep. "They're waiting on us to go in." He explained that a large local discount store had been held up by a man with a stun gun that morning. "A stun gun at Costco." Paula slid her sunglasses on against the afternoon sun. "Was he planning to stun every customer and employee he passed on his way out? Can you imagine the mob there on a Saturday morning?"

"No one's saying he's smart or clever. Just desperate. He said he's been out of cash for a while, since his taxidermy business went bust. The perp is Kevin Hawkins. Says his aunt owns Green Spring Farm and he lives in a cabin on the back acres."

Paula had always shivered a little when she'd passed those signs advertising TAXIDERMIST on that farm road. It seemed so old country, so Norman Bates. "And you want me along to check on the aunt . . . the one who owns Green Spring Farm?"

Chief Todd shook his head. "It's not Vera Hawkins we're worried about. It's this sister Hawkins mentioned. He calls her Sissy, and he said he's worried about her getting along if he's incarcerated. Asked us to check on her."

"That seems considerate of him," Paula said.

"Except our records show that he has no sister. Just one brother. No adult arrest record, but three sealed convictions when he was a minor for rape and attempted sexual assault."

"He's a sex offender?" That caught Paula's attention. "I don't remember any registered sex offenders in the Green Spring Farm area."

"That's because there's a loophole," the sheriff explained. "A childhood conviction doesn't stick. Even three childhood convictions. When Hawkins committed his crimes, the judge let him face trial as a minor on all three counts. Law says he doesn't have to register as a sex offender."

"That and the fact that he's not even living at a legal address. He keeps talking about a cabin behind the farm. You can't reach it by car, but it's a short hike down a trail." Hank shook his head. "That's not like any residence I know of in Mirror Lake."

Mirror Lake was not a place where people lived off the grid. She propped her sunglasses on her head to get an unfiltered look at Hank. She had known him for thirty-some years, since she'd started working for social services, and the man had excellent instincts. "What are we talking about here, Hank?"

He gave a shrug of those burly shoulders that held up the burdens of half of Mirror Lake. "Hawkins says he's lived in the cabin five or six years. If he's not completely deluded or lying, I'm thinking that puts us back around the summer that Lauren O'Neil disappeared."

Paula's interest shot up—way up. It seemed that everyone in the state of Oregon had participated in the search for the O'Neil girl. Paula and her son had volunteered more than once, helping the recovery teams search local farms and parks. "And you think that this fake sister—Sis—you think she might be Lauren? Right here in Mirror Lake?"

"Thinking . . . and hoping."

"Oh, Hank, I hope you're right," she said as the Jeep circled fast on a roundabout. "I hope you're right."

Chapter 6

Sis dropped the hoe and swiped her sweaty hair back with one wrist. Too hot. She hobbled back to the shed to wrap her hair into a coil. Using two chopsticks from a Chinese takeout place, she secured it at the back of her head, off her neck. Her wispy yellow hair was already lightening from the sun, turning pale as a wheat field. She used to hate her hair. She used to think people thought blondes were stupid. But she had come to love it—a glittery, golden part of herself that Kevin could not control.

That first year he had made her dye her hair, and she hated slopping the smelly stuff on. It stung her scalp and left brown patches on her skin.

"Why do you make me use this?" she had protested.

" 'Cause we can't have you matching the girl on TV."

Not that anyone ever saw her in the beginning. When they'd made the two-hour trip from the beach to his aunt's farm, she had been handcuffed in the back of his van. Those first few months, he wouldn't let her go out in public at all. Later, when he knew she wouldn't bolt, she'd been disguised by hair dye and glasses and these grandma dresses for the weekend and summer days at fairs and festivals and the Saturday market in Portland. Kevin would plunk her down at an easel with a sign that said: PORTRAITS FOR PENNIES: STARVING ARTIST PORTRAITS FOR SALE. Of course, the penny thing was sort of a lie, since Kevin wanted two thousand pennies for a simple pencil-sketch portrait. Still, people went for it. Anyone who asked was told she was his sister, but mostly he had kept her a secret. Sometimes it made her mad because she wasn't supposed to talk to anyone, but Kevin would put Mac on his hip and go around and visit with the other vendors like old friends. But at least she got to talk a little with the people she painted. Folks visiting from Chicago or California. Grandparents and young couples and families like the one Sis used to have.

Other than the portrait sketching, he didn't let her go on errands with him, and their compound was set back in a secluded area behind his aunt's farm. Sis had never seen a wanderer, though Kevin had brought a few women back here in the past year or so. That was good, because it saved her from being ridden. The only problem was that he didn't want her to see or be seen when his women were here. Most times, when a woman was here, Sis was relegated to the shed, locked in the cage once again like an animal in the zoo. Other times, she was princess of the compound, though that didn't mean much.

That was what he called it—a compound, even though it was only an old cabin with a slop sink, shower, and toilet. Outside was space for a garden, mounds of trash, and a shed that had once been used to store farming tools. Before Sis got here, Kevin had added a toilet and shower to the cabin, but the shed had no plumbing, which meant Sis had to use a bucket when she was locked in

there. Sis hated that, but Kevin teased her that she was
spoiled, expecting her own throne. Kevin liked to tease
that the compound was his kingdom, and he was king
of his castle. When he got high and mighty like that, Sis
didn't remind him that he was only here because his
Aunt Vera had let him move in when everybody else let
him down. Sis didn't know why the rest of Kevin's family
didn't help him. After six years, she didn't know anything about his family, and she had never even seen
Aunt Vera. She figured they were in Oregon because of
the familiar sky and plants and weather, but she didn't
know for sure.

"But where are we?" she used to ask him, not so much
because she thought she could escape, but because she
thought it would feel better to know where she was
pinned to the earth.

"You just want to know so's you can git away. And
then what would happen to ya?" he always asked her.
"You're ruined as far as everyone else is concerned.
Like a dirty, used tissue."

Although Sis knew it was true, she painted a pretend
world in her mind: a wonderland, a postage-stamp view
of the past in which her mom arrived on their block just
in time to rescue her from Kevin's van . . . or in which
her dad busted into the beach house that first cold
night and punched Kevin out like a hero in a cowboy
movie. Sure, she understood why her parents wouldn't
want her now . . . now that Kevin had ridden her and
made her filthy. And since she'd gone and gotten herself pregnant . . .

Those had been his words. "Now you gone and got
yourself pregnant, Sissy! You trying to ruin everything?"

At first she had felt guilty about her growing tummy.
But then, once there was a little flutter inside her, she
had thought of the chicks she'd seen hatching at

school, and she had starting liking the idea of a little chick of her own.

Her baby girl. Little Mac. Sis had been scared about having a baby, but once Mac was born, Sis could not love her enough. Mac had been born with blond hair like Sis's; only on Mac it was downy and fluffy like a baby chick.

Little Mac. Now Sis turned to the rise at the back of the compound. The tiny gravesite was marked by a wooden plaque painted with an angel. Sis had painted that angel with extra loving care, trying to capture Mac's little smile. Kevin had told her to write: R.I.P. Mac.

That stood for "rest in peace."

Sometimes Sis looked at it and wondered if a person had to die to find peace. Maybe.

As she was hoeing, there was a bang at the gate. Kevin . . . he was finally back, and mad, from the sound of it. Drunk? She hoped not. How could he find the money for whiskey when he said there was no more money for food? Since he didn't give a shout, she knew he didn't have a girlfriend with him, so she didn't have to hide in the shed.

There was a clank, and then the gate swung open. But instead of Kevin, two men peered in.

The hoe fell from her hands as she recognized their uniforms and stumbled backward. Police officers! She tripped over a ridge and landed in the grass.

She was in big trouble now. She could feel it as their angry eyes honed in on her as if she were a bull's-eye.

Lauren's fingers dug into the green, scraping up clover. If only she could disappear into the grass. Kevin would be so mad when he found out about this. And these men . . . would they lock her up in jail, as Kevin said. Jailbait, that was what he'd called her. They would crush her and toss her out like an old tissue.

A woman stepped in behind the two men. "Hey, there." Something about her reminded Sis of an angel. Maybe her silver hair, maybe her eyes, big and round and framed by smart black glasses.

But angel or not . . . Sis couldn't let them see her. This was against the rules. Kevin would be so mad.

She backed away, not sure what to do. It was too late to duck into the cabin or hide behind a tree. They had seen her. The two cops were headed right toward her.

"You okay?" one of them called.

Sis scrambled back, but there was no place to hide in this small, cluttered yard. There was no escaping.

"Hold on." The woman stopped the cops in just two words.

Was it that easy? Sis stared, awed by the woman's power.

"We've come to help you." Sunlight lit her silver hair like a halo. "Everyone here wants to help, even though it may seem kind of scary, with us bursting in here." The woman stepped forward, graceful but cautious. "So you don't need to be afraid. My name is Paula. What's yours?"

"My name's Sis." She grabbed the hoe and used it to lever herself up. "And this is private property. Not to be disrespectful, but you'd better get going. How did you get in here, anyway? Wasn't the gate locked?"

"It was locked." One of the cops, the leaner and younger one, held up a giant scissor thing. "We cut the chain."

Sis shifted her head down, afraid to look at the cops, afraid to let them get a good look at her. Her ankle throbbed at the thought of Kevin's anger. She would be blamed for this. This would mean another beating.

The woman stopped pressing forward, but she didn't take her eyes off Sis.

"Young lady? Can I ask you something?" The older cop with a big chest like a football player tilted his head as if he could understand her from a different angle. "How old are you?"

Keeping her head down, she swallowed back the smell of clover and fear. This was something she could answer. "Seventeen."

"That's young to be living here alone."

"My brother lives here with me. He went to town to get some groceries." She didn't explain that he had left two days ago.

Where *was* Kevin? He would know what to do with these people . . . how to handle them. She hacked away at the dirt, and then frowned up at the intruders. "So . . . yeah. My brother will be back any minute, so you'd better get going."

"This brother . . ." The older cop's badge caught a wink of the June sun. His uniform was dark and crisp, reminding Sis of a cop on one of the kids' shows Mac used to like. Those videos were still stacked in the cabin. "Is his name Kevin? Kevin Hawkins?"

Sis's heart stammered in her chest. Was this some kind of a trick? "That's him."

"We have him in custody, young lady. He's not coming back here anytime soon."

"He is? What did he do?"

"We caught him trying to rob a store. But the important thing is that he's confessed. He says he kidnapped you some six years ago."

Sis stared down at the dirt of the garden and retreated into herself as the world began to drop away around her. She was like a scrawny ant frozen in place as the hoe came down all around her, chopping her earth away.

"So we came here to help you," Paula said. "To rescue you. The worst is over, honey." The woman seemed kind. She had eyes as dark as chocolate and a softness to her plump figure that made Sis want to bury her face against her and close her eyes.

"Are you ready to come with us?" the older cop asked.

"No . . . no! I need to stay here." Lauren's whole body began to tremble at the thought of the trouble ahead. To the outside world, she was jailbait. Trash. A filthy slut. Kevin had warned her about going out there. If she just waited here in the compound, Kevin would be back to take care of her.

And then . . . then the woman called to her, real gentle.

"It's going to be okay, Lauren."

Lauren.

The name was like the breeze that cooled you off at night. A drink of water when your throat was dry. But it also made Sis hurt inside—one of those deep, dark aches that you never outgrow.

Paula reached out to her. How did the woman manage to inch so close?

"Come with me, Lauren. We're going to get you home."

With trepidation beating in her chest like a panicked bat, Lauren put down the hoe, took Paula's hand, and followed her out of the veggie patch.

Chapter 7

The sea of royal blue shrank as the graduates filed out of the high school gymnasium. Still sitting in the bleachers, Rachel and Julia held hands, their faces streaked with tears.

"Life is fickle, I'll give you that. I never thought it would be this way," Julia said. "I thought John and I would be looking forward to empty-nesting at this point. You know, getting ready to kick it together when we sent Nora off to college. I never dreamed that he wouldn't bother to attend his daughter's graduation because of a family commitment on his girlfriend's side. I thought Lauren would make it back in time to graduate. That's unrealistic, I know. A true delusion, coming from a licensed therapist. But she was always such a good student; she could have caught up."

"It's not deluded at all." Rachel sniffed. "Look at me, attending a graduation when my daughter never even made it to junior high." Tears blurred the dissolving river of blue down on the gym floor as she recalled Sierra's sharp words just last night.

"You're cray cray, Mom! Doesn't your therapist tell you that? Doesn't she tell you that you're crazy to keep acting like Lauren is going to turn up after all these years?"

Rachel had been tempted to argue that therapists were not in the business of telling people they were crazy; they had a million other ways of saying that. Instead, she had tried to keep it positive. "Honey, I just want to sing 'Tell Me Why' while we do the dishes. It's a women's tradition in our family. It's our thing."

"It's *your* thing. Yours and Lauren's, and you keep singing it because you know 'she's looking out at the very same stars at night.' " Sierra's mocking voice had been downright offensive. The little brat. But Rachael knew the responsibility was hers for neglecting Sierra while she scoured the earth for Lauren. It was a no-win situation, but Rachel had chosen to focus the bulk of her attention on the daughter who desperately needed it.

"Don't you ever think of her?" Rachel had asked. "You were so young. You probably don't remember."

"OMG!" With a grunt, Sierra had tossed a wet baking sheet onto the granite counter. "I try not to think of her because I am trying to live in the present! And I was six when she disappeared, not six months!" She wiped her hands on the dishcloth and tossed it into the sink before storming dramatically out of the kitchen. "I quit."

Left to her own devices, Rachel had leaned against the sink, searched the night sky, and started mouthing the song, minus the harmony. "Tell me why the stars do shine . . ." Singing in a low, soothing voice, she had scrubbed and dried and buffed the countertops to a reflective gleam. "Because God made the stars to shine. Because God made the ivy twine . . ."

Now, Rachel squeezed her friend's hand as Julia mentioned the grief John had been giving her about paying his half of Nora's college tuition. Talk about cray cray. This did not sound at all like the John Berton who had seemed like the model father.

Julia was still talking when Rachel's phone buzzed. Rachel pulled one hand away and saw that it was from the City of Mirror Lake. "Sorry, Jules, but I guess I should take this."

"Go right ahead." Julia waved her off. "I need to pull myself together before the festivities continue."

Rachel pressed the answer button. "Hello?"

"Rachel, this is Hank Todd from MLPD. Are you sitting down?"

"Well, yeah." Rachel scratched the back of her neck. "What's going on?"

"We found her."

Her confusion bubbled into joy. "Lauren? You found Lauren?"

A gasp from Julia, who began shaking Rachel's shoulder in a celebratory cheer.

"We're taking her into custody now," Hank explained. "Apprehended the alleged kidnapper this morning on another charge. She seems fine, Rachel. Scared, and a little shook up, which is understandable. But it was damned good to see her."

An image of her daughter, blond hair lit by the sun, burned in Rachel's mind. "You found Lauren, and she's okay? Our girl's okay?"

"That's what I said. Dave is on the phone with your husband. There's going to be some questions and social service protocol at the precinct. You want to meet us there?"

Bag slung over her shoulder, Rachel was already halfway down the bleachers. "I'm on my way."

*   *   *

Everything familiar and safe was falling away around her . . . pushing her to the big, bad world Kevin had always warned her about. Sis wiped her sweaty hands on her flowered shift, embarrassed as the two cops poked around in the shed. They would see her chamber pot. And the cage, that big, hateful kennel. Although she had draped flowered sheets over it to soften the cold metal look, it was still a human cage. She didn't want them seeing that, thinking of her as a smelly, dirty animal.

"Are the police arresting me?" she asked, limping along beside Paula.

"No, sweet pea. You didn't break any laws. You have nothing to worry about."

"Then why can't I stay here?" Sis stopped walking, tugging Paula to a halt. "I need to stay here."

They kept saying that they would take her home, but this was her home, wasn't it? Long ago, she had given up dreaming of the sort of home other people had, with a family and friends and dogs. A life with places to go and people to meet. Sis couldn't imagine sleeping anywhere but in her little tent beside the cabin. Even the cage in the shed was more of a home than anywhere in the strange world over the hillside.

The thought of walking over that hill reminded her of the day Kevin had forced her out onto the rocks in the ocean. The other side of that hill was a cliff, a drop-off to terrible things. Punishment and shame. Rejection from her parents.

"They forgot about you pretty fast," Kevin had told her years ago when she'd bugged him with questions about her family. *"You're lucky I found you, 'cause a man like me, I'll take care of you. And I'll never let you go."*

She hadn't chosen this; never, never, never would she have chosen to live here with Kevin. But there was a weird security in knowing that he would do his best to take care of her.

Clasping Sis's hands between hers, Paula faced her squarely. "Let's talk about this a minute. Can you tell me what's keeping you here? Why do you want to stay?"

I don't. I want to run away, bounce away, flap my wings and fly away like a strong bird.

Sis closed her eyes, trying to hold back the tears. Finally, after six years, she had her chance to leave, and she couldn't take it. She couldn't even squeeze out a word to this nice woman.

"You can't think of a reason to stay, or you're too overwhelmed to talk?"

Sis shook her head as a hot tear rolled down her cheek. "I don't know." Her lips warbled. Everything was wobbly and unsteady.

Paula patted her hand. "That's okay. You'll find the words one of these days, and when you do, they'll flow fast and furious like the Columbia. Do you remember studying rivers in school?"

The smell of chalk and stale peanut butter came to mind as Sis sniffed back a tear. There had been a lot of things she did not like about school—homework, boring recess, and a P.E. teacher who seemed heartless when kids got hurt. But all things considered, she would choose a dull school day over a day of weeding or toting water in this compound.

"Here's what I'm thinking." Paula kept talking to her as if she mattered. Sis liked that. "Change is hard. We all fight it, and leaving here means a huge change for you. But through that gate and over that hill are people who love you. They've been searching for you and praying for you for years, and they're going to jump for joy when they see you."

Paula was wrong about that. If her parents had

wanted to find her, well, they would have found her, plain and simple. But right now, Sis didn't see that she had much choice but to go along with the police, the men with guns.

"Is there anything you want to take along? Any clothes?" Paula looked over her shoulder toward the cabin. "I'll help you pack up."

None of the clothes Kevin had bought appealed to Sis. He had gotten them for her from thrift shops and discount stores. "Clearance sale!" he would crow, then show her some granny dress. But then she thought of Mac. He had taken most of her clothes, but she had hung on to her blanket and her magic shell.

"There are a few things I want to take." The words rasped from her dry throat. She was parched and tired and exhilarated, and she hadn't even stepped outside the gate yet.

Paula squeezed her hands. "Good girl."

She held onto the woman's hands a moment, thinking how good it felt to hear those words. Kevin was nice sometimes, but mostly he spoke when she did something wrong. Her gaze traveled from Paula's sturdy hands and up to her wrist, where a splotch of red blood dripped down her arm. She gripped the woman's hand and turned it, gently. "Are you bleeding?"

"Oh, dear, no. It's just red paint. I was painting a picture when I got the call to come get you."

"You were painting something red?"

"Three little red hens." Paula tilted her head back when she smiled. "A little too red, I'm afraid."

"I'm an artist, too." Sis felt shy and bold and wobbly, all at the same time, but there was no going back now. Besides, if anyone would understand, it would be this woman with fat black nerd glasses and paint on her arms. "I'll show you."

Inside the cabin, Paula admired her work. "Wow, you really kept busy." She stepped carefully over a rusted tricycle Kevin had brought home one day, her steady gaze following the tentacle of a creature Sis called Kraken.

"I always liked to draw. And the walls in here were so ugly that Kevin didn't mind if I covered them."

Paula told her nice things about the paintings as Sis scooped Mac's stuff into a shopping bag. And that was that. Six years, and everything that mattered could fit into one paper bag with room to spare.

The gate screeched as they followed the police officers out of the compound. Just a rust-hinged gate on an old wooden fence. How had it kept her here, all these years? It was cool and shady here under the cover of trees that had hidden her for all these years.

The path to the creek seemed short now. No one spoke as they crossed the large, smooth stones and made their way up the grassy hill, toward the world. Toward the future, Sis told herself, trying to put a bright face on it. She was curious. Whenever they left the compound, Kevin had kept her blindfolded in the back, though she had begged him for a peek, aching to see where she lived, wanting to know the tiny pin dot on the map where she belonged.

They climbed the hill, rising, rising until the crest, where they looked over a small valley of farmland encased by a busy roadway and a walking path.

Sis paused to gape at the orange and silver streamers that glittered in the wind over the crops, as if winking in welcome. The flicker of silver was dazzling, and for a second Sis thought they were party decorations until she realized that it was a way to keep the birds from picking away at the crops of Green Spring Farm.

Yes, Green Spring Farm, right on the border of Mirror Lake and West Green. She had visited here as a kid for a summer day camp and school trips. The farm was just a mile or two from where her family used to live. So close, and no one had thought to look here? Kevin was right; they had given up on her.

"You okay?" Paula asked.

"I just . . . I need a minute." Because she couldn't believe the life that had surrounded her. The whole scene held her rapt. Cars zoomed past in the distance. On the path, women pushed strollers. There were runners and kids on bikes and people walking their dogs. It was not as bad as Kevin said, not so bad after all. In fact, it seemed busy and alive, like a teeming ant colony.

Her eyes filled with tears at the realization that all these people, all this activity, had always been just over the ridge. Life had been just a stone's throw away.

Chapter 8

Earlier, at the farm, the adrenaline high had kept Paula moving, courting the girl, soothing her, and listening. Always listening.

She had listened as Lauren casually mentioned the child she'd born, and the older woman watched without judgment as the girl dropped a baby blanket, a sea shell, and a worn stuffed bear into a shopping bag. She had listened as Lauren described her daughter's sickness and death. She had detected the girl's sorrow but reluctance to dwell when she had pointed out the small grave across the yard, its wooden marker hand-painted by Lauren. She had listened as Lauren explained her paintings of phobias and whimsical creatures. She had watched in wonder as the girl had revealed a "secret panel" in the wall, the opening to a small closet where Lauren had painted a portrait of herself holding her baby, Mackenzie.

A child Madonna, with sprays of golden light around mother and baby.

"I like your halo," she had said, and Lauren had corrected her, saying that it was the light inside.

"Everyone has a single, beautiful light inside them," Lauren had said, as if this lesson were as matter-of-fact as instructions on hygiene or crossing the street. "And even when we go to heaven, that light keeps shining."

"That's beautiful." Paula had commented that she would remember to add a light the next time she painted a person. The girl had told her that she'd gotten lots of practice doing portraits. That was how she and Kevin made money, setting up a starving artist stand at farmers' markets and fairs and the Saturday market in Portland.

Now that they were back at the precinct, the adrenaline rush had subsided, but the mission remained. This little girl needed all the help and resources Paula could muster. Plucked from her neighborhood and raped at age eleven, pregnant at twelve, and a mother by the age of thirteen, and then burying her own daughter three years later, this young person had already survived a lifetime of hardship, and she wasn't even old enough to vote in an election.

Paula was committed to advocating for the best interests of Lauren O'Neil, who was jittery and tearful and overwhelmed.

Chief Todd knocked on the door and stepped in. "Hey, there. You really were thirsty." He nodded down at the empty bottle in Lauren's hands. "Do you want another one?"

Lauren looked to Paula for permission. "Can I?"

"Well, sure."

Lauren peeked at the chief, and then bent her head down again.

"Lauren, you don't have to be afraid of Chief Todd. He's here to help you."

"I know. I know him. . . . you." She dared to glance up at him. "You came to my elementary school. You were a cop then."

"Did I?" Hank's green eyes twinkled when he smiled gently, hunching down to Lauren's level. Hank understood about body language in communication. "That must have been some time ago."

The girl nodded. "Am I under arrest?"

"No." Hank's tone was gentle. "You didn't do anything wrong, did you?"

She took a deep breath. "Everyone has done something wrong. Everyone makes mistakes."

The girl was too wise for her years. "That's true," Paula agreed. "But you didn't break the law. Kevin Hawkins did. He's the one under arrest."

Lauren looked toward the door. "Is he here in a jail cell? Can I talk to him?"

"Right now he's at the county jail in Clackamas," Hank said, "but you don't need to worry. They'll be moving him down to a maximum security prison in Salem soon."

"But I need to talk to him." Lauren turned pleading eyes to Paula. "Can't I see him?"

"Why would you want to do that?" Even as she asked, Paula knew the answer. Kidnapping victims often became indoctrinated to go along with their kidnappers. The so-called Stockholm syndrome was not brainwashing, but an unconscious decision to go along with the captor in order to survive.

Lauren shrugged. "I need to talk to him."

That was not going to happen anytime soon. Paula knew the police, prosecutors, and FBI were scouring Hawkins's life and the evidence at the compound, and the suspect would be questioned extensively from here till the trial. "How about some more water?" Paula asked.

"I'll get it." Hank straightened. "And I have good news. Rachel and Dan O'Neil are here. Your parents. And they can't wait to see you."

"Not now." Lauren turned to Paula. "Do I have to see them?"

Hank's lower lip went stiff as he shot Paula a concerned look. "They're really eager to see you," he told Lauren in a cajoling tone. "Did Paula tell you how they've been searching for you since the day you disappeared? Your parents kept every cop here on his toes, looking for you. They love you a lot, kiddo."

Perfect, Hank. That's what she needs to hear. Paula turned to the girl, but saw no change in her demeanor.

"But they didn't find me." Lauren squinted, as if trying to do a calculation that didn't work out. "I was right under their nose—right here in Mirror Lake—and they never found me. It doesn't sound to me like they looked too hard."

"Green Spring Farm was searched," Paula said. "I was there, one of many volunteers, and we walked every field. The police checked those buildings in the compound, and there was no sign of you."

"But that was right after you were kidnapped," Hank said. "You say he kept you at a beach house for a few months."

Lauren nodded. "About six months I think. I didn't have a calendar, but it was fall, I think, because it wasn't so hot during the days, and the nights were getting cold." Hank rubbed a hand over his graying buzz cut. "He must have moved you to Green Spring later, knowing we had already searched the farm."

"But that doesn't take away from the fact that your mom and dad scoured the state of Oregon looking for you, honey." And they *were* Lauren's parents. By law, they were entitled to take her home tonight. Paula knew that wouldn't set well with Lauren, but she didn't dare go there yet. "The first step is for you to meet with them. How about I go out and bring them in?"

Lauren's mouth puckered as her eyes filled with tears. "Can't you talk to them? Tell them I . . . I can't see them now."

"I will definitely talk to them and fill them in on some of the things that you went through while in captivity. But come on, now. You're a survivor." Paula rubbed Lauren's shoulder. "I know this is beyond awkward, but they're your mom and dad. They love you, Lauren."

The girl shook her head. "After all this? I don't think so. I gave up on them a long time ago, and I just don't want to see them. Please, don't make me do it." Her pleading eyes tore at Paula's resolve.

"Let's take things one step at a time." Paula went to the door and paused. "You sit tight, while I go have a word with them."

"Where would I go?" Lauren's face seemed childish as she pressed her lips together, holding back tears. "I'm not going anywhere without you."

She's bonded with me. Paula knew there were good and bad aspects to that. "One step at a time," she said before heading down the hall.

Chapter 9

In the waiting room of the police precinct, Sierra watched as her mom tore DON'T STOP BELIEVING! flyers, all featuring a big photo of a smiling Lauren, from the bulletin board. Sierra took a flyer from her mother and stared at the big photo of Lauren—retouched by some computer nerd to make her look six years older.

"Do you think she actually looks like this?" Sierra asked.

Mom gave her arm a squeeze. "We'll see."

The bulletin board seemed bare now with only Kyron Horman, the nine-year-old boy who'd been snatched from his school, hanging there. Sierra crumpled the flyer in her hand into a ball and tucked it under her chin and closed her eyes as the news began to set in.

It was finally over.

The monthly searches, the awareness campaign, the recitals and car washes and auctions to raise money for more searches. No more spikey hawthorns scraping her legs. No more snakes slithering out of tall grasses along the edge of the walking path. Sierra would be happy to keep to the path from now on.

She slunk down low on the plastic chair and stared at her cell phone. On Facebook were fresh photos of Jemma, Isabelle, and Lindsay at Boondoggy's, posing with their vests on and laser guns pointed. Right about now they were probably in the middle of a laser tag game, making memories without her.

Why did Dad pull her out of there when she could have gotten a ride home with Isabelle's dad? It was great about Lauren, really great, but it still didn't make sense for her to be sitting here waiting when she could be hanging out with her friends.

KEEP THE HOME FIRES BURNING was the banner on the top of the flyer. Sierra had helped her dad design the first few, but then Mom decided they should all look the same. "We need to create our own unique brand," she'd said. Even though Dad was the one with OCD, when it came to Lauren, Mom had to have everything her way.

"I still can't believe it." Dad paced over to the doorway, peered down the corridor, then circled back to face Mom. "When can we see her? What's the holdup?"

"I know, I'm dying to see her, too." Mom stepped into his arms, flopping the flyers against his back as she hugged him.

God, they could be the couple in that mouthwash commercial.

"I just want to take our girl home." Mom leaned back, smiling at Dad. Then she flashed a look over at Sierra. "Just think . . . we're going to be a family again!"

Oh, God. Sierra snapped her head back to her cell phone to scroll down her Facebook feed.

"I'll be happy to say good-bye to this place." Dad reached over to straighten Kyron's flyer on the bulletin board. "But Hank says this will get worse before it gets better. The FBI is on its way to interview Lauren."

"And NCMEC," Mom added.

That stood for the National Center for Missing and Exploited Children. Those people knew their stuff, but Sierra had always been more impressed with the FBI agents—men and women in suits with guns and cool badges that were mostly concealed. Sort of like Men in Black.

"Hold on to your hat, because it's going to get crazy around here. I wish they could all just interview her at the house," Mom said. "She needs to get out of this sterile environment. I wonder if the cops scare her."

Dad shrugged. "I know we didn't find her ourselves, but I have to think that our relentless searches and awareness campaign kept Lauren's image in the public eye."

"The largest search in the history of Oregon," Sierra said without looking up from her phone. They all knew the pitch printed on every flyer. "With law enforcement from all over the state. Volunteers logged in more than 100,000 man-hours searching for Lauren O'Neil."

"I hope you're celebrating our success." Her mom's eyebrows arched in inquisition. "Because you sound a little sarcastic, Sierra."

"Of course I'm celebrating." She wanted it to be over. She just wasn't so sure about having a strange girl back in their house again. Would they have to share a bathroom? Yuck.

"What's taking so long?" Mom shot a look at Dad, then went up to the counter. "Pete," she said, addressing Officer Wolinsky, a cop their whole family knew well, "we need to see our daughter."

"I'll get Hank." He got up and went down the hall.

Yeah, bring out the big guns, Sierra thought as Officer Wolly went to get the chief of police. Hank Todd was a big man: kind and friendly with a good sense of humor. She understood why her parents liked him, why the whole town of Mirror Lake liked him. But it was awkward when the police chief was like family. Chief Todd had made a joke about that a few months ago when he'd found Sierra with a bunch of her friends, huddled off one of the park trails. Some joke about weed, which they *had* been smoking, though Isabelle shoved the pipe into her purse, lit and everything.

That was the problem when the cops in your neighborhood became like family—like aunts and uncles, on a first-name basis. Over the past six years they had gathered a few times a year to renew search efforts or stage some kind of service to keep the home fires burning for Lauren.

Officer Wolinsky came over to the chairs, where Sierra was waiting. "I just sent your parents in to talk with Hank. You need anything? A Pepsi or bottle of water?"

"No. I'm good, Wolly."

"Okay, then." He held up a hand and she fist-bumped him. "Bet you'll be glad to have your sister back."

"Absolutely," she said with enthusiasm she didn't feel.

"You let me know if there's anything I can get you." Officer Wolly went back to the dispatch desk.

And once again, Sierra found herself left alone.

Safe . . . but very alone. Even in a crowded room, Sierra was alone.

Chapter 10

In another time and place, Rachel would have liked Paula Winkler. With a cloud of silver hair, square black glasses, Frye boots, denim jacket, and a medallion of colored glass, the woman had a solid but whimsical vibe that was one part hippie and one part cowgirl. But at the moment, the social worker was the one thing standing between Rachel and her daughter. A ridiculous barrier after all these years.

"What's the holdup?" Rachel tried to press her point without revealing her agitation. "Why can't we see our daughter?"

Dan slid his arm around her as they huddled in the door of Hank's office, a far too familiar place from the past few years.

Paula leaned back against Hank's desk and folded her arms, her face projecting concern. "Please, bear with us for just a few more minutes. You're going to see her, but we want it to be on Lauren's terms."

"Her terms?" Rachel pressed into the office and dropped into a chair. "She's seventeen years old and we're her parents. Her legal guardians. We should be in there with her, protecting her from cops and social workers who ask too many painful questions."

Paula held up her hands. "Advocating for Lauren is my top priority, and right now she's overwhelmed. I'm sure you understand that assimilating after six years in captivity is difficult and complex. Just so you know, you all have a lot of therapy in your future. She's going to need time—maybe a lot—for debriefing and acclimation. You and your daughter have been through hell, and you're going to need support to make the journey back."

Dan leaned against the file cabinet, arms folded. "What kind of therapy are we talking about?" Rachel heard the cynicism in his voice; he was not an advocate of wasting time on a shrink's couch. Too invasive, too touchy-feely, and way too expensive.

"I'm going to get in touch with a friend of mine who specializes in reunification. Right now she's doing a lot of work with military families who need help adjusting when a veteran returns home. I think you'll want to work with someone like her. Someone who can help Lauren address her trauma and the changes in her family, as well as helping you deal with your own trauma. She focuses on things like developing coping skills and lines of communication."

"Yes, yes, of course." Rachel raked a hand through her hair and closed her eyes against the deluge of information. The three of them had been in and out of therapy since Lauren's abduction, without great results. Or had that been the one thing holding their marriage together? Whatever. Right now, she just wanted to see Lauren.

"So we'll do therapy with her—relocation therapy." She opened her eyes and leveled a beseeching look at

Paula Winkler. "We just want to take our daughter home. How much longer?"

The woman frowned down at her clipboard. "Rachel, I'm sorry to disappoint, but I don't see it happening today. The FBI and the folks from NCMEC need to see her, and then we'll be heading over to the Westridge Hospital. I noticed a limp when we were walking to the car. She says it's fine, but we'll need to get X-rays. But that's not the worst of it, and you'd better brace yourself." The social worker drew in a tight breath, her gaze shifting from Dan and Rachel, who pressed back in her chair.

Rachel knew what was coming.

The fodder of her nightmares.

"Lauren was raped. It started soon after the abduction. She bore a child when she was thirteen—she had a baby girl."

Rachel pressed a fist to her mouth to keep herself from crying out. Lauren had been a girl herself . . . a child bearing a child.

Dan's hand tightened on her shoulder. "So we're grandparents? Where is the little girl?"

"I'm sorry." Paula paused to give each of them a sympathetic look. "I'm so sorry, but you need to know. The child died shortly after her third birthday. It sounds like asthma or pneumonia. Lord knows, the baby wasn't allowed any medical care or immunizations."

"He's an animal." Dan's voice was eerily calm. "I hope he gets the death penalty. I'll throw the switch myself if they let me."

"Well . . . ," Paula cocked her head to one side, "that's for the courts to decide."

Right now, Rachel didn't have room in her thoughts for the man who had abducted her child. She had to stay focused on Lauren. "I won't waste time or energy on that monster."

Paula nodded. "You're right. You don't want to waste time on things you can't change. Lauren is still grieving for her little girl. She lost her in February, just after Valentine's Day."

The barbs were so fast and furious, Rachel was numbing over. "What can we do to help her now?"

"For starters, I think she should meet with you individually at first. This is all overwhelming for her, and that would help her to keep things focused and calm."

Rachel looked at Dan, and then nodded. "What else? How can we help her?"

"I can bring her favorite ice cream or one of her sketchbooks from home," Dan suggested.

God love him! Rachel would have hugged him if she had the energy to move, but this new wave of news had drained her.

"She says she's not hungry, but that would be a wonderful gesture," Paula said.

Dan was already at the door. "The ice cream or the sketchbook?"

"The sketchbook would definitely reach her. Your daughter is still an artist, and very talented. I saw some of her work in the cabin."

"Got it." He disappeared with a wave. That was Dan: man of action, firefighter, doer, and hero. She envied his ability to shed regret and fear by taking action.

Unlike his wife, who was left sitting here and wondering at the source of Paula's prevarication. As a teacher, Rachel had plenty of experience couching things in euphemisms for the parents of her students. She could read between the lines of Paula's hesitance. Why didn't their daughter want to see them?

*   *   *

Long tanned legs, thin, muscular arms, and a woman's body—this woman couldn't be her daughter. Dressed in a loose flowered shift, her golden hair coiled and pinned by two chopsticks, she looked like a model for some eclectic designer collection.

But as Rachel crossed the room in three long strides, the young woman lifted her chin to face her, and recognition flashed through Rachel at the sight of Lauren's exquisite amber eyes, Lauren's thoughtful, pouty lips, Lauren's squinty face, the expression that showed she was struggling to comprehend something.

"Mommy?" the young woman croaked, peering at Rachel.

Rachel nodded and the two hugged, but Rachel felt as if she were embracing a mannequin. Gently, she shifted away to examine her daughter once again. "Oh, honey! Look at you, so grown up." Rachel's throat was thick with emotion. "We've missed you so much."

Lauren's golden eyes brimmed over with confusion. "I had my own daughter, too. I was a mother but . . . but my little girl died," Lauren said, her heartbreak palpable.

"I'll bet you miss her."

Lauren nodded, leaning away from Rachel's scrutiny.

Give her some space and stop gushing. As Rachel took a seat across from her daughter, she sensed fear in those golden eyes. Everyone used to say that Lauren had Dan's eyes and Rachel's sumptuous mouth, but now . . . now these features had melded into a beautiful young woman who was a world apart. A beautiful, wary young woman.

Rachel tried not to crowd Lauren, but she couldn't help scanning her daughter from head to toe, making sure she was really there. Safe and sound, at last. "Words can't describe how happy I am at this moment."

Lauren squinted up at Rachel, then turned to Paula. "This is awkward." Her tone was pleading.

Like a splash in the face, reminders of Lauren's social awkwardness hit Rachel. A few teachers had noticed red flags, and there'd been talk of testing her for Asperger's, but Rachel and Dan had declined at the time.

Oh, Lauren, Lauren, baby, honey . . . you don't have to feel awkward around me.

"Sometimes reunions are awkward." Paula's intervention lightened the strain in the air. "It's not easy to communicate with people we haven't seen for years. And a lot has happened. I know you both have so much to say, but it'll take a while to get to that comfortable place where the words flow. Give it time."

Rachel felt Paula warding her off, and the unfairness of it bruised her. She had given six years, and so had Lauren. Why did they have to sit back and be patient?

There was a knock on the door, and Hank poked his head in. "Two agents from the FBI are here. Are you ready for them?"

Again, Lauren turned to Paula, who rose with her clipboard. "Bring 'em on."

"Is it all right if I stay?" Rachel directed the question more at Paula, obviously the one in charge here. "I may be able to help."

Paula cocked her head. "I think that's a good idea. Okay with you, Lauren?"

The girl shrugged, her eyes averted from Rachel. "Whatever."

The word was a dagger in her heart, but Rachel remained in her chair and folded her hands studiously. This was a start. Baby steps, but steps in the right direction.

Chapter 11

The officer moved the bright orange barricade aside, and Hank Todd pulled his Jeep forward, gravel crackling under the tires as he rolled toward the farm. It was strange to see Green Spring Farm vacant of the usual patrons—farm workers and golden agers, children and their moms, folks working a small parcel of growing space in the community garden run by Vera Hawkins. Today the buildings had been taken over by police cars and black sedans, the vehicles of cops and federal agents.

"Looks like it was a nice place," said Hapburg.

"It was a nice place." But not anymore. Hank wondered how the community would respond to a young kidnap victim being held behind their revered green space. Some folks would want to take a match to these buildings and plow over every field. Personally, Hank didn't blame the land.

"I've been through the compound out back. A real hellhole. What's the story on this farm?" As chief of the Portland-Salem region of the bureau, Mark Hapburg was the highest ranking official on the case. The boss. Mark and the federal prosecutor, whoever that ended up being, would call most of the shots on this case, and that suited Hank just fine.

"The farm is owned by an elderly woman, Vera Hawkins, who inherited it from family. The Hawkins family has been here for three generations now. Vera can't get out to the fields anymore, in a wheelchair now, but she's still involved in the family business. Most of the land is leased. There's a group of cooperative farmers who farm most of the acres. They use one of the barns; the other is leased to the city for meetings, workshops, summer camps, stuff like that. The old farmhouse is rented by a garden club and flower society. They've got an arboretum set up on the grounds, open to the public. All the flowers are labeled and tagged. It's nice."

The community garden stood atop the rise, many of the small lots dotted with scarecrows dressed in stuffed clothing. The place was downright creepy after dark; every Halloween, the Mirror Lake cops had to station a patrol car up here to ward off the ghoulish thrill seekers.

"So who are we interviewing?" Hapburg asked.

"Vera Hawkins herself." He steered to the end of the lane, an unobtrusive ranch house where Vera had moved when managing the big farmhouse got to be too much for a woman with her health issues. "She's the aunt of Kevin Hawkins. She's been refusing to talk to my cops."

"Was she aiding and abetting?"

"Don't know. As I said, she's not talking." Hank parked near the one-car garage and cut the engine. His hand was on the door handle when Hapburg stopped him.

"One more thing before we go in."

Hank turned to the man in the dark suit. Although they'd exchanged hundreds of e-mails, he'd met him only a handful of times over the past few years—not enough contact to be able to read him.

"The thing is, Hank, you know the lay of the land here. You've been working with the family all these years. I've got the resources to back you up, but you've got the experience and the know-how here. Stay on the case with me. Be my manager."

"I could do that." Hank rubbed his chin, studying Hapburg. "This doesn't sound like the complaints folks have about the FBI coming in and taking over their cases, elbowing them out."

"Would you believe that it's a kinder, gentler bureau?"

"No."

Hapburg snorted. "Okay, I'll be equally blunt. I've got a shitload of leave accumulated, and the wife has booked a six-week vacation in Europe. She's threatened divorce if I cancel again, and though that has its appeal, I'm leaning toward the trip."

It was Hank's turn to scoff. "This is about the Eiffel Tower?"

Hapburg winced. "Don't bust my chops. You manage and I'll give you all the backup you need. I've got a female agent coming in today to guard the victim. Bija Wilson. Do you know her? She's one of the best. Our forensic team is already processing the scene, and they'll stay on it until they get to the bottom of that trash heap Sanford and Sons accumulated. Honestly, I can bring in someone else from the bureau, but keeping you as the lead on the case, that just feels right."

"I'll do it." Hank lifted a hand to stop the pitch. "I wanted to stay on it anyway."

"Why didn't you just say so?"

"What, and miss you blowing smoke up my ass?"

Both men were grinning as they followed the flagstone path up to the side door of the simple, cedar-sided ranch house. The female officer at the door told them Vera was inside, alone and annoyed that the cops had overrun her farm and her home.

"That sounds like what I know of Vera." He knocked on the door, waited a minute, then pushed it open.

He recognized the redheaded woman in the wheelchair that blocked the path from the door. Vera Hawkins stared up at them with a hard-bitten scowl. "What's going on? You go barging into someone's home without being invited?"

"I knocked. I knew you were disabled, so I didn't want to make you come to the door." Hank introduced himself and Hapburg. "How are you doing, Vera?"

"That's a stupid question. You shut down my farm and the place is crawling with cops. It's not a good day." It was hard to guess at Vera Hawkins's age; her penny-bright hair was definitely out of a bottle, and though her face wasn't aged in terms of wrinkles, there was a dryness around her eyes and mouth that hinted at many years over rugged terrain. He figured sixty or seventy.

"I'm sorry about your business, ma'am," Hapburg said, not sounding at all apologetic, "but we've got to preserve the crime scene. You had a kidnap victim living on your property, and we can't have people wandering back to the compound."

"Nobody ever goes back there. That section is overgrown, covered with blackberry brambles. No one even knows that cabin is there."

"But you did." The FBI agent lowered his chin, his dead eyes homing in on Vera.

"Did you ever meet Lauren O'Neil, the kidnap victim?"

"Never met her."

"Because if you knew about the kidnapping on your property, that would be aiding and abetting." Hapburg was cheerful, as if he were explaining arithmetic to a child. "Under federal law, you'd be facing the same punishment as the kidnapper."

Vera turned to Hank. "Does your friend have a hearing problem? I said I never. Met. Her."

"But you knew about the compound?" Hapburg persisted.

Hank tried to keep his body neutral, not keen on the way the FBI boss was turning this interview into an interrogation. Hank found that you usually got more bees with honey than with law-enforcement vitriol.

"Let me tell you something, Mr. Hamburg. Around these parts, a farmer knows her land. I knew about the compound. That cabin was built as a foreman's quarters back in the 1940s when this place was a horse ranch. I had no use for it until Kevin came along, looking for a place to bunk and a job. That was some time ago. Seven . . . eight years ago. He'd been tossed out on his ear by his father. My brother never did have patience."

"Did you know your nephew had a history of sexual assault? That he was found guilty of three rapes?"

She cocked one brow. "Boys get into trouble. By the time Kev came to me, he was in his twenties, more settled. He was polite and grateful for a place to live."

"You said you gave him a job," Hank said quietly. "Is he still on your payroll?"

She waved the question off. "Not for years. Kevin wasn't cut out to be a farmer."

"What did you think he was doing for money?" Hapburg asked. "Aside from robbing discount stores?"

"I didn't give it any thought. He wasn't coming around here with his hand out, so it was no bother to me."

"Did you charge him rent?" Hank asked.

"It wasn't like I was going to get another renter back there. There's no kitchen, and the plumbing is raw. Not even a hot water heater."

"There is now. Apparently your nephew installed one. I guess he could be handy when the spirit moved him."

The grooves around her mouth deepened as she scowled. "Well, good for him, fixing up the place."

Hank brought up photos of the compound on his phone and showed them to Vera. "He also installed a wood-burning stove, and there was a small fridge and a hot plate. But the cabin wasn't really fixed up." He scrolled over to some exterior photos. "There were mounds of neglected trash, a leaking roof, and, well, general disrepair."

"And what the hell is this?" Vera pointed to a wall decorated with one of Lauren's murals.

"That's a painting Lauren O'Neil did to liven the place up. She's quite an artist," Hank said, though Vera's mouth remained crimped.

"Just about every wall and beam is covered with art," Hapburg added. "I guess that's what happens when an artist has a lot time on her hands. Six years." His eyes narrowed. "So what have you been doing for the past six years? You mean to say your nephew never brought her around."

"Never. I didn't know the O'Neil girl was back there until I heard it from that cop outside the door." Her beady eyes flicked from Hapburg to Hank. "I can't get back there anymore in this chair. And once I knew my nephew was bunking in the place, I gave up trying."

"Really. I thought that a farmer knew her land," Hapburg mimicked. "Around these parts."

Vera Hawkins swiveled the chair away from the man and wheeled herself down the hall. "We're done," she called without looking back. "Close the door behind you."

As the two men headed to the Jeep, Hapburg glanced back. "I don't think she likes us."

"It's you she doesn't like." Hank clapped Hapburg on the shoulder. "Good thing you're going to Europe." Although the FBI agent laughed, it wasn't really a joke. Hank figured he might get more out of Vera Hawkins when things cooled down. He just needed a chance to play good cop.

Chapter 12

Sis was scared by the men—the cops and agents and doctors—but the women weren't so bad. Especially Paula. She said she was a social worker, but she was also an artist, and Lauren figured that meant she understood more about the way Sis's brain worked than most people.

Paula was practical, too. She understood that Sis was too riled up to eat, but she got her water bottles and reminded her to stay hydrated. She sent the dad to get her a yummy chocolate milkshake that went down easy. And at the police station and the hospital, she always helped Sis find the ladies' room and let her go whenever she wanted. That was a relief, after Kevin's stinginess with bathroom time. With the way things were set up in the compound, she'd rarely had privacy, and on occasion she had been forced to dig her own latrine when the plumbing wasn't working.

At the hospital, when the doctor announced that Sis needed a cast on her left leg, Paula made sure that Lauren got to shower first, and she pressured the doctor to give Sis a waterproof cast in orange. Sis got to pick the color, and she thought it was festive, a way to celebrate her "recovery," which was what all the agents and cops were calling it.

Sis clung to the fact that Paula had not left her side. Sometimes she stepped outside the door to talk with the police, and she gave Sis privacy in the bathroom. But otherwise, Paula stayed with her the way she imagined a big sister or a mother would, and Sis began to feel safe with the older woman. Paula seemed old in a wise old owl way, but not aged like an old granny.

"How you feeling, kiddo?" Paula asked when they had been moved to a private room.

"Like a baby tucked in for the night." Sis had been settled into a crisp, white hospital bed, with her broken foot propped up in a sling. Leaning back against the pillows, Sis had actually dozed off for a bit. The strain of being questioned and facing the teams of people who had paraded in to meet her had zapped her energy. There had been the parents and the younger sister, police officers, FBI agents, doctors, nurses, and victim advocates assigned to her case. Aside from the family and Paula, Sis had already forgotten all the names, but Paula said that was okay. She would be here to help in the morning.

"So am I staying here tonight?" Sis asked, running her hands over the white sheet under her hips. So smooth and clean. This was the kind of bed she had dreamed of.

"That's the plan. The doctors want to take another batch of X-rays in the morning."

"And are you going to stay with me?"

Paula's eyes opened wide. "I'm going to head home, but I'll be back first thing tomorrow. And you've got your call button for the nurses and . . . and I bet your mom would like to stay with you. Should we ask her?"

"No."

"I think it would be good for you."

"No." Sis tugged the sheet up and wrapped a corner around her hand as that thickness clogged her throat again. It was all too much. Being alone here at the hospital. Being pushed at Rachel and Dan O'Neil, like she was a newborn baby being delivered into their arms. She worried about Kevin coming after her. She worried about what she would do without him to take care of her. Whenever Paula mentioned tomorrow, when she said "from now on . . ." as if Sis had just stepped into the Land of Oz, Sis felt that sour taste rise in the back of her throat.

"Lauren." Paula leaned over the bed. "You're overwhelmed. That's understandable. But you'll sort through this in time."

"Don't call me that." Sis felt her lower lip pucker in what Kevin called her "crybaby face." "I'm not her. I'm not who you think I am. I'm not their daughter or a good student or a good kid at all. That's not me."

"Then what should I call you?"

Lauren swallowed. "Sis?"

"Really. You want to go by the name *he* gave you? Do you really want to be the person he controlled, the person he tried to make you?"

She sobbed. "No."

"Then you'd better come up with a name for yourself. I don't care if it's Puddintain or Britney Spears. Just as long as it's your name."

"Puddintain?"

"What's your name? Puddintain. Ask me again and I'll tell you the same."

That made Sis sniff back her tears. She told Paula she would think about the name. But right now, she couldn't stop thinking of Kevin. She was afraid of what he would do when he found her here . . . and he would find her. Every time she had tried to escape, he had promised terrible revenge.

Last time, when she crossed the gates and went down to the creek to cool off during that hot spell in May, he had come after her with a wrench.

"That's how he broke your ankle?"

"This time. He's always gone for my left ankle."

"That explains the X-rays showing previous breaks in your tibia and fibula, left leg."

"Kevin always hits that ankle. He says he needs to slow me down, just in case I decide to try and run away. But I don't try to get away anymore. That's why it was totally unfair this last time. I wasn't even trying to get away, but he beat me and kept me locked inside the shed during the hottest hours of the day. I was miserable, and he was wrong, because I wasn't even trying to get away. I just wanted to cool off. I just went over the fence to cool off in the creek."

"Did you try to escape before that?"

Lauren nodded. "A few times. Not in the beginning, because then he kept me handcuffed and gagged when he wasn't with me. For the first few weeks he kept my ankles tied together, too."

Those days, those terrible, lonely days when she'd nearly choked on tears and that gag, when she'd had to pee her pants because she couldn't always get to the bathroom—that nightmare seemed like the life of some other poor girl. It hurt her to talk about that time, but she did. She had decided that she could trust Paula, and it felt good to unravel the tight ball of pain.

And Paula didn't scowl at her or judge her.

"Many kidnap victims learn that the only way to stay alive is to go along with the person who kidnapped them." Paula's voice floated overhead like a soft moon.

Sis closed her eyes to float along with it, to move in the night air and look down on herself, the scared, quivering eleven-year-old girl who wanted to go home.

The first time she showered, Kevin stood at the edge of the curtain, watching. She turned away, thinking that he was just standing guard.

Even the second time, when he gave her a razor and shaving cream and told her to shave everything, she thought that maybe he was trying to be nice. She liked the way the shaving cream puffed up, smooth and creamy, but she had never done this before, and she was so nervous about cutting herself.

"You look like you need some help with that." He started with her legs—just below the knee. "You cover everything with a thick lather, and then run the razor over it, nice and light."

She thanked him. Such a polite little kid. Her parents had taught her manners. She had told him thanks, and she would do the rest.

"Now I'm worried. You've never done this before. You're liable to cut yourself up, and I'm responsible for you now."

That was when he'd turned off the water and stepped in, cornering her. "I'll help you with the rest."

She thought she would die of mortification when he rubbed the shaving cream on her thighs. He was looking at her naked body, staring. He had warned her that he hated girls who cried, but she couldn't stop the whimper that slipped from her throat.

When he reached between her legs, she couldn't take it anymore. She banged on his shoulders with her fists and clawed at his face.

In a second, he was standing tall and pressing her against the fiberglass wall. "Cut it out! Don't you see I got a razor in my hand? I could slice you open like that. That!"

"I'm sorry. I'm—"

"Your blood would be running down the drain before you could even breathe that you were sorry."

Then in a flash, he left her alone in the shower. When she rinsed off and got out, he handed her a dress and a hoody, real calm. Scary calm. He shoved her out on that jetty, smacked by sea spray, and showed her the choices: Let him touch her, or drown in the dark, roiling sea.

There wasn't so much shame in telling Paula these stories, not like Sis had expected. Instead, she felt sorry for the girl she used to be.

"I didn't want him to touch me, but I didn't want to die. And that was the strangest thing, when I realized he didn't want to kill me. He liked me."

Paula told her that she deserved to be liked. But she also deserved to be free from his control. And his abuse.

Sis wanted to be free, but it all scared her. "What if Kevin comes after me? He's going to be really mad now. He warned me about something like this."

If I have to come after you, I'll be your worst nightmare. She shivered as his voice curled inside her.

"Kevin Hawkins is in police custody. With the amount of witnesses the police have in the armed robbery case, there is no chance that he'll be released anytime soon. Hawkins won't be hurting you anymore."

"I can't believe that. He's left me alone before, but he always comes back."

"Not this time. And he must know that, because he told the police where to find you."

"Why would he tell?" Lauren wondered.

"Maybe his conscience was bothering him."

"Or maybe he was getting sick of me. He's been complaining that I'm boney and frigid. A sad sack of bones, and it's true. I've been sad since we lost Mac. And he complained that I wasn't worth anything to him anymore. He was sick of having to take care of me, having to come up with ways to make money. He didn't like having me in the compound when he brought women around. Even with me locked in the shed. He said I was cramping his style."

"Did he bring lady friends home often?"

"Only recently. Since Mac died."

"Did you ever meet any of these women?"

"I talked with one girl, Gabby." Lauren pointed to her right cheek. "She has a tattoo of a teardrop right here. That always made me sad when I saw her. She talked to me a little when she was out in the garden, having a smoke. She said my paintings were nice, but her father would have killed her if she drew on the walls at home. She asked me how long my brother had owned this farm and where I went to school. I told her Kevin had been there a long time, and that I was homeschooled. That was the story I had to tell people." Sis let her head roll on the comfy pillow. Paula was making notes on her clipboard.

"Why are you writing that down?"

"They're case notes. I'm afraid we're going to need to go over all this again and videotape it. Sorry about that, but once we have it documented, you won't have to repeat your entire story for every district attorney or victim's advocate involved in your case."

"Do you write everything down?"

"Just pertinent facts. Memory cues." She pointed her pen to her head. "At my age, you need help remembering."

Lauren pulled the sheet up to her chin and sighed. "And me, I wish I could forget."

"I guess we make a good team," Paula said. "You can remember all the things I forget."

"Okay. That means you have to stay with me." The prospect of spending the night alone in this big room with shiny tile floors made Lauren's bones tremble. And she didn't want to lose Paula.

Paula chuckled. "Is this a clever trick?"

Lauren smiled. "Mmm-hm. Is it working? I bet those nice nurses can wheel a bed in for you, too."

Paula cocked her head to one side, looking girlish. Sometimes she seemed too young to have silver hair. "We'll see. The night is young."

Chapter 13

Dan O'Neil was no stranger to trauma. His unit was usually first on the scene for local emergencies: heart attacks at Mirror Lake's assisted living home, rollover car accidents in which victims needed to be cut from the vehicle, fires that swept through houses and filled the air with dense black smoke. Twenty years in the fire department and you figure you'd seen it all.

And then this . . .

To lose your daughter to some monster, to finally get her back, and then to realize that she didn't want to be back—at least, not with your family—all the training in the world couldn't prepare you for this.

"I don't know how to tell you this without causing you distress," the social worker had told them. She had corralled them into a conference room in Westridge Hospital while Lauren was having blood drawn. "So I'll be blunt: Lauren doesn't want to see you right now."

Rachel gasped and hung her head, more in frustration than surprise. They had suspected this; he and Rachel knew there was a reason they were being kept at bay, and in the little time they'd had with Lauren, the young woman hadn't expressed much interest or confidence in them.

Dan thought of the emotional baggage he had carried into that moment with Lauren. When he finally got in to see his daughter, he was so overwrought he could barely talk. Add to that his fear of touching her and seeming like a pervert, even though he was her father. The whole meeting must have looked more like a job interview than a survivor reunion or a "reunification," as Paula kept calling it. "You look like your mother when she was a teenager," he blurted out because it was true and he thought it might help to make a connection that didn't seem to exist in the static air between them. The young woman in the bed was polite, but cautious. She thanked him for bringing her old sketchpad. But then, as she leafed through the pages that he had studied over the years for traces of his daughter, she lamented that she'd been a pretty raw artist back then. "I thought you were remarkable," Dan told her. "I still do." Lauren eyed him warily and seemed to be taking her cues from the social worker. Who had told Lauren that Paula Winkler was the boss? "Thanks, Dad," Paula had said with enthusiasm. Lauren had nodded, refusing eye contact with Dan. "Yeah, thanks." Any thought of a hug was erased by Lauren's body language. "You're welcome," Dan said. A nurse came in with a tray of food, and Dan backed into the corner of the room, feeling guilty for being a man, the same gender as the monster that had repeatedly attacked his daughter, stolen her youth, and sucked away the spark in her eyes.

It had not been the bright reunion he had envisioned through the years. Still, he wasn't giving up, not by a long shot. And he wished that Rachel wasn't second-guessing the social worker who was trying to help Lauren now.

"I can't believe that after all this she . . . ," Rachel pressed her lips together as her eyes misted over.

Dan rubbed his wife's back, fielding the ball passed to him. "We felt this coming on. Has she told you why?"

"She hasn't articulated why, exactly," Paula went on, "but I'm guessing that she feels alienated. So many years away from you. She's changed, and so have you."

"True." Dan rubbed the back of his neck, assessing the situation. It was pushing eight, and Sierra had school in the morning. "We're probably better off heading home and returning in the morning, after we've all had a good night's sleep."

"No." Rachel shook her head. "I won't leave her alone."

"She won't be alone." The cold, industrial lighting sizzled on Paula's silver hair. "I'm staying with her tonight. She made me promise."

Rachel put a hand to her forehead, a gesture that said she couldn't deal with it.

"So you're saying she's bonded with you?" Dan said calmly.

Paula held up her hands. "Sometimes that happens. Sometimes hostages bond with the first rescuer who shows them kindness. It doesn't mean that she won't reattach to your family."

Dan raked back his pale hair. "Right. I'm sure you understand how disappointing that is for us. Our daughter is rescued after six years, you bring her in, and it's like she's not our daughter at all."

"I know. Believe me, I know." Paula tossed her pen onto the clipboard. "I have to admit, I'm a little over my head on this. I'm a licensed social worker with a degree in psychology—not a full-on psychiatrist. As I mentioned, I've reached out to a reunification specialist I know, as well as half a dozen others. There's a youth crisis center that we can use tomorrow, a place called the Children's Center. They have equipment to record and document interviews with Lauren, which will save her having to repeat all the difficult details for the cops, the district attorney's office, and anyone else who needs to hear it. They have trauma counselors there, some guys and gals that have tons more experience than I do with situations like this. Believe me, I'll be happy for the help. All day today I've been reaching for my proverbial toolbox and finding it one wrench short."

He put a hand on the table to stop her. "I didn't mean to imply that you're doing a poor job."

"No offense taken, Dan. I just want to confirm that if you think I'm under-qualified for this, I'm not saying you're wrong. I just happened to be the social worker on call today. I may not be the best with academics, but I've learned plenty in the school of life, and I'm going to give your daughter's case everything I've got."

"That's all we can ask of you." Dan stood up from the table. "I'd like to say good-bye to Lauren before we go."

Paula nodded. "Absolutely."

At least Lauren looked more comfortable now, settled in the hospital bed. She had the television on, a rerun of that sitcom where the three girls live in an amazing Victorian row house with their dad and two uncles. Mind candy TV was what Dan called it. Right now, Lauren definitely deserved some mind candy.

"We're here to say good night." Dan felt that sting at the back of his tongue when her eyes met his. Scornful eyes, as if punishing him for every bad decision he'd ever made. He hadn't ever expected to see that edge in his daughter's eyes. He hoped that therapy could erase it. "It's so hard to leave you here now that we finally have you back." Rachel leaned over the bed and pressed her lips to Lauren's forehead, and Dan felt one of those proverbial arrows piercing his heart.

Rachel was tucking in their oldest daughter. It was an event they'd been praying for. Only not in this way

It was a day of incredible highs and huge disappointments.

As the elevator doors closed, Sierra's fingers tapped away, her eyes on the cell phone screen.

"Isn't that against the rules, using a cell phone in the hospital?" Rachel asked.

"We're in the elevator." Sierra's disapproving tone did not waver. "And I don't understand why we had to sit in the waiting room all this time if we're leaving her here for the night."

"Can we not talk about it right now?" Rachel, tight as a double knot, kept her eyes on the flashing elevator floor number.

Dan offered a wary smile to the man in green scrubs, checking out Sierra from his place by the keypad. Just a friendly hospital worker, he reminded himself. Probably doing a study on family dynamics.

As he ushered his girls out on level P-2, he offered a silent prayer, grateful to have his daughter back, alive. A survivor. So often he'd been on his knees in church, begging God for relief, praying for Lauren's safe return or at least her safety. He had spent many hours pondering why bad things happened to good people like his innocent daughter. He would never know the answer to that, but he did know that the bad things were caused by other people, not by God Himself.

Evil lived in the hearts of men. Demons like Kevin Hawkins.

Chapter 14

On the way home from Westridge Hospital, Rachel told herself to stop feeling sorry for herself and focus on her daughter. Lauren's recovery was the important thing. Lauren's safety and her future . . .

Of course, Lauren was the priority, but at the moment, there was no denying the emptiness inside her.

She sank down in the passenger seat and let herself wallow in self-pity. "I should have been the one to stay with her," Rachel said loud enough for just Dan to hear. Sierra was in the back, plugged in to her music. "I'm Lauren's mother. I'm the one who should be with her right now."

"Right now Lauren is more comfortable with Paula," Dan pointed out.

"Perfect Paula." The woman was cheerful and down-to-earth, attentive and assertive at the right times. Paula was willing to take the lead but knew when she needed to rely on outside resources. "That woman is way too competent."

"She is."

"I hate her," Rachel muttered in a low voice.

"I know what you mean."

Sierra spoke up from the backseat. "Is it true that Lauren had a baby? That she really had a kid of her own?"

"It's true, but don't say anything to Lauren unless she brings it up, okay? She's still really upset about losing the baby."

"I had a niece and I didn't even know it. That's totally fucked up."

"Please! The language." How did middle-class twelve-year-old girls manage to mouth off like truck drivers? "But you're right. It is effed up."

"And why is Lauren staying in the hospital now? Because the guy raped her?"

"The doctors are keeping her for observation and tests," Rachel said, wondering how much of that was true. Was this a ruse to help Lauren avoid coming home with them? Was Paula on the phone right now, talking with her "resources," lining up a foster home for their daughter?

"Is she coming home tomorrow?" Sierra asked.

"We don't know," Dan answered.

"Do you think Lauren still likes us? I mean, she didn't seem like *thrilled* to see us."

Sometimes Sierra's bluntness was a relief.

"No, she didn't," Dan agreed. "But she'll get used to us. We need to give her time and space. And we're all going to have to go for therapy."

Sierra groaned. "Do I have to go? I am not going to tell my problems to a stranger. Especially a grown-up who doesn't remember what it's like to be me. I've got friends for that."

"This will be different. There's a very concrete goal here. We need to learn how to live together as a family again." Rachel explained about the reunification therapy.

"Just saying? I am not sitting in that creepy office with the giant fish and the dusty cactus."

"I'm with you on that," Dan said.

"Don't start putting up obstacles." Rachel turned to her daughter in the backseat. "I'm counting on you, both of you, to do what needs to be done."

The blue shadows of the car's interior gave just enough light for Rachel to see Sierra roll her eyes as she reinserted her earbuds. "Whatever."

Rachel turned back to the windshield and scraped back her tawny hair. "When do you think she will be coming home? I mean . . . wow. I guess this gives me time to put fresh sheets on her bed, but . . . it all seems impossible now. After six years in captivity, I don't want to force her to do anything, but I do want her home."

"Maybe our house is not the best place for her right now."

"Well, the hospital isn't exactly warm and fuzzy. I think she needs to come home, but right now she just doesn't realize how good it will be. Yes, she needs to come home. She's our daughter, a minor, only seventeen."

"Only seventeen, but she's survived more trauma than most people endure in a lifetime. Let's take it easy on her, mother bear. If she wants to live in some sort of middle place until she adjusts to her freedom, we can give her that time and space."

"Maybe a hotel. We could rent a hotel room and I could stay with her."

"I thought the point was to give her space."

"Hmph. I'm not letting Paula Winkler chaperone her."

"Actually, that's not a bad idea."

"Are you kidding me? Haven't you noticed how Lauren looks to Paula for approval before she answers every question? Paula has become her surrogate parent, and it's pissing me off."

"Rach, let's focus on what's best for Lauren. She's probably suffering acute post-traumatic stress. Would I like to bring her home with us tonight? The answer is yes. Is it a bummer that she's bonded with someone who isn't us? Yes. But I'm not going to blame Paula for being there to support our daughter. She's spending the night in the freakin' hospital to watch over Lauren. I applaud her dedication. And I have faith that Lauren will learn to trust us again. Give it time. We're going to turn this around."

Rachel wished she could share Dan's optimism.

"All the time that she was gone, we were hurting for her," Rachel said. "We were missing a piece. I dreamed of her coming back to us, but I never thought that this could happen—that she would no longer fit. We're all like puzzles pieces left out in the rain. Swollen cardboard. Nothing fits together anymore."

"Good metaphor." Dan kept his eyes on the road. "I get it, but we have to make the pieces fit."

Rachel imagined her husband shaving down the pegs of old puzzle pieces and sizing them up to make sure they interlocked properly. Dan was handy that way, and he had that conceptual gift. He could see how things fit together. Dan and Lauren used to stay up late, bent over puzzles on the homework table. "A thousand pieces!" Lauren would exclaim, marveling over the wondrous feat they were tackling. And Dan would remind her to do the edge first. "Always start with the border."

"I wonder if Lauren still likes puzzles," Rachel said.

"Let's hope so."

PART 2

Come In from the Cold

Chapter 15

In the hospital room, Sis couldn't sleep. She didn't want to leave the crisp, clean sheets of the hospital bed, but her fingers were restless, and her mind was spilling over like a river into a lake.

What was going to happen to her? Paula said she would have to go home with Dan and Rachel O'Neil. The mom and dad. But that didn't seem right. It wasn't her home anymore. The O'Neils didn't even live in the same house. Kevin had told her that her family had moved away, to another state. Washington, she suspected. That room was being used by someone else now. A TV room or the bedroom of an old granny.

But for a long time, that house had filled her dreams. How she had longed for it in those first awful months! She remembered her room, painted in a soft shell pink and beige, because Mom had thought that all pink would be over the top. But mostly it was her design, her room. She used to think of that warm, familiar little cocoon with her sketches and posters taped to the wall, her colored pencils on the desk, her creations from ceramics class set up like a fairy kingdom on one of the shelves. On the center of the bed sat her stuffed Mr. Toad. The bedspread matched her giant pillow, both a zebra print in hot pink and brown that brought the whole room together. She'd had a color scheme there, unlike the cabin in the compound that was such a hodgepodge of patch plaster and mold that Kevin hadn't cared when she started painting over it with her artwork. That house, the home of her childhood—why did they sell it?

Because they had given up on her? Because they wanted to make a fresh start in a place that didn't remind them of her. That was the explanation Kevin had given her before he told her to shut up about it.

Once upon a time, she had spent her lonely hours dreaming of going home to her family. In those early weeks and months at the beach, when he had kept her arms and legs bound so that she couldn't move—hogtied, he called it—she had yearned for home. She had wriggled toward the skylight in the upstairs cubby where he locked her in and watched the moon rise overhead. Moon and stars.

And then she sang that song that they used to harmonize on while they were cleaning up the kitchen. *Tell me why, the stars do shine. Tell me why, the ivy twine . . .* Back then she would have given anything to go back to the O'Neils because she thought they wanted her back.

Stupid girl, Kevin had scolded her. *They don't care about you.*

She had thought he was lying, sort of, just to make her trust him. Every night, as the moon rose, she told herself that tomorrow might be the day that she got rescued. She had kept hoping for a year or so, holding on to hope as if it were a tiny mouse in her pocket.

And then came the news that would change everything. One day when Kevin was done with her, he had pressed his palms to her belly, cupping the little mound that had grown there.

You're getting fat, he'd told her. She'd rolled away, telling him they ate too many fast food meals, too many milkshakes.

Yeah, well, you're gonna need the milk in those shakes, Sis, 'cause you got a bun in the oven. You're gonna have a baby.

Sis had burst into tears. It wasn't just the scary part about going through childbirth. She knew her life was over, her chance of going back gone. Now her parents would know the terrible things she had done with him. Everyone would know, and that was why she could never go back. Never.

Suddenly, the hospital bed felt wrong, as if Sis were a broken toy on display to anyone who walked in. She couldn't stay here.

Paula was asleep in the bed on the other side of the curtain; Sis had to keep quiet.

Moving silently and balancing on the weird heel of her walking cast, Sis went to the cubby where Paula had hung her dress. That old dress with fat flowers. She slipped off the hospital gown and put her old dress on. She had hated it since the day Kevin brought it home from the thrift shop. Now it was worn thin, the print faded to nothing. She tied the rope belt around her waist, picked up the plastic bin of free stuff and teetered a bit on the smooth floor. The walking cast threw her off balance. Better be careful.

Sis sat on the bed and went through the things they had given her, wondering how she could carry it all. A toothbrush and mouthwash and two pairs of footy socks with plastic footprints on the bottom for traction. Little plastic tubs for washing and lotion that smelled like lemons and mint. So many nice gifts in one day; she couldn't leave them behind.

This hospital wasn't such a bad place, not the madhouse Kevin talked about. Her lips puckered at the thought of what a hospital could have done for Mackenzie when she was sick. These medicines and clean sheets and nurses with knowing hands would have saved Mac for sure. But they couldn't do anything for Sis. All the doctors and nurses in the world couldn't fix the thing that had broken inside her.

Paula didn't stir as Sis found a big plastic bag in the closet, stuffed everything inside, and moved quietly out the door. She wasn't sure where she would go, but if she had to she could return to the compound. She knew her way around there, and Kevin wouldn't come around to bother her if it was true, what they said about him being locked up in jail.

And with the lock on the gate busted open, she could go down to the creek and soak in the cool water on hot days. She could probably survive until winter on the garden vegetables, and there were a few other staples stored in the other shed.

The hallway was wide, the floors and wall tiles shiny like a still lake. The cast made her limp even worse, but none of the people she passed tried to stop her. Up ahead she saw the main desk, with two people in scrubs lingering near it. Now those people were going to ask her questions if they noticed her.

Sis turned around and backtracked, following the red exit sign to a group of elevators at the other end of the hall. Pushing the down-arrow button, she thought about how much TV had taught her about the real world. Sure, she knew a lot of things before she had been kidnapped, but watching tapes of her favorite shows that Kevin had brought her had given her good lessons about how the rest of the world lived. How happy families lived.

When the doors whooshed open, she hobbled forward and came face to face with the bright eyes and pensive frown of Rachel O'Neil.

Sis's heart thumped in her chest as she considered bolting—running in the opposite direction.

"Lauren?" The mother stepped off the elevator, her smile smooth and sweet as a milkshake. "Honey, are you checking out your walking cast? Putting some mileage on it already?"

Sis looked down, caught, and unwilling to watch Rachel's expression shift when she realized that Sis was trying to escape. The woman seemed so hopeful, and Sis hated to be the one to disappoint her.

"Where is your hospital gown?" Rachel asked, a little more crisply.

"I took it off," Sis said, stating the obvious. She braced herself for Rachel to yell at her, the way Kevin would, but instead the woman put an arm around her and ushered her away from the elevator.

"I don't blame you. Those gowns allow zero modesty. I was thinking you might want to ditch the hospital gown, so I brought you some pajamas."

Sis squinted, carefully taking in each word as the woman guided her back down the hall, back to the room. Her touch was firm, but gentle, even though Rachel had to know Sis had been escaping. But Rachel wasn't mad. She wasn't going to punish Sis. She was painting over everything with a happy color—orange or pink—and acting like everything was fine.

"I brought some other clothes for you, too. I know it's late. I figured I'd find you asleep, and I planned to leave this stuff. But I made it to Target before they closed," Rachel went on as Sis's cast clunked rhythmically on the tile floor. "I guessed at the sizes, but I realized that you need everything. Don't worry if you don't like something. I'll take it back. I figure that we have a few shopping trips in our future, right? No rush, but it's always better when a gal can pick out her own clothes, try things on, develop her own sense of style."

A sense of style . . . it was something Lucy would say in *Seventh Heaven,* and Sis felt her throat growing thick at the notion that she might have a life like that once again.

Rachel ignored Paula asleep on the other side of the room curtain and began to spread clothes out on the bed. The woman had a million questions. Did she still like purple? Did she like ruffles or plain, a simple shift or denim shorts? Sis had trouble pushing words past the lump in her throat; she could only grunt dumb answers like "yes" and "sure" and "I guess."

The clothes were beautiful . . . like something D.J. or Steph wore in *Full House.* Flip-flops with pink jewels winking up at her and canvas tennis shoes as white as a puffy cloud. Besides jeans, leggings, skirts, and tops, there were two bras, one in hot pink, the other white, both with little satin bows between the lightly padded cups. Just the sight of them brought tears to her eyes. Kevin had bought her simple sports bras, always on sale, but these . . . these dainty bras were as sweet as candies. Bras for a young woman.

Sis swallowed back the tears as she fingered the strap of the pink bra. Rachel had been kind to go buy these things for her. Considerate. But it couldn't replace the years Sis had gone without a mother. She wished she could go back to being a daughter and sister again, but Sis couldn't get past the invisible wall between them—the constant reminder that her family had not saved her. *They're not even looking for you anymore,* Kevin had told her. *You're a lost cause.*

She felt gratitude, but that was it.

"Thanks," Sis muttered.

"I also got you these." Rachel dug into a smaller plastic bag. "Paula mentioned that you needed them right away."

Rachel pulled out a pile of underpants in rainbow colors. There had to be at least a dozen in the stack, some with stripes and bubbles and flowers and lace. Others were plain, soft cotton.

"Paula told me he didn't allow you to wear panties. I think these will fit."

Panties. Sis's vision blurred from tears. She wasn't sure what bothered her most, the fact that Paula had told this woman such an intimate thing, or the way this stranger wanted so much for Sis to love her.

Tears spilled onto her cheeks. Losing her resolve and balance, Sis turned and plopped onto the bed, right on top of a soft new hoodie.

"Oh, Lauren . . . ," Rachel sat beside her, and rubbed her back. "I know it's hard for you. No one can imagine what you're going through, but please, help me to see it. Help me know what you're feeling and thinking. I want to get to know you again."

The woman's gentle touch was soothing. Sis remembered a nighttime ritual, when her mother used to brush Sis's hair and make one big, loose snake of a braid down her back. Her mom was the only one who knew how to get the knots out without hurting her.

So long ago.

Surrounded by beautiful clothes and Rachel's arms, Sis sobbed. Rachel could not understand the fear and grief, the terror of the future and the loneliness for Kevin that filled Sis's heart.

Yeah, he was mean sometimes, even brutal, but Kevin was the only person in the world she could rely on. Sis cried at the prospect of the future. How would she survive without him? She was lost—helpless without him—and all the clothes and condolences from this very nice woman were not going to change that.

Chapter 16

The next morning, Dan was out of bed before his alarm went off. Outside the bathroom window, through the filter of fir branches, a swath of light streaked the sky. He smiled.

Lauren had been found. Lauren was safe.

It was going to be a great day.

As he pulled on jogging shorts and a T-shirt, he read Rachel's body language, curled up tightly under the covers. After her late-night shopping trip, she hadn't come in to bed until late. He wondered if the hospital had let her see Lauren when she got there. God, he hoped so. Rach was so stressed right now.

Not Dan. He believed that good things were going to happen now that Lauren was safe. He knew it. They would make lemonade out of lemons. They would get their girl the help she needed to recover and grow and become part of their family again.

Bending over and stretching his hamstrings as he laced his sneakers, he grinned. Finding Lauren changed everything. The axis of the planet had shifted. Things were going to be different from now on.

He pulled open the front door, stepped out, and paused before the lock could catch behind him.

What the hell?

The front lawn was fringed with a line of reporters, TV news vans, satellite trucks, and curious neighbors. It was not even six AM and the media army was here, reporting for duty.

The word was out.

"Holy crap." Dan cursed at himself as much as the media. He should have known better. As a firefighter, he'd dealt with reporters on nearly every rescue he was involved in. Hell, on slow news days, they sent someone out to cover the rescue of a cat up a tree. He should have thought about this, but he'd been so bowled over by Lauren's safe return that he'd gone blind to the world around them. Twitter and YouTube. Blog posts and TV nightly news. The media frenzy that demanded news flashes and sordid stories and human atrocities. Photos and video, even the grainy stuff shot by cell phones and amateurs.

"Dan?" Someone called from the edge of the yard. A dark figure held up one hand. "Dan, Jake Winthrop from the *Oregonian*. Got a minute?"

Leaving the door cracked open, Dan jogged toward Jake, who he'd spoken with a number of times. Jake had helped keep Lauren's name in the newspaper over the past few years, and Dan often spoke with him after fires or rescues. Jake was fair and factual, no spin or glitz. Dan wasn't so sure about the others, two of whom he recognized as on-air personalities for the local affiliates. He understood their need to do coverage, but he knew enough not to go on camera right now.

"Going for a run?" Jake asked.

"I was planning on it. Wasn't expecting the reception committee."

"Is it true that Lauren has been found? The sheriff won't make any statements until after the press conference at noon, and the hospital refuses to confirm whether that was her talking with your wife."

Dan scratched his head as the other media people on the street began to move closer, a slow-crawling wave.

"Come here a second." Dan had said the word, giving Jake permission to step onto his property. They crossed the lawn, pausing near the old-fashioned birdbath that had come with the house. This time of year it was coated with green moss, in need of a good scrubbing.

"So what's the word?" Jake asked.

"She was found by the police yesterday. I can't give any details from the law-enforcement angle; I wouldn't want to compromise the case against the kidnapper. The *suspected* kidnapper," Dan corrected himself, wary of tampering with the delicate justice system that allowed criminals to walk free because of technicalities. "She's alive and in fairly good health." He hoped that didn't diminish the fact that she'd suffered rape at that monster's hands. He didn't ever want Lauren to think that he minimized that atrocity, but he could not open that can of worms with the press.

"That's great news, man." Jake kept his voice low, probably less out of respect than out of a need to keep this news exclusive to his publication. A scoop, as if a person's secrets could be served up like globes of ice cream. "How did the police find her? Do you have the suspect's name? Was it someone you knew?"

Aware of cameras flashing and people calling from the street, Dan shifted away from the reporter. "That's all I can say. Well, you can add that Lauren's family is overjoyed and grateful for her safe recovery."

"It's nice to be able to report good news for a change." Jake extended his hand. "Congratulations, Dan."

They shook, and Dan made a broad wave toward the barking crowd on the sidewalk. "See you at the press conference at noon," he called with a slow smile for the cameras. They would know from his cheerful demeanor. They would see it as confirmation of the rumors, and that was okay. Lauren was back, and he didn't care who knew it.

"Is it a secret?" his mother had asked last night when he'd called with the news.

"Not a huge secret, but we're keeping the information close, trying to maintain some privacy for the next few days." Alice had agreed to keep it on the down-low, but she had agreed to contact the O'Neil side of the family, while Rachel's mom, Sondra, was going to make sure all the Lauers were informed.

Back in the house, Dan switched on the television and started a pot of coffee. The *Today Show* wouldn't be on for another twenty minutes, so he was stuck with local news. The grinder whirred through the traffic report. Then there was live footage from a news copter, showing Mirror Lake in the corner.

He shut off the water and took a closer look at the screen as the rhythmic chop of an overhead helicopter began to reverberate around the house.

"Here's the live aerial shot of Mirror Lake, where reporters are waiting to speak with the O'Neil family." The camera zoomed in, leaving the lake area and coming in closer and closer on Wildwood Lane, until the people and trucks in the street were evident. They switched to a reporter on the ground, Lucy Chong. With a colorful orange jacket and pink hat, Lucy appeared bright and perky in front of the neighbors' thick green laurel hedge.

"Just moments ago we saw Dan O'Neil, a local fire-fighter and the kidnap victim's father, emerge from his home. There was no statement, but he seemed in good spirits, leading us to believe that the news is true . . ."

The reporter went on to say that Rachel O'Neil, mother of the kidnap victim, was seen at a local hospital the previous night talking to "this young woman who some speculate to be Lauren O'Neil."

On the screen was a grainy photo showing Rachel guiding Lauren, one arm around her shoulders. The glare of the hospital tiles caused distracting light in the photo, and Lauren's face was shown in an opaque pro-file, thank God. Right now, Lauren needed privacy. It was too soon to have her image plastered on every media outlet.

So someone had snapped a shot of them at the hos-pital. Probably when Rachel had returned last night, judging by the jacket she was wearing in the photo. Well, they would have to be more careful from now on. Would the police give Lauren a guard? Hawkins was not a threat right now, but the media, they could be a prob-lem.

He checked the alarm system on the wall, wondering if Lauren would be coming home with them. He wanted her close, but now came the question of the media feed-ing frenzy. Had she been recovered from captivity only to be sequestered in this house, unable to take a step without being dogged by a different sort of jailer?

Chapter 17

The task force filled the conference room at the hospital, requiring extra chairs for some folks to sit away from the table, against the wall or windows. The organized chaos reminded Paula of a legislative hearing, where aides sat behind the big cheeses and everyone sought to make some important statement "for the record."

Just as long as we remember who we're here for, Paula thought as she hugged her coveted cup of coffee. Her third. Someone had brought a few big takeout vats of coffee to the meeting. God bless that anonymous donor.

From the head of the table, her boss at DHS, Truman Flores, pointed at task force members as he delegated assignments to the Mirror Lake police, Federal Bureau of Investigation, the National Center for Missing and Exploited Children, and the small team of therapists who had been brought in to work with Lauren and her family. Overnight, Truman Flores had grown some pretty big balls. In the midst of all these government agents and law-enforcement types, Truman stood out with his ringed ear and thin, gray pigtail. Considering his usual tendency to sit back and "let it flow," Truman was on fire today, and at the moment, Paula was feeling the burn as he took her to task in front of the entire task force.

"You should have deferred the case to someone with more experience," he said sternly.

Paula stood her ground, looking him in the eye. "I am so sorry it happened this way." A lie, a blatant lie, but Truman wouldn't know that. "I figured, when in doubt, do your best."

"No one is questioning your dedication," Truman told her.

They wouldn't dare, she thought, wiggling her toes at him under the table.

"But you don't have the credentials to counsel a client with issues of this complexity."

"So true." Paula nodded in easy agreement. "But I was the one on call yesterday, and when the client reached out to me, I couldn't tell her to hold on until someone better qualified came along."

Across the table, DHS's consulting psychiatrist arched his eyebrows in amusement, and Wynonna Eagleson, the reunification specialist known around the office as the Horse Girl, cracked a wry smiled.

"Still, she's bonded with you." Truman, a terrier with a squeaky toy, couldn't let it go. "And at the moment that's precluding her from making any meaningful attachment with our more qualified psychiatrists. It looks bad for us, and we can't afford that. The entire nation is watching this case."

"Thanks to a slip or two from the hospital," Paula said, glad to change the subject. "Any word on who sold that photo of Lauren and Rachel O'Neil to the AP?"

"That was unfortunate." Karen Rosenberg, the efficient but maternal ER doc who had caught Lauren's case, shook her head. "That's the problem with everyone having a cell phone on them. I don't think we'll ever be able to pinpoint the source."

"A story this monumental was bound to get out sooner or later," Truman said. "Now it's just a matter of protecting Lauren and maintaining her privacy.

"But the media should be reminded that Lauren is still a minor, and the victim of a heinous crime. Of course, her name and image were released years ago to facilitate the search. But now, her image should not be used without her permission."

Hank agreed, and one of the agents from the FBI backed him up. They agreed to make this point at their noon press conference.

Truman leafed through is papers. "What's the lodging situation? Is she going to be discharged today?" Truman directed the question at Dr. Rosenberg.

"Unless her morning labs show abnormalities, she'll be released," Karen said. "Her walking cast needs to stay on for at least six weeks, but we'll be following up in four."

Truman was shuffling papers. "And where are we taking her after discharge?"

"Her parents would like to have her home," Paula answered, "though that's problematic for a few reasons. One, Lauren needs time to assimilate." That was putting it mildly; last night, the girl had tried to sneak out of the hospital and return to that rat hole of a compound. "And the media camp outside the O'Neil house is not going to give Lauren the feeling of security and safety we want her to have."

"We can put an agent on her for round-the-clock protection." The heavyset man with dark hair and a dark suit who offered this was from the FBI. Stephen Good-something. Paula had written "Goodenough" on her notepad to remember how to say it. "But setting her up in the O'Neils' house is just going to attract more attention to the place. The family will have no privacy at all, and it won't be easy to guard the subject there. Another house would be better. Anyone looked at rentals?"

"I can do that," Paula offered. She had promised Lauren to stay with the girl as long as allowed. If Lauren was housed in a rental with an FBI agent for protection, DHS would probably want a rep with her, too. Paula wanted to be that person. Granted, some aspects of this case were way over her head, but if she was treading water, she wasn't alone. Who in this room had handled a kidnapping at all, let alone one in which the victim had been held captive for years? She would leave the protocol up to her boss and the capable FBI agents; her angle was to take care of Lauren. She had gained the girl's trust, and she was not going to let her down.

Hank Todd, the Mirror Lake police chief, leaned forward to catch her eye. "Talk to me after we wrap up here. We know some of the lake houses that are unoccupied right now, and I'm sure some of the owners would be glad to help. We might be able to make something happen for you."

Paula nodded. "Will do. Thanks." The chief held her gaze a moment longer, long enough for her to notice that his eyes were an exquisite shade of sea green, the shade of a Caribbean cove or a smooth piece of sea glass. Something twinkled in her chest as Hank leaned back into the line of men. Something sweet. A crush? At her age?

After all these years, attraction certainly chose an inopportune moment to strike. Well, maybe someday. Right now, she needed to get back to Lauren and find a safe house. If Truman would ever wrap up this meeting.

"Now, about the press conference." Truman looked over his reading glasses at Hank. "What do you think, Chief? Do you want to moderate, or should I?"

Paula took a sip of tepid coffee to stop folks from reading her dismay. Was that what this was about? Truman saw his first big photo op—his ten minutes of fame?

Hank said he was happy to defer to the FBI kidnapping specialist to introduce the case. The federal agent thanked Hank but told him it was really his bailiwick. Once again, Paula tuned out, focusing only on Hank's broad shoulders and wise green eyes. She had no interest in the press conference. When it happened, she would be miles away, probably at the hospital with Lauren, whom she could see right now in her mind, sobbing. Such a heartrending sight, to wake up last night and find the girl sobbing in her mother's arms.

But the tears had done Lauren good. Paula was a firm believer in flushing the system and crying out small pangs of pain, the way the body worked splinters out of the skin. This morning, Lauren had agreed that she felt a little better, but she wished that Rachel O'Neil hadn't come around with the clothes.

"Don't you like the clothes?" Paula had asked.

"The outfits are beautiful. I don't remember anything so nice since the black bomber jacket I was wearing when I was kidnapped. It's Rachel that's the problem."

Paula had cocked her head to one side, encouraging, listening.

"She wants to be my mother, but I don't think I can see her that way." Lauren's amber eyes had been heavy with guilt and shame. "I feel sorry for her, but I can't do what she wants. She's not my mother anymore."

"Legally, she is. You may not feel a bond, and that's understandable."

"I hate the way she looks at me. Like . . . like I'm a sick kitten."

"Pity?"

Lauren nodded. "I hate pity. I'm not a victim. I survived, didn't I?"

"Yes. Yes, you did. You're a survivor, girl, and you have every right to be proud of that."

Paula had let Lauren vent, but made a few notes on it later. For now, the O'Neils were going to have to understand that Lauren needed her space. And down the road, the reunification specialist would have her work cut out for her.

Chapter 18

Although Rachel sensed that Lauren did not want her family here, taking up space and sucking the air out of her hospital room, she held tight to the arms of her chair and tried not to stare at her beautiful daughter. Every time she sneaked a peek, her eyes misted over. In her lavender hoodie and black capri jeans, Lauren looked seventeen again. Her face had traces of a tan and the pink tint of health, and her hair was clean and brushed to a nice shine. The same honey gold hair as her father. Rachel had to restrain herself from wrapping her arms around Lauren like a manic octopus and never letting go.

"I don't understand why I need to watch this." Lauren yanked the sleeves of her hoodie over her hands. Her leg with its orange cast was elevated, even though she said that was annoying. Still conscientious, still following directions. Rachel used to think that was how you raised your children—to obey orders; now she wondered if she and Dan should have encouraged defiance.

"I don't understand why we can't be on TV." Sierra slumped in a chair, her cell phone poised in front of her. "If the press conference is about Lauren, she should be there."

"Should I?" Lauren asked.

Rachel had noticed that she seemed to be more open to Sierra's ideas than she was to her parents'.

"No, you should not be on television right now," Rachel said.

"But she's famous!" Sierra insisted.

"She's famous because someone kidnapped her." Dan rubbed his chin, choosing his words carefully. "We don't want to glorify the crime. And if you go on television, you'll lose your anonymity. Everyone will know who you are. Right now, we'd all like some privacy and peace."

"Well, I wouldn't mind going on TV," Sierra said. She was in that phase where she had to get the last word in. Rachel worried the cuticle of her thumb as she looked from her younger daughter to the older one. They had missed Lauren's rebellious stage. When she'd been taken from them, she had been polite and respectful. Back then, the crisis of the moment was her fierce resistance to the after-school program, which Dan and Rachel had thought necessary since neither of them wanted their children home unsupervised. "Please?" Lauren had begged. "I'll walk right home and I won't have any friends over. I won't answer the door or stop anywhere after school. Please, let me come home. I hate sitting in a classroom with those babies." She and Dan agreed that she had made a valid argument and she was trustworthy. They had agreed to let her walk home. On her own.

It had taken years of therapy for Rachel to accept

that it had probably been the right decision. A child could not thrive and grow in a bubble; she needed room to grow.

"Okay, let's watch." Dan held up a hand for quiet. "It's starting."

It was the oddest thing, watching a nationally televised press conference about your daughter on television. She and Dan would have been permitted to make statements about Lauren's recovery; however they had opted for privacy. Lauren's celebrity had come under terrible circumstances; her return was a matter for personal celebration. Her fame, well, one could only hope it would diminish over the years to come, allowing her to live a healthy, normal life.

A normal life. Rachel flashed to the very routine days in the classroom. Yes, some days were punctuated by a foul comment or a fistfight, but generally there was a predictable curriculum to follow. Each year began with rusty grammar skills and kids on the brink of growing up. Baby faces and guys who needed to shave, all mixed in the same class. The patterns of their progress, both academically and physically, were fairly predictable. Normal.

Rachel tried to imagine the new normal for their family, but the screen was eerily blank.

Hank Todd ran the show, giving the announcement the dignity it deserved. The cameras panned to photos of Lauren, the ones that had been used in the past on the MISSING flyers.

"I'm glad they gave Hank the show," Dan commented. "He's good people."

Sierra frowned up at the screen as if she didn't believe a word of that, and then went back to her texting frenzy.

The only time Lauren reacted was when an FBI sketch of the compound behind Green Spring Farm flashed on the screen. A mixture of fear and embarrassment flickered in her eyes as the FBI representative described the living conditions.

Rachel had to look away. It burned inside her, the irony, the feeling of ineptitude that her daughter had lived so close to them. Less than two miles away, at the farm where Sierra had taken riding lessons and attended a birthday party. So close, and yet, undetected.

Lauren's eyes remained fixed to the television as a photograph showed the garden and two structures in the compound.

"Is that where you lived?" Sierra asked in disbelief.

Lauren nodded.

"Was it awful?"

The question everyone was dying to ask.

Lauren fiddled with the tab of the zipper on her new hoodie. "It wasn't always bad."

Denial snapped in the air.

Rachel tasted bitterness on the back of her tongue. She had an utterly insane urge to argue with Lauren, to tell her that a monster had stolen six valuable years of her life. That she deserved so much better. That she had a family who had searched and cried and bled for her.

Dan must have caught the wildness in her eyes, because he caught her with a look that warned her to stop.

Taking a calming, deep yoga breath, Rachel tried to give up being fifty shades of crazy and focus on the other three people in this room. Her little family, reunited once again.

But she never expected this feeling of alienation. She and Dan were marooned on a desert island. This was not the way she had imagined her girls to be in their teen years. She longed for the little girls who listened to instructions, laughed at her jokes, and let her braid their hair with butterflies and bows. But those little girls were gone, and their mother needed to grow up, too.

It was time to learn the new Lauren.

Chapter 19

Sis rubbed the smooth sleeves of her new hoodie as she peered at the shiny eye of the video camera. Paula had warned her about it, telling her not to be intimidated, and she found she didn't mind it so much. It made her feel like a TV star, like the girls on *Full House*. Much as she loved the show, she knew it wasn't real, and sometimes she thought about how those actresses had spent so much time with their TV families playing out scenes in front of cameras like this.

Of course, they had happy things to say and she didn't. But she wanted to get the memories out. Paula said it would help with her rehabilitation, and after talking the older woman's ear off last night, she was beginning to believe it was true.

"That's a long list," Lauren said, frowning at Paula's pile of papers. "How many questions do you have?"

"As many as it takes to get your story, honey. But don't worry. We don't have to stick to the list. We can just talk, you and me."

The lady working the video camera, CeeCee or

DeeDee or something with two letters, had really short dark hair and a scarf that seemed to be squeezing its way out of her shirt. She had helped Sis prop her cast up on a stool, and then set out juice and water and cookies—animal crackers, like the ones they gave you in nursery school. She told Sis that she usually did these interviews, but today she was helping Paula. Sis wished the woman would leave and go back to nursery school with her animal crackers, but she settled in off to the side of the tripod with a creamy, distant smile.

"If it's not too hard for you, I'd like to start with the very first day," Paula prompted. "You told me you were walking home from school when you saw the van parked at the curb."

"I can talk about that. I've gone over it a million times in my head. Most of the time wishing that I could have done something differently. Just one thing might have created a chain reaction and changed everything."

If she had walked faster or slower. If she hadn't stopped to watch the hummingbird. If she had just stopped complaining and stayed in the after-school program with Sierra and the babies.

"We all second-guess ourselves," Paula said, "but we can't change the past. And it's not your fault you were kidnapped. So you stopped to watch a hummingbird? They are marvelous creatures, aren't they? Where did you see it?"

"On the Millers' porch. They were our neighbors, two doors down." Sis told Paula everything, moment by moment, as catalogued in her memory under the-day-my-sweet-life-ended. The amazing pattern of violets in the Millers' lawn that needed to be sketched. The man who seemed to be delivering a package. His piercing blue eyes. And then the stun gun. She even mentioned peeing her pants, and Paula told her that happened to a lot of people when they were subjected to that sort of electric shock. That made her feel better.

Paula wanted to hear everything, but today they were going to focus on a general time line of the six years she had been away.

"I'll do my best," Sis said, but some of the days and months were muddled in her mind. "I didn't have a calendar or watch, and my cell phone ran out of battery fast. Maybe I should have kept it, I don't know. But I was so frustrated that I tossed it away. I took it out of my pocket when we stopped in the woods for a bathroom break and hurled it into the trees."

"The police located your cell phone in the Tillamook Forest. The beacon from your phone launched a huge search in the area."

"Really?" Not huge enough, if they couldn't find her.

"Do you remember the first night?"

She told Paula about the windowless laundry room he'd kept her in at first, in the small house at the coast that he had called "the beach house." She recalled how she had screamed and cried and put up a fight when he touched her the first time. The bad touch. And then that scary trip to the beach, the threat of what would happen if she didn't follow his orders. "I thought about dying. I was so tired and scared, and I knew what he wanted to do to me was wrong. I thought about jumping into the ocean, but I didn't do it."

"I'm glad you didn't," Paula said quietly. "Do you remember what stopped you?"

Sis nodded. It was simple. "I wanted to live."

Paula nodded. "As I said, you're a survivor."

As the words spilled out, so did the memories.

That first night when he had released the handcuffs

in the laundry room, she had been surprised by the way
he looked. She had thought a kidnapper would be ugly,
with scars or a pinched nose or close, beady eyes. But
Kevin had pretty blue eyes and a nice smile. He was
strong and fit. Most times he tried to be nice. He apologized for putting the handcuffs on her. After the hard
metal edge bruised her wrists, he wrapped gauze and
padded tape around them, trying to help her feel better.

Those first few minutes and hours and days, she
thought her rescue would come at any moment. Her
mother had a stubborn streak, and Sis had been convinced she would not rest a moment until her daughter
had been found. And her dad, her dad saved people's
lives all the time, carrying them out of burning buildings or shocking their heart back to the steady beat of
life. Dad was a hero, and with each sunset she told herself that this would be the night when the door would
open with a bang and her dad would come rushing in.

Those days were torture. By day she had to close her
eyes against Kevin's physical assaults on the most private parts of her body. Riding her, he called it, but she
thought of it as splitting her spirit in half. Killing a unicorn, that was what he was doing. But knowing Kevin, if
she told him that, he would have tossed off responsibility, saying that everybody had to die sometime, or that
hunters killed animals all the time. Kevin had a way of
explaining his bad behavior. By night, it was just her, all
alone, so lonely. If a person could die of loneliness, she
would definitely be dead now. She stared through the
narrow skylight, searching for the moon and stars, telling
herself not to cry because she wouldn't be able to find
every wishing star with her eyes full of tears.

A few terrible months after she'd been taken, Kevin
loaded her into the van for another trip. It was a big

deal; she could tell because she rarely got to leave the laundry room, let alone go for a ride in the van. This time, the blanket on top of her wasn't so hot because of the chill in the air.

Autumn.

The summer had come and gone without her. Her birthday, too. One of those, hot, airless days in the laundry room had been her twelfth birthday.

The ride ended on a very bumpy road that made her feel like her brain was rattling around in her head. When the blanket was lifted from her, it was night, and they were outside surrounded by velvet stillness. The yard around them wasn't anything special, but it was a good size—bigger than the playground at her school—and the sky? It spread over them, a field of black into which God had flung handfuls of diamonds. She had stared up at that sky while he told her she could move around freely here, at least most of the time. There was a toilet in the house—no more pee bucket, thank goodness. Things would be good for them here, as long as she followed the rules. "Never go outside the fence—don't even try. And if you raise your voice or scream, I'm going to have to put a gag on you again and lock you up." He showed her the shed, which smelled of oil and fertilizer. At one side was a cage, a kennel for a big dog, he said. If she broke the rules, she was going to have to live in the cage. "Got it?" She understood that if she tried to leave, he would make her life miserable again. She would be a caged animal.

Maybe a smarter girl would have given up on escaping right then and there, but she tried again one gray day in the gloom of winter. Kevin had gone off with his truck to get rice and noodles for her to cook on the electric hot plate. She thought he'd be gone a while, but she was wrong. It took her a while to get over the fence, and when he spotted her, she hadn't even made it to the creek. She paid the price with a beating and days in the cage, and she vowed that she would never do that again. Her parents would just have to find her on their own. What was wrong with them, anyway? Why weren't they sending out search parties or following Kevin around? He always bragged about getting over on the government. Why wasn't anyone catching him?

That was when she had started giving up on her family and the police and the idea of a big, dramatic rescue from her heroic father. It was easier to let those dreams and hopes go than to wake up every morning sad and disappointed. By then, Kevin had discovered that she was an artist, and they were making regular trips to flea markets and festivals. Her hair was dyed a goth shade of black, and he made her wear goofy hats, but she liked drawing people. He bought her a white sketchpad and a fresh box of pastels for the work, and the smooth, soft texture was magic under her fingers. She found that when people sat for a portrait, they tried to let out that little glimmer of light that made them so distinctive. That singular light inside them. Sis never had trouble finding the light. After customers left the stand, Kevin made wisecracks and comments, but not Sis. That little flicker of connection put hope in her heart. She liked to think that it made her light shine stronger, but Kevin said that was a load of touchy-feely crap.

One day, after a busy day of painting portraits, Kevin rewarded her by letting her buy a tent. Unlike the little tent she had made out of blankets for sleeping, this one was tall enough the stand in and waterproof, too. She pitched it in a spot away from the house, and made it into her own little nest. A cocoon, like her room at home had been. Not a fan of camping, Kevin didn't care to come inside, so in her mind, the tent wasn't tainted by him. That tent became her escape within the compound.

Later in the summer, maybe it was August, and she'd been gone from home a year—that was when Kevin found the bump in her belly that showed she was pregnant. She had cried a lot over that. Twelve years old and pregnant! But mostly she cried because she knew it sealed the door shut behind her. She could never go home after this . . . this terrible shame.

But after Mac was born, the shame faded with the attachment that formed for her baby. Yes, it was hard caring for a baby and doing her other chores like gardening and cooking on the hot plate, but from the moment she was born, Mac won her heart. At first, taking care of the baby was like caring for a puppy. Mac relied on her for everything; Mac needed her. And for all the care she gave to her little girl, the love came streaming back to her in joyful ways.

Mac changed everything at the compound. Even Kevin lightened up. And when they went out to the flea markets so Sis could do money for portraits, Kevin would carry Mac around and show her off, like she was a trophy he'd earned. Sis wanted to think that he loved the little girl, but with Kevin you couldn't trust anything.

One day, while she was making portraits at the state fair, a female police officer started talking with her, just being friendly. The cop was young, and she complimented Sis's drawing skills. Sis drew a unicorn for her for free, and the cop told her partner she was going to frame it. In that moment, Sis realized she had a ticket out. This cop would help her escape from Kevin. But he was off wandering the fairgrounds with Mac, and Sis couldn't run away and leave her little girl behind. That was when she realized that she would never get away.

Even if she managed to escape with Mac, once she and her little girl got out, she didn't know where they would go. No one out there would let a teenage girl keep her baby. Kevin was always complaining about how expensive things were, how hard it was with another mouth to feed. And Lauren would sooner keep living in a tent, keeping putting up with Kevin, if it was the only way she could keep Mac. Mac was the rubber cement that glued her past shut. Forever.

Chapter 20

"We've combed most of the area, but it's still a crime scene," Hank Todd said that afternoon as they began the trek on the bald path behind Green Spring Farm.

Rachel stepped carefully in her black canvas Toms, a poor choice for a damp excursion on this overcast June gloom day. Since Lauren's afternoon would be taken up with the video interview process, Dan and Rachel had sent Sierra home with Dan's parents and accepted the police chief's offer to see the place where Lauren had lived. Hank had warned that the living conditions had been grim and squalid, but there was something special he wanted to them to see.

Gray, misty clouds slid along the horizon as they made the hike from the farm parking lot. Hank filled them in regarding Kevin Hawkins. Now twenty-nine, Hawkins had raped three girls in the Woodburn area more than a decade before. Hawkins had been fifteen years old at the time, and his parents had engaged a good lawyer, who managed to convince the judge to try

Hawkins as a juvenile and to seal the record. That explained why his name had not popped up in those computer searches of local sex offenders when the cops were looking for Lauren's abductor.

At the age of sixteen, Hawkins had joined the army and trained at a base in Colorado until he was dishonorably discharged after three years. When he'd returned to Oregon his parents had refused to take him back. His aunt, Vera Hawkins, had offered him a job on the farm and let him stay in the outbuildings on the back acres. Vera Hawkins said he had stopped working several years ago, but as far as she knew, he still occupied the outbuildings. When Rachel asked if someone like the aunt might have helped Hawkins, Hank had explained that the law-enforcement community thought that he had acted alone.

Alone . . . that always brought her to the question of how he'd handled it. How could one man manage to keep a young woman hidden and submissive for the better part of six years? She knew that the answer was control. Control gained through psychological and physical abuse. Logically, she knew that. But it was hard to wrap her mind around it when she and Dan struggled to "control" Sierra, with mixed results. And she was just twelve—not into the tough teen years yet.

Green hills and fields surrounded them. It was that lush, bright green that had attracted Rachel to Oregon when she'd first visited as a college student. As they made it to the summit of a low ridge, Rachel spotted Mount Hood, its crest crisp and white. It seemed close enough to reach out and scratch the ice of the glacier, though it was a good hour's drive away. A second later, the dark clouds tumbled past it, obscuring the view.

"It's the same view we have from our house," Dan noted.

"Which is just down the road. How could Lauren live within a mile or two of home all these years?" Rachel plodded ahead. "This close, but we couldn't find her. We beat every bush and scoured every path, every park."

"It was a combination of bad circumstances," Hank said. "This farm is private property. Yes, we checked it, but not repeatedly. Although Kevin Hawkins had a juvenile record, he wasn't in our system because a judge sealed it when he was a teen. The law-enforcement community—even the next neighbors down the road—had no idea anyone was living back here. And Hawkins's aunt had no idea her nephew was capable of such a crime. In many ways, it was the perfect storm."

And a cruel irony. "All the times we went to the farm, for parties or class trips, I had no idea this was back here."

"You can't see it from the road, and the walking path doesn't cross the creek." Hank led the way. "It was a pretty effective hiding place."

"I was here." Dan's voice was glum. "I was part of the search committee that swept through these fields in the first few weeks after Lauren was taken."

With information from Lauren and Hawkins, a time frame had been pieced together. Hawkins had kept Lauren in a house at the beach during the first five months of her captivity. Investigators were still trying to pry the precise address from Hawkins, who had gone silent once he realized that his "sister" was not going to be brought around to visit with him. Still, it was apparent Hawkins had kept Lauren well hidden at the coast until he was sure that every nook and cranny in this area had been checked out and cleared. Unfortunately, the constant news updates of the search for Lauren would have kept him apprised of those details. Once the search had expanded to other areas and more distant parks, Hawkins had brought Lauren back here, to his aunt's farm.

He had gauged his moves well, the bastard.

"I remember because the compound was fenced off and locked up," Dan went on. "We waited in the rain while one of the cops got the key from Vera Hawkins. Inside the fence was a cabin and a maintenance building with a slop sink and john and a shed. Mostly I remember the debris. Old chassis and auto parts abandoned in the dirt. It was a hellhole."

"Yeah." Hank scanned the gentle green hills, punctuated here and there by trees and lined by aging post-and-beam fences. "Don't expect it to be any better."

Because she had brought her students here on field trips, Rachel knew the history of Green Spring Farm, an institution in this part of Oregon for more than a hundred years. Originally an equestrian center, the farm had housed famous horses like Roy Rogers's Trigger and the Lone Ranger's Silver when they had been brought to shows in the Northwest back in the forties and fifties. Over the years the barns and buildings had been purchased and sold a few times and fallen into disrepair. The most recent owner, Vera Hawkins, had inherited the farm from her father, who had managed to restore it enough to turn a small profit by leasing the land to an organic farming cooperative. One of the big red barns was still used as an equestrian center, while the other was leased by the Town of Mirror Lake for classes, camps, and private parties. Not a gardener, Rachel had always considered the place to be a quaint touch of country in an otherwise growing suburb.

At last, they closed in on the cluster of trees that hid the compound.

Most of the fenced-off area was well hidden, surrounded by old-growth trees and bushes and blackberry brambles that were so overgrown, in some spots the matted snarls rose three feet above the path. Hank pointed to the prickly vines that reached over the path. "Watch your step. I already snagged my pants on those thorns."

Inside the big metal gate, Rachel was surprised to see a neatly tended garden with some early lettuce ready to harvest. At the far end of the garden, two men were scraping through the mud, one on his belly. The white letters printed on the jacket of the man facing away from them identified them as FBI.

Hank nodded toward the men. "As I said, it's still an active crime scene."

Off to the left was a one-story clapboard house, its roof green with moss. A wobbly brown tent stood beyond the house. To the left was a shed that was tilting dangerously toward the fence, and a mound of trash that was probably the source of the foul odor.

"The shed is falling down." Hank nodded toward the dilapidated building. "But the house has electricity, an old TV with a VCR, a prefab shower, and a sink. We think that Lauren was sleeping in the tent. We found a sleeping bag in there, along with some magazines and a sketchpad. It's all been photographed and vouchered for evidence."

"Lauren hated camping," Dan said as they scrutinized the tent like art lovers in a museum, seeking to experience and connect to the exhibit. "Remember when I slept out in the backyard with her that time? She was back in her room before midnight. She said the noise of the bugs in the grass was keeping her awake."

"She was not a fan of the outdoors." Beyond the creatures and flowers she had loved to sketch, Lauren had been an indoor girl. Not a hiker or a gardener. "But I guess she adjusted to the circumstances." *I guess we all have to adjust.* Rachel flipped up the hood of her jacket as a light drizzle began to fill the gray air. "It feels like we're a hundred miles from civilization."

"Which was probably Hawkins's intention," Dan added.

Hank explained that Hawkins had given Lauren free reign over the compound most of the time she was here. In the first few months at the beach, Hawkins had programmed Lauren to follow orders. By the time she arrived here, she had nearly given up trying to escape. "Kidnappers force their victims to relinquish control of their lives. Paula mentioned hearing about Lauren being locked in a cage, which we figure is the large dog kennel in the shed. Apparently Hawkins kept her in there from time to time when he wanted to keep her out of sight or punish her."

Rachel winced, and Dan kicked at a stone jutting through the mud. None of this information came as a total shock; Rachel had done some research about the psychological dynamics of kidnapping. However, picturing their daughter in this desolate patch of land would make for more tortured, sleepless nights.

Dan raked his pale hair back. "Have you been able to sit in on any interviews with him? Has he confessed yet?"

"His interrogation is being handled by the FBI and the district attorney's office. But last I heard, he's still pretty tight-lipped." Hank rubbed the back of his neck. "But I didn't bring you here for the grim images. You have to see the inside of the house."

Rachel rubbed her palms on her jeans, wishing she were anywhere else but here. In sharp contrast, Dan followed with vitality—almost a spring in his step. She had called him on it that morning over coffee. His cheerful tolerance of the situation with Lauren and the police and the social workers.

"Hold on a second," he'd said. "Are you mad at me because I'm being upbeat about finding Lauren? Because I could accuse you of being too rigid. Holding on to the pain. Stuck in the mire of regret."

"Honey, we're in the same boat," Rachel had said. "I'm just trying to get our daughter on board with us."

"For starters, we've had one daughter on board all along, but you seem to have forgotten that, and I think Sierra is beginning to feel a little left out."

It wasn't an accusation; it was simply the truth. "You're right. Did Sierra bring it up? Did she talk to you?" Rachel cupped her hands around her warm mug, trying to stay rooted in the moment, though her mind was spinning off in other directions.

"We talk every day, sometimes more than once a day. I know you've kept her at bay to focus all your energy on Lauren, but for Sierra, it feels like a rejection."

Dan was right. Rachel knew she was wound too tight lately, and though she sensed that it was putting Lauren off, she couldn't help herself. She felt like she was trying to force round pegs into square holes, pressing too hard because she was so desperate to make it all fit together, all the pieces of their separate, varied lives. Her attempt to talk with Sierra before the press conference had been met with that snappish "What do you want now?" attitude. At the moment, nothing was working. She wished she could be enthusiastic like Dan, but she did feel stuck in the muck. Nothing had moved forward since the moment they'd learned Lauren had been recovered.

Hank led the way toward the tired gray house with mildew stains running down the siding. "You have to see the inside of this one." Inside, he flicked the light on, and the walls came alive. Every single panel of plywood, every crossbeam, was covered with an illustration made by a combination of paint and Sharpie and crayon that seemed to have been melted and then layered on for texture.

"It's Lauren's work, and it's . . . amazing." Rachel went to one corner to follow the beanstalk into the crayon sky. "She must have worked on it all these years." There was a hopeful beauty to it, as well as lonesomeness and a heartrending sadness.

Rachel sighed in awe. It was a visual feast. Winged elves and butterflies and dragonflies. Peasant girls and catlike gladiators and insect-like robots. Spotted mushrooms and flowers and enchanted skies sodden with stars. Dragons and a beanstalk spiraling into the clouds and a veiled girl with a diamond tear sparkling on her cheek.

"It's Peter Max meets anime," Dan said. "Though I would have recognized the hand behind these illustrations anywhere. Thank God he let her paint and . . . what is this? Sort of a melted crayon texture?"

Rachel shrugged. "I guess she worked with whatever medium was available."

Hank paused in front of the painting of a woman bent over her hoe, the sunken lines of her shoulders and bowed head imitating a man-sized sunflower beside her. "All the gritty candor of Toulouse Lautrec with the vivid color and raw emotion of Van Gogh."

"What?" Rachel squinted at him. "I can't believe I heard you say that."

Dan chuckled. "You've been holding out on us, Hank." His lighthearted teasing eased the tension in the dim house.

"You know I'm a Duck," Hank said, referring to the

mascot of the University of Oregon, "I was a double major at U of O. Criminal justice and art history."

"Must get a lot of mileage in the locker room."

"Believe me, it's not discussed in the locker room. I keep it under my hat, usually, but looking at these paintings, I've got to say, your daughter has talent. That's why I wanted you to see these. It would be a shame for someone to paint over them."

"I wonder if there's a way to remove these without damaging the building's structure," Dan said, touching the raw edge of drywall that didn't quite meet the stud.

"I don't think damaging the building will be a concern. After the investigation, I think these buildings are going to come down. That shed is about to fall down; it's not structurally sound. And once the location of the compound becomes public knowledge, you run the risk of having looky-loos tromping around back here. I think Vera's going to take these buildings down."

"Do you think Lauren would want to save these?" Rachel bit her lower lip as she followed the long tail of a purple dragon that was cabled like a bungee cord around the ankles of a thin young woman who was swan-diving through a night sky speckled with stars. "I mean, it's extraordinary, but it might always remind her of a terrible time in her life. I don't know if she would be more attached to the art or more determined to cut the ties to the past and move on."

"I think that's a question that only Lauren can answer," Dan said, "and I don't think she's ready to do it just yet."

It felt good to debate Lauren's future, good to have a tangible connection to their daughter. "Well. If we're allowed to dismantle these walls, I would like to hold on to my daughter's creations." As Rachel began to take pictures on her cell phone, she wondered if all this drywall and plywood would fit in the garage. Maybe they could rent a storage space. She got Dan going with his cell camera, and soon the dim, one-room cabin was punctuated by flashes of cell phone photography.

"I'm reluctant to let go of anything that Lauren might find reassuring down the road," she said.

"But it might be a negative reminder of a terrible time. Maybe Lauren will want to burn these shacks to the ground. She might want to light the first torch."

Rachel nodded. Either way, they would support her. Her throat grew thick as she opened a swinging panel and found a portrait of a Madonna with an angelic infant in her arms. It was a reminder that the naïve preteen she'd lost, her baby girl, had borne a baby of her own.

With robotic resolve, she snapped the photo and moved on.

Chapter 21

The digital camera stood silent as a sentry on the tripod, an eternal witness to Lauren's animated description of how Mac used to tell her that she could only be tickled on Saturday.

"And one day, she was in my tent, and I kissed her and gave her a little tickle under the chin. And Mac said, 'No, Mama. Tickle me only on Saturday.' I told her it *was* Saturday, and she said, 'No. Saturn-day.' And since I had been teaching her about the planets in the solar system, I thought it was the funniest thing. We both laughed so hard we cried."

Paula cocked her head. "Sounds like you were a wonderful mother."

"Mac was a wonderful girl." Lauren went on to describe the little girl's fluffy blond ringlet curls, the chubbiness of her cheeks, the way she followed Lauren around the compound like a little duckling. "That's called imprinting," Lauren said. "I read about it in a book. The baby duckling follows the first one it sees, and that's usually the mother. Well, with Mac, I was just glad she followed me and not Kevin. It would have killed me to think that she liked Kevin better than she liked me."

Thank the good Lord, Lauren was a talker. She had answered Paula's questions, told anecdotes, described her feelings, and even reflected on her various incidents with a mature philosophical bent. Lauren had shared heartwarming details about Mac and annoying things that had made her hate Kevin even as she'd relied on him for her existence. That was the paradox for a kidnap victim: the love-hate relationship with the abductor. Paula believed that Lauren's insistence on being called Sis, the name that Kevin gave her, was symbolic of her allegiance to him.

It would take a while—a few months or even years—to unravel the complex relationship between Lauren and her alleged abductor. For now, it was up to Paula to make sure Lauren knew she would be taken care of, and that she did not need Kevin Hawkins anymore. Paula couldn't chance another getaway attempt like last night. Thank God Rachel had arrived at the right moment.

The girl had been talking for more than three hours when her voice began to squeak and Paula called a break.

"You're doing great, but I think you need to give your voice a rest for a bit. Stretch out. Hit the restroom. Get your circulation going."

While CeeCee plied Lauren with juice boxes and cookies, Paula ducked into the hallway of the Children's Center to sneak a look at her cell phone. As she'd expected, there were way too many phone messages and e-mails. She sorted through the e-mails first—finding what she wanted from Hank Todd. The two houses he had suggested for her were both available; the owners were even willing to let them go rent-free out of consideration for Lauren O'Neil. Hank had even sent one of his cops, Pete Wolinsky, to drive by both places and snap some photos so that Paula could get a sense of the houses.

Thanks, Hank, she tapped onto her smartphone, and then checked Wolinsky's e-mail. The two houses were beautiful, a sleek contemporary on a hill and a craftsman-style home on the lake. She liked the second one because it looked homey and the location on a peninsula would offer a certain level of privacy. Three bedrooms and three baths—that should be enough. She suspected she would be staying there with Lauren and an FBI agent. She wasn't sure if DHS would want to involve a therapist, too. She hoped that Truman was briefing the family about the house, because she barely had a minute to pee right now, but if not, she would deal with it later. She was good at picking up the pieces.

She sent a text to Hank saying the craftsman house was a go. Then she leafed through her notepad for the number of the FBI agent she had met at the meeting. There she was . . . Bija Wilson. She called her and left a message, passing on information about the house and asking if she would be the agent assigned to watch Lauren when she was discharged from the hospital.

So many things to line up. Early this morning she had sent a text to Courtney Brown, one of the other social workers, asking her to move or cancel all of Paula's appointments for the next two days. Courtney had responded with a quick "Will do!" That girl was on her game.

And Paula herself, she had not felt this alive in years. Oh, she'd handled plenty of cases that had broken her heart or engaged her resources and skills. But nothing like Lauren O'Neil's case. It was a gift, the challenge of a lifetime, and Paula felt right to be in the middle of it.

Sometimes, divine providence rang clear as a bell.

Back in the small office decorated in cheerful cinnamon chairs and a Pacific blue couch, she found Lauren and CeeCee laughing together. A good development. It showed Lauren beginning to open up to other people.

"How's your voice?" Paula asked. "Are you getting tired?"

"I'm fine." Lauren shrugged. The fine blond hairs on her forehead reminded Paula of a baby chick, and once again came that familiar rush of maternal love. Right now, Lauren needed so much, and Paula was happy to be the one to care for the girl. Of course, her personal issues were not supposed to be a part of her professional relationship. There were appropriate professional boundaries that had to be maintained with a client. But honestly, it was too late for that. This case was filling a need for her, and she was a good match for a girl who had spent the last six years in rural isolation.

"You're a trooper." She took her place in the chair beside the camera. "Are you ready to go on?"

"Sure. It feels good to get it all out."

"I'm glad. Telling your story is good therapy, but some people struggle to get it out."

"You're a very articulate girl," CeeCee added. "You know how to use your words."

"It feels good to tell the truth, after all these years. And Mac . . . he wouldn't let me talk about Mac anymore. He said I was getting too depressing, but I just wanted to talk about her . . . to remember her."

"Well, you can tell us anything, depressing or not," Paula said. "And before I forget, I wanted to fill you in on our plan for this evening. Apparently, there's been a pack of reporters camped out at your parents' house since early this morning. The police and the FBI are thinking that it's a good idea for you to keep away from there for now." She told Lauren about the idea of a safe house, and then showed her the photo of the lake house on her phone.

"It looks pretty nice." Lauren turned the iPhone and blinked when the photo moved. "How did you get a picture on your phone like that?"

"That's technology for you. So you're happy with the plan?"

"I'd be happy staying there forever. You'll be there, too, right?"

Paula nodded. "Along with an FBI agent. A female agent."

Lauren seemed to sit taller as she soaked that in. "And so I don't have to go back to Dan and Rachel O'Neil?"

"Eventually you will. That's the plan."

Lauren pulled the sleeves of her new hoodie over her hands and pressed them over her mouth. "That's the only part that makes me uncomfortable—living with the O'Neils."

"They *are* your parents. Your family." To watch Lauren, you would think they were terrible people, but Paula knew better. These people had been investigated years ago, when Lauren went missing. They had put their information out there, and they were genuine. But Lauren's feelings about them were complicated, all rolled into the tangle of her fear and loyalty for her captor. "Think of the imprinting . . . the baby chick following its mother. Once upon a time, that was you and your mom. You and your dad. They really want to be a family again."

"They don't love me. Maybe they did in the beginning, but it all trickled out and they stopped looking. If they hadn't stopped looking after the first few weeks, they might have found me hidden away right in their own backyard."

"Did you know you were living in Mirror Lake?" Paula asked.

"No. I told you. Kevin covered me up in the back of the van whenever we left the compound."

"It is a shame that no one thought to search Green Spring Farm a second time," Paula said. "But you're wrong about the O'Neils. They never gave up. They were vigilant . . . relentless."

"Your mom always believed you'd come back," CeeCee added. "And your dad, he led a search every weekend, through local parks and forests. I volunteered a few times with my husband." As CeeCee spoke, Paula made a note to gather some news clippings and video about the Find Lauren campaign her parents had run. Sometimes, seeing was believing.

"But Kevin told me that they didn't care anymore. That I was just a pretty butterfly that flew away. Something that makes you smile, but you forget about it a minute later. That's what Kevin said."

"He lied," Paula said flatly. She explained that the search for her had been going strong for six whole years. "It was on the news a few times a year. If you'd had regular TV, you would have seen your face on news programs every few weeks. You would have seen your mom and dad organizing searches and speaking about you at meetings and concerts and press conferences."

"If we had regular TV?" Lauren scowled. "That's like saying, if we lived in a nice house instead of a shack. If I had never been kidnapped. I learned you can't live your life crying over things that didn't happen."

"You're right." There was more than a touch of anger in Lauren's words, but Paula wasn't ready to explore that. Right now they needed to get the sequence of events on record for the police. She tried to switch to a more concrete topic.

"So what kind of things did you watch on your VCR?" Paula asked. "How did you get tapes?"

"Kevin found videotapes at thrift stores or flea markets. Real deals, he said. He got kiddy shows for Mac to watch and family shows for me. My favorites were *Full House* and *Seventh Heaven,* and I let Mac watch them, too. I wanted her to see happy families who laughed at their own mistakes and helped each other with their problems. Kevin never admitted to making a mistake, but he never let me forget mine. But the shows . . . the shows were an escape, and I thought they were good for Mac. Besides that, I let her watch some *Sesame Street* tapes and Disney movies and some other kids' shows that Kevin got real cheap from a yard sale. Her favorite was *Bear in the Big Blue House.* I liked it, too, because Bear is cheerful about everything, and he's friends with other animals and the sun and Luna, the moon. Have you ever seen Bear?"

"I have not, but it sounds great." Paula made a note to search for copies of Lauren's favorite shows on DVD. She could order them from the Mirror Lake Library during the next break and pick them up this evening. It would be good for Lauren to have something comforting and familiar.

Happy families who laughed at their own mistakes and helped each other with their problems. Healthy family relationships. It was a wonder Lauren still recognized that.

Chapter 22

Rachel knew it was time to get going, but it was hard to tear herself away from these tumbledown buildings that had been her daughter's home. She sensed that Dan felt the same way. Although their tour of the compound was complete, they stood at the edge of the garden, drawn to the ghosts that loomed in the whispering drizzle. Dan and Hank were nattering on the topic of the death penalty in Oregon, and Rachel tuned them out to focus on her daughter. Had Lauren enjoyed gardening here? The neat rows in well-tended soil spoke of a gardener who cared. Although the compound was surrounded by trees, the space was wide enough to catch a wide swath of sunlight in the growing season.

"We need to talk about Lauren's lodging," Hank said, garnering Rachel's attention. "A few points came up at our task force meeting this morning—Lauren's security being one. The FBI is assigning an agent to watch over her, and it was agreed that she should be moved to a safe house where—"

"What?" Rachel interrupted.

"Just temporarily. You saw those reporters outside your house this morning. Is that what you want for Lauren? Having to pass through a barrier of media people every time she wants to leave the house? Granted, she's still a minor and they probably will decline to publish her photo for the time being. But that doesn't mean they won't follow her every time she goes out to catch a movie or visit the dentist."

"We can keep her safe." Rachel looked to Dan for support, but he was shaking his head.

"Rach, you saw the trucks out there this morning . . . the people in the street. The cameras pointed at our car as we drove out."

"But a few small obstacles doesn't mean we just give up." Why was she so alone in this battle? "I think everyone is overreacting right now. We're not talking about protecting her from Hawkins or a killer. Hank, you yourself said that it looks like he acted alone. It's about privacy, which is important, I know. But at the end of the day, if someone prints a snarky article about her, what's the consequence? Bad press, but she'll still be safe. She'll be fine at our house."

Knuckles pressed to his lips, Dan frowned in concern. "Hank has a good point. Yeah, I want her home, too, but right now, for Lauren, safety is everything. We can't take any chances, Rach. If the FBI is willing to give us someone to protect her, I say we go with it."

Rachel shook her head. Her daughter was slipping away from her, and she was powerless to stop it. "So I'm outnumbered. Overruled." Both men remained stoic as she vented. "Why even bother to mention it to me? I don't even have a chance to speak my mind." She threw up her hands and marched in the opposite direction.

She paced the length of the garden in anger, and then let out a hissy breath. It was wrong to lash out at

Hank, the messenger. And Dan . . . had she really snapped at him this morning for being too cheerful and positive? Good God, she was off-kilter. A planet circling a star that had burned out and gone dark.

Find your center. She took a deep, yoga breath, then released it as she focused on the soil beneath her feet. Knowing her daughter had hoed and planted these neat rows of lettuce, carrots, peppers, and radishes, Rachel felt a connection as her shoes trod on the earth.

When she came to the end of a row, the sign on the little placard labeled BEETS was different—printed in slanted, scraggly letters instead of Lauren's rounded bubble letters.

His writing.

If this wasn't a crime scene, she would have gone over and ripped the sign from the ground. Turning away, she faced the FBI technicians. Although they were a good thirty yards from the rest of the action, they had been quiet this whole time, scratching and digging like archaeologists.

Just what were they digging for? Pressing a fingertip to the cuticle of her thumb, she imagined bodies . . . young girls. She squeezed her eyes shut against the agonizing vision.

Crazy thoughts, but she had to find out what they were doing. Although Rachel sensed that she wasn't supposed to engage the FBI forensic specialists, she cut across the garden and headed right over.

"Hey, there. How's it going?"

"Hold on there." The agent replaced the lid on a plastic bin and came toward her. "I need you to stay on the other side of the yellow tape. Got to preserve the crime scene."

"Oh." Rachel froze at the edge of the mud path. "Sorry."

The agent stepped over the low barriers and tipped

his baseball cap politely. "Mrs. O'Neil. How are you doing?" He had a broad smile and kind eyes.

"I'm sorry, have we met?"

He waved that off. "I just recognized you from television, the search campaign for Lauren. You've been in the media a lot these past few years."

Rachel's smile was halfhearted. "That's about to end, I hope."

He introduced himself as agent Mike Turk while Rachel surveyed the low beds of dirt and graded mud cordoned off in sections by sticks and tape. "It looks like you're digging for dinosaurs with those brushes and spoons. What do you expect to find?"

He rubbed his gloved hands together. "The chief didn't explain it to you?"

She sighed. "Maybe he did. Right now I'm on information overload."

"Well, I wouldn't want to make things worse."

She caught him with the stern gaze of a junior high teacher. "Tell me now, please."

"We're interested in anything Hawkins might have buried. We've gone over the grounds with a metal detector, but that led us to an old wrench and screwdriver. But this corner, we thought we'd find something more."

"Bodies?"

"One body. The remains of the three-year-old girl." Turk winced, clearly uncomfortable with having to be the one to give her this information. "When we came on the scene, there was a sign over in this corner. We thought it was a grave marker."

He opened a plastic bin and held up a wooden placard painted with a benevolent angel that could have been floating on the ceiling of the Sistine chapel. Beneath her billowing gown was written: R.I.P. Mac.

"Mackenzie?" The little girl . . . her granddaughter.

Of course, Hawkins would have buried her here; he didn't have the money to spring for a legal interment. She pressed a fist to her mouth, and then forced herself to pull it away. If she wanted Turk to take her seriously, she had to keep her cool. "They buried Mac in this spot?"

"So we assumed. But we were wrong." He opened another bin to reveal a small box—a shoe box. The cardboard was mottled with mold and caked with dusty soil, but there was no mistaking the exquisitely painted angel on the top as Lauren's artwork.

Rachel's voice dropped to a hush. "Is that a makeshift coffin? Mac's remains?"

"You wouldn't be here if that was the case." Detective Turk gave her a wary smile. "We wouldn't subject you to that. It's just a shoe box we found buried here. A few little baby mementoes inside. A pacifier and some clothes and what not. Two videotapes. *Sesame Street* and *Bear in the Big Blue House.*"

"They buried her belongings, but you haven't found a body."

He shook his head. "It's not here. At least not in this section, and I doubt that he put it under the garden."

A chill ran down Rachel's spine as a she shifted in the damp grass. "So it's not really a grave?"

"Doesn't look that way, though we're still digging. Digging very gently." Turk held up a few of the small tools—a brush and a small spade that resembled a serving spoon. "That's why it takes a while. If we end up checking the garden, we might be here for the summer."

Suddenly, the one-acre plot of land opened up around Rachel like an expanding ocean. What would it take to sift through all the dirt here, to carefully overturn the topsoil to screen for a small corpse? Such tedious work would take forever, and yet, it was important—vitally important—to find Mac's body. Without it, there wouldn't be much of a homicide case against Kevin Hawkins, and Lauren would have trouble finding closure on the loss of her little girl.

It was the kick in the pants she needed.

"Hank? Dan?" She motioned to the men. "Over here. Agent Turk is onto something essential to the case."

Chapter 23

Sis snuggled against the soft hood of her new jacket and soaked up the warmth of the mug in her hands.

It was chilly again, with that gray afternoon dampness that would hang in through the evening. Sis knew, because she lived in the weather now, outside whenever Kevin would let her. Well, out in the tent. She figured that was as close to Mother Nature as a person could get without waking up soaked in dew each morning.

But that wasn't true anymore. As of today, she'd be staying in this lake house, a safe house, with a social worker and an FBI guard to ward off anyone who came too close. That part was nice, but Sis didn't know how to explain her worries. They could keep her physically safe, but no one could fix the holes in her heart, the twisted emotions that dragged her down with guilt and fear. When she closed her eyes, there was no safety, no peace. Deep inside, she was broken.

But she was relieved for the time they would let her spend with Paula and Bija. She was leaning back in a lawn chair—an Adirondack chair, Paula called it—with her bright tangerine cast propped up on a little stool that matched the chair. She and Paula were talking, facing out toward the water when a goose flapped onto the lawn near her feet and let out an obnoxious honk.

"Silly goose," Paula joked.

They laughed out loud.

"Don't you know this is a safe house? You can't be here unless you have proper authorization. You have to be cleared by my case worker," Sis told the goose, repeating the warning she had heard Paula give to some people on the phone.

Undaunted, the goose honked again and waddled over toward the dock. Having dealt with a few geese at her grandparents' lake house, she knew not to be afraid. But she also knew that waterfowl were called that for a reason. "Go poop on someone else's lawn."

Paula chuckled again. "That's right." Her cell phone jingled and she looked down at it. "That's a text from Bija. Your parents are here."

"Oh, not them again."

"We talked about this, remember? You're going to keep an open mind."

"And you're not going to make me go home with them, right?"

"Not this week," Paula admitted. "But I think we should offer the extra room here to your mom. It would be a nice way to ease back into the relationship, spending some easy time together."

"Maybe tomorrow." Sis was determined to keep the O'Neils at bay as long as she could. It wasn't that they'd ever mistreated her. CeeCee, the woman at the Children's Center who had videotaped Lauren, had asked her about that a few times, which had begun to get annoying.

It had got her to thinking about that day when Kevin

took her. Walking home alone from school had been a pleasure, her treat, hard-won after she had finally convinced her parents that she could walk home like other kids her age and handle herself alone at home. She still remembered the steely look in her mother's eyes when they'd had the discussion. Dad had defended Lauren. He understood that it was humiliating and boring to be lumped in with the babies, and he reminded Mom that they had chosen to live in Mirror Lake because it was a safe neighborhood. "I think it's time to empower Lauren, time to let her grow up."

How many times after the kidnapping had she regretted that discussion? The horror of her mistake had stuck in her chest like an immovable pit, a stone that threatened to swell up until she could no longer manage a breath.

I was wrong, she had murmured, half confession, half prayer. I was wrong. I wasn't ready to walk home alone or defend myself from the world.

But there was no taking that back.

And it wasn't her parents' fault, though CeeCee had kept probing as if her next jab would hit gold. "The O'Neils didn't do anything terrible to me," Sis had said. "They're not bad people. I just can't live with them."

At least Paula understood that her feelings toward the family were complicated. She could not trust that Kevin wouldn't be coming back for her, coming after her family, which he swore he would do. In the back of her mind, she longed for her tent in the compound. And anyone who thought they could return to a family after six years away and just fit right in, well, that person was fooling herself.

"Hey, there!" Paula called to the people descending the deck and heading down the paved path to the lakefront.

In a television show, she would think they were a cute couple. Dan's hair was still the color of wheat, and he was trim and quick to smile, like the dad on *Full House*. Rachel had all the right features, shiny auburn hair, thick lips that now were more sour than sweet. Today, something must have sweetened for her, because the light was back in her eyes.

That single, beautiful light, Sis thought.

"We just came from the compound behind Green Spring Farm." Dan turned a chair toward Sis and gestured for Rachel to sit. "We were there with Hank. He noticed your artwork, Lauren, and he wanted us to see it."

The paintings.

The people and angels and creatures and plants that adorned every wall and beam in the cabin. Although artwork was a quiet companion, some of those paintings had helped her through dark times of doubt. Just the process of being able to brighten up a dingy wall with a unicorn or to layer melted crayon into speckled confetti over a splintered beam had given her hope and confidence in her worth as a person.

"That's right," Paula said. "I heard you decorated the entire house."

"Not so much decorating. I wanted to make something beautiful out of something ugly. And it filled the lonely spaces."

"You are a gifted artist," Rachel murmured, as if she were in church. "We always knew that. We saved every sketchbook you filled, every nursery school glitter star and grade school art project."

Sis tugged both sleeves over her hands, wishing she could vanish inside the hoody. This was embarrassing, but part of her was relieved that they liked her paintings in the house. The artist inside was always hungry for validation. "So the police chief wanted you to see my artwork?"

Rachel nodded. "He thinks it's important to let you decide what should be done with it. If you want to keep it, we can probably make arrangements with the farm's owner to remove it. If you want it destroyed, we'll respect your decision. Either way, it looks like the buildings of the compound will be razed in the next year or so."

So the compound would be flattened . . . that scared her. Where would she go, if she couldn't go back there?

"You can think about the artwork," Rachel said, leaning toward her with tenderness in her eyes. "There's time. But there's something else we need to ask you about, something that can't wait."

Sis looked down at the sodden grass, not wanting to face the inevitable question. The answer was no. No, she was not going back to live with them.

"I don't want to upset you, but we have to ask about the plot of land in the corner of the compound. There was a little plaque there that said R.I.P. Mac. You know what I'm talking about?"

Sis glanced up sharply. "Yeah. Mac's grave."

"Only it's not really her grave. The FBI dug up the area and they didn't find Mac's body. Just a shoe box that seems to be filled with her things."

"Well, yeah." Sis's mouth had gone sour, and she took a quick sip of cocoa, which was growing cold. "We couldn't bury Mac there, not really. When she got sick, Kevin took her to the hospital. He said they gave her medicine and oxygen and stuff, but she was just too far gone. When it was all over, people started asking a lot of questions, and Kevin got nervous. He didn't want anyone coming around the compound, snooping around, and besides, he didn't have the money to pay those medical bills."

Rachel's eyes glimmered. Were those tears? In the dying light, it was hard to tell. "So he left her body at the hospital. Is that what he told you?"

Sis nodded. "He said they would do the right thing. Respectful and everything."

"Do you know what hospital he went to?" Paula asked.

Sis hated that she never had the details. These people probably thought she was an idiot. "He never told me stuff like that. He said I couldn't be trusted." It had been a terrible time. Sis had been sick, too, with a raging fever and thick pain in her throat that had made it hard to swallow. Kevin had blamed her for getting Mac sick, blamed her for not getting up to take care of her girl, but how could she when her head weighed a ton and the room spun around her? He took Mac away sometime in her delirium. She had dozed off with a wheezing baby girl in her bed and awakened to velvety silence.

"I was sick when he took Mac away. I'll never forgive him for that. Yes, she was sick, coughing and wheezing, crying and fighting for every breath. But at least he could have let me come along to the hospital. I could have kept Mac calm, held her hand and rocked her." It still haunted her to think of her little girl leaving this world without her mama at her side.

Rachel shook her head. "That must have been so hard for you. Especially when you needed a doctor, too. Did he ever take you to see a physician?"

"No, but that time he brought me some pills. Said I had scarlet fever, and if I didn't want to die, I'd better take them."

"Oh, Lauren, I'm so sorry." Rachel leaned closer, and this time Sis didn't feel the need to back away. "You know, today when I found out that the grave was empty,

I actually had a moment of hope. Maybe it's crazy, but I started to wonder, what if Kevin lied about her dying? What if Mac recovered and she's out there somewhere."

The breath caught in Sis's throat. This idea—this was a dream she had spun in her mind a thousand times but had always tamped down as a wild wish. "I've thought about that. Hoping and praying. But then I realized that it didn't make sense. If Mac had gotten better, Kevin would have brought her back to the compound. I mean, what else would he have done out there with a three-year-old girl? Besides, Mac was attached to me. She would have wanted to come home."

"But would Kevin have cared about what Mac wanted?" Rachel's voice still held sympathy, but there was a flame of conviction that seemed to light the space between them. "He had already separated one girl from her family. I don't think he would have hesitated to do it again."

"Rach, let's not go down that road." There went Dan, playing the dad. "It's wrong to build false hope."

"We don't know that it's false," Rachel insisted.

Paula held up one hand to stop the conversation. "Before we jump to any conclusions, let's hear what Kevin Hawkins has to say. Chief Todd is going down to the prison tomorrow to try to find out what he did with Mac's remains. When we get more information, we can proceed from there."

With that, Paula wrapped up the visit. It was nearly dark as the four of them rose and headed into the lake house, where the row of yellow-lit windows on the bottom floor and the two windows upstairs made a smile pattern. A big, bright, shining grin. It reflected the tiny wiggle of hope inside Sis, the crazy idea that her little girl might still be alive and breathing and even laughing somewhere on this planet. It was something good to hold on to, something to pray for when she closed her eyes tonight in bed.

As her new white sneakers shuffled on the path, Sis watched clouds and mist wander in front of the milky moon glow. How many times had she sent a message to the moon, hoping it would bounce back from her parents and wake them into coming to find her? At the time, she hadn't known they were looking for her. Had they stared at the moon and sent her a message, too? When she had scrubbed dishes in the slop sink and sung that song she used to sing with Mom, maybe it wasn't just silliness she was feeling. Maybe Mommy had been thinking of her at the same time. She wanted to believe that her parents wanted her back, but Lauren couldn't get past the invisible wall between them—the constant reminder that her parents had not saved her. *They're not even looking for you anymore,* Kevin had told her. *You're a lost cause.*

Chapter 24

The sound of steel doors slamming in a concrete chamber in the Clackamas County Jail chipped away at Hank's composure. He had already surrendered and vouchered his gun with the property clerk, and now he sorely felt the loss of that familiar weight on his waistband. He never liked this part, locked in with men who had killed, raped, and sold their souls at the altar of crystal meth or heroin. Generally, Hank's job as Mirror Lake's police chief kept him away from prison corridors. His time was spent in the precinct, out on the streets, and in schools and communities. The grip and grin, Lieutenant Dillon called it. Hank was in his element when he was reassuring business owners about crime stats or reviewing safety precautions with grade-schoolers. But here, in the county jail, he was out of his element.

"You should let me do the talking." Bradley mopped his brow with a handkerchief as they followed the guard down the corridor. "I sat in on Elliot's interview with him, and this guy is a sociopath. Did you know he refused a lawyer? He was going to defend himself. He's that good. Or, at least he thought so." Bradley Trout-man seemed more nervous than Hank to be inside the prison. An assistant district attorney for Clackamas County, maybe Bradley was jittery to be entrusted this interview by the big cheese, DA Elliot Gustin. Or maybe it was just the finality of those doors sealing shut behind them.

"How are you planning to play it?" Hank asked.

"No games. I'm a straight shooter. Elliot told me to ask him the questions and keep it at that. In and out and back to the office."

"What if he doesn't answer your questions?" When Bradley squinted at him, Hank went on. "I'm just saying, men behind bars like to be cajoled and indulged. Especially sociopaths. Sometimes if you humor them, you can make a connection. Get them to talk. In the end, it's all about saving face."

"Shit, Hank. I don't want to have beers with the guy. I just want him to tell me where the kid's body is buried." Bradley's heart was in the right place; he couldn't help that he was young and inexperienced. Elliot should have known better than to send someone so green on a case this important.

"It doesn't work that way. He's got no reason to give you what you want. Especially if it means he's giving us evidence to charge him with a homicide. He hasn't even confessed to the kidnapping yet. He's still standing by the story that he saved the girl from homelessness. He thinks he's a hero because he gave up her location at the farm. He figures that, otherwise, she would have died there while he was spending a stretch in jail for the attempted robbery."

"A real humanitarian," Bradley muttered.

"Did he finally lawyer up?"

"The court assigned him someone. Elliot said this case is too big for the judge to risk a mistrial. Whether or not Hawkins takes the attorney's advice, that's his loss."

Even before Hank and Bradley were seated across from Hawkins and his lawyer, Hank sensed that the lawyer would not be an obstacle.

It was Hawkins who was the problem.

"I can't help you with that one, man," Hawkins answered when Bradley asked him the location of the little girl's grave. "I don't know anyone named Mac. Is that a girl or a dude?"

Bradley's lips curled in a bitter smile. "You know exactly who I'm talking about. The three-year-old girl who died this past February. Your daughter. Or do you not have an ounce of compassion for your own flesh and blood?"

"Whoa." Hawkins held his hands up in defense and mock shock. "If I'd wanted a sermon, I would have asked for the prison chaplain."

Although Hank wasn't surprised by the suspect's broad denial, the bravado and smugness irked him.

"We know about the little girl. Mackenzie?" Bradley stood his ground, but the sheen of sweat on his upper lip revealed his uneasiness. "You kidnapped Lauren O'Neil when she was just a girl. You raped her, and she bore your child, who died, we think of natural causes. I'm asking you to help us out here."

"Why would I want to help you?"

"If you give us the body, we'll knock down the homicide charge for Mackenzie Hawkins. Lauren says you tried to get her help at a hospital. Tell us where you took her and we could bring it down to negligent homicide, if you help us locate the body."

"You're so generous." Kevin Hawkins's smile softened his face, as if he didn't have a care in the world.

Hank read sarcasm. Kevin was a good-looking guy, with those blue eyes, an enviable head of hair, and a smile that could have won him a toothpaste commercial. The kind of smile women liked. Even the candy-cane striped uniform issued to the highest risk of the county inmates did not emasculate this guy. You had to wonder why Hawkins didn't go for a real relationship with a woman instead of a heinous transgression with a child.

"It's a good offer," Bradley said. "You want a few minutes to talk to your lawyer?"

"I would like to confer with my client." Leon Marino, a fiftyish guy with an East Coast look—maybe it was the suit, maybe the salt-and-pepper curls that seemed to be jelled and coiffed—turned to gauge Hawkins's reaction.

But the suspect did not acknowledge Marino's existence. "Here's what I'm going to tell you. That girl is crazy with a capital C. First of all, I never kidnapped her. *She* came to *me,* asking me for a ride. Begging me to take me away from the shit going on at home."

Hank's vision glazed with annoyance as Hawkins spun a tale of abuse in the O'Neil home. An obvious lie. After Lauren had gone missing, Dan and Rachel had been checked out thoroughly, and the firefighter and teacher had proved clean as a whistle. From his relationship with them over the past six years, Hank knew they were solid, good people.

"She was running for her life," Hawkins went on. "A runaway, not a victim. I just helped her by giving her food and a place to stay."

"And raping her when she was eleven?"

"That word—it hurts my ears." Hawkins winced. "Did she tell you that? I mean, is that the story she came up with? Because it's a lousy lie. First of all, you can't prove that I laid a hand on her, can you? I mean, in the biblical sense?"

"I'm not going to discuss our case with you." Bradley folded his arms and leaned back, a sign that he was closed for business.

Probably because Hawkins was right about proving the statutory rape. Hank thought of the doctor's report, the gray areas there. Even if the hymen wasn't intact, it did not prove that a woman had engaged in sexual intercourse, let alone born a child.

But the fractures in Lauren's leg were very real.

"She's wearing a cast from the multiple fractures in her left leg," Hank offered. He kept his voice low and calm, so low that Hawkins had to lean forward slightly. "I'd say that's pretty good proof of physical abuse."

"She's clumsy." Hawkins's blue eyes iced over as he looked at Hank. "She used to trip and fall all the time. Not my fault."

"Leaving all that aside for now, what about the little girl?" Bradley asked, reentering the conversation. "This is your chance to redeem yourself, Kevin. Tell us where you put Mackenzie's body."

Scratching the bristle on his jaw, Kevin squinted at the assistant district attorney. "Mackenzie, who?"

Chapter 25

It wasn't so bad, doing the interviews all day long. With Paula, her silver angel nearby, Sis felt protected, as if her own guardian angel had finally arrived after all these years of praying and wishing on stars. Also, with each story she told, new memories came bounding back, like a big dog racing across a field. It was good to get everything out, and the quiet room decorated like a nice living room gave Sis a chance to see herself in a different way, as if she were looking down into the compound from a cloud in the sky, watching the years go by in a fast-moving reel of film.

In her second day at the Children's Center, Sis was beginning to understand what a good idea this place was. Since they had taped her interviews with her social worker and the police chief, she would only have to go through most of these questions once. That was good, when it came to the embarrassing things like Kevin riding her and the sad things about losing Mac. It was okay to spill the details to Paula, but she couldn't imagine talking about that personal stuff in front of strangers like the cops and the people in suits from the district attorney's office.

The only problem was the closed-in feeling of being trapped by four walls. Sis has learned to like being outside. It was her escape. When things weren't going well, she needed to let her mind squeeze out the window and float off in the clouds. Paula understood that. She let Sis take lots of breaks so that she could go out in the back, on the swings, to get some fresh air. In Sis's mind, this was day two of freedom, and her body was relaxing into the comfort of sitting in a soft chair and sleeping in a real bed. And the textures of clean clothes and sheets, of a buttery croissant still warm from the bakery, of a fluffy, sweet-smelling towel to bury your face in.

The textures of this world could be soft and calm as a summer sky. This was one thing Kevin had lied about; it wasn't all condemnation and shame out in the real world. There were plenty of wonderful things that she had been missing.

Today, Wynonna was helping Paula ask questions, and though Sis felt a twinge of shyness around the lean, strong therapist, there was also a glimmer of admiration. Wynonna Eagleson reminded Sis of a Wild West hero like Annie Oakley, except instead of shooting guns Wynonna was an expert horsewoman. Wynonna had promised Sis that she could learn to ride as part of her therapy. Sis had always wanted to be around horses, mostly to study the musculature so she could draw her unicorns better, but to think that she might get better by falling in love with a horse, well, that warmed her heart.

The sun was out today, having burned off the marine layer of the morning. Sis closed her eyes and let her hair dip into the warm light as she stretched back on the swing.

"Who was your favorite character in all the shows you watched?" Wynonna asked, pumping her legs on the swing beside Sis.

Sis knew that answer right away. "Ruthie on *Seventh Heaven*. She's honest and she says what she thinks, like me. When I was pregnant, I hoped for a daughter like Ruthie, a little girl with a heart of gold. That's what I prayed for. And that time, I guess God was listening, because he gave me a little baby girl. At first I wanted to name her Ruth, but Kevin said it sounded too biblical, and that creeped him out. So I named her after the girl who plays Ruthie. Mackenzie is the actress's real name."

Wynonna had slowed her swing to a gentle sway. "Kevin controlled every aspect of your life. Do you see that? He even made you change the name that you wanted to give your baby."

Sis shrugged. "Yeah, but Mac did fit her."

"Even if it did, I'm wondering if you're aware of the way Kevin made you depend on him. It's typical of kidnappers; I want you to know that. They take away the subject's autonomy. You came to rely on him for food, clothing, shelter, and a place to sleep. For a prolonged period of captivity, you couldn't wash up or use the bathroom without his permission and instruction. It was his way of taking away your freedom and control."

"I know that. I couldn't stop him from controlling me."

"I know. For some people there's a safe feeling in letting someone else take care of everything. Other people hate to be controlled."

The metallic click of the stun gun made her quiver inside. She blinked and squeezed the chains of the swing. It was just a sound in her head, but it was embedded there, cold and vivid. Sis would never forget it.

"I fought him more in the beginning," she said, telling Wynonna about the way he had threatened to use the stun gun to keep her in line. "I learned the hard way, but I learned. If I didn't obey him, I would get a shock that would make me feel terrible for a very long time."

"And how do you feel about him now?" Wynonna asked.

"When I think of Kevin, I get all cold inside." She lowered her head. She knew he'd been mean to her, even cruel. But she still felt the need to protect him. "There are some things I miss. The compound—I hated that place, but it was home. I knew my way around. When he left for long stretches, I could take care of myself and Mac there. Part of me wants to go back, but then I remember how lonely it was. Just me and Mac, talking to the squirrels and birds. I'm not sure what to think. My feelings are a big, tangled mess."

"It will take a while to sort everything out; that's just the way it is. But in the meantime, we'll start focusing on you, dear girl. Helping you reconnect to your family and to the everyday parts of life that you're not accustomed to. Therapy and healing. And I've found that healing happens faster when you work with horses. They have a way of bringing issues out faster."

Sis twisted in the swing. "I want to work with the horses, but I don't want to lie back on a couch and talk to the ceiling."

Wynonna rose, grabbed the chains of her swing and pulled her legs up so that she was kneeling on the seat. "Is that what you imagine therapy to be?" When Sis nodded, Wynonna smiled. "Don't worry. I don't have an office, and you won't be stuck inside. If you're staring up at anything, it'll be blue sky." She motioned overhead, and Sis leaned back and breathed in the thin white wisps that crossed the field of blue. In that moment, she wished she could rise up to the sky and float there, free from Kevin and her family, from the reporters who wanted a picture of her.

This was a game she had learned to play in the years with Kevin . . . floating away on a cloud. It used to make him mad when he caught her daydreaming with her face to the sky, but in the past few years, he wasn't paying attention enough to notice.

Paula's voice pulled her from the open sky. "Come on in, ladies. I just got a call from the police chief, and we need to talk."

Back in the little living room with the comfortable chairs, Paula told them that the police chief had spent the morning at the prison, trying to get information about Mac. "It would really help if we knew what hospital he took her to, or where he disposed of her body. But Kevin was uncooperative, with a new twist. He denied ever knowing a child named Mac." She tilted her head down and looked at Sis over her black glasses. "Kevin is saying that you did not have a baby while in captivity."

"What?" Sis felt her face screw up in disbelief. "He can't do that! He loved Mac. Why would he pretend that . . . that she never existed?"

"He probably realizes that the DA will charge him with murder or at least negligent homicide if they find Mac's remains." Paula shrugged. "He's trying to save himself from some serious jail time."

"He can't do that. He can't just erase her like that. He can't just say she didn't ever live." Tears were streaming down her cheeks, but she swiped them away with her tight-fisted hands. Fury burned inside her. "How can he do that?"

Neither Paula nor Wynonna seemed surprised by Kevin's lies, but Sis couldn't believe he would deny Mac.

"How can he do that? To pretend that sweet little

Mac never lived?" Sis paced to the window and back to the couch. "That's so wrong!"

"That's who Kevin Hawkins is. He manipulates people and steals from them and tortures them and then lies about it." Paula's voice was soft, but the underlying truth made Sis quiver inside. "That's how he treated you, Lauren. It's no surprise that he's lying about Mac."

"But to say she didn't even exist?" Sis pushed off the couch and paced back to the window. "He's acting like it's all a lie. He's going to make people think that I'm lying, because that's what he does. Kevin is good at twisting things around and making people see things his way. Everyone is going to think that I'm lying and that Mac never, ever lived."

"We know Mac was real," Wynonna said quietly. "Even if it can't be proven in court, we believe you. And I'm grateful for your artistic gift, because we have a dozen wonderful sketches of your little girl. Sketches so good that the police are using them in their investigation."

Sis's chin was quivering as she turned from the window. "It's so unfair! How can he do this to me?"

"Kevin Hawkins does not have the power to turn people against you," Paula said. "But you are the only one with the power to turn away from him. That's your choice."

Sis sniffed, but in the muddled tears and confusion, she knew what Paula meant. She couldn't count on Kevin anymore . . . never again. And she had to give up thinking that he was going to protect her in any way. He never really had; he never would.

"I'm finished with him," Sis said quietly. "I hope I never see him again."

"I'm with you on that," Paula said. "And I know this is a confusing time, but I promise you, you'll never regret crossing him out of your life. So, for the record, would you tell us your name?"

Sis bristled. It was hard to shed her comfortable skin, but Paula was right. It was time to let the past go. And that meant losing the name he had forced her to use. "My name is Lauren. Lauren O'Neil." Saying it out loud, she felt something shift. Just a flicker of movement. Sort of like when the moon seems to move before your eyes, rising through the dark tree branches.

Lauren O'Neil. It still didn't seem to fit her, but there was a ring of truth to it.

"That's a very nice name," Wynonna said, "for a beautiful girl."

"Okay, then. Lauren O'Neil, I am very happy to make your acquaintance." With a wry smile, Paula extended her hand. "Welcome back to the free world."

Lauren uncurled her fingers and gave Paula her hand. "It's a scary world."

"I know that, and you've seen way too much of the dark side. But it is going to get better. That I promise you."

Chapter 26

Rachel could not stop her hands from shaking as the inquisition began. It was ludicrous; a meeting to decide the future of their daughter. As if they were not fit to care for her. All these years, missing her daughter, centering their lives on searches for her, Rachel never expected to be rejected when Lauren was finally found. Rejected by Lauren herself. Rachel pulled her hands under the table and shoved them between her thighs and the chair, feeling spent and hollow. She hated being the mother on trial.

"This is just an informational meeting," said Kate Engle, a facilitator from the Department of Child Welfare. "We're here to share information. No final decisions will be made today."

But they should be, Rachel thought. *Lauren should be coming home with us. We're her parents.*

Paula Winkler spoke up from across the table, thanking everyone for attending on this "beautiful summer day." Staring blandly, Rachel thought the woman had fabulous skin for a woman in her sixties. The sparkle in that thick, silver hair was enviable, and Rachel wondered if it was enhanced with color. After her fact-finding mission, that might have been one of the few things she did not know about Paula Winkler.

It had been the last straw for Rachel when Paula had blithely offered to stay on with Lauren in the lake house. A casual suggestion, as if they were sorority sisters on spring break. That had put Rachel in a witch-hunt mentality, looking for anything that could undo Paula's authority over Lauren's case. Against Dan's advice to "keep her cool," she had Googled the social worker, canvased Paula's neighbors, hooked up with a friend of a friend, talked with her boss—just about everything short of becoming her friend on social networks. It hadn't taken much digging to hit pay dirt. A neighbor had mentioned the terrible tragedy of her husband's death, and a book club friend had tipped her off that Paula no longer indulged in wine at their monthly meetings.

She'd soon learned that Paula attended a very different kind of meeting, nearly every day. Or at least she had until her life had been interrupted by Lauren's 24/7 emergency. Some ten years ago, Paula's husband had committed suicide. A Vietnam vet, he had struggled with post-traumatic stress disorder and fallen into alcohol and drug addiction. Paula had been the one who'd found him, and the grief from his death had cracked her resolve and started her drinking.

Having probed that tragic sore spot, Rachel had stopped her investigation. She didn't know the whole story, but clearly Paula Winkler was sober now— sober and optimistic and supportive of Lauren. And dammit, Dan had been right. Rachel had been hell-bent on finding some skeleton to prove that this woman was not fit to care for Lauren; instead, Paula's life crises had made Rachel utterly sympathetic.

Paula Winkler was a saint. If anyone was a vindictive bitch . . . well, Rachel wasn't spending too much time in front of the mirror these days. She didn't know what to do with these feelings of anger and helplessness. Fury with a system that kept her daughter away from her, coupled with the knowledge that it was Lauren herself who wanted to be kept at bay.

Dan tried to tell her that this was a temporary obstacle; he believed that Lauren had bonded with Paula, the first female who had come to her aid. As time and therapy began to heal the wounds wrought by Kevin Hawkins, Lauren would open up to other relationships.

I hope he's right, Rachel thought. For now, Rachel was supposed to stand by and wait for her daughter to come around—a role she struggled with every day.

"You and your husband are doing a great job, giving Lauren the space she needs," Wynonna had told her during their brief meeting.

"It doesn't feel like a good job. It feels like we're not taking care of our daughter."

"This is a confusing time for her, but we've already started her therapy, and she works well with the horses. I'm sure you're sick of hearing it, but right now the best thing you can do for her is to continue giving her breathing room."

Here in the conference room of the Children's Center, Rachel wondered if Lauren would ever accept them. She would turn eighteen in May; then she could tell her parents to get lost, cut them off for good. Glancing over at Paula, she didn't think the social worker would lead her daughter in that direction, but Lauren did have a stubborn streak. At least, the old Lauren had.

Looking around the table, Rachel saw genuine concern and thoughtfulness in the people assembled. Seated beside Paula, Lauren kept her eyes on the table most of the time, reminding Rachel of how hard it had been for her eleven-year-old daughter to look people in the eye. That slight social awkwardness, along with Lauren's obsession with her drawings, had raised a few red flags. Back then, the possibility of an Asperger's diagnosis— or even being "on the autism spectrum"—had been so devastating that Rachel and Dan had chosen to avoid testing and address the problems as they arose. Now, the notion of dealing with autism seemed a welcome relief from the torture their family had endured these past six years. *The devil you know*, she thought.

Wynonna Eagleson introduced herself as the owner and founder of Spirit Ranch. "Lauren and I are doing daily sessions, and we would like to start family therapy this week, if possible." She mentioned that Lauren had chosen equine-assisted therapy, which dated back to the ancient Greeks. "For patients with physical disabilities, horseback riding provides neuromuscular stimulation; that rhythmic motion that mimics human walking does wonders. For a client like Lauren, this therapy gives us a way to unblock obstacles to healing, build her confidence, and establish a relationship of trust between horse and rider. We have found that therapy with the horses tends to illuminate issues more quickly. It's the great accelerator."

Lauren lifted her chin to give Wynonna a meek smile. It was a hopeful moment, albeit fleeting.

Wynonna talked about the course of therapy that Lauren would be pursuing on her own, and then added that family therapy was vital to reunification.

Rachel glanced beside her at Dan. He gave a helpless shrug, indicating that he would participate, despite his aversion to the therapist's couch. She touched his thigh under the table, and he covered her cold, shaky hand with his. Thank God for Dan.

As the therapist talked about the goals of reunification therapy, Rachel tried to enumerate her own list of things that showed progress. Lauren wanted help. She had eagerly begun her sessions at the ranch. Lauren was honest. There was no masking her feelings, no manipulative backstabbing. This young woman was so true to the little girl who had sometimes offended people with her honesty. *Mommy, what are those lines beside your eyes? Daddy, why is hair growing in your nose?* Or the classic moment Rachel and Dan had laughed about for years, when four-year-old Lauren pointed to a gentleman sporting an obvious toupee as they waited in line at the bank.

"Mommy, what's that furry thing on his head?" Lauren had asked at full volume, causing most of the customers to turn and look.

Head down over her daughter, Rachel had answered: "It's anything he wants it to be."

Rachel was drawn back to the meeting when Wynonna deferred to Hank, who gave an update on the media encampment outside the O'Neil home. The crowd of reporters had diminished since the press conference and the agreement that new photographs of Lauren were not to be published without written consent. An alleged rape victim and a minor, Lauren was supposed to be protected from exploitation in the media, as least as far as her image went. Of course, that didn't temper the voracious appetite for information, but for now, the media did not know the location of the safe house.

"There's also the matter of the accused's recent statements about Mackenzie Hawkins, namely, his categorical denial that the child ever existed." Hank nodded toward Rachel. "The O'Neils are eager to launch a search for the little girl, but we cannot make that search public without revealing Hawkins's statements, and the prosecutor isn't ready to do that. We're in the middle of building a case, and for a multitude of reasons, we want to withhold this information from the public as long as possible. So I'm asking you to sit tight for now, Rachel."

Rachel nodded. She was itching to do something about it. Finding the little girl's body would help give Lauren closure. She had half a mind to start her own campaign and search, but she wouldn't dare cross the prosecutor and take a chance of messing up the case against Kevin Hawkins. Still, it would be so nice to be a hero in her daughter's eyes. She so wanted her daughter to like her . . . to *love* her. How pathetic was that?

"We're still searching the compound," the police chief went on, "and though we haven't found the child's remains, we've collected other evidence that might be helpful."

"Like what?" Dan asked. "Can you prove that Mac existed?"

"Not ready to go into detail on that yet, but I can tell you the labs are on overtime processing crime scene evidence, and I'm working with detectives to pursue alternate theories."

Under the table, Rachel picked at the cuticle of one thumb until it stung. What was taking these investigators so long? Lauren needed to know what had happened to her little girl. She deserved validation that Mac had even existed, but still, the investigation was hush-hush. Well, Rachel was going to do something about that. *What,* she wasn't sure. But she wasn't going to sit around and watch her daughter suffer anymore.

"I'm sure the press will have all kinds of speculation, but I know this team will keep private information confidential." Kate turned a page in her folder. "Let's visit the issue of Lauren's living situation. How's it going at the lake house?"

Another timid smile from Lauren. "It's fine."

"The house is a wonderful transition spot," Paula said. "The owner has waived rent as a donation. Our friends at NCMEC are footing the bill for groceries, and it certainly helps to have Agent Wilson on the premises."

The lake cabin was the stuff of a dream vacation. Rachel had been in grander houses on Mirror Lake, as well as small cottages like the home Dan's parents still owned on East Bay, but the safe house struck just the right note between comfort and luxury. No wonder Lauren didn't want to come home.

"I understand we're working toward getting you home, Lauren." The facilitator made the statement sound so feasible, so doable, Rachel wanted to hug her. "Aside from getting the media and satellite trucks off your front lawn, are there any preparations we need to help you with so that Lauren can move home?" Kate asked Dan and Rachel.

"I think we're good to go." Dan turned those earnest golden eyes on their daughter. "Whenever you're ready, Lauren, we're looking forward to having you home."

They had decided Dan would make that pitch; Rachel had worried that she might slip into her psycho mom persona, complete with weeping and begging.

"Working at the firehouse, my schedule is flexible, and Rachel's about to go on summer break from school. At least one of us will always be around to help you adjust. But till then, we wanted you to have this."

Rachel watched Dan open up the laptop in front of

him, and click it onto the FIND LAUREN O'NEIL Web site, where the opening page was a field of those bright pink balloons surrounding an old photo of a smiling Lauren with a banner that said: FOUND! Rachel had forgotten about the Web site, but of course, Dan had updated it in his neat, efficient way.

"You can keep this laptop. Right now, it's on the Web site we made when you went missing. See all those pink balloons? That used to be your favorite color. We launched them just two weeks ago, on the anniversary of the day you went missing. And all those people in the field there? They came out to help search for you."

Lauren's face opened like a lens as she followed Dan's instructions, clicking the mouse and typing in words. She seemed mesmerized by the screen.

"Your mom and I, we realized you've missed all this technology, and figured you might want to start playing and exploring." Dan glanced around the table. "I don't want to take up everyone's time with this, but I'll show you more after the meeting. We'll get you navigating the Web in no time."

"Thank you." Lauren was still staring at the screen.

"For now, let's close it up." Dan gently folded the laptop screen. "It's kind of rude to play with electronics in front of other people."

"Oh. Okay."

That caused two of the people at the table to look up from their cell phones.

Rachel swallowed and pushed back her chair. It was her turn. "And I brought these for you. Some of your old sketches." She picked up a flat plastic bin from under the table and slid it over to Lauren. "I know it's been a long time, but you used to get so much joy from your sketches. Having seen your amazing artwork inside the cabin at the compound, I know that you've really grown as an artist. I thought you might want to go through some of these."

Lauren peeked into the bin, nodding.

"And just to let you know, there are about a dozen more bins like that in the attic, all filled with your art."

A few folks at the table chuckled, and Lauren smiled. "I filled eleven sketchpads. Remember that?"

"I do, and we kept every sketch." Rachel went on to add that her teaching experience would come in handy when it came time to homeschool Lauren. Wasn't it time to start catching up on some of the education she'd missed? If they worked together over the summer, Lauren could probably attend high school in the fall.

Wynonna agreed that homeschooling was a viable option; however, she wanted to focus on reunification therapy for now. "There are a lot of basic social interactions that are still new to Lauren. Shopping for groceries, going out for a meal, making a simple purchase, or attending a concert or sports event. I think re-immersion will be the focus of our summer."

"Of course." Rachel's pulse was thumping in her ears. Why was she trying so hard? She added that she'd begun a journal when Lauren went missing, detailing every development and discovery. She had also included newspaper clippings about searches and the police investigation. "You're welcome to take a look, if you ever want to fill in the blanks and see what was happening on our side of the fence."

Lauren thanked her, but the exchange felt way too polite and distant as Kate began to wrap up the meeting.

"So we're going to start family therapy ASAP," Kate said. "I trust you've all been looking at your calendars and penciling in some dates?"

It sounded so impersonal, booking a meeting to try and connect with your own daughter.

"We're on it," Dan assured Kate.

"And we should schedule a time for Lauren to visit the O'Neil home." Kate turned to Lauren. "I think that's a good idea. Familiarize yourself with the surroundings before you make the next big move."

A visit to the house, . . . Rachel's heart lifted at the small window of progress that had been flung open. A small window, a welcome gust of fresh air.

Chapter 27

After the meeting, Lauren sat beside Dan O'Neil and followed his instructions for pointing and clicking, filling in boxes with words she wanted to search, and closing things by clicking on the "X" in the corner.

"I remember some of this stuff," she said, clicking on little symbols he called icons to see what would happen. "I had inputting class in school."

"No wonder you're so fast on the keyboard. Funny, what we remember."

She remembered thinking computers were lame because it was too hard to draw with that little paintbrush on the screen. She remembered wondering why her parents were so interested in their e-mail when they barely cared about the real mail that the postman delivered each day.

Kevin had ranted about computers, complaining that people lived through electronics. "Just climb into the box," he would grumble, "because that's where you want to be! Head in your phone! Fingers glued to your damned laptop. Man is losing to the machine!" She didn't know why he was yelling at her about it. Sometimes she worried he would take the television and the VCR away from her, so she tried not to watch too much when he was around.

Now Dan guided her through setting up an e-mail account of her own, with a password that was to be kept secret.

"So, now your mom and I can send you messages. Check in with you. And you can answer back, if you feel so inclined."

"Okay. Thank you." She didn't know if she would ever use this e-mail thing, but it was nice of him to try and help her.

"That's it in a nutshell." Dan patted her shoulder, and she found she didn't mind. He smelled good, like lemony soap, and his voice was calm but bubbly, as if every word from his mouth was a new discovery. "If you run into any problems, Paula or Bija can help you out. They can help you connect to the wireless at the lake house. So go forth. Have some fun with it."

It was magic, the way one click of the arrow opened up new boxes with pictures and words. But the way it worked was secondary to the way it could open up whole books of information for her. Dan had moved quickly over the FIND LAUREN Web site, but now she scrolled back to her history to find it again, haunted by those balloons and sad but hopeful faces.

When had the bright balloons been launched? About two weeks ago, Dan had said.

That sounded about right, about the time when she'd spotted a single bright pink balloon floating in the sky. A light breeze had almost blown it into the compound, but it had been swept to the side and lodged in a tree just beyond the fence. Though she'd longed to climb up, extract the balloon, and read the little card dangling from its ribbon, her ankle had been throbbing that day, a reminder of what Kevin would do if he caught her outside the compound again.

It was ironic that one of the balloons had almost reached her. But then, what good was a balloon to a girl locked behind a fence with her captor breathing down her neck? A balloon couldn't save her. It had been too little, too late.

Lauren had never imagined that you could do therapy outside. On rainy days, she and Wynonna sat in the gazebo with lit candles and talked as rain dripped quietly onto the grass around them. Sunny days found them out on the ranch working with the horses, mirrors of the soul, Wynonna called them. She had learned that from a wise teacher she once had, a man named Buck.

"Horses are sensitive creatures. They pick up on what is bothering us through our body language. I find them really effective as therapists because they don't hear our lies. If you say something is fine and it's not, I might accept your answer, but a horse senses the anxiety or depression inside you."

"Does Yoda know what I'm feeling right now?" Lauren stroked the gray horse's neck, wondering if that kind, serene eye could really see inside her.

"I think so."

Lauren gave the horse a good rub, loving him up, as Wynonna called it. With his dappled gray hair, so thin that his skin could sometimes be sunburned, Yoda was not the prettiest horse at Spirit Ranch. Still, Lauren felt a special bond with him. He stood out like a sore thumb among all the other majestic brown horses, just the way she felt that she stood out in a group of normal people.

He had been patient and calm when she'd struggled to climb onto him for the first time. And he was so enormous! A giant draft horse with the tenderness of a little mouse.

Yoda was content now, but Wynonna explained that his life had not always been peaceful. As a colt, he had been turned loose down in Arizona, abandoned by an owner who could no longer afford to feed his horses. When a rancher found him wandering the desert with a few other stragglers, he had been thin, dehydrated, and suffering from a rattlesnake bite. The veterinarian had wanted to put him down. Instead, Wynonna, who had been visiting her cousin in Arizona, took him home.

"Even after we got him physically healed, he was always bucking and whinnying," Wynonna said. "He would let me get close, but he reared up when someone else came near him."

"Why did he do that?"

"He was afraid. He didn't understand that we weren't going to abandon him and make him suffer. He was afraid to trust anyone."

"But he's so calm now. I think he trusts me."

"He does. He understands how it feels to hurt inside. He's been there himself."

Lauren let her hands drop away. How could a horse understand what she'd been through? She folded her arms, closing herself up. If she wanted to, she could clamp shut the door to her soul and keep her own experiences inside. She could keep the misery to herself—and the brief moments of joy, too.

Wynonna turned to her and laughed. "Even I can read that body language. Are you having second thoughts?"

As if he were teaming up with Wynonna, Yoda swung his head toward Lauren and pressed his muzzle against her.

•

"Hey!" She stumbled back, slightly off balance.

"Told you." Wynonna's smile was wide and open, like the Oregon sky. "He won't let you get away with much. You can try, but you won't hide your feelings from Yoda."

Turning back to the horse, Lauren pressed her face into his bristly hair and hugged his neck. "I'm sorry, boy. You really do understand, don't you?"

His answer was in his relaxed nostrils, his low-hanging neck, his soft, loving gaze.

She took a deep breath and sighed against him. Finally, someone got her.

Chapter 28

"**M**y two-piece is falling apart. Can I get a new one?" Sierra asked as she pushed a red shopping cart down the wide aisle at Target.

"You have half a dozen suits, but Lauren needs one or two for swimming in the lake." Mom put her hand on Lauren's shoulder and guided her into the swimsuit section. "Look at that one—pink and purple polka dots. What do you think? Or would you like a halter top?"

With her head propped on the handlebar of the shopping cart, Sierra scowled at them. She couldn't hear Lauren's answer because her sister was whispering like a spirit in a ghost movie, but Sierra really didn't care what kind of suit Lauren got, as long as she could get one, too.

But no, it was Lauren's day . . . as if that were a national holiday. Already the cart was half full with shorts and jackets and sweats and jeans—all for Lauren. And Sierra? Apparently, she was just here to push the cart.

"When the hell is it going to be Sierra Day?" she muttered under her breath as she scrolled over her cell phone to check her Facebook page. "Oh my God. Mom? Jemma and Lindsay are going tubing on Jemma's boat. Aren't we done here? If we leave now, I can go with them."

"Sierra?" Mom looked up from a rack of bikini bottoms. "We are in the middle of shopping."

"We got enough. If we leave now, I can go with them. Please, please?"

"Absolutely not. This is a day to spend with your sister." Annoyance sizzled in her words. "There'll be plenty of opportunities to go tubing with your friends."

Biting back tears, Sierra pushed the cart aside and slunk down against a shelf of folded T-shirts. She was close enough to hear Lauren's soft voice now.

"It's okay if she wants to go. That's enough clothes for me."

Sierra sniffed. Even Lauren was willing to end her misery!

But Mom clamped down again. "Sierra's fine. Trust me, she'll forget about tubing and get into the shopping again."

Oh, no I won't. I will never forget this.

They moved on to the T-shirts, where Mom found some cool tank tops for Lauren in neon orange and pink. Jealousy swirled as Sierra watched Lauren get anything she wanted. Even the cheap clothes looked good on Lauren's trim body, while Sierra couldn't go near tank tops and tight tees. She knew she needed to lose ten pounds—baby fat, she hoped. She could only wear certain styles. No form-fitting tees for her. It was not fair. Yeah, she felt bad about what Lauren had gone through, but look at her now. She was freakin' gorgeous and skinny.

At the checkout counter, Lauren asked if she could buy some candy bars. Mom said yes, even though everyone knew where they would go. Skinny Lauren wouldn't eat them. No, she was stockpiling them under her bed at the lake house. Paula had shown Mom the stash and warned her that this was typical behavior for kidnap survivors. Their way of taking back control. Bottom line: No one was supposed to touch Lauren's stash. But if Sierra tried to take a bowl of chips to her room at home? Yeah, Mom would have a major freak-out. It wasn't fair.

After they loaded up the car, Sierra figured they would head home. She was texting Jemma that she would be there soon when Mom pulled up to a fancy-looking store with brass sculptures of ducks and horses by the door.

"What is this place?" Sierra asked.

"The Outdoorsman. We're all going to need some riding gear if we're going to be doing therapy with horses."

The delay pained her, but Sierra liked the prospect of getting some new clothes. "Can I get some of those leather pants with fringe?" she asked as she held the heavy glass door for Mom and Lauren.

"They're called chaps, and no, jeans will be fine. You're not going to spend the summer rustling cattle."

"What about a jacket?"

"In June?"

Lauren was holding a western boot with a heel as if it held the key to life inside. It wasn't really fancy, but since western stuff never went out of style, Sierra would look cool in them, clicking down the corridor at school.

"We need boots," Sierra said.

Mom paused, frowning down at them. "Yes, we do. I haven't ridden for twenty years, but I remember that sneakers do not work well in stirrups."

At last—something she could buy! The salesman was a talkative know-it-all who told Sierra she was putting her boots on wrong. Whatever.

When they finally figured it all out and took the three pairs of boots to the register, the salesman blinked at Mom's credit cards.

"Rachel O'Neil? I thought you looked familiar." He smiled as he scanned a box. "I recognized you from television." He nodded at Lauren. "And your daughter from those flyers, way back when."

Lauren's eyes grew wide as she stepped back, knocking into a rack of boot polish.

"Welcome back, Lauren." The man gave her a little two-finger salute. "You're a mighty brave girl, with all that you went through."

"We're glad to have her back," Mom said firmly, as if she could will the man not to look at Lauren the ghost.

"So you're going to do some horseback riding? Whereabouts?" he asked.

"Eastern Oregon," Mom lied smoothly. "My parents have some land out there." Lie number two. Sierra understood that no one was supposed to have information about their family activities, but still, it was a little weird the way those lies rolled off Mom's tongue.

Lauren stood there like a duck in hunting season, just because the guy had recognized her.

And the man kept on yapping about the great happy ending to the kidnapping story. Sierra was getting sick of that. Everyone kept making a fuss over Lauren, acting like she was some kind of hero when she had been living in a shack not far from their neighborhood for six whole years. People acted like she was a total victim . . . but she could have just climbed over the fence and run to the main road. Someone would have called the cops and gotten her home. She had been two miles from home! Why was no one else seeing how ludicrous that was?

Chapter 29

Three days later, Rachel and Sierra cut through the narrow aisle of booths in the Portland Saturday Market amid scents of sausage and peppers mingled with burning incense and marijuana. Rachel pushed back the straw fedora her husband had worn to deejay the school auction and guided Sierra away from a display of glass pipes, bongs, and incense. She figured if the paraphernalia was for sale, the drugs probably were, too. In less than ten minutes at the outdoor marketplace she was reminded of the reasons Mirror Lake moms rarely made the short trip into Portland.

"This is so cool," Sierra said as she fawned over a field of pinky rings with sparkly colored glass. "Mom, they're three for ten dollars. Can I get some?"

"Sure." Rachel dug into the pocket of her jeans for some cash. No purse today. She had dressed in jeans, an old white-collared shirt of Dan's, and a denim jacket, trying her best not to look like a middle-class Mirror Lake mom who usually spent her weekends at soccer games and backyard barbecues.

With only a twinge of guilt that she was using her youngest daughter to make vendors more affable, she handed her daughter the money. Wanting to make amends with Sierra, who had been sidelined since Lauren's recovery, Rachel had suggested the Saturday market excursion and had been a little surprised when her daughter jumped on it. Had she been that deprived of rings and henna tattoos?

While Sierra debated the merits of ruby glass versus amber, Rachel studied the vendor, a lean young man who was eating out of a white takeout container. "Hey, how's it going?" Rachel asked.

"It's going good. You let me know when you decide," he said, then shoved in a forkful of noodles.

This is your chance, Rachel thought. "Love the rings," she said. "Have you had this booth long?"

He shook his head, swallowing a mouthful. "I've been here two weeks, a summer hire."

"What about the owner? Is he around?"

The guy—probably a college student, now that she got a closer look—wiped his mouth on the sleeve of his hoody. "He's spending the summer in Thailand."

Okay . . . so no information here. Rachel shot a glance down the aisle, taking in displays of wind chimes, knives and blades, T-shirts, metal sculptures, and handbags. The overabundance of drug props and weapons seemed a bit contradictory and alarming. Who needed such an endless supply of rolling papers and bongs? And when did Oregonians develop an appetite for exotic blades and samurai swords? Which of the booths were regulars at the market? She couldn't be sure. She hadn't been here since she'd been a college student, getting her West Coast cool on while a student at Lewis and Clark. Back then, the smell of burning incense and skunky raw weed in the open streets of the city had seemed rebellious and exciting. Today, it made her feel cranky and hopelessly over the hill, in both age and philosophy. One hearty sniff and she would probably fail the random drug test administered by the Mirror Lake Board of Education.

She had come here to learn something about Lauren and little Mac. Frustrated with the lack of information from Hank and the FBI, she had decided to take some initiative and ask around at the Saturday market. In all the times that Lauren had sat at an easel selling portraits while Kevin and Mac made the rounds at the market, someone must have seen them. Lauren had even mentioned that Kevin seemed to befriend some of the regulars here. Rachel figured that the police may have already checked out this avenue of information, but she couldn't sit back one more minute and watch her oldest daughter suffer the humiliation of being called a liar. So she had put together a hippie-chick costume and recruited Sierra to come along on a little fact-finding mission.

While Sierra checked out woven handbags, Rachel chatted up the vendor. The bearded man who sold woven blankets and jackets told Rachel that he was here "all the time." Rachel thought the emerald stud in his nose was attractive, but she had trouble taking her eyes away from the wide-gauge holes in his earlobes—hollow plates that exposed a hole through the center of the lobe. Was he in constant pain? What sort of tool was used for such a piercing?

She tried to get herself back on track by tracing her index finger along the jagged pink line woven into a blanket. "Do you remember a portrait artist named Sis? She worked here in the market. Usually came with her little girl and a man named Kevin."

He scratched the back of his head, a tentative glint in his eyes. "Are they in trouble?"

She considered lying, but didn't want to complicate things. "He is. Sis isn't." Would he not have seen the head-lines or news stories about Kevin Hawkins, kidnapper? It seemed unlikely, but then she didn't see any signs of technology in the booth—no portable television or even a cell phone. It was a cash-only booth. Maybe this man was one of the eccentric Portlanders who prided them-selves on living urban but off the grid.

"Must be big, because you're the third person who's asked about them lately. The others were cops." He sneered. "You don't look like a cop."

"I'm not. I'm . . . I'll be honest. I'm Sis's mother."

He squinted up and down. "Yeah, I see the resem-blance. I saw them around."

He had seen them. Did he mean all three—Mac too? She thought about showing him the sketches in her pocket but didn't want to seem pushy or too official.

"Mac, too? Do you remember the little girl?"

"Sure. I can't say I knew them or anything. Fact is, I thought little Mac was his kid, the way he toted her around. And I figured Sis was his sister. Just the way it seemed."

"Did you ever talk to Sis?"

"Few times. Nice girl, and a good artist. People were always happy with her sketches."

"She is talented. Did you ever speak with them?"

"We probably talked about the weather and the cops."

Reminding herself to keep cool, she said, "Right now I'm looking for information about the little girl."

"Little Mac? I'd say she was better at small talk than

Kevin. Sort of stuck on himself, that one. But the kid was cute. Smart without being a pest. How's she doing?"

Suddenly, it was hard to swallow. "I wish I knew. It's little Mac I'm looking for. She's gone missing."

"Really? Well, that sucks. Nobody's ever safe, are they? Got to watch your back, that's what I say."

"Mom?" Sierra came over with a small shoulder bag trimmed in leather. The woven strands of red, purple, and pink reminded Rachel of Valentine's Day colors. Wasn't that around the time that Mac had been taken from the compound? Strange, how certain images resonated. "Can I buy this bag?"

"How much is it?" Rachel asked the perennial question.

"It's fifteen, but I'll give it to you for twelve."

Rachel knew she should have offered ten, but she didn't have the energy to barter. She forked over the money. When the man opened his fanny pack for change, he also extracted a business card. "This is me, Ben Juza."

There was no phone number on the card. No address, either. "Thank you, Ben. If some other questions crop up, how can I reach you?"

He shrugged. "I'm always here."

She knew for a fact that the market was closed for two months of each year, but she wasn't going to argue with a stranger who had given her some precious information.

As they made their way through the market, Sierra searched for bargains, and Rachel scrutinized vendors for signs of longevity in this locale. A duo of men tromping heavily down the closed street caught Rachel's eye.

Was that Hank Todd, Mirror Lake's police chief? He was walking alongside an armed, uniformed guard.

"Sierra!" Rachel waved her daughter over. "Come, quick."

"But I want to get a paper lantern."

"Later." Rachel grabbed her daughter by the arm and hustled her toward the street. "Hank?" she called, pulling Sierra into a jog as she saw the Max train whispering toward them, eerily silent. Didn't they have warning bells or beepers on those things?

"Mom?" Sierra looked back at the train, as if they had just dodged a monster. "Are you crazy? You almost got both of us killed."

"I just spotted Hank Todd, and I didn't want to lose him. Hank!"

Now that the train had passed, Hank heard her, turned, and gestured for the other man to pause. Arms akimbo, he stared at Rachel and Sierra as if they were trespassing.

Moving her daughter along, Rachel kept her voice firm. "Hank, what are you doing here?"

"I could ask the same of you, although Sierra seems to have racked up some purchases."

"And out of uniform. Are you working undercover?"

Hank winced. "Sort of. I'm out of my jurisdiction, but yes, I'm working on the case." He looked over his shoulder. "Can we not talk about it here and now?"

She pointed to the market on the other side of the tracks. "Hank, I just talked to a man who remembers Lauren and Kevin and Mac. He really remembers. He thought Lauren was a talented portrait artist and he says Mac was cute. Do you know what that means?"

Hank held up his hands and drew a deep breath. "Don't tell me. You talked with Wheatie Steger, the child pornographer."

"What?" Sierra winced. "Gross!"

"No, we did not. His name was Ben J-something."
She pulled out the card. "Juza."

"The anarchist and cop-hater. Well, I'm glad he opened
up to you. Unfortunately, hearsay evidence is inadmissible
if we can't get him to go on the record. And being that
he is anti-just-about-everything . . ."

"Hank, he'll go on the record for me . . . for Mac.
Don't you see? It's evidence that she was real. Hawkins
can't keep denying that she existed."

He sighed. "Ladies . . . we know about Mac. Right
now we're trying to get to the next level, trying to find
out what happened to her, and I really can't have you
working at cross-purposes here."

The crackling noise of voices on a radio made the
uniformed guard beyond Hank shift impatiently. "Repeat location," he said into the mouthpiece clipped to
his collar. He listened, and then turned to Hank. "I
need to handle this. You can find your way. The tie-dye
lady, Crazy Mary, and the Stained Glass Sisters are your
best bet for information. If you have time to talk, Ernest
at the Portland game of life might have something for
you, but he's an investment."

"Thanks, Pike."

As the cop walked off, Rachel seized her chance.
"We're going with you. We haven't been to the vendors
in Waterfront Park yet, and a woman is less intimidat-
ing. Besides, there's a definite anti-cop vibe going on
here."

Hank shoved his fingers into his pockets. "You noticed?" He shot Sierra a concerned look. "How's it
going there?"

"Good." She walked ahead, pretending that she was
on her own in the riverfront market.

Hank lowered his voice for Rachel. "I'm not comfortable doing investigations with teens on my task force."

"Sierra is the reason these people are going to talk to us," Rachel assured him. "This girl is a serious shopper."

One look at the tie-dye vendor, and Rachel understood how the woman had earned her nickname. It was all in the eyes—the wounded, wary eyes that shifted nervously. When Hank identified himself as law enforcement, a little moan escaped her throat. "Oh, my gosh. Oh, my land. It wasn't me, whatever you're thinking."

As Sierra disappeared into her booth, Crazy Mary snapped out of her paranoia for a moment to call: "Let me know if I can help you find something."

When Hank showed her the pictures, she moaned again, a pup in distress. "They were here. They used to be. But they're not here anymore."

"Do you remember the little girl?"

She nodded. "And the other girl—the teenager— she used to smile at me. A nice smile."

That sounded like Lauren. Even in captivity, her light had shone through.

When Sierra emerged from the narrow booth with a shirt of pink, green, and purple circling a red heart, Rachel smiled.

"That's cute. Why don't you get another one with the heart for Lauren?"

Sierra's face crumpled. "I don't want to match her. We're not twins."

"You don't have to wear it at the same time."

"No way, Mom. Can I get this or not?"

"You can get it, as long as you get another one for your sister." *Your sister.* That sounded weird. With a sigh, Rachel forked over the cash. All the better to butter up Crazy Mary.

It seemed to work.

"I wish I could help you find your people," Mary said as she tucked the cash deep into a front pocket. "I'll keep an eye out for them. I have good eyes."

They thanked her and moved on to the Stained Glass Sisters' booth, where only one of the two sisters was in town today. Holly Cannady was a spare, no-nonsense woman with a short-cropped haircut and enviable biceps. Rachel could imagine her wielding a blowtorch and bending metal or cutting glass with crisp precision.

"We saw them around," Holly said when Hank showed her the sketches of the girls and the photo of Kevin. "When you're a regular vendor, you get to know the others."

"Did you ever notice anything odd about them?"

Holly tucked her hands into the deep pockets of her denim overalls. "We don't condemn or praise. So no, we didn't notice anything. Did we see Kevin's photo on the evening news and put two and two together? Yes. But that was only after you had arrested him."

"Looking back, do you remember anything unusual about them? Maybe your sister remembers."

"Heidi doesn't pry. It's not our job to judge, Officer Todd. We coexist."

Rachel thought a person could coexist but still have opinions about other people.

But despite Hank's questions, Holly Cannady was as cold and austere as her dark, gothic stained glass creations.

After another hour or so of canvassing vendors, Hank decided they should wrap it up. He begrudgingly admitted that folks had loosened up when he had Rachel and Sierra along, but he told Rachel to please leave the investigation to the detectives.

At the edge of Waterfront Park, Rachel paused and stared out over the dark waters of the Willamette. She imagined little Mac, with her wide dark eyes, blond ringlet curls, and button nose.

"Where do you think she is?" she said aloud. "If he didn't bury her at the compound and he didn't leave her to die at the hospital, what did Hawkins do with Mackenzie?"

Hank followed her gaze to the waterfront, frowned. "Honestly? The possibilities are as endless as that river is deep."

The bleak prospect put a damper on her good news for Lauren. *We know you had a baby; we just have no clue what happened to her.*

Chapter 30

A week after the meeting, Paula told Lauren it was time to visit the house she had grown up in—a prospect that filled her with dread, though she was not sure why. Dan and Rachel had been good parents, and Sierra had been a cute and pesky little sister when she lived with them. It had been a very good life.

The problem was not the past, but the future. There was no going back to the way they used to live, and the O'Neils didn't seem to understand that.

But Wynonna did. In Lauren's first session at the ranch, the therapist had shown her three candles in colored jars outside on the gazebo. The candle in the red jar was for her past.

"Red for the past, because I want you to think of a stoplight," Wynonna had explained while Lauren had lit the candle. "The past is over and done, and no amount of regret or wishing can alter what has happened. When we talk about your past, we'll try to understand the way the events have molded your behavior."

The candle in the green jar represented the present.

Green for action, for everything going on today. For the future, Wynonna had chosen purple, "A color that hints at mystery and spirituality and creativity. The future is a mystery to all of us, but with some thought and guidance, we can modify our behavior and our way of thinking to live a life of joy."

"Joy," Lauren had murmured as she'd lit the purple candle. She had always liked that word. Joy was bubbling fountains and fireworks and graceful unicorns.

"That's right. When you come for a session, you can choose which candle to light to let me know what you want to talk about."

The colored candles appealed to Lauren, maybe because it was a way to communicate with her therapist without words. A sort of shortcut in their relationship.

Lauren imagined that glowing purple candle of the future as the O'Neils' car rolled toward the house she had grown up in. When Dan turned down Wildwood Lane, a knot formed in Lauren's throat. They were coming up on the Millers' house, the spot where she had first spotted Kevin, a deliveryman, she thought. The green lawn dotted with purple flowers, too delicate and perfect to ignore. It was on that patch of green that her life had changed, forever.

The past, she thought. *Let it burn behind you.*

"The reporters are gone," Sierra said from the backseat, "but Dad says they could still be hiding."

"You never know."

"Mom calls them vultures. It was kind of exciting, having them out on the street all day. Sort of like a block party. But Dad says it's not cool to have our pictures on TV or in the newspaper. He might see them in prison—or even some other creep. So I guess it's good that they're gone."

Lauren had never thought of this connection to

Kevin—that he might read about her or see her photo from prison. The thought of him sitting in a prison, hearing about her on a news broadcast struck an odd chord of longing in her. Would he think of her fondly? Did he miss her? Maybe it was crazy, but she wanted there to be some connection between them for the six years that she'd been away from the rest of the world. Yes, she had told everyone she was done with him, but still, didn't she deserve a flicker of affection from the man she'd spent six years with?

Dan pulled into the driveway and waited until the door on the attached garage rolled up. They plunged into the shadows, and the engine cut off.

"Do you recognize the house?" Sierra asked.

"Sure." She didn't mind Sierra's questions. They didn't have the same anxiety and pressure of Rachel's questions about the photos in the scrapbooks she had dropped off at the lake house. "Did you see the photos with Gran and Grandpa? Do you remember your friend Nora?" Of course, all the photos were familiar, but they didn't help her feel a new connection to this family or their lives.

The big door rolled closed behind them as they got out of the car. The smells of oil and potting soil reminded Lauren of the small shed at the compound.

The small door opened to the sweet smell of baking and to Rachel, haloed by the kitchen light. "Oh, good, you're here. Come on in."

Carefully placing her cast on the wooden stair, Lauren stepped inside and hoped that Rachel wouldn't expect a hug. Although Rachel held back, Lauren could tell that she wanted so much. She wanted Lauren to be happy, to adjust, to come home, to get her high school degree. Rachel's wants were overwhelming, like a big ocean wave that swept over your head and sent you somersaulting under the surface. And when Rachel went out of her way to do things, like finding people in the market who remembered Mac, Lauren felt even more deeply indebted to her. Yes, it was good that the police and everyone now knew that Mac had been real, that Kevin was lying.

"Are the cookies done?" Sierra asked.

"I just took them out of the oven." Rachel backed up, rubbing her palms on her jeans. "Careful when you bite in."

Sierra broke a cookie on the wax-papered counter in half and steam rose. "Still gooey. Do you want one, Lauren? Mom made them for your welcome home."

"Thanks." Holding the warm cookie with both hands, Lauren took a tentative bite. Melted chocolate and buttery flavor made her go soft inside. She had forgotten about the smell and warmth and brightness of a real kitchen. The meals that were brought in to the lake house were good, but nothing quite matched something hot from the oven.

"So what do you want to see first?" Sierra peeled another cookie from the wax paper. "The upstairs, the downstairs and . . . well, that's it. It's a pretty small house, but you probably remember that."

"Don't push her." Rachel put the cookie tray in the sink and ran the water. "We're not in any rush."

"That's okay." Lauren found that she liked Sierra's blunt approach. She didn't try to soften things or decorate them with curlicues, like the pictures in the photo albums Rachel had sent. "I guess the downstairs. I remember the room where we used to sit and watch TV." Or everyone else used to watch shows while Lauren stretched out on the floor and drew things. For a time

Sierra used to fill in coloring books with crayons, as if competing with Lauren, but she usually gave up after a half hour or so and flopped on the couch.

"Well, we finally got a flat screen," Sierra said.

"Finally," Dan said quietly. "We couldn't stand another minute watching that old box."

"Dad, it was awful and you know it. The new one's not even that big, but it's HD. It's in here."

Lauren popped the rest of the cookie into her mouth as she followed her sister into the den. The TV room seemed smaller than she remembered, as did the living room and the dining room with its six wooden chairs that once had seemed hulking and heavy.

Without fanfare Sierra moved the house tour upstairs, showing off her room, recently painted apple green with her name in carved pink letters on the main wall. There was a poster of a boy singer with droopy pants and a sweet smile, and her bedspread was a patchwork of dark green, white, and pink.

"That's a pretty quilt," Lauren said.

"And I made the bed in your honor." She looked up at Rachel. "Mom made us clean up for you."

"I hardly think pulling the quilt over the pillow constitutes cleaning. And your room looks very nice with your clothes off the floor."

"Do you want to see your room?" Dan asked Lauren. "Your mom made sure that no one messed with it while you were gone."

Rachel's smile was tight but full of hope as Lauren passed her and followed Dan down the hall. The pink and beige of her old room felt like the inside of a candy store at first, but as she paused, then crossed to the single bed and sat on the edge, the cocoon of memories closed around her.

How she had longed to return to this room!

She used to feel so cozy there. As promised, all her things had been left as they were, giving the room the eerie sense of a person missing not for six years but only six days. Her box of broken charcoals. The shelves containing very rough statues she had sculpted in a ceramics class: a stiff horse, a circular pile of snake, a duck without feet. There was an open tin of colored pencils—special pencils with colors that came alive when you brushed them with water.

Even her stuffed toy Mr. Toad was there, resting on the bed. She picked it up, immediately thinking that Mac would have enjoyed the ugly creature with the huge grin and bulgy eyes. "Do you remember teasing me about Mr. Toad?" she asked Dan. "You used to say that someday I would kiss him and turn him into a prince."

Dan rolled his eyes. "Was I that corny?"

She nodded. "And I would answer that I didn't want a stuffed prince sitting on my bed."

"Oh, that sounds like me." Chuckling, Dan moved next to Rachel and put his arm around her.

Lauren closed in on the shell-pink wall where her artwork seemed silly and whimsical. The art of a child. A dragon with glittering scales. A winged horse. A poster Lauren had made for a contest, in which it won first prize. It showed a silhouetted girl leaping through the air, and inside the silhouette, where her heart would be, was a glowing flame. She ran her fingers over the caption: A Single, Beautiful Light. It was something her mother had told her about.

"Do you remember this?" She turned to Rachel. "You used to say that every person has their own light inside them, and that it was up to you to learn how to let your light shine."

"That's right. A single, beautiful light."

"I used to wonder what Kevin's was." At the mention

of her abductor, a chill descended over the room, but Lauren plodded on. "Even though he was nice to me sometimes, it was a false sweetness. Like he was wearing a mask, and that mask could come off in an instant."

"We should have taught you to be more on guard," Dan said.

"I'm so sorry, honey." Rachel stepped forward, but Lauren moved away before her mother could touch her. She didn't want pity pats or gushing sympathy. She wanted them to face the truth, face the future. "I've learned that there are some bad people in the world," Rachel said. "Bad apples. I'm so sorry that I didn't prepare you for that, but I thought we could protect you, at least until you were older. I was wrong, and I'm so sorry."

Lauren wondered if she would ever feel safe and happy again, the way she did when she lived in this room. She was afraid that Kevin had taken that away from her. He had robbed her of happiness, and there was nothing she could do but mourn the shell of her past, like a wimpy little hermit crab without a home.

The white dresser seemed impossibly small. Its crystal knobs belonged in a dollhouse or a little princess's room. When Lauren gripped the small knob and pulled open a dresser drawer, she found that it was stuffed with T-shirts, just the way she had left it.

"Are these my old clothes?"

Rachel nodded. "Just as you left them."

She stared at the neatly folded shirts, mostly white, with some pink and black mixed in. "I didn't think my room would exist anymore. I thought you would have changed the furniture or maybe moved. Kevin told me you moved."

"Honestly, the idea of moving did come up," Dan admitted. "A therapist told us that it might be good to start fresh in a new house, and I thought we should give it a try. But these gals wouldn't consider it."

"I was worried that you would come to the door and find us gone," Sierra said.

"And your mom put her foot down," Dan added. "She was the one who preserved everything in this room, keeping it intact.

"She wouldn't even let Grandma sleep in here when she visited," Sierra said.

Lauren looked to her mother, who was suddenly quiet. Rachel hadn't given up. None of them had.

Lauren plucked a T-shirt from the drawer and held it up to herself. It seemed like a doll's shirt against her small breasts.

"That's way too small now!" Sierra scoffed.

Of course it was. Lauren was not the person she used to be. And she was not sure if the person she had become belonged here in this house.

"None of this is going to fit."

As if reading her mind, Rachel grabbed an armful of T-shirts from the drawer and tossed them onto the floor. "We'll make space. We'll adjust to the new you. Whatever you need, honey. Whatever it takes to welcome you home."

"Hold on a second, I've got something." Sierra ran out the door and returned with a tie-dyed T-shirt. "This'll fit you, right?"

Lauren held it up to her chest and smiled when she noticed the heart shape at the center. "It's cute."

"We got it for you," Sierra said. "But it's not like a trap gift. You don't have to move back here just because you want the T-shirt."

"Sierra . . . ," Rachel sounded annoyed.

"Well, it's true." Hands on her hips, Sierra faced her mother. "Can't you tell she's still uncomfortable here? She's not ready to come home."

Thank you, thank you, little sister. Lauren held the shirt to her face, taking in the oddly familiar scent of incense.

"Lauren?" Dan touched her shoulder. "Are you okay?"

"I'm fine," Lauren said, instantly thinking that Yoda would know she was lying. "I . . . I just need to go now."

Dan took a set of keys down from a rack in the kitchen. "I'll drive you back to the lake house."

"Thanks," Lauren said, "for everything."

On the way out, she avoided meeting Rachel's eyes, not wanting to see the disappointment there. Horses weren't the only creatures that could see into the soul.

PART 3

Jump Up Behind Me

Chapter 31

Sloping green hills, bold blue skies, a fringe of white-capped mountains, and sunshine that could blow you out of bed in the morning—this was the sort of summer Dan O'Neil remembered from growing up in Oregon. He sat on the steps of the ranch gazebo and watched his daughters straddle the post-and-beam fence to lure the horses closer. Lauren was amazingly agile in her bright walking cast, but then she'd had a few weeks to get used to it.

"Come here!" Sierra waved her arms wide, as if flagging in a jumbo jet. "Over here, you big lug."

"His name is Socks, and he's kind of sensitive because he was in a car accident. You'll be able to see his scars when he turns around." Lauren leaned over the fence, beckoning with her sad smile. "Here, boy."

How could a horse resist?

But the brown horse with white legs kept his wide posterior facing them, swatting flies with his tail. There must have been some hay or oats to chomp on in the lean-to.

The girls turned their attention to two other horses that seemed to be contemplating life in the corner of the paddock. An enormous tan horse that seemed to be shadowed by a brown and white pony.

"Penny! Here, Penny!" Lauren called. "Why isn't she coming?"

"How do you know all their names?" Sierra asked.

"Because I've been working with them, and they all have personalities, like people. But I don't know why they're not coming over."

The girls couldn't attract the horses, so they decided to skirt around the paddock fence to get closer. Dan was amused to see the two of them working together on this: Lauren the practical one with some information about the horses, and Sierra the instigator who needed to make a connection now.

This was Lauren's choice—family therapy in the form of equine-assisted therapy. Wynonna had gone over the history and goals when he and Rachel met with her. Dan could see she was a person who believed in her horses and her program.

"Equine therapy has been effective in helping trauma victims and seniors, and most recently I've had success working with veterans. The goal is to create a bond between the client and the horse. Since horses are prey animals, they're very sensitive to human behavior and intentions. There's a certain immeasurable 'feel-good' sensation a lot of our clients report when they learn how to care for and handle a horse. When clients learn to understand and guide a horse, they, in turn, learn to understand and guide themselves." The therapist had explained that learning to ride was not Lauren's chief goal; the focus was on learning to communicate with the horse, and eventually with others.

Dan knew jack about horses, but he was glad his

daughter had picked Spirit Ranch. Anything out in the open air, even air tinged with horse dung and sweet hay, was preferable to being stuck in an office with pallid gray walls and a leather sofa as slick as a black hole. Dan had never liked therapy. To start with, an office was a stifling environment for him—one of the big reasons he'd chosen his profession as a firefighter. Being outdoors was key. And Dan didn't like therapists on principle. If a person had one friend they could trust, they shouldn't need to dish out cash to spill their troubles to a stranger, should they? He trusted Rachel with his life. And his friends Sully and Tuna were great sounding boards for issues that Rachel wasn't inclined to understand.

But this therapy was designed to get Lauren back on her feet. To heal her heart. To help the family learn how to love and support her. To launch her back into the world that she'd missed during some crucial growing-up years. Yeah, his attitude about therapy was shifting. Thank God for Wynonna Eagleson and this amazing ranch. Sitting here on the steps, gazing off at the glacier peak of Mount Hood, he could find his own piece of serenity.

Two horses with riders appeared at the edge of a field of tall-grass wildflowers. Dan recognized one as his wife. Rachel had come out earlier to meet with Wynonna, and apparently their session had turned into a horseback ride. Dan's wife had been a horse girl back in New Jersey; though she'd never owned a horse, she'd traded off grooming and stall-mucking for the chance to ride. So that was probably good—two women riding together. He didn't know much about horse etiquette or female bonding, but being a firefighter, he understood how adventure bonded people together. That was one of the distressing aftermaths of Lauren's captivity—the way she defended Hawkins from time to time. It made him sick to think of his daughter forming an emotional attachment to that monster, but it had happened. And now, it was time to deal with it—even if that meant getting up on a honking big Budweiser Clydesdale and riding down the main street of Mirror Lake.

At the edge of the corral, Rachel and Wynonna dismounted and handed the horses over to one of the hands. When the dark-haired boy spoke to his mother and led the two horses back to the barn, Dan recognized him as one of Wynonna's teenage sons, working on the ranch for the summer. With family security and privacy a priority, the therapist had made it a point to introduce the O'Neils to all the ranch staff, from the horse handlers to the cleaning lady. Dan had gotten a solid hit off Wynonna's husband, Vic, and their sons, though the teenage boys, Jazz and Chance, were a little too good-looking for his comfort. When he'd noticed Sierra's wobbly smile, it was a reminder that those years of heartache and hormones were right on his doorstep.

"Hey, Dan." Wynonna tipped her Stetson back. "I'm thinking we'll start inside the round corral, if you want to head on down."

He rose from the steps, thinking that this outdoor therapy might be better than their last vacation at Disneyland. Definitely shorter lines.

The family looked like a scrappy circle of cowboys in their straw hats as they gathered round Wynonna listening to her instructions.

"We'll start simple. I want each of you to catch one of the horses here and slip a halter on." She pointed to the leather strappy things sitting on the fence.

"Something tells me it sounds easier than it looks," Dan said.

Wynonna's smile seemed to hold mystery. "Sometimes."

"Do the horses bite?" Sierra asked.

"Some of them might snap if they think you have a treat for them, so don't tease them. But these horses are gentle. Lauren, do you remember the names of these four in the corral?"

"There's Penny, the pony, and Flicker. Hero is the chocolate brown stallion, and the brown horse with white socks is Socks, of course." Lauren's eyes were bright with enthusiasm.

"Good. So . . . ," Wynonna gestured toward the open pen. "Have at it."

As he grabbed a halter with the others, Dan assessed the horses, all four of them now hanging around the lean-to. He would have liked to go after the smaller pony, but being the only man in the group he felt obliged to take on a bigger challenge.

He swallowed, taking the measure of the three taller horses.

"Can I have Penny?" Sierra asked as the four of them crossed the corral. "I'm the smallest one here, and so is she."

"You can try," Lauren said. "But sometimes the horse chooses you."

Words of wisdom, Dan thought, as the four horses stirred and began to scatter at their approach. The big tan horse, Flicker, loped off to the back of the pen, and Penny followed, as if trailing her mama. That drew the two girls away in pursuit.

"I'll give you twenty bucks if you catch and halter my horse for me," he muttered to his wife.

Rachel's chuckle eased his worries. "Don't be a big baby. You got this, O'Neil."

It turned out she was right, but only because his horse was a pushover. He later learned that Socks, the horse he chose, was one of the most docile of the group, having been injured in a car accident and nurtured back to health by Wynonna's family. The horse waited patiently, even willingly, as Dan slipped the halter over its head, realized it was upside down, and then got it right on the second try.

"Piece of cake," he said as he finished with the last buckle.

Rachel and Sierra also had quick success, but the exercise wasn't so easy for Lauren, who had trouble capturing Flicker, the alpha horse of the herd. Every time Lauren approached her, the mare turned and scampered away.

Dan felt a pang of regret that Lauren had ended up with the difficult horse; hadn't she dealt with enough difficulties in her young life?

Sierra tried to help by chasing Flicker toward Lauren, but the horse was far too quick and smart to fall for that one. Lauren's face was ruddy, her hands balled in fists of frustration.

"Why don't you take my horse?" Dan called over. "I'll do a trade with you."

"I can't do that. I'm not a quitter. I just need to get this halter on Flicker."

The corral was quiet for a moment as the breeze blew up red dust and helplessness.

"Why don't you play hard to get?" Rachel suggested. "Get close and turn your back on her. That might pique her interest."

"Yeah, Mom." Sierra was skeptical. "Or maybe she'll ignore her for a few hours."

"It's worth a try," Dan said. The friction between Sierra and Rachel could scrape at his patience, but he understood the source. Sierra was pushing for independence but also feeling abandoned by Rachel's obsession with Lauren's recovery. But wasn't this exercise about showing mutual support?

"Okay." Lauren took a shaky breath and turned away from the big tan horse. "Okay, Flicker. I'm not going to chase you anymore. You've got to come to me." She folded her arms and frowned. "I can't believe I can't even get a halter on a horse. I've been here a lot more times than you guys. I should know how to do this by now."

"But you're just learning," Sierra said as she patted the pony's neck. "We all are. And you know lots more about the horses than we do."

"But I can't even catch a horse." Lauren sniffed and scratched at her cheek. Was she wiping a tear?

Dan shot a look of concern at his wife, who winced. This was all going south; he had to stop it, now.

Just then Flicker stirred and swept her head toward Lauren, as if just noticing her.

"Hold still," Rachel said. "Looks like you've caught her interest."

They stood stock still and expectant in the midday sun. A light breeze rattled the back of Dan's shirt as Flicker inched closer to Lauren.

"Getting closer . . . ," he narrated, "closer . . ."

At last, the mare lowered its head in submission and nuzzled Lauren's back.

"Who is that?" Lauren asked, turning slowly until she was staring into one eye of the big horse. "Was that a sympathy nudge, or do you like to be courted?"

Dan grinned as Lauren lifted the halter and slipped it onto the horse. She had to rise onto her toes to loop the band around Flicker's neck, but she managed.

"Yes!" Dan cheered, and Sierra let out a whoop as they all applauded.

"Great job, everyone," Wynonna said, crossing the

corral. "Lauren, I noticed that you let your sister take the easiest horse, but did you know you chose the most difficult one? Flicker here is our prima donna. She's the dominant horse of the group—the bossy one."

Lauren skated her orange cast over the dirt, sending a spray of golden dust into the breeze. "I think I knew that. I just figured that she liked me, so she wouldn't run away."

"Just because she gave you a hard time doesn't reflect how she feels for you. Flicker likes to play. She likes to be fussed over, just as you said." Wynonna rubbed the horse's shoulder. "Don't you girl? You're a tough one to snag, but you're worth it."

"Like some challenges in life?" Rachel suggested.

"That's right." Wynonna tipped her hat back. "I also noticed that you didn't ask for help, Lauren. You're used to being on your own, independent. But you have a family now, and they want to help. Did you see how they tried to help? Chasing the horse for you and giving you suggestions."

"It helped," Lauren said, "but I wanted to do it myself."

"That's what you're used to. But it's a good adjustment to make—letting other people in. Letting your family help you with problems."

Dan's throat knotted up as he watched emotions chase over Lauren's face like racing clouds. God love her, she was so earnest, so eager to please, so determined to do the right thing. She'd been through some bad times, but she was coming through. Sure as they were all standing here, Lauren was going to pull through this, a stronger and wiser person.

He swallowed hard, proud of his daughter. Stubborn as ever, she was a survivor.

Chapter 32

My name is Lauren O'Neil and I am trying to find out who I am after six years of living some-one else's life.

I am seventeen years old and I don't have an ATM card or cell phone. I am learning how to use e-mail on a computer, but even my own sister says I'm a dinosaur. That means I'm extinct; a creature whose time has come and gone. At first I cried about this, thinking that I was a big, awk-ward brontosaurus who would never fit in this world. But then Wynonna pointed out that I can adapt. I have already gotten used to some things about this new life. Wynonna says that it's okay to be a techno-dinosaur.

I am seventeen and I don't have any friends. There is one girl, Nora, who has come by the lake house, but only because I think her mother made her. She's a nice girl, and I remember when we used to hang out together, making cupcakes or having sleepovers when we were in grade school. But now, when she looks at me, I think she sees a victim. For her I'm a sad girl who a terrible man stole away and abused for six years. Her eyes always flick away from me fast. I call it the nervous look.

I have never been to high school, and it scares me to think about being around hundreds of kids who might make fun of me or give me the nervous look.

I have never driven a car. I have never kissed a boy or had a boyfriend. I have never fallen in love or had a crush, unless you count Jesse from *Full House.* Proms, football games, concerts, vacations . . . these are some of the things I missed. My mom wants me to try school in September so that I can experience some great moments. The social building blocks of life, she calls them. But to me, that feels like I would be going backward, and that is one important thing I know in my heart. You have to let the past sit behind you.

Sometimes there's an ache when I think about all the things I have missed, and sometimes I get angry and sour about it. My grandma used to call Sierra and me crabby Appletons when we got cranky. That's how I feel when I think about high school or best friends. I think I am the world's crabbiest crabby Appleton.

But my logical mind knows that feeling sorry for myself isn't going to help. Again, all those things I missed are in the past, and once that candle is blown out, the light is gone.

So when I feel bad, I try to think of the horses, especially the ones who have had rough lives, like

Socks, who was hit by a car, or Yoda, who was abandoned in the desert when he was a baby. Sometimes when I'm brushing Yoda, I think of how sad he must have been, sad and sick from dehydration and that rattlesnake bite. It's a wonder he didn't die of a broken heart. But he didn't. He's got a light inside him that kept him going. In so many ways, he's like me, only he's a lot more patient than I would be when Jazz and Vic bring the feedbags out.

I really, really want to learn to ride, but Wynonna says that ninety percent of riding is your bond with a horse, so we need to work on the ground first. Again, I'm not as patient as Yoda, but does a horse ever want a person to jump on his back? I don't know.

Another big thing Yoda and I have in common is that we both need to learn how to play. That sounds funny, right? You might think that everyone loves to play games and laugh. But I guess it's something you forget how to do when you lose practice, and fun was not something that happened much at the compound. The closest I ever came to playing was watching Mac. The way she would line up cukes from our garden and pretend they were cars waiting to leave a parking lot. When I gave her a bath in the slop sink, she would play with clusters of bubbles, giving us both bubble hairdos before she blew at them and narrated the wonderful places they were headed as they floated away. And the stories she would make up about talking buttons and wiggly fingers and magic shells. Mac knew how to have fun. But Yoda and I, we're going to learn together.

* * *

"Did you write in your journal?" Wynonna asked as Lauren lit the past candle and leaned back onto the built-in bench in the gazebo.

Lauren unzipped her backpack and removed the blue notebook. "I did. Do you want to read it? You already know everything I said, anyway."

Wynonna smiled. "That's because you try to be honest, and I'm grateful for that. Your therapy will go faster if you keep pushing for the truth." She gestured toward the flickering red flame. "So we're going to talk about the past today. Have you found that forgotten memories are coming back to you?"

She let her eyes stray to the distance, where Mount Hood stood, silver gray and strong. "Memories of Mac. All the good things that are happening to me, all the new clothes and being around the horses. Swimming in the lake and getting to have what I want for dinner. Those things should be happening to her, too."

"And you feel guilty about that? That you have a better life now?"

"I feel so sorry that she never had a good life. She never had her own bed to sleep in. Sometimes Kevin would buy her popcorn or ice cream when we worked at a market or fair, but I know she wasn't getting the right foods. No visit to the doctor for her shots. Maybe if Kevin had spent some of the money on doctors, Mac wouldn't have died of that awful cough."

"That's true. He made a string of bad choices that hurt so many people, and you and Mac were at the center of his cruelty. But we can't change the past. We can't bring Mac back."

"I know. But now, when good things are happening, I think of Mac, and suddenly it's not so good because she can't enjoy them, too."

"That's Old Man Guilt for you. He'll come along and fasten himself on you like a big pair of scissors."

That was how it felt, like a sharp clamp on her heart. "How do you get rid of him?"

"First, you need to know that it's not your fault. You would have given Mac the world. You did everything for her. You loved her, and it sounds like she adored you. Didn't she follow you around the compound, like a little shadow?"

She had.

"And though Kevin took her around at markets and fairs to show her off," Wynonna added, "Mac didn't always like that, did she? She wanted to be with her mother. The person who loved her and took care of her."

Lauren swallowed, but it did nothing to ease the knot in her throat. She would never stop loving Mac. Never. "I know the past is behind me, but I don't know how to give up thinking about Mac."

"You don't have to. Right now, you're still mourning the loss of your little girl, and remember how we talked about the stages of grief?"

"Denial. Anger. Bargaining." That one always made Lauren think of the Saturday market, where shoppers haggled with the vendors, negotiating for a better price.

"Depression and acceptance, but not always in that order."

Lauren shook her head. "Maybe my life doesn't fit that mold."

"Maybe it doesn't. Grief is unique. Every person has a different experience."

"Well, we can forget about acceptance, because I'm never going to be okay about what happened to Mac."

"That's understandable. For now, do what you need to do to grieve. Be angry with Kevin. Be furious. Sit with the guilt and sadness. But I hope you can get to a point where you don't feel guilty about the good things that are happening to you. Someday, we want to get you to a point where you have more good days than bad."

"But I already have good days," Lauren admitted, tears blurring her vision of the mountain. "I just feel bad about them."

"Old Man Guilt." Wynonna leaned over and blew out the candle of the past. "I think I hear Yoda calling your name from the barn. It's time to play."

Chapter 33

Rachel rolled onto her back, propped her knees up and moaned. After a week of regular horseback rides with Wynonna, every muscle in her body ached.

Including her heart.

"Can't sleep?" Dan's presence beside her was so pure and serene, she envied him the simple peace that was his nature.

"Everything aches. I'm going to have to ask Wynonna to move these therapy sessions to a couch . . . or a hospital bed. She thinks I'm a better rider than I am."

With sweeping breath, he sat up and touched her shoulder. "Roll over."

Muscles screamed as she shifted to her belly and gave herself over to the sweet agony of Dan's massaging hands.

"Why do you and Wynonna do those sessions on horseback?" he asked.

"She's preparing me to do some special therapy with Lauren. It's called back-riding. Supposedly, it's a way to connect with her."

"Well, if it involves horses, I think Lauren will be quick to make the connection. Watching her with Yoda and Socks, I can't get over how sweet our girl is. Even after all she's been through, she's got a heart of gold."

"And I'm ever the shrill bitch."

"What? Who said that?"

"Everyone seems to be miming the message without saying the words. Am I the problem?" she asked as Dan pressed into the tense muscles over her shoulder blades.

"Come again?"

"Lauren is leery of my take-charge, controlling nature. Wynonna told me that, in the gentlest of terms. And Sierra says that her sister would come home if I wasn't always, and I quote, 'the boss of everything.'"

"That sounds like Sierra. She doesn't hold back, does she?"

"Our daughters are honest to a fault."

"What does Wynonna say?"

"She says that I'm the scapegoat in Lauren's mind, and nothing I do will change that. Lauren has to be the one to come around. It's going to take some external factor—whether it's therapy or some event—for Lauren to see me in a new light."

"So what are you supposed to do?"

"Back off. Lay low."

"Not your forte."

"Nope."

"Mmm. I like Wynonna, but that doesn't explain why Sierra is so down on you. Isn't this the age when kids start to question everything their parents do? They hate us for a while, but it will all pass. Give it a few years and they'll be swearing that you're the best mother in the world." He ran his fingers down her spine, and then pressed a kiss to the back of her neck. The sweetness of the gesture, coupled with her worry, made her tear up.

"I don't want to wait a few years." She knew she sounded pathetic, but this was Dan. No filters with him. "I want them to love me *now*."

He slid down beside her and she turned toward him. The faint glow from the clock allowed just enough light so that she could see the beautiful planes of his face. "Sorry, babe. Can't make those girls do anything right now. But I love you." He pushed the collar of her sleep shirt down and pressed his lips to her bare shoulder. "And with a little persuasion, I can show you just how much."

The next morning, Rachel was popping ibuprofen in the entryway at Spirit Ranch when Lauren and Paula arrived.

"I think she's got a little crush on Jazz," Paula said under her breath as Lauren followed the therapist's son into the kitchen for a glass of juice. "And why not? He's sweet, adorable, and good with horses. Everything a seventeen-year-old girl should be dreaming of."

Rachel watched as her daughter crossed the wooden floor, barely a limp despite her orange walking cast. She and Jazz disappeared under the barrel wood ceiling leading to the kitchen in the Eaglesons' home. "He has a girlfriend, doesn't he?"

"So I've heard. A girl at college, but nothing is permanent when you're nineteen."

Rachel's aching muscles tensed. Her daughter was into a nineteen-year-old? The bond between Lauren and Jasper Eagleson had been plain as day, but Rachel had assumed it was the love of horses that they shared. "She's never mentioned him to me. Does she talk about him?"

"No, but I've noticed how she lights up when he's

around. The other day, when Wynonna asked her if she wanted to earn some money helping out in the stables, Lauren asked if she'd be working with Jazz. How's that for straightforward?"

"Lauren doesn't mince words." Rachel ran her palms over the sides of her jeans. "But I'm not sure I'm ready for teen romance. She's so vulnerable right now."

"You can't stop it, mama bear," Paula advised. "Heartbreak and head-over-heels—it all comes with the territory of love." She checked her cell phone. "I'd better get going. I told Hank I'd go with him to interview a client." She lowered her voice. "Kevin Hawkins's brother. Bound to be interesting."

"I'll call you later to find out how it went," Rachel said.

Down in the barn, Yoda was saddled up and ready for Rachel's first ride with Lauren. Yesterday Wynonna had explained about a technique called the Horse Boy Method, a type of therapy designed for children with autism.

"When you mentioned you'd considered having Lauren tested for being on the spectrum, I thought of this. It's really pretty simple, and we can try it because you're an experienced rider, and because both you and Lauren are petite. The two of you will need to sit in one saddle."

"I think we can manage that. I'll hold my breath. But the horse will be moving, right? This is Lauren's chance to learn horseback riding?" It had been one of Lauren's new goals before everything had been pushed back in the interest of finding Mac.

"She'll finally get to ride her buddy Yoda. It's called back-riding. You'll ride with Lauren in the saddle in front of you."

"And that will make her feel safe?" Rachel had asked.

"There's a long list of benefits. There's a theory that the rocking motion created by the rider helps produce feel-good hormones like oxytocin. With you sitting behind her it's nonconfrontational—no need for eye contact. But at the same time you can communicate by talking right in her ear, managing the experience. And the pressure of having two arms holding the rider close gives many kids on the spectrum a feeling of security. It's one of those things that is simple and complex at the same time."

The notion of riding with Lauren in her arms, nearly in her lap, had stirred memories and emotions that had kept Rachel up until late last night. And when she had fallen asleep, images had appeared in her dreams like photos in a scrapbook. Baby Lauren, with wrinkled pink lips and a whisper of downy hair on her little bald scalp. Lauren pulling up on the coffee table. Lauren holding on to Dan's extended arm like a baby monkey swinging from a tree. The white dresses of baptism and first communion. The Christmas photos taken in front of the tree.

Sorting through those memories in her mind, she had tried to determine the last time she and Lauren had snuggled together, physically close. Granted, before Lauren had been kidnapped she had been shedding the bonds of physical affection for the superficial aloofness of adolescence, but that was no excuse for the fact that she could not remember the last time they'd shared a hug.

Now Wynonna was coaching Lauren on the procedure. "We'll let you both mount from this block, since it's hard to swing into the saddle with someone else sitting there." Although she went on to explain that this was a very specific form of therapy, which she thought Lauren would enjoy, Rachel could see that her daughter's mind was already in tune with the thrill of riding her favorite horse out in the beautiful green fields and hills.

Lauren went first, sliding the leg with the orange cast over the horse as if it were light as a feather.

As she plopped onto the saddle behind Lauren, Rachel let out a laugh. It was a tight fit. "We're like two sardines in a can."

Lauren stiffened. "It's weird. Am I squishing you?"

Although Lauren was stiff as a cement block in front of her, Rachel hoped the ride would loosen her up. "I'm fine, but you'll probably be more comfortable if you relax."

That made Lauren's body even more rigid. "I'm just holding on."

"I'll have my arms around you, like a seat belt."

When Lauren shrugged her shoulders and settled back with a sigh, Rachel could imagine the determined frown on her daughter's face. Years in captivity had taught her stoicism.

"You guys look good up there." Wynonna handed Rachel the reins and lightly patted Lauren's bad leg. "You still up for this, Lauren?"

"Yup." Lauren planted her hands on the saddle horn. "I think I've been waiting for this all my life."

As Rachel reached around her daughter to take the reins, she had to turn her head to avoid a mouthful of Lauren's thick, honey-blond hair, which now smelled of lemon and flowers—a delicious shampoo. Far from the baby-faced girl of her dreams, this was a young woman in her arms, tough as leather but delicate as a spring blossom.

Gripping the horse with her heels, Rachel steered him to the left and they were off. Lauren called good-byes to Wynonna and Jazz.

The posture was certainly intimate. The horse beneath them did set their bodies to rock in a natural rhythm, and in the bowl of the saddle, Lauren had no choice but to ease her tight stance and succumb to the gentle rhythm. With her daughter in her arms, Lauren leaning back into her breasts and belly, maternal longings swelled inside Rachel. This was her child—a young woman now, but always and forever her daughter. She thought of the haloed figures Lauren had painted in the compound, Madonna and baby, and she wondered at the things Lauren understood intrinsically that had yet to be unlocked through therapy.

Spectacular scenery rolled out around them as Yoda plodded down the path. This land was one of the things that had drawn her to stay in Oregon after college—this gorgeous corner of the planet, along with a gorgeous man whom she could not live without. Lush green fields banked by gentle hills that gave way to the two majestic mountains, Mount Hood and Mount St. Helen's—"old flat-top," Dan called it. The slopes were punctuated by dark green Douglas firs that towered into blue sky. Many of the trees were more than two hundred years old, a fact that inspired wonder for the years of sunshine and rain synergized into their dense trunks. When Rachel had first come out west in college, she had thought of the tall evergreens as natural cathedral spires. She talked quietly about the trees, narrating the landscape as they rode. She told Lauren about her first trip to Oregon, how the plane descended over a wide river flanked by evergreens so tall they'd made her jaw drop. How she let out a whoop anytime she drove down Mirror Lake's Main Street and found that it was so clear she could see Mount Hood ahead, a diamond in the rough, hunkered down at the end of the street like a pot of gold at rainbow's end.

And somewhere along the gentle trail, Rachel sensed the one body they had become—horse, mother, and daughter melded together, rocking softly in unison. It was a momentary bond, a fleeting instant, but that rare quality made it that much sweeter.

With eyes wide open, Rachel breathed in the life around her and seized the moment.

Chapter 34

"I don't know why you bothered coming." Kevin Hawkins leaned back in the chair and folded his arms across his red-and-white striped prison shirt. "I'm not in a talking mood, and you're not pretty to look at. You're not even FBI or a federal prosecutor. Who the hell are you again?"

"Hank Todd, Mirror Lake's chief of police."

"What's that, like a chief with no Indians?" Hawkins snorted. "You're a waste of my time."

"Ya think?" Hank slid a folder over to Hawkins's attorney, who slipped on a pair of reading glasses with a silent frown. The file was so thick, Hank himself wasn't sure where to start. With the nineteen-year-old girlfriend, Gabby Haggart, who had seen Lauren on the farm but had not realized she was a prisoner? With Gabby's sister Eleanor, whom Hawkins had tapped because she worked at an adoption agency—a place rife with eager parents who would do just about anything to locate a child in need of a home. With Hawkins's aunt, who claimed to know nothing was going on in her backyard for six years? Or maybe Kevin wanted to hear what his friends at the Saturday market had to say about him.

"Oh, you brought paperwork?" Hawkins laughed. "And I'm supposed to be impressed?"

"You should be. It's a detailed list of the people we're going to depose. Basically, they'll be preparing statements that can be used as sworn testimony."

Hawkins rolled his eyes. "You got testimony from that shrink? Does he say I'm a sexual predator? That I need intensive therapy?"

"I don't give a shit about your mental state. But I've got plenty of people who saw you taking three-year-old Mackenzie around. That puts you with one minor who's now dead and another you kidnapped and sexually assaulted."

"Yeah, well . . ." He faked a yawn. "So you got me on kidnapping. Guess I'll be here a while, but there's something to be said for three squares a day and a roof that doesn't leak."

"Don't get too comfortable. Capital punishment is legal in the state of Oregon. We've got thirty awaiting execution." Hank pointed to the open file. "Soon to be thirty-one."

"You're bluffing."

Hank shook his head. "I know a judge who's willing to unseal the records from those rapes you did when you were a kid. Add those to the crimes of kidnapping, sexual assault, and homicide, and you're going to meet your maker. But don't worry; they say lethal injection is painless. Out like a light."

"But you don't have Mac, right? No body, no sign that she even existed."

"We have the records from the urgent care facility where you took her, claiming she was Eleanor Haggart's daughter. Only because you knew Eleanor had health insurance. Oddly enough, the insurance didn't go through when their date of births didn't match; Eleanor was twenty, and Mac was, well, definitely not twenty."

Hawkins shook his head. "I brought little Eleanor to the clinic. Can I help it if her mother gave me the wrong insurance card?"

"There is no little Eleanor, but there are plenty of people who saw little Mac, from the vendors at the market in Portland to your dear Aunt Vera."

Hawkins's jaw clenched as he shot a look down at the open file beside him.

"Nice lady, Aunt Vera. She took you in when your parents wouldn't let you back in the house. I mean, not even back on their property. I don't know what you did to them when you were growing up in Salem, but it must have been a doozy. They're still refusing to speak with the police."

"They're crazy."

"Be that as it may . . . you go to your Aunt Vera and she gives you a place to live, rent-free. A piece of land with a rustic cabin at the back of her farm. A rural paradise. And you repay her with this? Keeping an innocent girl there for six years. And when things get out of control and the little girl gets sick, you take her to your aunt, thinking she'll fix everything. When the truth of the matter is, she's not an MD, and by showing her the kid, you made her an accomplice to your crime."

"I didn't tell her anything—just that Mac was sick. I told her Mac was mine, but she didn't know about Sis. Vera didn't do anything wrong, so get her off your list. She's good people. She's in a wheelchair. You can't arrest a woman in a wheelchair."

"We can, and we will."

"That's my fault, but I was desperate. How was I supposed to know how to take care of a three-year-old? And she could barely breathe. I thought she was going to die in my arms."

Hank rested his chin on his fist and scrutinized the suspect. "I think she did. And at the very least, that's negligent homicide." He tapped his fingertips on the table. "It's all in the file, but it does make for some pretty dense reading. You may want to take it back to your cell with you. Check it out before lights out. I'd say it's worth a look since we're looking at a death penalty conviction."

"That's not going to happen," Hawkins snapped impatiently. "Is it?" He turned to his lawyer. "You're supposed to be defending me. Could I really get the death penalty?"

Marino frowned, reading. "We should discuss it in private, but yes, it is possible."

"Shit." Hawkins's face screwed up so tight, his eyes nearly crossed. "Shit! I didn't kill her, and she didn't die. You'll tell them that for me, right? Tell the FBI and the prosecutor. I ain't no killer. Just a sick man with a problem." He pressed two fingers to his temple. "Twisted from my childhood. Can't help that, can I?"

"Everyone has problems. Lot of kids have it tough. Obstacles to overcome." Hank spoke so softly that Hawkins had to lean forward to hear. "But even with problems, it's not okay to kidnap an eleven-year-old and kill a three-year-old. Our society looks down upon actions like that. Thank God."

Hawkins was nervous now. His eyes shifted from Hank to the file and back again, and fine beads of sweat had formed on his upper lip. "You gotta help me here, help me convince the cops that I didn't hurt her. Maybe I didn't always do the right thing. I'm flesh and blood, a creature of sin, like any man. But I never would have hurt a little girl."

"You're so full of shit. Like you didn't hurt Lauren O'Neil?"

"Well, nothing permanent. I'd never kill a kid, and definitely not little Mac. No one could hurt her. She was a special kid, real smart. I didn't want her to get hurt."

For the first time, Hawkins's words and tone seemed genuine, his eyes earnest. Hank almost believed him. Almost. His logical mind reminded him that trusting Hawkins was like playing with fire. Brush too close to the flames, you get burned.

"You didn't want Mac to get hurt, so you saved her? How'd you manage that?"

"I just did, okay? And she's better off for it. She's free from this mess, living a better life."

Like, in heaven? Hank frowned. "You're saying you killed her."

"No! You gone deaf with those big ears? I would never kill her. I sent her to a better place, that's all. And that's all I'm saying."

Rolling his fingers on the table, Hank considered the possibilities. Had he sent the little girl to live with his parents in Salem, his brother the traveling rodeo rider, or Aunt Vera? Doubtful, because the task force had checked out Kevin Hawkins's relatives. Anyone with the last name of Hawkins had been wrung out and hung out to dry.

If Mac wasn't dead, then who else would he have given her away to? Some scalawag in Hawkins's small circle. Or had he tried to make some money on an illegal adoption? It was intriguing that the girlfriend's sister, Eleanor Haggart, happened to work for an adoption agency.

"So you gave her up for adoption. Or better yet, you realized you could make money on the deal." Hank was pleased at the way the suspect's face seemed to implode. It appeared that he'd hit a vein. "Did Eleanor Haggart's agency broker the deal? And where'd you put the money, Kevin? You don't have any bank accounts in the area, and we never uncovered your wad of cash stuffed under a mattress or inside the van."

A cool glaze dropped over Hawkins's eyes. "I got nothing else to say."

"I think you do, if you don't want to revert back to that murder charge. Three strikes and we're looking for lethal injection."

"She was adopted, okay? She's safe somewhere, and I didn't kill her."

"But where? You want to save your skin, we need to prove that you didn't hurt Mac." Hank knew his logic defied the "innocent until proven guilty" precept, but neither Hawkins nor his attorney lodged an objection.

"What if I don't know where she is?"

Hank tapped his fingers on the table again, realizing the gesture seemed to rattle Hawkins. "Are you suggesting you trusted someone else to handle the whole deal? Even you wouldn't be that stupid."

"I'm done here." Hawkins scowled at his attorney, who had watched the exchange with only a trace of distaste. "And you're useless."

As Hank watched the prisoner march to the door of the conference cell and call for the guard to open it, he wondered if he'd been wrong. Maybe Hawkins *was* that stupid. Maybe he'd given Mac up to someone else to broker the deal. *You handle the deal, as long as I get my money.* Blood money.

Chapter 35

Sprawled on her left side, sketching lake scenes with her right hand, Lauren was the first to see the police chief making his way down to the dock. "Hank's here," she said, rhythmically tapping her cast against the dock.

"Oh, good." Paula put the cover on the box of pastels they were using and rose from her cross-legged position on the dock. "He's just in time to save me from overdoing this lily pad. Monet would roll over in his grave."

"No, he wouldn't," Lauren said. She didn't care that Paula's objects looked thick and cartoonlike, because the warm, bright colors always filled her heart with light.

These days, a visit from Hank Todd was a daily occurrence, as he liked to personally deliver updates on the case against Kevin Hawkins and the mystery of what had happened to Mac's remains. Having gotten over her fear of a person in uniform, Lauren had come to like the kind bear of a man, probably because she realized that Paula liked him, too. When she'd asked about it, Paula had gazed at Lauren over her glasses and admit-

ted that she did like Hank. "He's good people. I have to
say, the more I get to know him, the more I like him."
And they'd left it at that.

Recently, Lauren had wondered if Hank Todd might
want to start keeping Paula company when Lauren had
to leave her. Not that Lauren wanted to think about moving in with the O'Neils, but both Paula and Wynonna had
told her that it was the right thing to do, an important
step in reunification. "A stepping-stone to your future,"
Wynonna had said, pointing to the glowing purple "future" candle in the gazebo. In her therapy sessions with
the family, Lauren had come to see their good intentions. Sierra had a talent for reducing problems to their
emotional core, and Dan was so good-natured he reminded Lauren of one of the ranch dogs, a golden lab
who had taken to following her around to protect her.

The problem was Rachel. Mom. It was awkward, thinking of her that way. When Lauren pictured herself moving into that house on Wildwood Lane, she found it
hard to breathe because of Rachel. Her need to control
things could zap the air from a room.

"Everyone needs to feel some sense of control in her
life," Wynonna had pointed out.

"But why does she need to control mine?" Lauren
had asked. She had argued that the house would become another prison, except that instead of being
ruled by Kevin, she would be controlled by Rachel.

Wynonna understood. "Children are expected to
obey their parents. That's part of the social order. But
in that model, the parents take care of their children,
giving them food, shelter, and love." She had pointed
out that Lauren was close to an age of independence.
"In a year, you will legally be permitted to leave home

and make your own decisions. Not that I advise it for you yet, but the need for independence you're feeling is normal for a young woman your age."

Lauren had argued about that. She didn't want to be independent; she wanted to stay right here in the lake house with Paula. Lauren didn't care if that was unrealistic. She didn't want to hear that the agency money and donations would run out, and that the FBI was going to transfer Bija to another assignment, now that it was clear that Kevin had acted alone and Lauren was no longer in jeopardy. Lauren had been through too many changes in her life. She was going to stay here as long as she could.

Now Paula brushed her hands against her boxy gray shorts and gave a wave. "Howdy."

"Ladies. I see you're taking advantage of the beautiful day." Hank's square chin and broad smile reminded her of a happy parrot.

Trying to be graceful with the orange clunker on her leg, Lauren pushed herself up to a cross-legged position and leaned back into the late afternoon sunshine.

"I just came from the state prison." He squatted down on the dock so that his eyes were level with Lauren's face. "I talked to Kevin, and I have some news."

The thought of Kevin made her bristle. Part of her therapy included learning more about the real Kevin Hawkins—as much as she could stand. But in the last few weeks, as the many ways he had wronged her gelled in her mind, her curiosity and odd loyalty to Kevin had given way to revulsion. "What did he say?" she asked in a dull voice.

"He's changed his story on your daughter."

"Mac?" It still hurt to say her name, unless Lauren

was half asleep, in that dreamlike state where she believed that Mac was still alive and that she would come running in the door any minute to report that she had spotted a rabbit in the garden. Or tired Mac, crawling into Lauren's arms and twirling Lauren's hair around her fingers while she sucked milk from a sippy cup.

"It turns out that Mac didn't die at the hospital, as he said. We think he took her to an urgent care clinic on Boones Ferry Road, where she was given antibiotics and released."

"What?" Lauren closed her sketchbook as jumbled memories pricked her mind. Worries about Mac's terrible cough. Her little blue lips. Fury when Kevin plucked her from her weak arms. Guilt over letting go, letting her little girl slip from her arms. She never understood why she had let him take Mac that night; she supposed she was all mixed up and delirious, as she'd been burning up with fever, too. Still, when she looked back, she hated her weakness. What kind of mother was she, letting someone take her child away?

"I don't want to give you false hope," Mr. Hank went on, "but there is another possibility the police have been exploring."

Paula peered over her square, black glasses. "You think Mac is alive?" When he nodded, she pumped a fist in the air. "By golly, I had a feeling. This is good news."

"Mac is alive?" Feeling as if someone had just tossed her in the air, Lauren scrambled to her feet, wobbling a little when she remembered the walking cast. "I need to see her! That's . . . that's the most wonderful, awesome news."

She could see her little girl, chubby cheeks and blond curls, giggling with delight. She thought of Mac splashing in this lake. She would have to learn to swim, of course. And the good wholesome foods she could have—fresh fruits and vegetables. And the horses and dogs at Spirit Ranch! She could imagine her daughter rolling the ball to Ludwig, Wynonna's golden retriever, who would roll the ball right back to her. Mac would laugh and clap at that. And Sierra and Dan and Rachel . . . a family. Finally, Mac would have a real family.

"Where is she now? Lauren asked. "I mean, if he didn't bring her back to the compound, where did he take her?"

"That we don't know. But we're working on finding her. We're interviewing Kevin Hawkins's family and connections, following every lead. I can only promise that my department will stay on this twenty-four seven until we find her."

"Oh." The little cry escaped Lauren's throat as her gaze swept over the lake's surface—water all around them, dark and deep beneath the silver surface—and it all seemed so vast and hopeless. The world, the "out there" that Kevin had warned about, was closing in around her, and somewhere in the process, it had swallowed up her little girl.

"Lauren? Honey, this is good news." Paula's hands were on her shoulders, warm and consoling, but not enough of a tether to safety.

"She's out there . . . all alone." Her mouth puckered as tears stung her eyes. "She must be so scared and lonely. I know how that feels, and I've got to find her." She turned to Paula. "We've got to find her."

"We will," Paula said.

As the police chief described the plan, his words shrank away, so small that Lauren couldn't catch them. She shivered, suddenly cold. The sun had shifted, putting them in shadow, turning the lake water to gray ink. Only a small patch of sunlight remained, glinting against a window in a cottage on the other side of the lake.

A distant light—that was Mac. Lauren knew she had to catch that light before it faded, but she didn't know how to do it. She sobbed, staring at the glimmer across the lake until her tears made it all a blur.

Chapter 36

A low-profile search.

Rachel understood the need to keep the investigation a secret; if Mac was living in the area, they didn't want to tip off her adoptive parents that the search was on. That was the logic; in practice, it felt like they were sitting on their hands, waiting, wishing, and fooling themselves that a positive turn of events was just around the corner.

Darkness fell over their small group as Doug O'Neil inched the boat under the low, narrow bridge. The inlets leading from East Bay to the main lake were narrow and tight in spots, but Dan's father managed the straits with the ease and precision of a man who'd been boating on Mirror Lake for thirty years.

While the boat was still drifting at low speed, Sierra popped out of her seat in the back and moved forward to sit by Lauren and Rachel in the front of the boat.

That left Dan alone in the rear. "What?" He lifted his arms and pretended to sniff one armpit. "I showered this morning."

His mother swiveled her captain's chair back toward him. "That's what happens with teenagers. They don't want to be seen with you for a few years."

"Why don't you come up here, Dad?" Lauren called.

Had she said *Dad* or *Dan*? Rachel looked at her husband, but was unable to read the expression beneath his sunglasses. It had sounded like Dad. Another inch of progress. Although Lauren was understandably tense and anxious about her daughter, she maintained a kind, polite attitude toward the family. Rachel had to give her credit; if she were in Lauren's shoes, she would be on the verge of a major meltdown.

After Dan moved forward, his father put on his captain's hat with a grin. "Everybody in a good spot?" His bushy gray brows twitched up. "Okay, gang. Hold on to your hats and I'll get you there in one piece."

The boat sped up, sending jets of water spraying back on both sides. The girls shrieked in delight as they soared around the island and proceeded across the main lake. On an ordinary summer day, the family might go tubing or swimming or out for lunch along the downtown strip. But today, their destination was Phantom's Bluff, where Dan's father had reported seeing a little girl who "looked just like Lauren when she was a kid."

Ever since Hank had pressed Hawkins at the Oregon State Penitentiary, "little Mac" had been a flame of hope dancing in every heart. Rachel knew she wasn't alone in her desperation to recover the little girl; still, she had to fight every day to keep the mission from becoming an obsession. Divide and conquer—that was what she did best. It was hard not to make the search her own, but she was working hard not to be the controlling "boss of everyone," hated by her daughters and avoided by the police. Rachel was trying hard to be a team player.

These days, she and Paula worked well together, and Lauren seemed a little more open to her ideas when it came to finding Mac. But often Lauren seemed more lost than ever, overwhelmed by a sense of helplessness as she thought of the difficulties they faced in finding her little girl. Rachel desperately wanted to break through. If only she could get Lauren to see that she understood the torture of worrying about a missing child. As the boat shot over a swell, Rachel pulled back her wind-tossed hair and rethought that. It really didn't matter so much that they commiserate together. None of that would matter if Lauren got her daughter back. That was the true goal.

Now that the search was on, their days often ended with a small gathering at the lake house, with Hank stopping by to give them the latest. It was hard to focus on anything else with the prospect of Mac out there—another child who needed to be rescued. But as Wynonna insisted, the therapy had to go on. Lauren needed to re-learn the world and define herself; it would make her a better mother when Mac was finally located.

After maneuvers that included bumping over a few wakes, spraying the passengers, and turning in a wide circle, Doug cut back the engine and grinned. "Nobody overboard? That's always good. But the evening is still young."

The girls exchanged a wide-eyed look and Sierra giggled.

"So let's see." Dan stared at the coastline. "We just passed Half-Moon Bay. See that house with the curved roof that looks like a Safeway? That's my landmark for Crescent Bay." He pointed out a few other landmarks as they chugged along. Lauren had never been out on the lake, and Sierra had never taken notice of the lake houses. A stone-covered mansion, complete with turrets and towers, had been dubbed the Castle. A small contemporary home that seemed to be built into the hillside was known as Hobbit Town. There was the Tudor, the Japanese Garden, the Resort, and the Beach House, complete with its own shoreline of trucked-in sand. "And this half bay here is known as Phantom's Bluff."

"Where did you see her, Dad?" Rachel asked.

"Over to the left. See that paved patio that leads out to the dock?"

Everyone looked over to a lounge area with a small building that probably contained a bathroom. A bright red umbrella sat open, as if someone had been hanging out recently.

"Do the people live in that little building?" Sierra asked.

"That's just a pool house," Dan explained. "See the two-seat contraption a few steps up the hill? It looks like a double swing? It's a lift, sort of like a ski lift. Takes people up and down the hill so they don't have to climb that path with all the switchbacks."

It was one of those lots built on a cliff. Mirror Lake had quite a few of them. A hundred feet above the shore, the houses featured magnificent views of the lake, the trees, and the sky. The only drawback was getting down to the lake. Even with switchbacks evening out the trail, it was a steep climb.

"Have you ever ridden on one of those lifts, Grandma?" Sierra asked.

"A few times," Doug's wife, Alice, said. "We used to have friends in a cliff house. The view was nice, but they didn't really use the lake much. Just too much work to get down here."

"You can't even see a house up there," Lauren said.

"It's hidden in the trees, but it's there." Dan rubbed his chin, looking up. "I think that's the cathedral house."

Rachel nodded. The dark, gothic house set back from the road had lots of stained glass, gargoyles, and a spire visible from South Shore Drive.

"That's right." Dan's mother narrowed her eyes. "I've heard the place is stunning and brutally cold. My friend Haddie always jokes that it's occupied by some ex-nuns."

"Do you know who really lives there, Grandma?" Sierra asked. "Maybe we can knock on their door."

"Nope. I've never even seen a car turn into the drive."

"But there are signs of life down here." Doug tipped back his hat and stood up to lean over the boat's windshield. "Too damned bad they're not here right now. I'm telling you, I've seen the lady and the little girl down here the last three times I took the boat out." He turned to Lauren, apologetic. "Sorry, but when I heard about Mac, well, I just wanted you to see this little girl."

"It was worth coming out, Dad," Rachel said. "And that's what we have to do right now. Everyone keep your eyes open, check out every lead."

"We can come out another time," Doug said, squinting over toward the empty terrace. "First time I laid eyes on that little girl, I swore I saw a family resemblance right away. It was you as a toddler, Lauren."

"Did she have blond hair that curled around at the end?" Lauren asked hopefully.

"She did."

"And chubby little cheeks?"

"Like a chipmunk. The girl's as cute as a button. Seemed to be around three or four now."

"Mac turns four September first." It sounded so hopeful, the way Lauren said it. It made the little girl seem so real.

"I still think we should knock on their door," Sierra said. "Or tell Chief Todd. He'll make the police storm their house."

"The cops try not to barge into homes without a war-rant," Dan said. "Remember that historic document called the Constitution?"

Lauren looked from Dan to Sierra, watching curi-ously.

"I never liked history," Sierra said.

"Well, I'm sorry we didn't get to see your little friend," Alice teased her husband. "But we're going to keep pray-ing for her, praying to find her."

Praying for a miracle, Rachel thought, as everyone took their seats for the return trip. *Praying for a second miracle.*

The next day she met Lauren at the ranch for an-other back-riding session. This would be the first time Lauren would ride without her cast. She had been to the orthopedist, and since the X-rays had shown the bone healed, the orange cast had been removed. Checking her messages on her phone, Rachel hung back by the door of the stables while Lauren and Jazz saddled up the horse.

As she brought the saddle blanket over to Yoda, Lau-ren moved without a trace of a limp. In her matched pair of cowboy boots, she looked trim and healthy and confident—so different from the girl who had been res-cued a month ago.

"Do you need help with the saddle?" Lauren called to Jazz.

"I got it." His voice was slightly strained from the weight as he hoisted it from the fence. Lauren moved beside him to help lift it high enough to sit on Yoda's back. "Thanks." He shifted the saddle, making sure it was secure, while Lauren went to stroke the horse's neck.

"Pretty soon, I'm going to be riding you on my own," she told Yoda.

The horse gave a gentle snort, as if answering her.

Lauren leaned into him. "Oh, Yoda. Mac would really love you."

Jazz pulled the saddle strap tight under the horse's belly. "That would be so cool to have Mac here. We used to do riding classes for little kids, but now Mom focuses on veterans mostly. Sometimes the little kids get scared by the horses."

"Mac was fearless. She wasn't scared of bugs or animals. Sometimes when I was working in the garden, she would sit and watch ants crawl in a line, doing their thing. But with Yoda, I think I'd be the one a little scared, seeing her on top of a tall horse like him."

It was such a maternal reaction; this was something Rachel understood.

"I guess she could start with Penny," he said.

"I guess so." Lauren took her helmet from the post. "Of course, she would have to wear one of these."

"Yup." He wrapped his hand around the saddle horn and tested it. "How's all that going? I mean, I know it's a secret and all, and maybe I shouldn't butt in."

"That's okay. It's all up to the police to find her. I'm supposed to just keep doing my therapy, which would be fine, except I can't stop thinking about her. I wish I could go looking for her."

"You want me to take you some time? Mom would let us use the Jeep. Where would you look for her?"

Lauren tugged the riding helmet on her head. "That's the problem. I don't have a clue."

That day, Lauren's body offered no resistance as they rode along the ridge. Girl, woman, and horse were like one big muscle, flexing and releasing as Yoda followed the path between green fields and tall fir trees.

"You've really learned how to sit a horse," Rachel said. "Look at you. Cast gone and you're gripping Yoda's sides like a pro."

"Therapy at the ranch is the highlight of my day."

Because of the horses? Rachel wondered. *Or because of a certain boy?*

"I hope Wynonna will let me ride on my own soon."

"I'm sure she will. Although that will be bittersweet. I'll miss this."

"Me too."

The words were a sunrise, a slow dawn in Rachel's heart. Wynonna had been right; the blame was lifting.

"I heard you talking to Jazz," Rachel said before she lost her nerve. "I'm not supposed to be pushy, and if I'm over the line, just tell me to back off. But I want you to know, I'll take you out looking for Mac. I'll take you to the ends of the earth, if that's where the trail leads." She wanted to tell Lauren that she understood her desperation; she knew the feeling of violation—the sting of someone having stolen your soul.

But she couldn't push. And Lauren's pain may have been different from her own. It might seem selfish to assume she understood what her daughter was going through.

"I don't know." Lauren paused; silence yawned. "Where would we even look?"

Rachel let out the breath she'd been unconscious of holding. "We could start with Kevin's girlfriend . . . the young woman you met? And her sister, who works at the adoption agency. And Kevin's Aunt Vera."

"Didn't the police talk to them?"

"Yes, but they may be willing to tell you things they wouldn't mention to the police."

"But won't Hank get mad?"

"Learning about Kevin is part of your therapy. And you're supposed to be doing more outings, interacting with the public. It makes sense to me."

"Okay." Lauren's voice sounded small, but decisive. "I have to learn something from my therapy. Wynonna says I have to accept help from people I trust. Let's try that—the girlfriend. Do you know how to find her?"

Rachel felt herself misting over behind her daughter's back. "I can figure it out. I'll track her down."

"And Mom?"

The word *Mom* seemed to echo through the fields and trees.

"I think it's time for me to move home."

Home. Rachel breathed in traces of summer grass and horse and shampoo and hope.

Hope came along in surprising ways.

Chapter 37

Sierra could not believe that Lauren was really home. After almost a month of keeping her distance from the family, Lauren had packed her new clothes in shopping bags and transferred them to her old room upstairs. Dad had said he wanted to bring Lauren home with a minimum of hoopla, and since the local media had agreed not to publish or air photos of Lauren or Sierra because they were both under eighteen and Lauren was a sex crime victim, their dad sort of got his wish. The day Lauren came home, Dad did a press conference with Chief Todd and some dude from social services—a balding guy with a stringy ponytail in the back. Turned out he was Paula's boss, Truman. Anyway, they did the press conference at the police station—a diversionary tactic to draw the media away from the house while Lauren pulled into the Wildwood Lane driveway in Paula's car. That had been an awesome trick. It had reminded Sierra of some stroke of sabotage by one of the competitors on *Project Runway*.

Mom had hung a giant yellow ribbon around the

tree out front, and Sierra used butcher paper to make the banner taped to the stairs that said: WELCOME HOME, LAUREN! Her name was surrounded by tiny foil heart stickers, which Sierra added on at the last minute because the bubble letters took her so long to color in.

And one of the weirdest things had happened when Sierra was wildly trying to finish the poster and make it look good. Mom had come in and picked up a crayon and helped. Okay, that wasn't so weird. But then Mom had started opening up. She told Sierra she was sorry.

Mom had actually apologized for focusing so much attention on Lauren. "Not just recently, I mean in the last six years . . . since she went missing. You know I love you, honey. I admire your adaptability and grace. Who else could excel at soccer and piano?"

Sierra kept her head down, her eyes on the poster so Mom couldn't see the raw emotion in her face. Had Mom really noticed her all these years? Yes, her mother had never missed a big soccer game or a piano recital. But much of the time Mom had been there in body only. Her mind was usually on other things: her new batch of students, the next rally to find Lauren, the broken vacuum, or the seminar on missing children.

Although Sierra wanted to brush the topic aside, she couldn't resist a jab. "You know, Mom, I used to think you love Lauren more."

"What?" Mom's hand landed on her shoulder. "No!"

"And then I realized that it wasn't about me. It's really about you, Mom. You tuned everything else out to focus on searching for Lauren. I guess that was what you needed to do. And now that Lauren is back, now you're just noticing that I'm still your daughter?"

"Sierra, no. I was never that far away. Distracted, yes, but I wasn't emotionally unavailable."

Whatever, Sierra thought as she kept coloring in the giant L. Mom would always see it her own way, but Sierra knew the truth. Tragedy could crack a family in half like the San Andreas Fault. Still, she gave Mom credit for trying. It was still an apology, right?

In the first few days, Mom and Dad did their best to help Lauren adjust, but Lauren mostly latched on to Sierra. During meals, Sierra felt her sister watching and following her motions like a shadow. Fork down between bites. Napkin on her lap. Second helping of beans . . . whatever Sierra did, Lauren mirrored.

At first it was annoying. It was like Lauren was trying to climb inside her skin. Then, on the second night at dinner, Lauren reached for the ketchup Sierra had just put down, and she knocked Dad's water over. In seconds, Dad's plate and half the table were swamped with liquid and melting ice.

Lauren's hands flew to her face in horror. "I'm so sorry. I . . . I'll clean it up." She rose from her chair too fast, knocking it back to the ground behind her.

Dad and Mom were saying it was okay. Dad joked that he liked his burgers extra juicy. But Lauren was too freaked out to hear them. With the cry of a wounded animal, she fled up the stairs.

Mom gave Dad the worried look. "Want me to go?" he asked. "And you do the cleanup."

"I'll go." Sierra stood up, a little surprised by her own initiative.

"That's okay, honey." Mom waved her back down, but Sierra was already backing away from the table.

"She'll talk to me. If you haven't noticed, she imitates everything I do. I think she looks up to me, even though I'm the little sister."

She bounded up the stairs, not sure what she would say, though she knew that anything would be better than the drizzled honey that would come from Mom or Dad.

Lauren was in her room facing the open window.

Sierra couldn't see her face, but she was pretty sure she'd been crying. "Hey. You okay?"

"I can't do anything right. I can't even sit at the table and eat dinner like a normal human person."

"You're nervous, right?" Sierra said, taking a wild guess. "You probably feel like everyone is watching you, and you're sort of right. Mom and Dad can be that way, staring. Like they're picking you apart in their minds. I always yell at Mom when I see that look in her eyes."

"It's not their fault. It's me. I don't belong here. I don't know how to act. All these things—sitting at a dinner table or shopping at the store. When you don't do them for six years, you botch everything up. It's awkward. Seventeen and I can't drive or work a cell phone. You said it yourself, I'm a dinosaur."

Sierra was cocking her head to the side, forming a sympathetic look, when the words sank in. Had she really said that? Well, yeah, maybe, but it had been a joke. Mostly because Sierra couldn't believe someone wouldn't know how to use an iPhone.

"I didn't mean it that way," Sierra said quickly. "And you've used a cell phone. You had one with you when you were kidnapped."

"Not a smart phone! It was a stupid phone." Lauren's irritation was showing. "A stupid phone for a stupid girl."

"Nobody thinks you're stupid." Sierra stood next to her sister, staring out at the treetops illuminated light green by the evening sun. This was the season of long days, sunlight from six in the morning to after ten at night. Sierra loved the sun. She had already decided that she would only apply to colleges in sunny places.

The sight of the tall trees and the talk of cell phones made her think of the Tillamook forest. "I remember when the police followed the beacon to your cell phone. Do you know they traced it to the Tillamook forest?"

"Yeah." Lauren sighed. "We stopped there for a bathroom break, and when Kevin wasn't looking I gave it a toss with all my might. I didn't realize we were already way off the main path. Mom said it took days to find it."

"That was really smart of you to leave a clue. Everyone said so. The police said you did the right thing." She swayed against her sister, giving her a bump with her shoulder. "That's how smart you really are. So don't beat yourself up about the little things."

"How do you separate the little things from the big things?" Lauren asked slowly.

That was when it clicked, when Sierra realized that her sister really, really needed her. "Easy. You just ask me."

Chapter 38

Crazy thoughts

Ever since I found out Mac is alive, I can't sleep at night. Crazy, crazy me. As soon as my head hits the pillow my thoughts go to her, and I can't sleep. It's like I can't rest until everything is right with her, and I know it's not.

I am so mad at Kevin for taking her away from me. It's like he stole my life a second time when he took Mac away. I don't understand why he would do that to her or to me.

Last night, my window shade looked sort of bright. When I opened it up, I saw it was lit by the moon—a big orange moon with the laughing man's face. I remembered looking up at the moon through that skylight in the beach house laundry room, just after I had been taken from my mom. Mac is a lot younger than me, but last night I was thinking the same thoughts of years ago.

Is she looking at the moon now? Same moon, same stars.

What if Mac is being held in a house near here, just like I was? What if she's back at the compound? I mean, it's possible she would find her way back there if she got away from whoever has her. She's almost four. Is it really possible? I don't know! I have to go check the compound.

I miss the tent I used to sleep in. It was small but cozy. Mom says we can get this drapery thing from Ikea that will hang over my bed. It's nice of her to try and help, but a pink net is not a tent.

Isn't it weird that Sierra is now about the same age I was when Kevin snatched me away? If I was still eleven, I could go to school with Sierra and have a normal high school experience. I know that's trying to change reality, but that's why I called this section crazy thoughts.

I can't do it! I can't sleep alone in my old bedroom. It's too lonely at night, too quiet, and I keep wondering about Mac. I started going into Sierra's room to sleep on the floor, and she caught me. But she didn't seem mad. She said I could sleep in the bed with her. I just want to be close to someone else. The soothing sound of her breathing reminds me of having Mac nearby at night. When I hear the breathing sounds, I can almost trick myself into believing that everything is okay. Almost.

Chapter 39

The first few nights after Lauren's return, Dan had barely slept. Like a zombie, he'd risen from bed in the middle of the night and plodded downstairs to check door locks and windows. As if that would ward off further evil in his daughter's life. As if she had been stolen in the night from her crib instead of snatched while walking down the street.

"If you want to be really safe, you'll move to another house," one of the guys at work had warned him. "Your place has been on the news a hundred times. People know it. It only takes one crazy copy-catter to lock on to your house and come after Lauren. I'd get out of that house. Get the hell out of Mirror Lake. Go somewhere out east where no one can find you."

The air had locked in Dan's lungs at the man's insinuation. Was he really telling Dan to turn his family into fugitives on the run because of the existence of evil in the world?

"Yeah," Sully had joined in, sliding a sponge over the table in the firehouse break room. "You can't be too safe." He winked at Dan. "You could even be targeted by aliens with two beauties like that. Better lock the girls in the house. Don't ever let 'em out."

"I'm just saying, you can't be too safe," Trevor Van Allen said, with a scowl for Sully.

Later, Dan and Sully had both expressed relief that Van Allen usually worked an opposite shift. "That kind of careful, I can live without," Sully had said, though the underlying message was one Dan had heard over and again. You could never be too safe. But you couldn't live in a bubble either, and the therapist's warning on that point had been clear. Lauren had been held in tight spaces, but over time she had come to enjoy the open space of the compound. Keeping her penned up in the house was not an option.

So Dan checked the windows and doors and peeked into the girls' rooms after they were asleep at night. When he'd checked on Lauren her second night home, he'd nearly had a heart attack at the sight of the empty bed.

"Holy crap," he breathed.

He checked the floors and closets. The window was cracked open, but the screen was intact. Hoping he'd missed her slipping downstairs for a snack, he began a search through the house.

Thank God he didn't have to look for long. Lauren was in Sierra's room, a small tangle of comforter and pillow on the deep pile carpet between the bed and the window.

His pulse slowed as he crept into the room. Sierra was out like a light, but Lauren's head turned to follow him as he approached.

He squatted down and whispered: "Hey, I've been looking for you."

"I can't sleep," she said softly, her hair silver in the

dim light from the hallway. "I can't stop worrying about Mac, and being in here with Sierra, hearing her breathing, it reminds me of sleeping with Mac."

She looked so small in the fat comforter, small and vulnerable. He wanted to take her in his arms and rock her like a baby and tell her she would always be safe, but of course, he couldn't.

He sat down on the rug and leaned close. "You know what my mom used to tell me? Never worry alone."

She frowned. "What does that mean?"

"That you should share your problems with someone who cares." Dan noticed a box on the floor beside Lauren's pillow. A box of Pop-Tarts. Paula had told them that Lauren still felt the need to keep a stash of food nearby, though she rarely tapped into it at night.

"I bet you forgot that I make a pretty good ice cream sundae," he said quietly. "Should we go down and raid the kitchen?"

She popped up to her knees. "Sure."

Down in the kitchen, the ice cream was like a brick. As Dan set it out to thaw and assembled sundae fixings, he got her talking about Mac. Dan realized that there were many topics he could not discuss with her, things that had happened to her that he couldn't bear to think about. Most people thought he was remarkably easygoing about the whole ordeal, but Rachel understood. She knew that Dan could keep moving ahead and smooth over the surface wounds as long as he was spared the horrific details of the trauma. The same went for Mac; he had not been able to let his mind go there when he'd thought the little girl was dead. But now . . . now he faced the prospect of meeting his first grandchild with curiosity and anticipation.

Lauren described Mac as cheerful and industrious. "She could make a game out of a handful of pebbles,

and she had a great vocabulary." Lauren told the story
of how, one spring evening, she lifted Mac out of the
slop sink where she'd bathed the little girl. "It was chilly
that night, and she had goose bumps on her arms. She
shivered and started poking at the little bumps, really
upset about them. She asked if she had a disease, and I
said no, that it was just goose bumps. She shook her
head, insisting that it was impossible. 'But Mama, I didn't
bump into a goose!' "

Dan chuckled as he chiseled away at the edges of the
ice cream. "Makes perfect sense to me."

"Even before she had her words, I knew she was
smart," Lauren said as she snitched a chocolate chip
from the sack. "When she was really little, not even two,
I think, I was doing a project with old crayons. Kevin
found a bucket of them somewhere. I was melting the
crayons down to paint them onto the wood, and Mac
kept taking a blue crayon and trying to put it in her
mouth. I took it away, over and over again. Finally, I told
her to stop putting it in her mouth because the crayon
wouldn't taste good. She said, 'Okay, Mama." And then
she picked up a yellow crayon and said, 'This color taste
better?' "

They laughed together, the buzz of connection filling the kitchen.

"She sounds like a great kid," Dan said. "I know it's
hard to think of her out there, but trust me, the worry
thing can zap your energy. I'm not saying you can't
worry about Mac, but you need to take care of yourself.
Food and sleep, they're important for a kid your age."

"But Dad, I can't forget about her, not for one minute."
Lauren folded a napkin into tiny strips. "When I was gone,
you and Mom didn't forget about me. I know that now. I
saw the articles and reports about the searches you orga-

nized and all that you did. It's my turn now. I need to look for Mac."

Dan paused and put the scoop down. "Lauren, we can't go public with this search."

"I know that. But I was thinking we should go back to the compound."

Dan turned to the sink to rinse the scoop. That place had sickened him, knowing what had transpired there. The perversion. The violation. The pain. "Why would you want to go there?"

"I think, if Mac got away from these people, that's where she would go."

"Geez, Lauren. She's not even four. How would she even get there?"

"I don't know. I don't have all the answers, Dad, but that's where I need to start looking. It's the only place I can think of. Will you and Mom help me?"

Looking up at the young woman seated across the counter, her amber eyes confident, he felt a mixture of pride and intense wariness. It was a brave, bold move for Lauren to return to the compound, but shouldn't he be the one to protect her from the unnecessary torture of an ordeal like that?

In the end, the supportive father won out. "Of course, we'll help you. I've actually been thinking about that place. I got a call from Hank, and the lady who owns it, Vera Hawkins, she wants to tear it down."

Lauren's eyes grew wide. "Why would she do that?"

"Too many rubberneckers sneaking back there. There've been a lot of pictures of Green Spring Farm in the media. It's giving her place a bad reputation. She wants to put an end to the negative attraction out there. She was kind enough to ask if we want to keep any of the walls—your artwork."

Lauren frowned. "What do you think we should do?"

"I don't know." He had wanted to ask Lauren that question, but he hadn't wanted to bring up that hellhole. Now he sprayed a swirl of whipped cream on one sundae and slid it over to her. "But don't worry about it. I don't want to add to your list of worries."

"Thanks, Dad. I'll think about the artwork."

He nodded. "You know, there's this thing called the serenity prayer. Have you ever heard of it?" When she shook her head, he tried to think of it. "I can't remember how it goes." He picked up his phone and searched for it. "Here it is. 'God grant me the serenity to accept the things I cannot change; courage to change the things I can; and wisdom to know the difference."

She sucked on a spoonful of ice cream. "It sounds simple when you put it that way."

"It is simple." He sprayed a swirl of whipped cream on a sundae. "But that doesn't mean it's easy. It's like trying to get a scoop of rock-hard ice cream. You saw how that worked. You scrape away at the edges and let it melt a little. Simple, but not easy. Persistence and patience."

Chapter 40

My heart is bursting with love for Mac! I'm glad people are asking about her now, and suddenly I'm remembering lots of stories about little things she did and said. I can see her holding her magic shell to her ear and telling me the stories that came out of it. And the way she used to sing along with the TV, with Bear and Elmo. But one thing I can't talk about is those last few days I had her with me. She was so sick!

It started as a little cold—that's what I thought. She told me her nose "was leaking." That was what she called a runny nose. But then she started coughing, and the cough hung on. Sometimes she would cough for long spells, and when she breathed in there was that quacky sound, like her lungs were collapsing. I started to press Kevin to get her to a hospital, but as Mac started getting really sick, hot with fever and

*turning purple during her spells, I became sick,
too.*

*Through my fever, I recall my little girl seized
with coughing, tears on her cheeks. "The crows!
Stop the crows!" she kept crying. Mac and I spent
a lot of time gardening, and it was her job to
chase the crows from pecking away at our seed.
When I asked her what she was saying, she said,
"The crows are pecking on my heart." I guess
there was a terrible pain in her chest from the
cough.*

*Sometimes when I close my eyes, I see her little
face, cheeks tinged with purple as she rides out
the cough. And when it finally subsides, she
grabs at me, begging me to make it stop. "The
crows!"*

*And that's the last thing I remember her say-
ing.*

"I can't sleep." Sierra flopped over in bed beside
Lauren.

Ever since Sierra had nearly tripped over Lauren,
sleeping on the floor beside her bed, the younger girl
had told her she could sleep in her room. "Mom and
Dad got me this double bed for sleepovers," Sierra had
explained. "So, *you* can sleep over." Sierra was trying
hard to be nice to her; Lauren could see that, and she
was glad to have a sister here to keep her from being
the only "child" in the house. Living with two parents
was like sitting in a glass case, on display all the time.

"Maybe we should sing," Sierra said. "What songs do
you remember?"

"I don't know." Lauren didn't lift her head from the
pillow. She didn't want to admit that she would never,

ever forget the "Tell Me Why" song with its beautiful three-part harmony. She had taught it to Mac, without the harmonies, and she promised herself she wouldn't sing it again until Mac could join in.

With a sigh, Sierra rolled out of bed and lifted the blind. There was that moon, a sliver of light in the inky sky.

"This always happens to me in summer. I sleep too late, and then I want to stay up late, and Mom and Dad give me a curfew."

Her eyes on the curling light in the sky, Lauren was only half-listening. "Mac's out there, somewhere, under the same moon."

Sierra oohed as she breathed in. "That is the sweetest thing, and it's true, too. Mom was obsessed with finding you. I can see her looking at the moon with longing. You're so wise."

"I didn't just think of it. When I was first kidnapped, back in the first few months, I used to stare at the moon and think of Mom, looking up at the sky at the same moon. I was sure she was thinking of me."

"She was!" Sierra insisted. "She was a crazy person, looking for you."

"Then why didn't she find me?" Lauren asked in a small, monotone voice.

"I don't know. Nobody knows. And when they found you so close to home . . . ," Sierra picked up her stuffed elephant and stroked its silky ears. "We all felt awful about that."

Me too, Lauren thought, a bitter taste at the back of her throat.

"Lauren? Can I ask you a question?"

"Of course." Lauren propped her head on one hand.

"Why didn't you leave?"

A scrim of annoyance glazed Lauren's eyes, but when

she looked over at her sister, Sierra's face was awash
with sincerity.

"You could have climbed the fence and walked home."

"I didn't know that. I didn't know where I was. He
covered me with a blanket every time we went in and
out of the compound."

"But what about the times at the Saturday market . . .
or the state fair? There's always police at those things,
and you could have gone up to someone and told them
that you'd been kidnapped."

*Help me, please! My name is Lauren O'Neil and this man
kidnapped me. Please, get me away from here before he comes
back!*

"I tried, in the beginning. I screamed and hollered
and kicked and punched him. But he . . . he threatened
to kill me. He was going to let me drop into the ocean,
down deep." Her lower lip jutted out. "And I was afraid
you guys would never even find my body!"

"Lauren, I'm sorry. I didn't mean to—"

"It's okay. You need to know why, and I'm supposed
to talk about it." *As much as you can stand,* Wynonna always
said. Mom and Dad had been allowed to see all those
videotaped interviews, so they knew it all, but Lauren had
learned that sometimes Sierra was overlooked, kept away
from the harsh truth because of her age. "I know people are confused about it. There were stories about me
being a runaway, but that's not true. Not at all. I wanted
to get away. I wanted to come home, but he made me
believe that could never happen." She swallowed.
"Wynonna says that the same thing happens to most victims. There's this sort of brainwashing, and the kidnapper keeps reminding you that you need him to stay
alive."

"Was he mean?"

"Not always, but yeah. I realize now that he was very

self-centered. When I was drawing portraits and the customers complimented me on my work, Kevin got mad. He couldn't deal with me getting more attention than him."

Sierra's eyes were wide with amazement. "Did he ever tie you up?"

"He handcuffed me in the beginning. My wrists were bound and I was locked into a room. It was hard to move, hard to pee and all that stuff. When he finally let me sleep without those uncomfortable handcuffs, I was so grateful that I didn't want to do anything to lose that privilege. There were a few times when I thought I might be able to get away. I made it over the fence once, but by the time I got to the creek, he was there. He beat me, usually with a wrench, on my ankle. It was a spot that could be covered up with leg warmers and granny dresses if I had to go out in public. I learned not to try and get away. It wasn't worth the pain. And then . . . by the time I got to leave the compound for fairs and stuff, I was pregnant with Mac. I didn't think anyone would want me if I escaped and made it home."

"How could you think that with all the searches going on all the time?"

"I didn't know about that." Lauren plopped back on to the bed and stared at the wall, which was painted a pretty shade of peacock green. "I didn't know anything."

Sierra came over and sat on the floor by the bed, eye to eye with Lauren. "You're a brave girl. I used to be jealous of you, but I got over it."

"Jealous of me? Why?"

"Can't you see it? Mom and Dad are obsessed with you. Mom gave up her teaching job for two years because she wanted to spend all her time focusing on the search."

"She did?" It was the first time Lauren heard that part.

"Yup. The only reason she went back was because the therapist told her she needed a distraction from the search. She called her obsessive."

"Wynonna said that?"

"The other therapist. Avery something. She had a slippery leather couch and a big tree dying outside her window. Yeah, they made me go too. I was so bored, I used to wish that tree would die already and come crashing through the window during our session."

Therapy? She hadn't thought of them needing therapy while she was gone. She had suffered alone, but her family had also gone through a lot, missing her.

"I know Mom can be a pain in the ass," Sierra said with that language that always caught Lauren's attention. "But she does mean well. She loves you a lot."

As Lauren bunched the pillow under her head, the image came to her in a flash.

That mother and baby she had painted in the cabin: at the time she had thought she was painting Mac and her, but it could have just as easily been Mom and her. Mom knew what she was feeling, her little girl torn from her side. She rolled over and groaned. Why couldn't she let her mom love her?

Chapter 41

Leaning her elbows on the kitchen island, Rachel pretended to read the front page of the *Oregonian* as Lauren sat at the counter, digging around in a large bowl of oatmeal. Rachel looked at her watch, trying to think of a subtle way of hurrying Lauren along.

"I should get going. I want to catch Heather before the students arrive," Rachel said.

"But I want to go with you." Lauren pressed a napkin to her mouth and looked down at the bowl with some distress.

"Honey, are you full? You don't have to finish that."

"I hate to waste it. Dad makes good oatmeal."

"But look at the size of that bowl!" Grinning, Rachel hoisted it to the light. "Weighs a ton. Your dad served you a supersize portion. He so enjoys feeding you, but he's got a thing or two to learn about portion control."

Lauren smiled with relief. "As long as he's not mad."

"First of all, he will never know." Rachel scraped the remainder into the sink and ran the water. "Besides, you don't need to force yourself to eat something to please someone else. When you feel full, you can excuse yourself from the table."

Lauren slid off the barstool and smoothed down her black cotton skirt. What a transformation. Her skin had taken on a golden glow, despite plenty of sunscreen. Rachel's stylist had trimmed her split ends and cut side bangs that framed her delicate features. Her face had filled out so that her high cheekbones and her broad smile replaced that wan, ghostly look.

Such a beauty, inside and out, Rachel thought wistfully.

Lauren shifted uncomfortably. "Mom?" Lauren scraped back her hair and let it swing down her back. "What's wrong?"

Caught staring, Rachel turned away and grabbed her keys from the rack by the door. "Just smitten with you. Sorry, but I've got a few years to make up for, and you are a wonderful sight."

"Sometimes you embarrass me," Lauren said.

"Sorry, but I do believe that's part of a parent's role." Rachel felt almost giddy as she backed out of the driveway with Lauren beside her in the passenger seat. The beautiful young woman sitting shotgun was her daughter! Rachel couldn't remember such a feeling of freedom and independence since she'd gotten her driver's license.

Something had shifted—the planets, the invisible barriers between them—and the resentment Lauren had felt for her was fading. Although Rachel remained on guard against her desire to take control of everything, she felt generally at ease with the even flow of conversation and the change in their household. No, things were not perfect, but no family ever was, and in her time with Wynonna she had learned that the lead horse of the herd had to pick her battles.

The Little Red Schoolhouse was quaint, a residential building that had been converted to a school with offices upstairs. Rachel cruised past the building and found a spot on the street, knowing that the parking lot would fill up at drop-off time.

"Are you coming inside with me?" Rachel asked. Sensing Lauren's insecurity, she added, "I'm sure Heather would like to meet you. She's a friend. We used to teach together before she switched to early childhood education."

Reluctantly, Lauren came along, following Rachel dutifully and shaking hands with Heather.

"I met you and your sister when you were little at a backyard barbecue, but you probably don't remember. I think you were more engrossed in Popsicles and Supersoakers," Heather teased, rolling up the sleeves of her bright red shirt.

There was a flicker of response in Lauren's eyes. "I do remember the Supersoaker phase." She smiled. "I was always getting in trouble for drenching Sierra."

As the women sat down together on tiny chairs, Lauren wandered the classroom, checking out the paintings on the wall and the various play stations.

"I'm looking for information on the registration process," Rachel said.

"Oh?" Heather's eyebrows shot up. "Do you have a little one on the way?"

"Not exactly. I'm wondering how much accountability you have to the Board of Ed with children in your school. I'm not asking for confidential information. Just wondering what you need to supply."

"That's simple. They want the birth certificate and immunization record."

Rachel nodded. That would be helpful. If Mac, who was turning four September first, was going to attend school in Oregon, she would need a birth certificate, either real or fraudulent.

"Oh, and you know about the photo records now, right? We now put a copy of the child's school photo in their file. It's something that law-enforcement agencies advised. Helps them track missing children."

"Really?" Rachel's eyes went wide as possibilities opened like a lens. Could Hank or the FBI agents get copies of all those photos—all the preschool children registered in Oregon schools—so that Lauren could look through them? Oh, maybe this would be the most direct way to find Mac! And what about the state of Washington . . . and California, and Idaho?

"Does the state have a database of this information?" Rachel asked.

Heather picked up a crayon from under a cushion as she considered. "That I don't know."

"I can find out." Rachel would talk to Hank.

"What's this about? Or am I being too nosey?"

"I can't really say right now." Rachel was watching Lauren make her way through the room, restacking blocks and looking through picture books. Outside, she heard the chipmunk voices of children greeting the other teacher. "But I appreciate your help. And I guess we'd better get going. I think some of your students are here."

"No problem." Heather rose and joined Lauren over at the sand table. "What do you think, Lauren? Does it bring back memories from when you were in pre-K?"

"I know a little girl who would love this," Lauren said fervently.

"And we'll get her here," Rachel promised. There were photos . . . files . . . birth certificates to be checked. A child could be stolen, but she could not live in isolation forever. Mac would be enrolled in a school, somewhere, and as soon as she was brought forward, they would snatch her back.

Chapter 42

From Lauren's Journal

There is a nursery school nearby that is so cute! My heart melted a little when Mom took me there so that she could talk to the woman who runs it about checking to see if Mac is registered for school in the fall. Rachel is really smart with things like that. I'm glad I got up the nerve to ask her to help search for Mac. But the school—they have a sand table where you can build things with squishy sand. There are regular blocks and Legos. There's a reading corner with a big Winnie the Pooh chair to sit in. There's a theater to do little puppet shows and a mini kitchen so Mac could pretend to make me a meal. Mac loves pretending.

It's funny, but I forgot that my mom is a teacher. I know she teaches older kids in junior high, but hearing her talk to the lady about the little kids, it reminded me just how good Mom is with kids. I know that I've backed away from her a lot, but that's mostly because she needed to see me as an adult, not a little kid anymore. But seeing the way Mom talked to the little kids who were coming into the nursery school, I could just imagine her with Mac. They will really get a charge out of each other. I don't know why I ever worried about Mom and Dad accepting my little girl. That was probably Kevin's negative voice whispering in my ear.

Here's the big thing: Seeing that little school-house, it was the first time I could see Mac living here on Wildwood Lane and having her own little place to go. I'm letting my heart and mind believe that this is going to happen, because I want to be positive. Wynonna says that sometimes we can make our dreams come true, but that we have to create the dream first. Well, that's my dream. Mac playing with other kids in the yard of the little red schoolhouse. When I saw that school, I began to see possibilities for Mac. I just hope and wish that I am seeing the future.

Chapter 43

Dan and Lauren led the brown stallion known as Hero around the arena against a sky split into two. Overhead, the bright expanse of pale blue was streaked by fast-moving clouds. In the distance, a field of gray and purple swarmed like a cauldron—a brewing storm that looked spectacular from this safe distance.

For three weeks they had been participating in family therapy at Spirit Ranch. This time of year the sessions were held outside under the bold, blue Oregon summer sky. Even Dan, therapy skeptic, had been won over by the clear-eyed therapist, the magnificent surroundings, and, of course, the horses.

Their family sessions included a group forum in which they took turns sharing their thoughts and concerns while wearing a ridiculous horse hat. They also spent time on group exercises, often activities as simple as rolling a ball to play catch with one of the horses. If they wanted to play, the horses would manage to nose or kick the ball back across the corral. The Eaglesons' dog, Ludwig, a canine Michael Jordan, often nosed his way into the activity, making it a threesome. This game could be a real gut-buster, especially because Ludwig was tireless when it came to jumping up in the air to return a flying ball. Some of the horses didn't care for the ball activity, but once Lud got involved, they usually got sucked in to the fun.

Besides the group meets, there were private sessions that allowed each person to work on a goal with a partner horse. Early on, Wynonna had matched each family member with a horse. Lauren worked with wise, slow-moving Yoda. Sierra was on a mission to break Penny, the pony, of her habit of always following other horses around the corral. "If the other horses jumped off a cliff, would you follow?" Sierra asked the pony, sounding like very much like a parent. "The answer is yes," Wynonna said, "but we're going to work on adapting that behavior." Rachel was assigned Flicker, the giant draft horse who was the self-appointed boss of the herd. And Dan was getting to know Hero, a chocolate brown stallion with a touch of neuroticism.

Usually Hero was a willing partner, but when he got spooked, he bucked and jumped a few steps. Your basic horse freak-out. And any sudden noise or movement could set Hero off, including a flapping tarp, a piece of trash blowing in the wind, or the noise of a motorcycle or thunderclap. Wynonna told them of horses who got spooked by things as basic as mailboxes or puddles. "You can imagine what a challenge they are to ride." She also explained that Hero's reaction to his fear had improved. "He used to go galloping off when he was frightened. Now, as you see, he'll react, but not as violently."

Violent or not, when a half-ton of horse started jumping around, you did not want to be in the same corral. So Wynonna and Jazz had been teaching Dan how to manage Hero better in a crisis.

"Horses are linear thinkers," Wynonna had explained in the first days of working with Hero. "They can only focus on one thing at a time. So if we can get Hero to think about doing something else when he gets spooked, even if it's just looking down or turning to the side, he'll be dealing with his fear in an acceptable way."

"A lot of people try to soothe their horse when it gets spooked," Jazz had said. "People try to pat the horse and tell him it's okay, but that really just tells the horse that it's good to get spooked."

The therapist had outlined three steps to help Hero modify his behavior.

"First, we want to redirect Hero's focus when he gets spooked. It would also be good to teach him a cue to calm him down. Maybe we could teach him to turn away or drop his head to the ground when he gets scared. Horses don't rear or jump around when they have their head to the ground. And the third factor is the rider, who needs to stay calm when Hero gets spooked. The more confident you are, the more confident and brave he will be."

Dan loved the logic of the training. "But I'm a little confused," he'd said to Wynonna. "Who's in therapy here, me or the horse?"

Her dark eyes gazed out over the horizon as if to say that the answer was in the clouds, the sky, and the mountains.

So far, Dan had mastered the art of controlling his horse from the ground. He had learned how to get Hero to stop and put his head to the ground instead of rocking and stamping around when the horse was afraid.

But today Wynonna had wanted to expand the lesson by bringing in Lauren. That pleased Dan, who had admitted to being a tad envious when Rachel, with her superior riding abilities, had started riding with Lauren. He wanted that same closeness with the daughter who had disappeared as a girl and returned as a woman.

"You've done a good job with him, Dad," Lauren said as the horse walked alongside Dan with barely a touch to the halter. "He trusts you now."

"And watch this. This is the 'calm down' cue I've taught him." Dan paused and gently pulled the harness down. "Drop down, Hero."

The horse stopped walking and lowered his head, nearly touching the ground.

"Good boy. Good boy!" Dan stepped close and praised the horse, rubbing his neck.

Lauren smiled and reached up to pat the horse's flank. "Perfect! You are both excellent students," she said in a confident tone that reminded Dan of their teacher and therapist. "Did you move close to try and block his view?" she asked.

"That's part of it. If he gets scared by a moving squirrel or a piece of blowing trash, one of his big triggers, I can partially block his view of the thing that scares him. Of course, that won't work if he gets startled by a loud noise like thunder. Can't really put earmuffs on him."

"Right." Lauren smiled and gave the horse one last pat. Then Dan cued the horse to lift his head and continue walking.

"I see you two are ready for the true test," Wynonna called.

Dan turned to see the therapist and her younger son open the gate of the corral. Jazz held one hand behind his back, hiding the dreaded fear trigger.

"Isn't it mean to scare poor Hero deliberately?" Lauren asked.

"It's necessary so that we can teach him how to respond in a safe way," Jazz answered. "We're not hurting him, and this lesson could save him or his rider from danger. Without the ability to calm down, a horse can go out of control. He can hurt his rider and himself, too."

"It's okay, Hero," Dan told the big brown giant. The horse stared at him with soft brown eyes. Trusting eyes. "We're gonna get through this."

Wynonna motioned Lauren to the gate, where they exited the corral to watch in safety. Lauren climbed the fence and leaned her elbows on the top plank.

"Ready?" Jazz asked.

"Go for it." Dan took a calming breath, knowing that the slightest scent of fear on his part could amplify the fright factor for the horse.

On cue, Jazz brought his hand out and tugged on a string attached to a wrinkled section of newspaper. He waved it through the air, as if trying to launch a kite. The airborne paper had all the rattle and unpredictability to send the horse into a nervous frenzy.

Dan felt a tug on the lead as Hero pawed at the ground with his feet and started to back toward the fence.

"Hero, drop down." As he gave the order, Dan pulled down on the horse's halter.

Immediately, the horse's head dropped to the ground as the rest of his body stilled.

"Good horse!" Dan said, loving him up. "Good job."

"Nice!" Wynonna called. "Why don't you try it a few more times so we can be sure he really gets it?"

They took Hero through the exercise twice more. The last time, Dan held the horse in place while Jazz actually twirled the newspaper over the horse's back. Poor Hero's flanks were quivering, but the horse kept his head down.

When Jazz removed the trash "threat" and the ladies came into the arena, Dan loved the horse up with sincere pleasure and trust. Who knew it would be so satisfying to keep repeating a simple lesson with a half-ton hunk of horse? But it was.

"Nice work, Dan." Wynonna tipped her hat back. "What does this tell us about dealing with fear?"

"Try to distract yourself?" he said.

"Sometimes that works. The thing is, we cannot remove the threat from a horse's life, just as we can't always remove the things that scare us from our lives."

Dan thought about Lauren's worries over Mac, fears that kept her up at night. He thought of his own basket of fears, his worries about his girls, the fear that he could not protect them in this world.

"We cannot stop the thunder or the stray leaf from scaring Hero. But now we have a way to help him deal with his fears. You know, a lot of people have a tendency to try to soothe an animal out of fear. When they get scared, we stroke them and say it's all right. But that just reinforces them getting frightened. Instead, we need to distract the horse, just as you did, Dan, and save the praise for when he gets himself to a safe, relatively calm state."

"So are you saying we don't always have to face our fears?" Lauren asked.

"We don't. Some fears may seem irrational, but they're rooted in logic. Fear is nature's way of warning us that something is a danger to us. If we see a man with a knife coming down the street, we feel fear and we run the other way. At least, we should. The gift of fear is our instinctive way of saving our hide."

*   *   *

Later that day, everyone assembled in the sunroom as rain poured down the glass walls all around them. Dan wore the horsehead cap with its ears turned down in a sign of sadness. "Mom and I are in a quandary. We've invited some close family and friends to your grandparents' lake house for the Fourth, but now we're not so sure the party should go off as planned."

"You want to cancel because you're concerned about Mac?" Wynonna asked.

"Well, yeah. It seems wrong to be celebrating without her."

"Are you planning to spend the evening out searching for her?"

Dan and Rachel exchanged a look of doubt.

"No. We wouldn't be searching at night unless there was a good reason," Rachel said. In fact, the search for Mac felt like an adventure into darkness, a river voyage into the heart of a suburban jungle in search of an unknown, unseen child.

Wynonna pressed her lips together, deliberating before she spoke. "You can have the gathering, or cancel it. Either action isn't going to affect your search for Mac. You may feel better keeping a low profile and not having to entertain. Or you might find comfort in the company of people who care about you."

Dan was impressed, though he half-expected the horse whisperer to add: "That is all, Grasshopper."

Chapter 44

When she'd agreed to attend the Fourth of July barbecue at Doug and Alice O'Neil's lake house, Paula had no idea there'd been some matchmaking behind the scenes. Very few people knew about her ties with Hank. She had been honest with Lauren only because the girl had asked, and Paula believed that a client had a right to some personal information about the caretaker she had attached to. Well, Lauren must have spilled the beans to Rachel and Dan; no sooner had Paula arrived than they rustled her down to the dock with a tale about the fabulous lake tour Hank gave on his boat.

And though the yard was filled with more than half a dozen teens playing badminton, how curious that they weren't interested in heading out on the water. Nope, it was just Hank and Paula, chugging out of East Bay on his shiny red boat.

"Come sit beside me. I need a copilot," Hank said, reaching out to her. She moved from her seat at the back and took his hand.

"Lake tour my ass. We've been set up." She sat beside him as he kissed her hand. So gallant. Hank had been alone a long time too, and he'd admitted his insecurity about how corny he became when dealing with the opposite sex.

"It's like one of those reality shows," he said, navigating through the tunnel. "Only there's just one bachelor and one bachelorette."

She sneaked over and sat on his lap in the dark. "One, my dear, is all you need." Their lips met in a sweet kiss, and then she was back in her seat, hands in her lap. It wouldn't do for the Mirror Lake police chief to be seen necking in a boat on the Fourth of July. She and Hank were going to have to break this to the community gently.

They plunged from the shadows to the sunshine of the main lake, and she let out a whoop as Hank gave it some gas. Add the need for speed to his protective nature, gentle hands, and prowess with a pistol. Yes, this was love.

With the wind lifting her hair and the gentle spray of lake water cooling her arms as Hank cut the boat right and left, Paula reveled in a youthful joy that took her back to the days before she'd lost George. Their halcyon days, their Camelot, when each day ended with them watching the sunset from the porch, ice-cold martini in hand, while the kids played in the backyard. Although the future had seemed ripe with possibility, the present had been equally plentiful with the sense that they had faced the most atrocious obstacle of their life and won. George had served in Vietnam, survived the killing fields, the napalm bombings, the constant fear, and the maze of land mines. He had survived—returned home intact—and they had been granted a chance to enjoy each other and their children in the blessed peace and green space of western Oregon.

Damn, but those were good days. She had thought they'd last forever, George and her. She'd been too wrapped up in her own world—the kids, the job, dinner and dishes—to notice that George was suffering post-traumatic stress at a time when most psychologists had no name for the disenfranchisement and depression that plagued Vietnam veterans. Looking back, she was glad that difficult chapter of her life had ended. Over and done.

She had moved on, and now, this week, she was moving on once again, transitioning from full-time caretaker back to artist and social worker. She would miss Lauren, but this wondrous girl had blown her out of the water. Paula had no idea how empty her life was when that girl walked in. Sure, she had her art, and her job—so much paperwork and babysitting. Her grandchildren were delicious little things, but they lived down in the Bay Area, too far to be a regular part of her life. She had thought her life had been full, satisfying . . . self-actualized. But working with Lauren had shown her how far she had removed herself from the daily cares of the rest of mankind.

And Lauren had taught her that growth and transition were still a viable possibility. Paula couldn't even measure how much Lauren had progressed in one month. The wounded waif who had become her shadow from the day of recovery had evolved into a more assertive young woman, a person who had learned to question authority while maintaining a sensitivity that could warm the coldest heart.

Yes, she would miss her needy companion, but she was grateful for the young woman she could call her friend.

And then, there was the other relationship that had developed through her involvement with Lauren's case: Hank. At this stage in her life, Paula had not been looking for love, but, oh, she'd found it in this warm teddy bear with a grizzly bear exterior.

The lake was unusually rough from the wakes and swells created by the water traffic. After a few loops, Hank decided they might be better off taking the boat out when it was less crowded.

"I will definitely take you up on that invitation," Paula said.

Hank headed back, cutting the boat's speed down to a whisper when they noticed that the teens were now jumping off the dock and paddling kayaks and stand-up paddleboards out along the bay.

After they tied off, Hank headed into the house, but Paula stayed back, claiming that she was unable to resist the "delicious sun" still lingering on the dock. She plopped herself in an Adirondack chair, closed her eyes, and listened. She had thought it might be good to lend some moral support to Lauren, but from the dynamics of the conversation, it was clear that Lauren did not need to be saved.

Most of the girls were keenly interested in Jazz Eagleson, Wynonna's son. They wanted to know about the ranch, about the horses, but he kept deferring to Lauren.

"If you really want to know about horses, Lauren is the one to ask. I've never seen anyone get Yoda's undivided attention the way she does. Yoda used to be the lazy man of our herd. Sometimes, you'd take him out to trot and he'd just pull up and freeze like a figure in a wax museum."

"Your mom told me that story, but I can't believe it," Lauren said. "Yoda is such a sweetheart, and he wants to please. He tries to do what you say."

"Maybe for you," he teased. "You've got the magic touch."

The other girls eyed Lauren with envy, but Lauren didn't seem aware of it. She just leaned back on the dock and splashed her legs in the water.

Upstairs on the deck, the adults were talking shop once again. Rachel was selling Hank on a plan to scrutinize birth certificates for girls Mac's age registered for nursery or preschool in the fall. Not a bad idea. Hank answered that they were in the process of reviewing the paperwork of all legal adoptions that had taken place in Oregon in the past six months. Wynonna's husband, Vic, was discussing grilling techniques with Doug. Dan was talking about the canine dogs he'd seen in action on search-and-rescue missions.

"They're so well trained," Dan said. "Great workers. I grew up with dogs in the house, and I miss that unconditional love. Dogs don't see the color of your skin. They don't know pretty from ugly or fat from thin. But they seem to know when you're having a bad day. A dog, he just knows it. And he'll come right over and put his nose to your knee and love you up."

"That's it!" Wynonna shouted as she rose to refill her lemonade. "You need a dog! Two dogs. They make great home therapists for you and your kids alike."

"Oh, no, no!" Rachel interrupted her conversation with Hank to add her two cents. "If we get a dog, *I* get the privilege of walking it, feeding it, and cleaning up after it."

"Rachel, sweetheart." Dan put his arm around his wife with a wide grin. "The therapist recommends it. How can you say no to man's best friend?"

"Easy. I just say no."

Laughter rippled through the group as the debate about adopting a dog carried on. As Paula helped set up for dinner, she shared her observations about the youth dynamic on the dock with Rachel and Wynonna.

"How is Lauren doing with the group?" Rachel asked tentatively. "She's not used to social situations with people her age, let alone so many. I thought it would be nice to invite Nora; I never expected that she would bring a handful of friends, but that's what happens when you have a party on the lake."

"It's something Lauren needs to learn to handle," Wynonna said evenly. "She knows she can back off and take a break if it begins to be too much for her."

"When I was down there, she was doing just fine. All the girls are fawning over Jazz, which is understandable with a guy that adorable," Paula said, shooting a look at his mom, "but Jazz seems to be sticking by Lauren. I don't know if he's trying to boost her self-confidence or if he really enjoys her company that much."

"Jazz is not a game-player," Wynonna said. "He says what he means and stands by his word."

"And he's a man? How refreshing," Paula teased.

"But doesn't he have a girlfriend at college?" Rachel asked.

"He did. I think they broke up, but we haven't really discussed it. He's working the ranch for the summer, and I've heard no mention of any visits from friends."

Rachel sighed. "Maybe it's a moot point. Lauren told me they were just friends, that she was glad he had a girlfriend because that takes away the strain of even thinking about a romantic relationship."

"That's very mature of her," Wynonna said.

"Mature, yes," Rachel agreed. "But I don't know if it's true."

"Listen to us, talking about their relationships like old busybodies." Paula shot a look out the window to the dock, where the kids were out of the water and wrapped in towels. Some headed up to the house to change for dinner. Squinting, she saw that Jazz and Lauren were the last two on the dock. Sitting side by side, they shared a big towel that was spread across their shoulders like a blanket.

Good kids. Paula didn't know what would come of their relationship, but she felt confident that the outcome would not harm Lauren. Whether she became the heartbreaker or the heartbroken, wasn't the value in the relationship itself?

The voyage. The journey. Whatever the destination, Lauren was on her way now, a traveler on the road of life. And she was going to be just fine.

Chapter 45

"It's not such a bad place," Lauren said, as if the ramshackle compound needed defending.

She walked along the edge of the garden, some parts now overgrown with weeds as tall as Mac, while other areas bore the scars of the extensive digging that had been done during the search for the child's remains. Hank said that they'd ended up bringing a bulldozer in, to be absolutely sure, and Lauren found herself wondering what she might have grown back here if she'd had a bulldozer. The plot of land had been much improved by the removal of the rubbish heaps and the old rusty car that she had finally gotten Mac to avoid after the little girl had scraped her arm on the door.

The cabin was stained with dirt and mildew, and the shed still leaned precariously, as if a good, stiff wind would put the small structure out of its misery. The grounds were mottled with the scars of digging, but sunshine rained down on the open plot, redeeming it in the most natural way.

"It's not as bad as I remember it," she told her mother, who had been careful to walk alongside her, as if she expected Lauren to faint or burst into tears or something.

"Can't put any blame on the place," Mom said quietly. "You were a prisoner here. Terrible things happened to you here." She scanned the fenced-in area, the garden, cabin, and shed. "And I can only imagine how lonely you must have been. But I don't think that makes the land tainted."

"It's hot back here." The sunlight was stark, and the breeze didn't make it past the trees that surrounded the compound, blocking it from outside view. Lauren shoved her hands into the pockets of her jeans, which she'd worn for the trek through the brambles outside the fence. They'd been good protection, but now she was hot and her throat was dry. She figured she could get water inside the cabin, but she didn't have the nerve to penetrate the darkness yet.

"Don't get upset, Mom, but there was a time when I wanted to come back here. It was familiar and safe for me. I mean, I knew what I had here." Her sneakers scraped over the spot where her tent had been set up. Now just a patch of compacted dirt, it had been her private home. Kevin usually left Mac and her alone in there, unless he had some crazy scheme going on.

"And now?" Her mom slid the small pack from her back, zipped it open, and handed Lauren a bottle of water. "Does it offer you any comfort now?"

She frowned at the shed. Was the giant crate still in there—her cage? Or had the police removed it. The cabin . . . it was bound to be dark inside and smelling of mold and echoing with terrifying memories. "There's no comfort here. And it's not safe." Kevin had tricked her into believing he'd made everything right for her, but it had all been an illusion. A string of lies. "It was never safe at all. But I think we need to check inside. I know the police were here, but I just need to know that Mac didn't come back here." A crazy thought, but then Wynonna had taught her that sometimes you had to float crazy thoughts out there to find out if they had any merit.

A noise at the gate told them that Dad was there with his friends from the firehouse, who had volunteered to help them take any artwork that was removable. Sully had a big truck for hauling, and Tuna did construction work on the side. Among the three of them, Dad figured they would know what could be removed and how to do it. As the three men paused inside the gate, Lauren felt a stab of embarrassment. What if these men took one look inside and laughed out loud at her creations?

She need not have worried. Inside the cabin, both men were awestruck.

"This is amazing," Tuna said, staring up at the painting of a woman arching through a starry sky, anchored by the tail of a purple dragon coiled around her ankles.

"You really got some talent, Lauren," Sully pressed on the edges of a wall, which shifted back. "Oh, yeah, this will come right out, no problem. So Lauren, have you ever thought about art school?"

"I used to think about it," she said, glad her voice sounded steady. She still wasn't used to talking to strangers, but over the past few weeks she had seen enough of Dad's friends to gain some ease around them. "I still love to draw and paint, but the idea of being inside a classroom makes me feel too closed in. I need to be outside."

"I hear ya," Sully said. "I could never work in an office. I need to see the sky, even when it's gray and rainy."

Tuna moved over to one of the beams, which was textured with crayon that Lauren had melted. "As far as these go, I'm not sure." He removed his hat and scratched at the fringe of hair behind one ear. "If the structure is coming down, we could slice through the joints."

"Vera Hawkins has told us to take anything we want, just as long as no one gets hurt dismantling the cabin," Mom said. "These buildings are going to be torn down next week. That's why we wanted to get in here and save Lauren's art."

"Yeah." Dad swiped away some cobwebs with an old broom that had been left there. "Vera wants to be done with all this. Done with us, too."

Lauren sensed that her parents were angry with Vera Hawkins for letting her nephew live back here, but Lauren didn't hold a grudge. Having never met the woman, she believed Vera's story. The woman had been trying to help Kevin, and she had no idea Lauren was being held in the back acres of Green Spring Farm.

Tuna turned to Lauren. "I don't know if you'd ever want to do this, but I bet some museum would love to make an exhibit out of this art. It would appeal to young people, and old guys like us, too."

"Speak for yourself, Tuna," Sully said. "I'm not old."

"You're older than me," Tuna countered.

"Still, I'm not old. Old is when you lose your hair."

"Come on, brother," Tuna teased, his blue eyes twinkling. "Old is gray hair."

Sully ran a hand over his thick, silver crew cut. "Listen, buddy, I'd rather have snow on the roof than no roof at all."

Dad shook his head, but Lauren could see a hint of a smile. "You guys should take that act to a comedy club."

"You can see us at the firehouse, Saturday night," Tuna mimicked a drum roll. "Ba-dum-bum."

Mom chuckled. "You guys are too much."

A small laugh bubbled up inside Lauren as the guys chuckled. This was something she had missed: the easy camaraderie of friends. Granted, she hadn't been that social when she was eleven and wrapped up in her art. But she enjoyed the easy chatter Dad had with his friends. It made her heart feel light, even in this dark cabin, oozing with some painful memories.

Did she have any possibilities for friends now? There was Jazz. She could be herself around him, and she loved watching him care for the horses. Horses could bring out the true nature of a person, and inside Jazz was golden, kind and strong and responsible. Sometimes she wondered if she might be more than a friend to him. Sure, he had a girlfriend at college, a girl named Dallas, but he hadn't seen her for weeks, and he never talked about her. Well, even if he didn't like her that way, she was grateful for his friendship. That part felt real.

Nora was in a different mind-set, a world with priorities and a language Lauren did not understand. The talk of boys and college, clothes and drunken parties didn't strike anything authentic inside her. She felt more at ease with Paula, who was probably sixty years old, or Sierra, who was only twelve. Maybe being a dinosaur wasn't so bad.

Before anything was removed from the compound, Dan organized the guys to search in nooks and crannies, looking for any sign that Mac might have returned here after the police left. The men did discover some drug paraphernalia in the shed, probably from some kids who'd found their way in. Otherwise, there was no sign of Mac.

It took most of the afternoon, but the men managed to extract almost two dozen different panels and beams from the cabin. Everything was loaded into the truck, except for the panels with the mother and angel baby, which would go to the garage at home for now. Sully had brought special padded blankets to wrap things in, and Mom had rented a space at a storage facility in Mirror Lake. They managed to salvage a lot of Lauren's art, and though Lauren wasn't sure what they would do with the pieces, she was glad it had been saved. The paintings documented a terrible part of her life, but her own emotions were mixed into the swirls of color and texture, and that part was good.

She had learned that certain pieces from the past held intrinsic value, even if the emotion they represented was dark or sad. In therapy, she had learned about yin and yang, the two opposing sides in human nature.

Male and female, darkness and light, cold and hot, evil and good. At first she had told Wynonna that she wanted to be only yang, the sunny side of the slope. But Wynonna pointed out that the sun always moves across the slope, obscuring what was revealed and revealing what was hidden. "You want to be eternal sunshine? Endless day. Relentless heat?" Wynonna had asked.

"Well, not exactly."

"The nurturing instinct is strong inside you," the therapist had told her. "That's yin. There's a little bit of yin and yang in all of us," Wynonna had explained. "Yin and yang don't exist separately, and there's always interplay between them. That contrast makes for many of the juicier moments in life. The serenity of night is sometimes what we need. And at times we appreciate the sunlight more when we've been living in darkness."

That is why I need to be out in the sunlight, Lauren thought as she stood back while the guys loaded up the last of the pieces. She understood what Wynonna meant about balance, but she was ready for the light now. After six years in this prison, she was ready for the sunlight of the soul. It was time to breathe in some yang.

Chapter 46

Lauren looked around the office and wondered why no one put colorful paintings or decorations on the walls. There was so much gray, a person could die in here, just from lack of contrast and definition.

"Here are some more cuties," Rachel said as she scrolled through files on the computer at Mirror Lake's Board of Education.

From the sound of Mom's voice, Lauren knew it was not a photo of Mac, but she gazed up at the computer and focused on the picture of the smiling first-grader. Freckles were sprinkled across her nose, and she was missing two teeth. Lauren bit her bottom lip. The kid was cute, and she looked at the camera with such trusting eyes. Eyes that said: My world is a happy place!

If someone captured Mac in a photo, would her eyes sparkle with that childlike bliss? Lauren wasn't sure. But the more photos of schoolchildren they screened, the more convinced she was becoming that they were not going to find Mac this way.

"Is that a no?" Rachel asked.

"It's not her. First grade would be too old for Mac, anyway."

"True, but we finished screening the kindergartners last week, and the pre-K kids were done in the beginning of July. This is a long shot, I know, but sometimes those big gambles pay off."

"What happened with those little kids who didn't have photos or birth certificates?" They had come across three files that were incomplete, which Rachel had flagged.

"I pointed them out to Hank, and he took the information. Last night I looked up the addresses on MapQuest. Two of them are in that development on the other side of Mirror Lake, and one is right on the lake—a big piece of property, but I can't tell which house. Google Maps wouldn't give me a picture."

"Can we go to those houses?" Lauren asked.

"Maybe. We'll keep an eye on them as more information comes in. How about this one, just registered? Carrie Scott."

Lauren frowned. "Too old. Mom, Mac is way too young for first grade."

"But it sounds like Mac has an excellent vocabulary, and you never know. If the kidnapper is making up a fake birth certificate anyway, he or she might have decided to lie about Mac's age to throw off a search like this."

Lauren shook her head slowly, hating the chill of the air conditioner. She wanted to be outside in the sunshine, brushing down Yoda or taking the kayaks out with Sierra on the lake. One thing she'd learned about herself in therapy: indoor work put her in a bad mood.

Still, this was important. She watched the screen as her mother scrolled through more files, each with a child's image embedded in the upper-right corner. Mom was good at moving around on the computer, and she knew she could rule out boys or children who did not come close to matching the portrait Lauren had drawn of her daughter. Besides, part of the deal was having Mom and only Mom—a teacher in the Mirror Lake School District—actually use the computer. The superintendent's argument that these were confidential files had been countered by the police chief's assurance that this was an ongoing criminal investigation and that an employee would be handling the confidential information.

They were so secretive, so protective of these children, Lauren thought as she shook off another photo, a sweet girl with a Dutch boy haircut. She was glad for the security they had in place, though she wasn't sure that what had happened to her could have been avoided. Kevin had told her that he'd been watching her walk home from school, clocking her afternoon route, for weeks.

"Lauren?" Mom cocked her head to one side to study her. "Are you okay?"

"I don't think we're going to find her this way, Mom. If the person who kidnapped Mac has her in Mirror Lake or one of the nearby towns, they're probably not going to let her go to school at all."

Rachel sighed. "That's probably true, but we can't stop trying."

"No. I didn't mean that we should stop. I just—"

"Lauren." Rachel swiveled around in the chair and put her hands on Lauren's shoulders. "We are not going to stop until we find her." She frowned at the computer. "It looks like we're done here for the day, but this isn't our only resource." She checked her watch. "You're supposed to be at Wynonna's by three, but I guess we have time."

"Time for what?"

Rachel logged off the computer and stood up. "I got an address for Gabby Haggart."

Gabby . . . "Kevin's girlfriend." The one who'd been smoking outside in the compound.

"That's the one. I couldn't get a phone number, so I figured we might have to drop by and hope to catch her."

"Okay." Lauren rose from the chair, a mixture of surprise and wariness churning inside her. She did not like walking into unfamiliar settings, but with Mom guiding her, she thought she could handle it. "Do you think she'll want to talk to us?" she asked as she followed Mom out the door.

"Probably not," Mom said. "But we'll persist. If you haven't noticed, I can come on pretty strong when I need to."

Lauren laughed as they pushed open the double doors and stepped into the sunshine.

Chapter 47

What was she dragging her daughter into? Rachel began to have second thoughts about this adventure as she faced the middle-aged woman with painfully short hair and a mouth pinched tight in disapproval.

The woman didn't spare a smile as she leaned into the shadow behind the door. "I got no time to talk about Jesus. Let's leave it at that."

Rachel looked back at Lauren. In their skirts and blouses, they'd been mistaken for door-to-door missionaries.

"Oh, no, we're not trying to convert you. We're looking for Gabby Haggart." The girl with the teardrop tattoo. Was this woman her mother? Did she approve of the tat? "Is she home?"

"Who are you?"

"Rachel and Lauren." Rachel knew that if she explained, this woman would slam the door in her face. "Gabby knows Lauren. They met. A few times." It wasn't a lie, but it didn't endear the woman to them.

"I'll tell her." And the woman disappeared, slamming the door behind her.

Rachel stepped down from the porch, joining her daughter in the packed-dirt driveway. "I can't tell if that meant she was home or not." She turned toward the house, an ill-kept ranch with a trailer home parked in the driveway. The bottom of the front door was scuffed from so much kicking or the scratching of a dog. The windows were covered with yellowed newspaper that had been taped up inside. "Should we come back another time?"

"We're here." Lauren kept her eyes on the front door. "We might as well wait. I need to feel like I'm doing something, anything, to get closer to Mac."

Rachel could understand that, but perhaps trespassing on the Haggarts' property was not the best approach.

A minute later, the door opened and a round young woman emerged from the house and descended the steps. Ignoring them, the woman walked to the shiny car on the dirt lawn.

Was that her? Rachel didn't see the teardrop tattoo. "Gabby Haggart?" she asked.

The young woman shook her head. When she smiled, a gap in her front teeth was evident. "I'm her sister Eleanor. Gabby'll be right out, but we have to go." Eleanor got into the car and turned on the radio. A country pop song. She sat there waiting for three minutes, then cut the engine, got out, and yelled into the front door of the house. "I told you, I'm not gonna let you make me late for work. If you're not here in ten seconds, you're taking the bus."

"Wait!" someone called from inside the dark crack of the door.

"I already did!" Eleanor yelled. She began to give the door of the house a slam, then caught herself when she noticed Rachel and Lauren watching. She flashed them that odd, gap-toothed smile, then let the door close softly and got back in the car. With the radio blasting once again, she checked herself in the mirror, frowned at the dashboard, and put the car into gear. The cute little Kia crunched over the dirt driveway, then sped onto the road with a gust of red dust.

Lauren's eyes widened. "That's not very nice, leaving her sister behind."

"It's not," Rachel agreed. "Though we don't know the whole story. It can be frustrating to always be waiting for someone who's chronically late." She knew firsthand. Sierra was in that stage where she couldn't pull herself away from the mirror.

Thirty seconds later, the front door opened and a young woman scowled out at the driveway. Gems sparked on her fingers and ears, which were prominent due to the short, wild haircut that was moussed to bright orange spikes. "Dammit, Eleanor!" She hitched a batik print tote bag on one shoulder, then hurried down the steps, right past Rachel and Lauren.

The telltale tattoo dripped down her cheek.

"Gabby?" Rachel called. "You got a minute?"

"Not really." Gabby's gray eyes, flashing inside dark circles of eyeliner, were piercing. "I have to get to school, and now I'm going to have to take the bus."

"We wanted to ask you some questions about your boyfriend, Kevin." Lauren stepped up, her voice engaging and kind.

Her sincerity and poise surprised Rachel. Apparently, it disarmed Gabby, too, because the young woman paused.

"Kevin used to be my boyfriend." She looked back at the house. "I don't date prisoners."

"My name is Lauren, but he used to call me Sis." Lau-

ren's amber eyes were open and friendly, nonjudgmen-
tal. "We met at the compound behind Green Spring
Farm when you were visiting."

Gabby's eyes grew wide. "I don't know what you're
talking about. I've never been to that old farm, and right
now I gotta go or I'll be late for cosmetology school. So,
yeah. . . . see ya." She cut between Rachel and Lauren
and strode down the driveway to the street.

"She's lying," Lauren said quietly. "She came to the
compound with Kevin. More than once."

"Yup. You hit a nerve." Rachel had an idea. "Let's follow her. Maybe if we offer her a ride to school, she'll
open up a little more."

As Rachel slowed the car along the sidewalk, Lauren
stepped up once again with an earnest offer of a ride
into Portland.

Pausing on the sidewalk to squint down at the car,
Gabby seemed perplexed, but interested. "It's over on
Hawthorne," she said. "Do you know how to get to
Hawthorne?"

When Rachel assured her she could figure it out, the
young woman hopped into the car. In the rearview mirror, Rachel saw her staring sullenly out the window. She
figured it would be best to let the girl warm to them.
She asked questions about beauty school and listened
as Gabby talked about not being sure where she wanted
to end up.

"All I know is, I've always been good with hair and
makeup, and I know I need a job. So I figured I'd get
hooked up with a salon and cut hair, only you need to
finish this program and get a license."

Lauren complimented Gabby on the orange in her
hair, and as the girl talked, she seemed to relax. They
were already in Portland, heading for the bridge to

Hawthorne, when Gabby leaned forward between the two seats.

"You do look familiar," she told Lauren. "Maybe I do remember you. But either way, I can't help you."

Lauren's voice was clear and calm. "Did you ever see my daughter, Mac, at the compound? She's three years old."

Gabby turned to look out the window. "Maybe. I mean, I know I met Kevin's kid. I don't remember where."

"We're trying to find her. I miss her a lot."

"Hold on. Did you say Mac is your daughter?"

Rachel felt Lauren nod.

"Well, that . . . ," Gabby huffed out a breath. "Kevin is such a liar. I swear, I never knew Mac was your baby. I would have dumped Kevin in a red-hot second if I knew. He told me Mac was his . . . that her mother had died in childbirth. It was a heartbreak, he said. He was crying, I swear. He was that convincing."

"Do you miss him?"

Good question, Rachel thought. Lauren had a gift for making Gabby know she wasn't out to hurt her.

"Yes. No. I miss what I thought we were going to have. We were supposed to get married. He promised. We were going to get married and find a place to live."

Rachel bit lips together to keep from commenting. It was best to let Gabby roll.

"After he got money for Mac, he figured baby-making was our ticket to ride." Gabby shifted back, touched the ruffles of her maroon shirt, and rubbed her belly. "You can't tell, can you? The thing is, he got me pregnant, too. He said he'd pay for the hospital and all as long as I agreed to sell the baby, just like Mac. He said lots of people were willing to give good money for a healthy white baby of their own, and that the baby would have a better life, too, living with rich people on the lake or with big farms in the country."

"And you were willing to go along with this?" Rachel asked.

"I was thinking about it. The money would be nice, but something about it didn't feel right. I mean, I didn't want to spend the rest of my life crying in my beer because I made a mistake I couldn't fix." Gabby explained that Kevin had said they would have a baby they could keep when we were both ready. "After I finished cosmetology school and he got out of that hellhole behind his Aunt Vera's farm. He said he'd pay for me to get an abortion, but, I don't know. I just couldn't do it, you know?"

Rachel slowed the car as they approached the school. She knew this was valuable information, but she didn't know if she and Lauren would be able to convince Gabby to go on the record and talk with the police. Gabby and Lauren were talking about babies as she pulled up in front of the beauty academy.

Gabby glanced at the school entrance and sighed. "Shit. I don't even want to go inside. They said I'd be able to work with celebrities. That I could do Rihanna and Britney's hair, and I thought, I know I'm good enough. I can do this. But it's all a lie. There's no celebrities around here. The only thing this school prepares you for is sweeping the floor at Quick Cuts."

Rachel shot a glance at her daughter, who winced and shrugged. Of course, she couldn't expect Lauren to have a solution here. Rachel put the car in park and turned to the young woman in the backseat.

"Gabby, I appreciate your being so forthright with us," Rachel said. "You really don't want to go inside, do you?"

"Hell, no. You got a better idea?"

"I do." Steeling her nerves, Rachel put the car in gear and pulled away from the curb. "And if you don't mind missing school, there's someone I'd like you to meet."

There was an air of reverence in the conference room at the Mirror Lake Police Station; it was as if everyone could feel the shifting planets, the new spin of the Earth that brought them closer to Mac.

Hank did most of the questioning, with a video camera rolling and a female police officer, Candace Evans, taking notes. Although Rachel and Lauren had been asked to wait in the reception area, Hank had made an exception when Gabby had said she was "down with" having them present. "Why would you kick them to the curb when they're the reason I'm here in the first place?" she'd asked Hank. Rachel took that to mean that Gabby felt more comfortable with them in the room.

"So he made a deal to give Mac up for adoption in exchange for money," Hank said. "Did he use the adoption agency where your sister works to make the deal?"

"Eleanor didn't do anything wrong, if that's what you mean," she said. "Sure, he went to her first. He kind of got the idea from her, because she's always talking about these rich people who will give anything for a baby. So she talked to someone at work about it, and they freaked out. Apparently there's all kinds of laws and regulations about adoption, and you can't even get paid to give up your baby, except for money for medical bills and stuff. I mean, how stupid is that? Why give up the kid if you're not getting anything out of it?"

"So Hawkins didn't use Eleanor's employer?" Hank looked down at his files and added, "The Kellerman Agency."

"Nope. No money there. So for a while he and Eleanor

were putting their heads together and trying to decide what couple Eleanor should go after. You know, someone who'd applied to the agency but maybe wasn't going to get a baby? Eleanor was going to find someone desperate and loaded, and then either call them or stop in at their house and offer up Mac."

"When was this?"

"That was, like, January or February. But then Mac got sick, and Eleanor didn't like the plan anymore. She says that people want infants, not three-year-olds, and besides, there was no way she was going to make money on a sick kid. People who are putting up good money want a healthy baby."

And a child with a legitimate birth certificate, Rachel thought. It was hard to keep her barbed comments to herself, but she didn't want to interfere. Gabby Haggart was actually quite gabby, and the girl was a wealth of information on Kevin Hawkins's adoption plans for Mac.

In the end, she didn't know who he sold Mac to. Last she knew, he was giving the little girl to his brother to take her to Utah. "There's barely any adoption rules in that state. Kevin said Steve would handle it all for a cut of the action."

"Did he give Mac to his brother?" Hank asked.

Gabby said she didn't know. She helped him take Mac to the clinic back in February, and that was the last she saw of the kid. When she asked, Kevin said the deal was done, and he wasn't spilling the details for her. "He told me what I didn't know wouldn't hurt me. He had to cut the money down to thirty-five hundred because she had that bad cough, but he got the money. Bought me this diamond earring." She turned to reveal a diamond stud at the bottom of four other gold studs. Gabby described how Kevin worked on her over the next few months, saying they should make a baby so that he could make another sale. "He was so pushy. But I figured if I got pregnant, he'd change his mind. I knew he wouldn't give up our baby. So one thing led to another. Come April, I found out I was pregnant, and Kevin was all over Eleanor, telling her we'd have a good, healthy, white baby to sell." She folded her arms. "I was pissed.

"Next thing I know, I see his mug shot on the news, with him holding up a store. At first I thought he did it for our baby, and I thought it was sort of sweet." She touched her belly, barely visible under the frilly burgundy shirt. "Then, the kidnapping stuff was all over the news, and I started hearing how the girl at the compound wasn't his sister." She gave Lauren a sad look. "I'm sorry, but I thought you were a little slow, that's what he said. And I never lied to you," she added, facing the police chief. "Maybe I didn't tell you the whole truth, but then I never swore on the Bible or anything."

After the interview, as she drove back to the house, Rachel told Lauren that she'd been impressed by the people skills she'd demonstrated dealing with Gabby Haggart. "You really stepped up."

"It wasn't so hard because I had something important to say." Lauren ran her hand over the seat belt, tugging it away from her neck. "I think we make a good team, Mom. I'm the good cop. You're the bad one."

Rachel laughed. "That's the junior high teacher in me."

"Do you think the police will be able to find out who Kevin sold Mac to?" Lauren asked.

"I do. I think it's just a matter of time."

"I hope so. It's weird, but I feel sorry for Gabby. She's

not a very smart girl. I was kidnapped by Kevin, but she chose to be his girlfriend. What's going to happen to her and her baby?"

Rachel didn't know, but she felt a thread of pride in the daughter who had compassion for a girl like Gabby, whose prospects were bleak. "Gabby did make some bad choices, but I think she turned a corner when she refused to sell her baby to someone else. Maybe that was a step in the right direction."

Lauren nodded. "I hope so. It would be terrible if Kevin ruined her life."

Like yours? Rachel thought.

No, honey, no. Your life isn't ruined. It's just beginning.

Chapter 48

In the cool shade beside the barn, Lauren reached up with a sponge full of cold water and rubbed it over Yoda's flank.

"How does that feel, boy?" she asked, washing him down to relieve the excess heat of the stark summer day.

In answer, he blew a gentle breath through his nostrils. *That feels great.*

"I knew you'd like that. It's hot out there, and we don't want you to get overheated."

It was the last week of August, and summer had staked its claim on western Oregon. With temperatures in the nineties, Jazz had warned her that all the horses taken out for any strenuous exercise would need to be cooled down when they returned to the barn. "Although I'm not sure how strenuous it is for you to give Mom and me a ride at the same time," she said as she rubbed down his left side with cold water. "I'll bet it feels awkward with two people on your back, but you don't seem to mind."

As Lauren moved around the front of the horse to wash down his right side, she couldn't resist pausing to press the sponge between his eyes and toy with the little tuft of hair that fell down between his ears like bangs.

"You don't mind me fussing over you, do you? You like a little love and attention," she said as she stroked the hair into a clump, then let it feather back over his head.

"Nah, I don't think he minds your fussing at all," Jazz said from behind her.

"Yoda can speak for himself," she teased without looking back.

"Yeah, I know. He says that when you're done cooling him down, your friend Jazz could use a little love and attention."

She laughed, surprised and excited at the meaning behind his words. "Oh, really? I didn't know you spoke his language."

"We have an understanding. It's a guy thing."

She reached down into the bucket and saw his boots pause in front of the horse. When she looked up, there was Jazz, his cowboy hat propped back so that she could see his hair, damp with sweat, his golden skin a contrast to his white teeth as he smiled. Sweat and dust and grime had never looked so good until she had met Jazz here on the ranch.

"It's good that you're washing him down," he said. "Yoda's extra vulnerable in the sunshine. Did Mom tell you we use sunscreen on his nose?"

"Yup. And I rubbed on some more before we went out, just to be safe." Wynonna had explained that fair horses like Yoda could get sunburn, especially on his sensitive pink nose.

Jazz scratched the horse's neck. "You are one lucky dude."

"Don't be jealous." She leaned down to the bucket again. "I can cool you down too." With that, she put her hands together to cup some water and splash it onto Jazz.

"Hey!" He turned away and the water splashed over the back of his T-shirt. "Ahh." He sighed, then turned and faced her with his arms stretched wide. "Do it again, please."

Laughing, she shoveled two more handfuls of water at him.

"That is awesome. Except I probably smell like horse now."

"Nothing wrong with that. We work in a stable."

"Yeah, but we have to remember that we're the humans. We get to shower."

Smiling, she continued washing down Yoda as they joked about everything and nothing in particular. That was the way her days went here on the ranch. Therapy often had her digging deep into the past or searching inside her heart, but when she was out here caring for the horses, the talk was lighthearted and the work was satisfying. She had come to love the horses, she felt a strong partnership with Jazz, and the hard work distracted her from the problem in her life that she felt helpless to fix: the constant anxiety over her little girl.

She was just finishing up, gushing cold water over Yoda's hindquarters, when Vic called over to her, telling her that Wynonna wanted to see her in the gazebo.

"A summons from the boss," Jazz teased. "I'll finish up here."

"No shortcuts," she said. "This horse doesn't get turned out until he's cooled down and brushed."

"Yes, ma'am," he drawled in a cowboy accent.

As she plunked on her hat and headed away from the barn, Lauren smiled to herself. Where did she learn

to talk to a guy that way? Sometimes she couldn't believe herself lately, but then again, Jazz wasn't some
strange boy she was trying to impress in school. He was
Jazz, her friend, her coworker, her buddy.

She thought about his teasing comment. "Love and
affection?" It sounded sort of romantic, like flirting.
Had he been flirting? Did he like her?

Lauren couldn't tell. But if he felt something special
toward her, well, it wouldn't be a bad thing. Not bad at
all.

Her parents sat opposite Wynonna in the shade of
the gazebo, three plastic glasses of iced tea on the table
before them. Her boots clicked on the wood until she
paused, sensing from her parents' faces that something
was up. Dad looked nervous, almost apologetic, and
Mom was forcing a brave smile.

"What's wrong?" She wiped her hands on the sides of
her jeans. "Did they find Mac?" The words stuck in her
throat like a bitter pill.

Wynonna shook her head. "No, but Hank Todd had
another meeting with Kevin Hawkins, and we wanted to
talk with you about it. Have a seat." She reached forward and poured Lauren a glass of iced tea. That was
Wynonna, always smooth and gracious.

Grateful, Lauren took a long drink of the tea before
facing her parents again.

"Hawkins seems to be feeling some remorse about
what he did to Mac." Her father's face was stern. "He's
promised to give us information about her whereabouts
in exchange for a visit from you. He says that he'll talk,
if he can see you."

"Oh." Lauren's heartbeat was loud in her ears. "I
don't want to see him again."

"We know that, and I don't want you to feel pressured to do this," Dan said.

Mom shook her head. "I don't want you to go. We can protect you from this. We . . . ," Her lower lip wobbled, and she took a breath to compose herself.

"Rachel, I know this is difficult for you, for everyone concerned, but there are other factors to consider." There was a touch of concern in Wynonna's eyes, but otherwise her face was a moon of peace. "First, Hawkins is offering information about Mac that could be instrumental in her rescue. I know this is important to Lauren."

"It's important to all of us," Dan added.

Wynonna nodded. "Yes, and since part of Lauren's therapy is for her to learn as much about Kevin Hawkins as she can stand, it might give her some closure to confront him in prison." She turned to Lauren. "It's something for you to consider. You don't have to decide today."

"I'll do it," Lauren said before fear could eat away at her resolve. "I'll do it for Mac."

"Honey, you don't have to," Mom said. "It will mean visiting a prison. You'll be safe. We would be with you, and there would be guards, but it's bound to be traumatic."

"I've been through trauma," Lauren said. "Look, I wish I could be sure I would never see Kevin again in my life, but he knows about Mac. I can't say no. I need to get my little girl back. You've got to understand that."

Rachel reached over and took Lauren's hand, "I do," she said before tears overtook her.

"I'll tell Hank to set it up," Dad said.

As he left the gazebo to make the call, Lauren's gaze fell on the three candles representing past, present, and future. With this meeting, she might be able to change

Mac's future. Resolve settled within her as she thought of the serenity prayer, the part about fixing things that could be changed.

The courage to change the things I can.

Dear God, please give me courage.

Chapter 49

Lauren was lost—alone in a crowd of strangers in downtown Mirror Lake.

The clinking melody of a xylophone in the Labor Day Parade made the cyclone of people shoving around her all the more surreal. Why had her parents dragged the family here? Who liked parades, anyway? For Lauren, they ranked right up at the top of the creeper list with clowns and guys who drove vans. But Mom said that Mirror Lake always put on a good parade, with marching bands and street jugglers and acrobats. And some of the guys from Dad's firehouse were rolling out their shiny new fire truck. The family was committed to the parade and a backyard party at Nora's mom's house afterward.

And then Sierra had gotten permission to go off with her friend, and while pausing to look at the tall Uncle Sam on stilts, Lauren had gotten separated from her parents. Caught in a sardine can of people.

Panic made her heartbeat race, her palms sweat. How could she fix this? She realized that as she moved away from the street, the crowd began to thin. She squeezed past families and gum-chewing teens until she cleared most of the mob. In the middle of the block, there was a statue of tires with rubber balls shooting out the top, and she climbed onto the cement base to get a better view around her. There was Dad's red baseball cap bobbing in the pack, moving up the slight hill along the parade route.

"Dad!" she shouted, then realized how lame that was with dozens of dads on this block alone. "Daniel O'Neil!"

But he didn't turn around. He seemed to be talking with Mom. Engrossed, probably.

She took a calming breath. It was okay. She would catch up with them. And she had her cell phone. Her cell phone! Why didn't she think of that in the first place? With an easy breath of relief, she took the phone from her pocket and called Mom.

As it was ringing, she looked out over the parade. Some guys in hardhats were walking down the street, waving and tossing candies out to the crowd. From here she had a clear view of the bare street and the opposite side, where a group of boys sat on the curb, an old man sat in a wheelchair, and a little girl swung herself around a lamppost.

The phone was still ringing as she watched the girl, a cute kid with hair that golden shade of Mac's. The girl seemed to be singing to herself, despite the chatter of the crowd and the noise of an approaching marching band, a cacophony of brass and drums.

Lauren smiled. Did all kids sing to themselves?

Wait.

Flashes of Mac, swinging on a post of the fence, singing to herself.

Holding up a hand to shield her eyes from the sun, she saw the truth.

It was Mac. Her Mac.

Her face had thinned out a little. Her chubby cheeks were more girl-like, not so babyish anymore. But her silver blue eyes and fine-boned face were unmistakable. "Mac!" Lauren cupped her hands to her mouth to try to get her daughter's attention, but no one could hear over the passing high school band.

She jumped from the platform and dove into the crowd. People protested when she squeezed in front of them, but she there was no time to explain. She peeled between two men and pushed through, stumbling onto the pavement beside some boys sitting on the curb. Cinders scraped her palms, but she scrambled up to find Mac.

From here she could see across between the rows of legs marching in red pants. The lamppost was right across from her, but she didn't see Mac.

She scrambled to her feet and raced across the street as soon as the band marched past. People yelled and laughed at her as she honed in on the lamppost and paused.

Where was Mac?

The man in the wheelchair was still there, but he shook her questions off. No one else on the street corner had noticed Mac, though one nice lady offered to help her look.

"No, thanks," Lauren said.

There was one thing she knew for certain: Mac had been here in Mirror Lake this afternoon. Her daughter was nearby.

After the parade, Mom and Dad used both cars to drive slowly through the neighborhood, but there was no sign of Mac. Dad insisted on putting ointment on

Lauren's hands from his first aid kit, while Mom called the incident in to Hank Todd.

After the anxiety of being lost and just missing her daughter, Lauren was wiped out. "Can we just go home?" she asked her parents.

"Let's make an appearance," Mom said. "Julia is probably my best friend, and she really wants to see you. Besides, I know she's invited Jazz."

Lauren steeled herself to make it through the party for Mom's sake.

The backyard barbecue was in full swing by the time they arrived. The kitchen table and counters were loaded with salads and desserts.

Mom's friend Julia gave Lauren a big hug. "I hope we get a chance to talk later. I've got some funny stories you can tease your mom about."

Julia directed someone to check the downstairs fridge, then pointed to the salads. "All the perishables are in here. Drinks are in the coolers outside, burgers and hot dogs by the grill."

Outside, rock music mixed with laughter and conversation in a garden edged by thick patches of flowers.

Julia told Lauren that the teens were over in the garage around the side of the house. "They've got music and a Ping-Pong table set up in there. Oh, and Jazz is there. He was asking about you," Julia said with a smile.

Lauren couldn't wait to tell him that she'd seen Mac.

From the backyard, there were stone steps and a path that led down the hill and around the side of the house to the garage. This side of the house was well shaded by a stand of tall yew trees that allowed a lot of privacy from the neighbors and the street.

The door of the single bay was open. Lauren peered into the shadows at the old chair and couch, table, fridge, and dartboard. Three kids sat on the couch, kids who had come to the get-together on the Fourth. The one guy, Andy, was laughing, while Kiki was drinking from a glass vase and the other girl was dozing with her mouth open.

"Hey." Lauren stepped into the dimness to let her eyes adjust. Scented candles were burning, and Lauren got a whiff of sweet cotton candy mixed with burnt cherry.

"How's it going?" Andy said with a wary glance.

Lauren stared at the glass vase and suddenly realized it was some sort of pipe. These kids were smoking. Marijuana? She wasn't sure. For all his craziness, Kevin didn't do any drugs. Beer, yes. Not drugs.

She shifted, uncomfortable, but not wanting to sit down with them. She thought about the time she'd spent with them at the other party. They had been sort of standoffish, though the girls all seemed to like Jazz. Now she wondered how much they knew about her, about the kidnapping and her time in the compound. About what Kevin did to her, which everyone was curious about. Were these kids discussing the sick details when she wasn't around?

She did not want to hang out here. "Have you seen Jazz around?"

The guy pointed a thumb to the wall behind him. "Around the side," he said, taking the glass pipe from the girl.

"Okay. Thanks."

A small barrier of spruce trees blocked the side of the garage. She walked down a few feet to a small space between the trees that seemed to be used as a passageway. Peeking through, she saw Jazz leaning against the wall of the garage, talking with Nora, who had her back to Lauren.

"I can understand you feeling sorry for her," Nora was saying. "I mean, yeah, I get it. But I can tell you two

aren't serious. My mom says that rape colors every relationship you have in your life. Lauren isn't going to go
there."

Jazz said something, but his voice was so low Lauren
couldn't make it out.

"I just don't want you to be hurt," Nora said, step-
ping closer to him so that he was backed against the
garage. "The thing is, you deserve better. Someone new
and sparkly." She put her hands up on his shoulders.
"Someone like me."

Stunned, Lauren stepped out from behind the spruce.
She needed to see the assault, the flash of the blade, the
plunge of the knife.

But her appearance caught Jazz's attention, and he
turned his head toward her just as Nora rose on her
toes to kiss him.

"Lauren!" He stiffened and his arms shot out awkwardly, pushing Nora off balance.

Turning quickly, Lauren squeezed through the spruce
barrier and fled up the path, taking the stone steps two at
a time.

"Lauren, wait!" Jazz called after her.

Her vision blurred with tears, but she swiped them
away to survey the party guests. She had to get out of
here, now.

Dad was over by a bright patch of flowers, talking
with some men. Where was Mom? She spotted her moving away from the crowd, heading for the deck stairs.

Sniffing back tears, Lauren darted over. "Mom?"

"Hey, honey, I was just heading into the kitchen to—"

"Take me home." Her voice was thick with conges-
tion and tears.

Rachel squinted as she caught on to Lauren's state of
mind. "What happened?"

"Just . . . just take me home, please."

"Okay." Mom's voice was a calm whisper as she put an arm around Lauren and pulled her close. "I know a secret path through the garden so we can avoid the kitchen and the garage." She guided Lauren steadily, bright and sure as the North Star. "You just hang on and I'll have you home in a flash."

Chapter 50

Rachel stared at the closed door of Sierra's room, her mouth dry, her heart aching. Inside the bedroom that Lauren and Sierra now seemed to share, Lauren was crying. Sobbing.

Something was very wrong, but Lauren wouldn't talk about it. She had maintained her composure in the car, thanking Rachel for taking her home. And once inside the house, she'd lied, saying that she would be fine, that she needed time alone. Rachel wanted to respect that, give her space. She had learned to treat Lauren as the young woman she had become, not a malleable little girl anymore.

Damn time alone.

Rachel leaned toward the door, broke down, and knocked. "Lauren? I'm coming in." She wasn't going to give her a chance to say no.

Inside, evening sunlight lit the fine tulle sheers with purple flowers embroidered at the bottom. Lauren sat huddled on the bed. Hunched over her legs, she wiped her nose with the back of one hand.

"What happened, Lauren?"

"It doesn't matter. You can't fix it, Mom. No one can."

Rachel paused, an island in the center of the room. "But if you tell me the details, we can discuss it and search for insight. Try to find solutions together. That's what families do."

"So you can call your good friend Julia and tell her to keep her daughter on a leash. Her daughter who was smoking pot with her friends and kissing Jazz and telling him that he's wasting his time with me because I'm a . . . a used up old . . ." A sob cracked her voice and she turned to the wall.

Rachel pressed her palms together in prayer position, her fingertips to her lips. "I won't call Julia," she said firmly, "but I can't believe Nora would stoop so low."

"Well, she did." She picked up Sierra's' stuffed elephant and pressed it to her face. "She said terrible things about me, Mom. And the thing is, I know lots of people are thinking those things. And Jazz, I thought he was different, but when I got there I . . . I think he was kissing Nora back."

"Oh, Lauren." Rachel had to tamp down the fury she felt toward the young people at the party. Nora was a huge disappointment; Jazz, too. Couldn't they see how vulnerable Lauren was right now? She had come so far over the summer. She had grown strong and independent. She had found her voice. It seemed so unfair that her first forays into friendship would be met with backstabbing and rejection.

Rachel longed to take her daughter in her arms and rock her like a baby. Maybe that instinct would never evolve, but Rachel had learned how to approach her wary daughter without making her bolt. She went to the bed and tapped her thigh. "Scooch over," she said. When Lauren did, she sat beside her, her eyes looking away in a nonconfrontational stance. When she sensed Lauren softening against her, she put an arm around her shoulders and held her close.

"Tell me what happened."

And Lauren did, every painful detail, in her blatantly honest manner. She didn't exaggerate; she didn't need to. The truth was loaded with drama.

"And now I'm beginning to see it in the way people look at me. The perverted, sick things they're imagining when they look at me. It's like I'm wearing a scarlet letter. A big *K* for kidnap victim." Lauren sniffed. "No one is ever going to love me. I'll always get the nervous look. People look at me and they remember what Kevin did to me. They know he ruined me. They know I'm scarred inside. Ruined. No one will ever love me."

"But I do." Rachel struggled to keep her voice steady. "I look at you and I see the light inside."

"Of course you see it," Lauren said dismissively. "You're my mother."

"But I'm not alone. There's your dad and Sierra. Other people see it, too. They don't see Kevin Hawkins or what he did to you. They look at you and see a bright, honest, beautiful young woman who has battled through more obstacles in six years than most of us face in a lifetime. They see a survivor."

"I'm just so sick of being damaged."

Lauren's words tore at Rachel, but at the same time Lauren snuggled against her, yearning for comfort and reassurance. That, Rachel could do.

"You spent six years in a terrible place. And you've been working hard these last three months to heal from it." Rachel stroked Lauren's golden hair, gathering it away from the damp nape of her neck. "I know that parts of your heart have healed already, while others will take time. But time will change other people, too. Some will get to know you and be attracted to who you are. Others, people on the fringe, over time they'll forget what happened. Your connection to the kidnapping will fade away to a whisper of memory."

"I hope you're right. I don't want to be broken for the rest of my life."

"Honey, we're all broken in some way. What matters is the care we take putting the pieces back together. And half the time, the re-creation is more wonderful than the old teacup we started with."

"I hope you're right, Mom." Lauren's chest swelled as she took a deep breath. The air stirred against Rachel's neck, reassuring, as her daughter exhaled with a new glaze of calm.

Hugging her daughter close, Rachel closed her eyes and let her mother love flow. It was going to be okay. Oh, there would always be more storms to weather, but holding on to each other, they could wait for the break in the clouds. The bright patch of blue. As long as they kept holding on.

Chapter 51

The moment her boots hit the gravel of the ranch driveway, Lauren headed straight for the barn to find Jazz. She had a session scheduled with Wynonna, but she didn't want to lean on Jazz's mom to pick up the pieces and sort out Lauren's relationship with him. This was her relationship—a friendship, at the very least—and though her face tingled with embarrassment already, Lauren knew she had to take responsibility for straightening things out.

She found him in the barn, working with the farrier who'd come to replace the horses' shoes. They were in Flicker's stall, where the farrier stood bent over with one of the horse's rear hooves propped between his legs.

"Jazz." She kept her voice low, pretending to be calm. "Do you have a minute?"

"Sure." Jazz backed out of Flicker's stall. "Be right back."

"Hold on." The farrier looked up. He was a tall man

with a mustache and no hair on his shiny head. "Is this the girl who's been taking care of Yoda?"

"It is. Lauren O'Neil, meet Dusty Jenson. He already put some new shoes on Yoda."

Lauren nodded at the man, whose eyes seemed stern.

"Lauren, I want to know where you learned to pick out a horse's hoof."

She shot Jazz a nervous look. "Right here. Jazz taught me."

Dusty shook his head. "I've never seen a frog looking so clean, especially after a few days of rain and mud. Good job, girl. Keep at it."

Relief and pride lifted her spirits. "Thanks, Dusty."

Without speaking, the two young people went to the side of the barn that was out of view of the house.

"Did you tell your mother?" she asked.

He shook his head. "I will, but I wanted to square things with you first. I called your cell and left you two texts."

"I know. I don't feel right talking about important things over the phone." Neither of them was looking at the other. It was as if a river flowing between them was tugging them off to the side.

"I didn't kiss her," he said. "I didn't even want to go to that party, but the lady, Julia, she called and told me you'd be there. I only went for you."

"You don't have to explain to me, Jazz."

"But I do. I do care about you, Lauren. A lot. Sort of like a sister, but sort of more than that, too. But when you put a label on it, everything sounds kind of strained and lame. You know what I mean?"

She did. "I'm in about the same place," she said earnestly. "I don't think of you as a boyfriend, but it hurt me to see you with Nora."

"That would have been a betrayal," he said. "But it wasn't the way it looked. She sort of cornered me. I guess I should have seen it coming, because I knew she was flirting when I saw her on the Fourth. But a lot of people flirt. No harm in that. I just . . . I don't know. I feel like an idiot, getting myself into that situation. Even if you hadn't come along, which was awful, I would have had to peel her off me. Awkward. I shouldn't have let it get that far. That's my bad."

She shrugged. "You didn't break any rules. I mean, you're not my boyfriend."

"No, but . . . we have an understanding. At least I thought we did. The way we work together and talk and all. We're like two trees in the wind, bending in the same direction, swaying into each other. Two trees that stand beside each other."

The image struck Lauren as beautiful. "Did you read that in a book?"

"Hell, no." Jazz took off his hat and raked back his hair. "There's something else. I'm not sure how much you heard, but Nora was saying some pretty nasty things about you." He shifted, his mouth screwing up on one side. "I don't even want to repeat it. I just have to tell you, I'm not hanging anywhere near that girl again, and I don't think she's a true friend to you."

Lauren nodded. "No. She's going off to college next week. No great loss."

"Yeah." He stuck his hat on and stepped toward her. "So are we cool?"

Looking up into his dark eyes, she saw trust and concern and respect. Beautiful eyes, a window to his noble soul. "We're good." On a whim, she put on hand on his shirt and rose up to the toes of her boots.

His eyes flared as she brought her lips to his, just for a quick touch. He leaned forward and deepened the kiss, sending her floating a few feet off the ground. When it ended, she thought she might crumple to the ground, but his arms came around her and held her to him.

"I don't think my mom is going to like this," he said. "But I sure do."

"She'll get over it." She ran her hand down his chest, intrigued by the ripple of muscle beneath his T-shirt. "I am seventeen."

"Still at that in-between age. Not an adult yet, but no longer a kid."

Lauren smiled up at him. "Sometimes I feel like I've lived a million lifetimes. My mom says I was always that way. A wise old soul."

"A Yoda. *Stand not in the shade when the sun brighter shines,*" Jazz said in a squeaky voice. "Or something like that. Yoda always talks in puzzles."

"I know. I used to be a sci-fi nerd."

He blinked. "Really? Wow. We'll have to get you up to speed with recent releases. And the *Iron Man* movies. Have you seen any of those?" When she shook her head, he added: "You've got some movie marathons in your future."

"Sounds good." As she leaned against his chest and breathed in the smell of leather and soap, she wondered about Jazz's place in the purple light of the future. She knew he would always be her friend, but she wanted more.

How high can you soar? Her parents' words emerged from her memory. And what was her answer?

To the stars.

Chapter 52

Lauren gaped at the jailhouse corridor that loomed ahead of her, a dead chamber with floors and tiled walls that shone. It had taken a week for Chief Todd to set up this meeting, a week of anticipation and dread. Now that the time had arrived to meet her abductor, Lauren's resolve was weakening. Her legs trembled, and her chest felt so tight it was difficult to breathe.

"This is really scary," she whispered as she waited her turn to walk through the metal detector.

Dad turned to her, his eyes reading her anxiety. "We got this," he said. "Just follow me."

She passed through the metal detector behind him and nearly fell into his arms. Why were her legs so wobbly?

"Remember what Wynonna said about fear?" Dad asked. "It's there for a reason, and we don't always have to look it in the eye. Now walking through here, it's going to be just like the exercise we did with Hero. You're going to keep your head down." He slipped an arm around her. "Just hold on to me, press against my chest, and I'll guide you, okay?"

She looked over at Mom, who was nodding. "Hold on to your Dad. We're going to stick with you, honey."

Lauren closed her eyes and tried to think of things that calmed her. The sound of her sister's breathing at night. The mountains that sat guard at the edge of Spirit Ranch. The nickering sound of horses. Diamonds of sunlight on the lake. When she closed her eyes and pressed against Dad, she could almost block out the guards' voices, the buzz of alarms, the click of high-tech prison doors. It wasn't so much the idea of prison that scared her as the knowledge that he was here. He was the fear she did not want to face.

But Dad kept her safe as long as he could, until they landed at the meeting room. The therapy trick they had taught Hero worked. The only problem was that it didn't make the danger disappear.

And so she sat at the table, half-listening as the guard explained that her parents would be watching from behind a two-way mirror, along with the prosecutor and Kevin's lawyer. There would be a guard in the room with them, so she didn't need to worry about Kevin hurting her. That was what the guard told her. Didn't he know? She wondered. Couldn't he see that the damage had been done?

Goose bumps pricked her upper arms as she heard their footsteps at the door. She pulled her black cotton sweater closed and folded her arms, bracing herself.

A sliver of revulsion sickened her as he walked in, hands cuffed behind him. He had gained some weight and was growing a beard that made him resemble a billy goat. Or maybe the devil. The guard pulled out the chair for him and pressed his shoulders to guide him onto the chair.

That was when he snagged her with his eyes. Cold, piercing eyes. "I knew you would come."

"I'm here for Mac." She would have liked his apology, too, but she had discussed that with Wynonna and realized it was highly unlikely. No, she would stick to her mission to save her daughter. "Where is she?"

"Where is she?" he mimicked. "Is that how you say hello? Don't you want to tell me how much you miss me, Sis?"

The old name, the name he had given her, pierced her resolve like a fat thorn.

"Why did you sell her?" she asked. "If you couldn't afford to take care of us, you could have let us go."

"It wasn't about that. I wasn't the one who let Mac down. It was you. You didn't know how to take care of her. Letting her roam around in dirty clothes. Getting her so sick she needed to go to the hospital. You were a god-awful mother."

Lauren wanted to argue that it wasn't true. She's been a good mother; she knew that now. But then she remembered the way Kevin had won every argument they ever had, because he was in control. Right now, she couldn't give him control. She was here for Mac. It would be great if she could also get closure, but she was not going to get it by fighting with Kevin Hawkins.

"So it was all on you, Sis. If I took it to court, I think what they'd call you is an unfit mother." He spoke with authority, as if he really could have filed a case against Lauren. Now she could see how ludicrous it was, but three months ago, she would have believed him. "You gave me no choice. I gave Mac away to save her life."

"You sold her."

"Just some cash for my troubles, is all. And I set her

up good with a mother older and wiser than you. Someone with the money to take good care of her."

"Who?"

He swatted the question away. "I set her up good and made some money in the process. I was supposed to sell her for five grand, but I had to settle for less because she didn't have a birth certificate. I shoulda printed one on Aunt Vera's computer, but I didn't think of that." He shrugged. "Woulda-coulda-shoulda."

"Did your brother sell her for you? The one in Utah?"

He squinted at her. "Now where'd you hear about Steve?"

She stared at the table, not wanting to think about the gross people who'd come through this room. "The police have been investigating you."

"I bet they have." He shifted in the chair, wincing. "Damned cuffs. Yeah, I was thinking about using my brother. Did you know they call Utah the sewer pit of the adoption industry? Nobody cares about the babies moving through that system. I was going to let Steve take her there and make the sale, but then Mac got sick, and even with the antibiotics, she was crying and coughing like crazy. Steve backed off. Hell, everyone backed away."

"Like Eleanor Haggart?"

"Well, aren't you Nancy Drew? Yeah, Eleanor got cold feet. *'No birth cert and now she's sick? Forget it!'* " The mimicky voice again. "She was in the wind."

He was dragging this out, painfully, and Lauren wanted to cut to the chase. She tried flattery. "I don't know how you pulled it off, with Mac being so sick. How did you manage to find someone to take a sick little girl?"

He tilted his head to the side, the cocky pose. "I hit

gold at the Saturday market. One of the vendors there wanted to adopt her."

"The Saturday market?" Lauren checked to see if he was lying, but his eyes were clear, his hands steady. "So you sold Mac . . . at the Saturday market in Portland?"

"Well, it's not like I set up a booth or anything." He grinned, his lips thin as worms. "But yeah. Some lady there was interested. But she didn't come to me about it. Wanted to keep it anonymous, so if anything ever happened, no one would be able to trace Mac back to her."

"So you don't know her name?"

"Nope."

She sensed that he was telling the truth, and that would be terrible. This wasn't going to get her to Mac. "How did you turn Mac over to her?"

"We used a third party. She paid one of the other vendors to broker the deal. That way, I couldn't come after the family if I changed my mind or wanted more money. And she didn't want you finding out about it and coming after her. Though I guess that's what you're doing now. Only I don't have her info." He pressed two fingers to his temple. "Pretty smart, wasn't she?"

Images of the Portland Saturday Market flashed through her mind. The bright banners, the booths of blades and jewelry and drug paraphernalia and colorful blankets. Who were the vendors that Kevin used to talk with there—the eclectic handful of people whom Kevin considered to be his friends? She didn't really remember. She'd been too busy trying to make money with the portraits to pay attention to Kevin gallivanting around the market with Mac on his hip.

"As far as I know, Mac's long gone. Living like a princess in some rich lady's castle, far away from here."

No, you're so wrong about that. Mac is right here in Oregon. Right in Mirror Lake. She's close . . . so close.

"Snap out of it, Sis. Can't you stay focused for two minutes? You always were a lazy, daydreaming fool."

"Who was the vendor—the one who made the deal?"

The direct question, so on track, took him by surprise. "Some guy. Not really my friend, you know, but he said he could make things happen fast, and he did."

"What was his name?"

"Ya think I remember?"

She nodded.

"It was the blanket man, the guy with the freak holes popped through his ears. Juicy something. Jewzer. I don't know. It's not like I'd ever use him again when I can get a lot more money going through other channels. I let him make the deal because I was in a bind. Mac was sick and all, coughing and crying, and I knew if I brought her back to you it'd be hard to get her away again." He rolled his eyes. "I guess I'm not as cold as you thought. I was sort of attached to that kid, too."

Lauren wanted to laugh in his face. He'd been attached? The man who sold a sick child through a flea market? For the first time she glanced toward the mirror, thinking it was time to go. She sensed that this was all the information she could pry from Kevin. Was it enough?

"I need to go," she said.

"Hold on there, Sis. Fair's fair. I told you what I know about Mac. It's your turn now. You need to tell the police the real truth about what happened with us." He leaned forward, whispering, "Tell them about us."

His vacant, icy eyes and pointy beard reminded her of the devil. Satan. Evil itself.

"I've told them everything."

"Not the true version. How you ran away from home and begged me to save you. You came along for the ride. You pursued me. I was the victim, Sis. A good guy trying to help a wayward girl like yourself."

She turned away, but his words crawled up her shoulders.

"You could have left. You could have climbed that fence and walked straight home any time. But you didn't, and I'll tell you why. You stayed because you wanted to. You wanted to be with me. You realized how nice it is having someone else take care of you. Someone to do all the work and figure out money and all. You had it good with me, Sis. Damned good. And that's what you're going to go out there and tell those guards. Tell the prosecutor and all those other dry balls cops who think they know it all. Tell them you wanted it." He lowered his voice. "Tell them you were a cute little whore, and I had no idea you were under age."

The venom in his voice scared her, but she couldn't fall down now. She had come too far to let him reduce her to the wounded sparrow who cowered under his barbed wing.

"I won," she whispered.

He squinted. "What?"

"I won." She spoke and her voice was there, firm and smooth. "I just want you to know that. You tried to break me. You hurt me. You violated me. But in the end . . ." She shrugged. "I won. I'm healing. I'm still a whole person, and life is good. It's very good, without you."

"You bitch . . ."

She rose and went to the door. She walked without a limp, her soul as light as a cloud. Watching her, no one would guess at the cruelty and abuse that she had overcome. It was a healing moment for Lauren, knowing that this man hadn't snuffed out the beautiful light inside her.

"Good luck out there, Sis," he snarled. "Good luck living in the real world, because you'll never get anything right. You're never going to be happy without me, and you know it."

As the guard opened the door for her, she turned back, wanting the final word.

Facing his sour slash of a mouth and crazy eyes, she changed her mind. He could have the last word; she was sure he'd have plenty of rotten words about her, for the rest of his life. Why argue and waste her breath?

Instead she flashed him a little smile and tinkled her fingers in a wave, just the way she'd taught Mac when she was a baby.

The bye-bye wave.

Chapter 53

On the drive back home from the state penitentiary in Salem, Rachel argued with Hank on the phone. She told him that she knew Ben Juza, the vendor who'd brokered Mac's adoption, and she was going directly into Portland to find him.

"You can't do this alone. This guy is no saint."

"He talked to me and he gave me his card," Rachel said, though she wasn't sure why the man had opened up to her, even a little.

"And Juza has a reputation for dissing the police. He's not going to talk to you. You may not even find him there anymore. Rachel, do yourself a favor and stay away from the market. Let the police handle it."

"I can't. I can't sit around another minute if there's a guy downtown who can tell me where to find my grand-daughter."

From the backseat, Lauren leaned forward and pat-ted the console between the seats. "You tell him, Mom."

"All right, let's compromise," Hank said. He would

swing by to pick up Rachel, and together they would head downtown and try to locate this Ben Juza.

By the time Hank Todd and Pete Wolinsky picked Rachel up, Hank had heard back from the admin office of the downtown market association, who confirmed that Juza was not only still a vendor; the man had upped his profile by taking one of the more permanent booths in Waterfront Park, closer to the river. That Saturday, the smell of chicken skewers was mixed with sandalwood incense as they moved through Waterfront Park. Just me and four cops, Rachel thought. Watching Lauren's difficult meeting with Hawkins had exhausted her, but now, on the verge of finding Mac, a new sense of exhilaration carried her along. She pictured the little girl in Lauren's arms and prayed that it would become a reality.

There was no sign, but colorful woven blankets hung from ropes made up walls that defined Ben Juza's stand. As rehearsed, Rachel approached the booth first.

Ben Juza was talking to another customer, telling her how his merchandise was superior to another vendor's across the market and his prices were lower. His dogged chatter bordered on badgering, but the woman argued right back. Watching them, Rachel couldn't take her eyes off those large plates that exposed huge holes in the center of his earlobes. Ouch. It reminded her of *National Geographic* photos of some long-lost tribe.

When he finished with the woman, he shot her a look. "Let me know if I can help you find something."

"Actually . . . ," she pushed away a woven jacket hanging on a rod and cut to the chase, "I'm hoping you can help me. I'm searching for my granddaughter. She would have just turned four. Mac is her name. Last time I stopped by, you said you remembered her."

"Always came by with the dad and the sister who was the portrait artist?"

"That's right. You do remember."

"I've got a photographic memory. It's a blessing and a curse."

"That's impressive. But I'll let you in the true details. The portrait artist was actually her mother. My daughter, Lauren. And she's desperate to find her little girl. Can you remember anything, anything at all that might point me in the right direction?"

He winced. "Wish I could help you, friend, but I got nothing for you."

"Really." It was easy to let the friendly facade slip. "How about you tap into that photographic memory and come up with the name of the woman you sold my granddaughter to."

Ben's eyes glazed over. "I don't know what you're talking about, lady."

"The deal you brokered, back in February? Selling a three-year-old for cash."

That had his attention. He was backing away, jittery eyes on Rachel as he pressed into the display of woven purses.

"I'm not sure if you'll be tried as an accessory to kidnapping or human trafficking," Rachel said. "I just know that once the police get you, you're going to be in prison for a long time."

"Who are you?"

"I'm Mac's grandmother, and I've had it with the lies." She could feel the junior high teacher emerging, the take-no-prisoners, oh-grow-up impatience. "Tell me where she is."

Rachel sensed a presence behind her. She turned to see that she was flanked by Hank and Officer Wolinsky. The uniformed Portland cops hung back a few feet away.

Ben Juza saw them, too. He held on to one of the purses, watching and calculating.

"Don't even think about trying to bolt out the back," Hank said quietly as he flashed his shield at the man. "We've got you covered, dude."

Juza's jaw hardened as he lifted his hands in surrender. "You got it all wrong, lady. I was saving your granddaughter. The way Hawkins trotted her around here, showing her off to strange men and making her kiss the pervs—he had plans for that kid. Sick plans, and we all knew it."

"Are you saying Mac was sexually abused?" Rachel asked.

"Not yet. But we could see how he'd worked over your daughter. Like a wounded bird." He scowled. "Mac was a good kid. I didn't want to see it happen to her."

"Oh, God." Rachel pressed a hand to her heart. "You know about Lauren. Did you recognize her? You knew! Why didn't you get a cop? Report him!"

"I only knew that something was majorly dysfunctional there. If I called to report every dysfunctional asshole out here, there'd be no one on the streets."

"Where is Mac now?" Hank asked, getting to the point. "Who paid to adopt her?"

"The Stained Glass Sisters, Heidi and Holly Cannady."

Chapter 54

"What a harrowing afternoon," Alice O'Neil said. "You were very brave to meet him, Lauren, and it sounds like you didn't take any crap from him."

Lauren smiled. It was weird to hear her grandmother talk that way. "I tried not to, Grandma."

"I just hope this information gets us somewhere with little Mac," Doug O'Neil said.

"I think it's a good break," Dan said. "We know Hank's doing his best, and Rachel, she's relentless."

Lauren and her father were sitting out on the deck with her grandparents, enjoying the September sunshine as the stress of the day drained away. The meeting with Kevin had loomed over Lauren's future since she'd known she had to face him, and now that it was over, she needed to re-energize. As her fingertips traced the pattern in the tablecloth, she felt the desire to sketch for the first time in months. In the quest for therapy and healing, she had put her artwork aside, thinking it was too solitary and too much a reminder of the dark days in Kevin's control.

But now . . . now alone-time didn't seem lonely.

"Isn't that your phone?" Dad asked, interrupting her thoughts.

"Oh, yeah." She wasn't used to having a cell phone like everyone else. She pulled it from her pocket and saw Rachel's photo. "Hi, Mom."

"Rachel, are you still at Grandma and Grandpa's?"

"Yes. What happened?"

"It's the Stained Glass Sisters in the cathedral house." Her mom sounded breathless. "They have Mac."

No one spoke as Doug O'Neil pushed the boat to full throttle across Mirror Lake. When Mom told her to have Grandpa take them by boat to the cathedral house, Lauren had nearly fallen down the deck stairs. She couldn't get there fast enough. Her pulse was thumping with a driving rhythm, telling her to move. To go. To get her girl.

Now as the wind rushed over her and they all looked ahead, she hoped and prayed that Mom and Hank were right. Mom said that Ben Juza had admitted to setting up Mac's adoption by the two women who owned the stained glass shop, Heidi and Holly Cannady. Mom and the police had rushed over to the stained glass booth, but the women weren't working today. Their employee admitted that they had adopted a little girl in the past year. But then Mom learned that they lived on Mirror Lake, right at the spot where Grandpa had seen the little blond girl. "I knew it had to be Mac," Mom had said on the phone.

As far as Hank knew, the sisters were law-abiding citizens, but he was worried that they would try to flee with Mac if someone from the store tipped them off. The police chief sent a patrol car to the top of the hill. That would stop them from leaving by car. And Mom suggested that Grandpa take the family down by boat, just in case the sisters tried to leave that way.

"They couldn't get too far, Rachel," Dad had argued as Grandpa chugged out of East Bay at the excruciatingly slow speed limit. "Sure, they might make it to the city docks, but it's not like they're sailing up Hudson Bay." Whatever Mom had said, Dad had agreed, then hung up. "Rachel is right. No use taking a chance of letting them slip away."

As they passed through the tunnel, Grandma had talked about how Grandpa used to have to drop everything and go on rescue missions like this back when he was in the Coast Guard. Lauren tried to picture her grandfather as a young man, coiling ropes on a boat or throwing a life preserver to someone in the sea. The happy image lasted only a few seconds before the cold-water panic came rushing back in and she bent forward to hug her knees. Dad gave her shoulder a reassuring nudge, but nothing could lift her from this agony. Nothing but Mac.

The boat hopped and rocked over wakes in the lake, but Grandpa kept the boat at top speed until the looped shoreline of Phantom's Bluff was in sight. Staying low, Lauren moved to the front of the boat and squinted over for a better view of the patio with the small little beach hut and sitting area. She saw movement.

"There's someone there," she shouted to the others.

"The boat house door is up." Dad pointed. "Looks like they're getting ready to take the boat out." The boat was slowly chugging backward, driven by a woman in a baseball cap.

"And look. Someone's coming down the lift," Grandma said.

The double seat held another woman and a little girl with curly blond hair and a distinctive tilt to her chin.

"Mac." The word was so soft when she should have screamed it across the lake, but everyone had heard.

"Take us over to the dock, Dad."

But Doug already had the boat moving forward, as fast as he dared without risking slamming into the dock or the other boat, which was also trying to dock.

"Get back!" the woman called from the boat. "This is private property." She kept steering right and left, apparently not an experienced driver.

"We're coming in, ma'am, by order of the Mirror Lake chief of police." Grandpa sounded so official. "That child is a kidnap victim."

"Kidnap?" Even more flustered, she steered right, banging the boat against the dock. "That's impossible. She's our daughter. I've got adoption papers to prove it."

"Amateur," Doug mumbled under his breath. "We'll tie up and talk about it."

"No, no! And you get your boat out of there right now! You're keeping me from docking mine."

"Too bad, ma'am. We're coming in." With calm precision, Grandpa steered the boat in.

As it floated next to the dock with a gentle touch, Dan jumped off with a line and extended a hand to Lauren. "Let's go get your girl."

She hopped ashore and raced up the steps to the lift landing pad. The chair was dropping slowly, still a good twenty yards away, but Mac and the lady had noticed the activity below, and Mac's face lit up as she started jumping in the chair.

"Mama! Mama!"

Lauren soaked up the wonderful sight of her little girl. "It's me, Mac!" she called, blowing kisses and waving like a crazy person. Even the obstacle of the woman sitting beside Mac could not stop Lauren's heart from bubbling over with joy.

"It's really her." Dad was beside her, looking up at the little girl who was now chanting for her mama, despite the annoyed woman sitting beside her. "Wow. She looks just like you, when you were little."

Once the chair landed, Mac had herself unbuckled and out of there before the woman could scowl at her one more time. Lauren knelt down on one knee with open arms as Mac, all golden curls and button eyes and wild smile, flew at her.

"Oh, my sweet girl." Lauren caught her and held her close, breathing in her curls and soft skin and warm neck. "Mac. I've missed you so much."

"I know!" Mac exclaimed. "Where have you been, Mama? I've been looking all over for you."

Lauren let out a breath. Mac's spirit didn't seem to be broken. "I've been busy looking for you."

"Well, no wonder. Heidi told me you went away to heaven, but I knew you wouldn't go anywhere without me."

Lauren smiled. "I missed you so much."

In that moment, Lauren knew it was going to be okay. Everything they'd been through, all the pain and loneliness and shame, one day it would all be a small ping in the back of their minds. They had each other, they had Mom and Dad and Sierra and the grandparents, and they were going to be just fine.

Out on the lake, the one sister's boat was spinning in circles as she yelled at Grandpa and tried to navigate to the dock. Grandma paced on the patio, giving Mom an update on her cell phone. The other sister on the lift was arguing with Dad, saying they had papers, legal documents, all kinds of proof.

Dad stood guard over Lauren and Mac, keeping the woman at bay.

The whoop of police sirens sounded from up above, and Lauren noticed police officers making their way down the zigzagging path.

Amid the chaos, Lauren knelt beside her girl, checking her button nose and shell-pink ears, her honey curls and monkey arms, perfect for holding on to her mom. "Still got two arms and two legs," Lauren said. "How are your feet doing?"

Mac did a little hop and stretched out one foot decked in a red canvas shoe. "I got new shoes," she said proudly.

"I see that.

"Promise me you never do that again," Mac said, pressing on Lauren's nose.

"I promise. I was sad without you, but from now on, we're going to be together, and you're going to love your new family."

"Like on *Seventh Heaven*?"

"Sort of. Maybe better because they're real." She started telling Mac about her Aunt Sierra and her grandpa who drove a fire truck and her grandma who liked to bake cookies. They could swim in the lake and paint pictures together and ride real horses. And Grandma had already found a wonderful little school for Mac.

"So I can go to school, just like on *Full House?*"

"Exactly," Lauren said, remembering how, just months ago, her favorite television shows had been the frame of reference for "normal" and "happy."

"Oh, Mama." Mac touched Lauren's cheeks, her eyes just inches from Lauren's face. "I'm so happy."

"Me too, honey." It was a smooth, sweet feeling Lauren had given up on. The ability to fly after years of slogging through mud. "I'm happy, too."

Chapter 55

Rachel paused in the doorway of Lauren's room and chuckled. She had come up to check on Mac, but found her daughters stretched out in bed on either side of the sleeping girl. She went over to the bed, swallowing against the bite of tears in her throat. "You look like an O'Neil sandwich," she whispered.

"We're three peas in a pod." Lauren lay on her side with her body curved around Mac's. Her face glowed with a new peace. Total contentment.

Rachel got that.

"Don't tell me you three are sleeping in this bed," Rachel said. "There are plenty of sleeping bags, a pull-out sofa in the den, and a perfectly good bed in Sierra's room."

"But we're having a sleepover." Lovingly, Sierra wrapped one of Mac's golden curls around her finger. "All the O'Neil girls, together at last."

"It is something to celebrate." Rachel perched on the bed and smoothed the comforter over Sierra. "But you have school in the morning, Sierra. Don't stay up too late."

"We won't."

Lauren nuzzled into the pillow. "I'm tired. What a day, Mom."

"What a day." Lauren had that knack for minimal summary. What had begun with a trip to the county jail for Lauren to face her abductor had somehow spiraled into a rescue mission on the lake and now—little Mac, here in their home. Her home, now. There were still a million details to straighten out with the Department of Human Services and the police. Officially, Mac should have been removed from the Cannady home and sent to foster care until all the legalities were dealt with. However, considering the circumstances, Hank and Paula had been able to cut through the red tape so that Lauren could take her daughter home tonight.

"Good night, cuties." Rachel gave kisses all around. By the time she closed the door, the girls were already giggling about something else.

Downstairs, she found Dan settled into the family couch across from the gas fireplace. He smiled up at her. "All good?"

"All good." She stretched out on the sofa and leaned into his lap.

"Do you realize that by the time Mac goes to college I'm going to be fifty-nine, pushing sixty?"

Rachel chuckled. "No, I hadn't made that calculation yet."

"You do realize that we're going to need to share some of the parenting with Lauren." Dan stared into the fire, ever the planner. "She couldn't possibly handle raising a child alone."

"I welcome the journey. And I love that you're so responsible." She lifted his hand and kissed his knuckles.

"We'll have to take care of each other so we can be around to get Mac through college."

He smiled. "That's a deal."

"I still don't know what to make of the Cannady sisters." The women claimed that they would have surrendered Mac had they known she was a missing child. When Rachel had arrived at the cathedral house with Hank, she had listened carefully as Heidi had explained their situation. They had argued that they had legal custody, since Kevin Hawkins, the child's father, had signed away all rights to Mac in a document drawn up by their attorney. They seemed like reasonable people, and once the police arrived, they cooperated.

"My sister and I have gotten very attached to Mackenzie," Heidi had said. "I don't want anyone to think we're weirdoes. We've been on the county's foster family list for years. A dozen kids have come through this house at different times. Good kids who needed a break that we could give them. That was what we saw in Mac. Kevin Hawkins . . ." Her eyes had iced over at the mention of his name. "That man is trouble. When we heard he was giving Mac up for adoption, Holly and I stepped up. Yes, we offered to give him money if he would sign the papers and leave us alone. And we used Ben as a middleman to keep Hawkins away. He is not a trustworthy man. We knew that if we took Mac on, we would need to protect her and ourselves from the likes of him."

Well, Rachel thought, they were right on that score.

"Do you think they'll go to jail?" Rachel asked Dan as she relaxed against the warmth of his body.

"I don't know. I don't completely buy their altruistic image. I'm relieved to let the justice system deal with people like Ben Juza and the Cannady sisters."

"And their claim about saving Mac makes me wonder about Lauren. If they were leery of Kevin Hawkins's possible abuse of children, why didn't they intervene on Lauren's behalf when they saw her being forced to peddle her art in the marketplace?"

Rachel knew that the Cannady sisters were not alone in their neglect. Ben Juza had pegged Hawkins as a psycho, yet Juza did not think to help Lauren. Nor had hundreds of customers moving through the market . . . or, for that matter, cops.

"Portland has its fair share of homeless and runaways," Dan said. "I don't want to think that Lauren was overlooked because she blended with that group, but it's the truth."

Another harsh truth. Rachel sighed. "We can't solve the problems of the world in one day."

Dan chuckled. "But I have to say, today we sure came close."

Epilogue

"Silent night, holy night . . ." Lauren, Rachel, and Sierra sang the Christmas carol in harmony as they made cookies.

Sitting on a high stool at the kitchen island, Mac stopped decorating a reindeer-shaped cookie to watch and listen. Enthralled, she swayed her hands through the air in time to the song.

Lauren grinned, almost missing a note over Mac's antics. Her little girl was such a ham.

The cookies, icing, and colored sugars were set up in the expanded kitchen—part of the renovation done to the house when it became clear that their family had grown. Now a new hall off the dining room led to a two-bedroom suite for Lauren and Mac, all funded by Lauren's art.

When a few auction houses had come around with offers, Lauren had decided to sell most of the artwork from the compound, relieved to part with the pieces that reflected the loneliness of those difficult years. She realized that its monetary worth was inflated because of her celebrity as the survivor of a six-year-long kidnapping. That label would probably always stay with her—her public image—but the people who knew her personally recognized her as a loving, creative, generous person. A person centered on joy—the union of the black and white yin-yang swirl.

Over the past few months, they had begun to build a life. Mac was a star pupil at the Little Red Schoolhouse. Lauren worked at Spirit Ranch, caring for the horses, loving up Yoda, and assisting with children's riding lessons. She missed seeing Jazz every day, now that he had gone back to college, but soon he would be off for an entire month during the Christmas break. And she had gone back to her art. Some evenings after supper, Lauren and Mac would set up two easels and paint together. Lauren believed that Mac had the gift, but then she believed Mac brought magic to everything she touched.

At first, Mom had been disappointed that Lauren wasn't planning to go to college, but she had come to see that her daughter needed to follow her heart right now—and play to her skills, as Wynonna often pointed out. In a few months, when the sun returned, Rachel and Lauren would start working together toward a GED. Lauren figured she could do that much, as long as they could study in a classroom under the sky.

When the carol ended, there was a moment of silence, lovely as new-fallen snow. Then Mac clapped.

"Mama, can I ask you something?"

Lauren smiled. As if there were any stopping her. "Sure."

"What pole does Santa Claus live on again?"

"The North Pole," Lauren answered.

"Oh, yeah." Mac hugged the post at the end of the kitchen island. "Is it like this pole?"

"The North Pole is a place. I can show you on the globe," Lauren told her, realizing she had never talked to her parents about Santa Claus. At eleven, she had known he wasn't real, but had wanted to keep believing. Now, she could keep it all going for Mac.

"And it's really cold there. It snows all the time," Lauren added.

"I think it's time to break out the Christmas movies." A puff of flour rose from the marble slab as Rachel dusted the ball of dough. She explained how Santa lived up north in a magical place with Mrs. Claus. "And every Christmas, Santa travels around the world in his sled to deliver toys for good girls and boys."

"I know the part about the toys," Mac said. "And they have poles there made of striped candy canes and cute little people who work, work, work with little hammers to build toys." She mimed pounding away with a hammer the size of a toothpick.

"That's right," Lauren said. "Santa's elves."

Sometimes Lauren felt bad for all that Mac had missed. Her family knew about her worries. "My poor baby girl was born in a shed," Lauren had told them.

"So was baby Jesus," Sierra had said. Though she had been quick to point out that Mac was no angel. Just a cute kid.

And Rachel had pointed out that children were flexible. Lauren could see that in her daughter's quick transition to this new life. She was a wonder. Mac's experiences made Mackenzie O'Neil who she was, just as Lauren's past was a part of her.

The purple glow of the future glimmered in Lauren's mind as she smiled down at her daughter. They'd been through so much, but their lights were still shining. That single, beautiful light inside.

Please turn the page
for a special Q and A with
New York Times bestselling author Rosalind Noonan.

Q: Most of your novels have been set on the east coast. *All She Ever Wanted* takes place in Westchester County, and *The Daughter She Used to Be* is a New York story. What prompted you to set this novel in Oregon?

A: Since I moved to Oregon nearly a decade ago, my editor, John, has been encouraging me to set a novel out west, and I felt I'd gained enough cultural competence to embrace this locale in a story. The wide open spaces out here lend themselves to a tale of abduction, as there are acres of land that would make good hiding spots, unlike the urban/suburban areas along the east coast that are well-populated. When I lived in Queens, New York, it was hard to imagine how a kidnapper could hold a victim captive without a neighbor or relative finding them. Now I get it.

When I knew I would be writing the story of a girl who'd been imprisoned near her home, I became aware of the gullies and forested acres that surround our city. Nearly every day I walk a trail that cuts through farmland near my house. It's a public trail, built for runners and walkers and dogs. The area is full of wildlife, with flocks of birds that swoop from tall fir trees, circle neat rows of vegetation, and then loop back to their nests. The farm is open to the public, and some towering ponderosa pines cast deep, dark shade that hints of secrets and fairylands. It's a lovely path, but much of the land along the trail is clumped with brambles and bushes, stands of trees and old outbuildings half-covered in vegetation. One small house that is obviously occupied has an odd configuration of cloth hanging in the window—some sort of makeshift curtains. Every time I pass by I am sure those are the pajamas of a young girl.

I'm probably wrong about those curtains, and with the number of cars parked outside that house, it's clear that people are coming and going all the time. Still, I feel a chill from the bushes some afternoons, and I wonder how long it would take to find someone who has been tied up and pulled off the path and dragged into the scrub. At the dip in the valley the path goes over a bridge, and in the rainy season the watershed below becomes a swamp. What might be hidden in the tall, dense grasses there? This is a dangerous question to ask a writer.

Q: This is your fifth novel with Kensington Books. Since your plots mirror life, do your friends ever worry that you might turn their lives into a story?

A: Usually I get the opposite reaction. Some of my friends come to me with amazing stories they want to see in print and others are always looking to see if their name has been dropped into a book. My cousin Karen, whose New Hampshire home inspired parts of my Christmas novella in *Making Spirits Bright*, would love to see her name in print, along with her husband, Dave, who is such a steadfast romantic he could inspire an entire romance series. My friend Moira was hinting around about seeing her husband, a New York City police detective, in a book, and so he appears in this novel, working for a different law enforcement agency. When I do drop in a name or story thread, it's just a small homage. I would never try to draw a full portrait of someone I know; fiction needs to morph into its own shape and size.

Q: Much of the backstory of *And Then She Was Gone* echoes the high profile kidnappings and recoveries of victims like Jaycee Dugard and Elizabeth Smart. Did you research their stories?

A: Early on, when I was pulling together a thumbnail

sketch of this novel, I studied the profiles of those kidnappings, as well as information from the National Center for Missing and Exploited Children. The NCMEC has an excellent website, and I appreciated the open, earnest way that Jaycee Dugard recalled her experiences in *A Stolen Life: A Memoir*. Dugard's memoir is a testament to her personal courage, resilience, and wisdom.

Throughout my research, a handful of questions persisted in each case I studied. How did the kidnapping happen? What motivated the captor? How was the girl treated? Why didn't she escape? This last question about escape is not meant as a judgment; it simply seems like the obvious solution for a captive who is not tied by physical bonds. Many asked this question about Elizabeth Smart, who reportedly denied her identity when police questioned her nine months after her abduction.

I learned that the dynamics of a kidnap victim's relationship with her captor are complex. Many captives stay because they fear for their lives, and would rather live in captivity than die. Furthermore, abductors create an atmosphere of alienation. They physically and mentally dehumanize victims and rob them of their identities. Victims are often given new names and forced to wear disguises. Victims begin to think there is no way to return to the world because their former "self" no longer exists.

The traumatic bond created between victims and kidnappers often keeps them together. This dynamic, this psychological chokehold, makes the actions of Amanda Berry, one of the young women kept captive in a Cleveland house, quite extraordinary. After nearly a decade, she dared to break out and seek help. What an amazing young woman. The news of these three women in Cleveland broke just after I had turned the manuscript of this novel in to my editor. For me, the timing was uncanny. It's one thing to play the "what if" game and write about terrible turns of events; quite another to read of terrible crimes against three young women.

Ultimately, my goal was not to tell the story of a kidnapping; I was focused on the aftermath. Recovery and reunification. The struggle to let go of regrets, fill in the blanks, and find the new normal. A story of heartbreak and hope—that's the backbone of the O'Neil family's journey.

Q: Do you see yourself in any of the characters of this novel?

A: There's a small piece of me in all the characters. When I write a scene, I try to get under a character's skin. Sort of like method acting. It's important that every character have his or her own voice, and the action must be colored by the character's distinct point of view. Dan's love for his daughter is different from Rachel's complicated relationship with Lauren. Paula's viewpoint is somewhat more clinical and a hell of a lot more down to earth. Sierra's perspective, which I enjoyed writing, is more impulsive and unfiltered. Maybe I got some help from my teenage daughter on that.

My writing voyages have taken me to some interesting places. Through my characters I have served as a soldier in Iraq, saved lives in a hospital emergency room, and tangled with a serial killer. So when my son asks me how my day went, occasionally I share what I learned about branding cattle or tracking down an infant abductor or defusing a roadside bomb. You might say, "It's not brain surgery." Well, actually, some days it is. All in a day's work.

Sisterhood has a price . . .

Pledging to Theta Pi at Merriwether College seemed to offer Emma Danelski a passport to friendship, fun, and popularity. But the excitement of pledge training quickly fades, as does the warmth of her so-called sisters. What's left is a stifling society filled with petty rules, bullying, and manipulation. Most haunting are the choices Emma makes in the wake of another sorority sister's suicide . . .

It doesn't matter that no one else needs to know what Emma did, or how vastly different life at Theta Pi house is from the glossy image it projects. Emma knows. And now, with her loyalties tested, she must decide which secrets are worth keeping and how far she'll go to protect them—and herself . . .

Please turn the page for an exciting sneak peek of
Rosalind Noonan's
PRETTY, NASTY, LOVELY
Coming soon wherever print and
e-books are sold!

Chapter 1

It was over.

It had been a hellish night of blood and pain, but at last, it was done.

With hands clammy from sweat, I reached for the door to the basement lounge known as the "babe cave" and pushed in. In the eerie glow of orange jack o' lanterns and Halloween lights, suspicion filled the air as the small group of Theta Pi sisters stopped talking. The Lily Council had assembled, and all eyes were on me.

"You scared the shit out of me." Courtney flopped back against the couch, her hair pale against the brown leather as she adjusted the silver cone cups of her "Material Girl" costume. "For a second I thought you were the cops."

"Don't be paranoid," Tori snapped at her, combing through one of her blue-and-white pompoms. She had spent the evening dressed as a Dallas Cowboys cheerleader, and it was hard to believe that her hot pants, tiny vest and boots were still snow white considering the level of partying that must have gone down in the meeting room. "The police are never going to hear about this. Emma will make sure of that." She folded her arms imperiously. "Right, Emma?"

Tori's words were thick with accusation.

I nodded, struggling to swallow the bitter regret at the back of my tongue. My eyes burned and every muscle in my body ached. How had I fallen into this? My evening plans for a costume party with dance music, orange-pumpkin shooters, and drinking games had given way to a night of screaming and cursing, crying and . . . and all that blood. I hadn't expected that.

"I have to go back to my room." What time was it? In the red haze of agony, I'd lost track of everything. The muted light peeking through the edges of the curtains on the small windows told me it was morning, and I knew I had a quiz and an assignment due, if I even made it to class. Right now even my most difficult sophomore classes seemed like trite indulgences compared to the trauma of the night.

But we had survived, my sisters and I. Every bone in my body ached and my muscles were screaming, but I had made it through the night. Now my body desperately craved sleep and solitude. "I'll see you guys later."

"Emma, wait." Tori was suddenly at my side, guiding me back into the room. "Come. Sit."

They sat me on a folding chair used for meetings, the boney chair strategically placed in front of the flat-screen TV. The hot seat. Although the sun had risen outside, the curtains were closed, and the only light came from Halloween decorations and candles.

Ritual candles, I realized. Who had gotten these out? The glow of votive candles cast peculiar shadows on the girls' faces as they, the Lily Council of Theta Pi, sat facing me. Someone handed me a white taper.

The candle of truth.

My throat felt raw and dry as I squinted though the flickering candlelight, trying to find the door behind the pretty faces marred by scowls. Although Lydia's vampire-dark hair fell over her eyes, I could feel the hot mess of emotion there. That girl was on fire. Or maybe the image of fire came from the red satin cape she wore – my Red Riding Hood costume. Had she lifted it, or had she asked to borrow it during the chaos of the night?

I couldn't remember.

Tori's beautiful mouth was a fierce slash of disapproval as she sat her shimmering pompoms in her lap. Courtney echoed the stern look just as she mimicked everything Tori did, same leg crossed, hands on hips, shoulders raised in that camera-ready pose.

And Violet, looking delicate and leggy in a fringed, beaded flapper costume, showered me with thick pity. "Bless your heart, but you're a mess." Hers was the voice of our rituals: soft, with a southern lilt and firm backbone that shut down argument. "First of all, no one can ever know about this. Now we're all going to swear an oath of silence. Swear on our loyalty and love to the sisters of Theta Pi."

We all pledged secrecy, but I was the one holding the candle of truth. The vow would burn deep. "Can I go now?" I felt like a heap of sodden laundry, wrung out and abandoned when the owner found that all the dorm dryers were full. I was so exhausted I was beyond caring about the festivities that I'd missed tonight. "I'm so tired."

"Don't you think we're tired, too?" There was condemnation in Lydia's voice, stern and imperious, as she flipped up the red hood of the cape and scowled at me.

I wished I could simply rise from the center of the circle and slip out. Vanish in a curl of smoke beneath the door frame. Escape seemed so simple, but appearances were deceiving. Reality was twisted and thorny and complicated, and it kept me in that chair.

Now I belonged in this ring of fire. I had pledged this sorority, vowing to remain loyal and true forever. As the song said: *I'm Theta born. Theta bred. And when I die, I'll be Theta dead.*

Death seemed like a restful option.

"I really have to go." I handed the candle to Courtney, who blew it out and plunked it on the table without hesitation.

"Poor baby," Tori cooed, with half-closed eyes that twinkled with blue glitter shadow. She looked way too good to have stayed up all night long. Had she sneaked off for a nap in the middle of everything? "You need rest. But before you go to beddy bye, tell us, what did you do with . . . *it.*"

I squinted. "What are you talking about?"

"You know." Courtney leaned closer, wincing. "The body."

Those two words stole away my last ounce of energy and hope. This night had been the worst of my life, and it refused to end. "I didn't . . ." I shook my head, not wanting to think about it anymore. "I left her there." I pointed toward the room where I'd left the body wrapped in a towel and tucked into a laundry basket, as if she were asleep. She had seemed too peaceful to move.

"Wait." Courtney's mouth dropped open. "You left it in the suite? That's disgusting!"

Violet was shaking her head and Tori was getting all puffed up with indignation. "That cannot happen," Tori said. "What if Ol' Jan sees?"

"She's not going in there." Our house mother wasn't in the habit of barging into girls' rooms.

Violet stared as if seeing me for the first time. "Bless her heart, I don't think she gets the enormity of the situation. Look at me, Emma. Sweet pea, you've got to get rid of it."

A wave of emotion crashed over me and I had to bite my lower lip to hold back the tears that formed when I thought of the baby — so tiny, with velvet mini-fingers— wrapped up in that fluffy towel like Itsy, the doll I used to bathe when I was seven. "I couldn't move her. She seemed so peaceful."

"Oh, no. No, no. We will *not* have that *thing* found in Theta House." Suddenly Tori stood beside me, hustling me to my feet. "You need to get it out of here. Pronto."

"I can't." I knew the baby couldn't stay here, but I couldn't bring myself to touch her again. "I can't do this. Get someone else."

"Like who?" Lydia chimed in, her dark gaze fixing on me like a leech. "Who wants to get stuck with that?"

I stared back at them, wanting to shrink away and disappear. After all I'd been through, how could they expect me to handle this horrible task? "Why are you ganging up on me?"

Violet gave a whimper of a sigh as she adjusted the skinny strings of her spangly dress. "Bless your heart. We're just trying to help you."

"You're not thinking clearly," Tori said.

That part was true. I was a hot mess.

Tori forged on. "We have bent over backwards to help you. We're like, all 'Go, Emma!'" she said, jiggling one pompom in the air. "But we can only do so much, and what would be the point of us jumping in to finish off what you started? You created this mess for yourself, and it's your responsibility to clean it up. Get that body out of here. Now. Put it in a shopping bag or hide it in your laundry bag and toss it in a hole. Bury it deep or throw it in the ravine. I don't care, as long as you get it out of here."

It was a *her*. Didn't they get that? And she was a living being. Well, she had been living a few minutes ago.

I was crying now. Silent tears, though I could feel my mouth crumpling in that pathetic frown that, Violet insisted, caused creases. "I can't do this," I murmured. "I can't."

"You can," Tori said steadily, "and you will."

"I can't even . . ." I shuddered, hot and cold and dizzy at the same time. "Why do I have to do this?"

"Silly, boo." Tori granted me a condescending smile, her teeth superwhite against her tanned skin. She leaned so close I could feel the heat from her skin. "You know this is the consequence of your actions. This is what happens when you kill your baby."